FURY OF A DEMON

ALSO BY BRIAN NASLUND

Blood of an Exile
Sorcery of a Queen

FURY
OF A
DEMON

BRIAN NASLUND

TOR

A TOM DOHERTY ASSOCIATES BOOK
NEW YORK

FURY OF A DEMON

Copyright © 2021 by Brian Naslund

Map by Jennifer Hanover

A Tor Book
Published by Tom Doherty Associates
120 Broadway
New York, NY 10271

www.tor-forge.com

Tor® is a registered trademark of Macmillan Publishing Group, LLC.

Library of Congress Cataloging-in-Publication Data

Names: Naslund, Brian, author.
Title: Fury of a demon / Brian Naslund.
Description: First Edition. | New York : Tor, 2021. |
"A Tom Doherty Associates book."
Identifiers: LCCN 2021010724 (print) | LCCN 2021010725 (ebook) |
ISBN 9781250309709 (trade paperback) | ISBN 9781250309693 (hardcover) | ISBN
9781250309686 (ebook)
Subjects: GSAFD: Fantasy fiction.
Classification: LCC PS3614.A757 F87 2021 (print) |
LCC PS3614.A757 (ebook) | DDC 813/.6—dc23
LC record available at https://lccn.loc.gov/2021010724
LC ebook record available at https://lccn.loc.gov/2021010725

Our books may be purchased in bulk for promotional, educational, or business use. Please contact your local bookseller or the Macmillan Corporate and Premium Sales Department at 1-800-221-7945, extension 5442, or by email at MacmillanSpecialMarkets@macmillan.com.

First Edition: August 2021

Printed in the United States of America

0 9 8 7 6 5 4 3 2 1

For my brother and sister.

Himeja
PAPYRIA
SOUL
SEA
Floodhaven
ALMIRA
Deepdale
THE
HEART
JUNGLE NATIONS

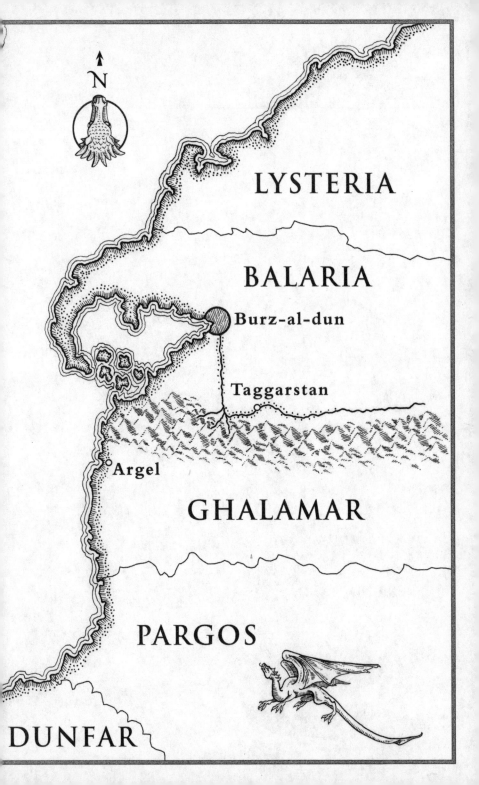

PART I

◆

True progress has a cost. Few are willing to pay it.
—Osyrus Ward

1

PRIVATE RIGAR
Dainwood Jungle, Sector Two

Wormwrot scouts found the mud totems an hour before dark. Lieutenant Droll called a halt.

The men crowded around to get a look. There were about fifty of the little bastards, pinched from the earth like miniature demons, twisted into positions of suffering, and adorned with all manner of unsettling decorations: Broken fingernails. Shattered bone fragments. Human eyeballs.

The grisly scene made Rigar's skin crawl.

"Fucking animals," mumbled their sergeant, Grotto. "Just got no decency at all."

That meant something, coming from Grotto. Before the reformation of Wormwrot, he'd been muscle at one of Commander Vergun's gambling dens. Apparently, his favorite punishment for catching men cheating at dice was grabbing their fingers and tearing them off with his bare hands.

"Wouldn't say they've got zero decency," said Lieutenant Droll, scratching at one of his wild mutton chops, which had streaks of silver amidst the dirty black mane. "They just don't dole much out to foreign soldiers encroaching on their land."

Grotto gave Droll a cold look. The men didn't care for each other, that was known. If the enemy didn't kill one of them soon, Rigar was fairly certain they'd kill each other.

In that event, Rigar privately hoped that Grotto turned out to be the murdered party. Droll was a strict commander with no tolerance for laziness, cowardice, or panicked behavior during a fight.

But he was generally fair with his men, and he'd kept them alive this long. Grotto was plain evil—here for the blood and the violence as much as the money. He'd inflict pain on the enemy when they were available. When they weren't, Grotto's ire often shifted to his own men.

"Should we turn back to an extraction point?" asked a new recruit, whose name Rigar hadn't bothered to learn. He'd only been with them a week. At this point, Rigar didn't learn anyone's name unless they proved they could survive for a month in the Dainwood.

Given how bad the last few months had been, half the men in the unit were anonymous to him. They'd most likely stay that way.

"You scared of some mud figurines, soldier?" Grotto asked him.

The recruit shrugged. "Don't they got magical powers? Or command forest monsters or something?"

"Forest gods," someone down the line corrected.

Grotto spat. Sighed. "These two idiots."

Droll stepped in. "They don't have magical powers. But the fact those eyes haven't been stolen by crows means they're recent. That means we stay on the ground till we root 'em out. We'll head to Fallon's Roost for the night. Hunker down with the skeleton crew posted there."

"Fuck that," said Grotto. "I say we—"

Grotto stopped talking when a long shadow fell over him and stayed there.

Their unit's acolyte had come up the line, and now towered over them. Horns made from dragon bones jutted from his scalp. His eyes glowed an unnatural, orange color. Apparently, the earliest acolytes all wore masks that hid their disturbing faces, but the latest war models didn't need them.

Strange as they looked, they all had simple, numeric identifiers. This one was 408.

"What is it?" Acolyte 408 hissed. His voice was raspy and stressed. Reminded Rigar of burnt meat crackling over a fire.

"More of their mud statues, sir," said Droll.

In general, Wormwrot wasn't big on sirs and salutes. Long as you followed your orders when the steel was out and the blood was flying, Vergun allowed his grunts to keep things pretty informal. But Osyrus Ward was their employer on this contract, and his terrifying acolytes tended to illicit a stiffer response from the men.

"Figured we'd make for Fallon's Roost to pass the night, then go searching in the morning," Droll continued.

Acolyte 408 surveyed the totems on the road for a moment, then stomped through them, flattening a significant number with his swollen feet.

He headed toward Fallon's Roost. They followed.

The acolytes were a mixed bag in Rigar's opinion. Terrifying as all hell—and known to murder Wormwrot grunts for no discernible reason. If a man took a piss in a place that an acolyte didn't like, he could get his head torn off for the infraction. But they were gods in combat. Rigar had personally seen Acolyte 408 send thirty-three wardens down the river—tore 'em apart like chaff with the razor-sharp spikes that popped from his fists during a fight.

The memory still gave Rigar nightmares.

They walked for an hour before Fallon's Roost came into view. It was one of the largest holdfasts along the northern rim of the Dainwood.

When they got within a hundred strides of the fortress, that same new recruit stubbed his toe on something metallic.

"Ow, shit!" hissed that recruit, frowning at the offending object, which was a bunch of armor balled up around a skeleton. "What the fuck is that?"

"Dead Jaguar," said Rigar.

The recruit frowned. "How'd he get all balled up like that?"

"You don't know?"

The recruit shrugged. "Tell me."

Rigar sighed. The prospect of a night in the jungle behind proper walls had relaxed him enough to tell the story. Which he could do, since he'd been there.

"This here's the site of the biggest victory we've won against the Jaguars to date. Wormwrot took control of the holdfast early in the war and we'd been using it as our forward deploy. The Jaguars took offense to that, and attacked, which was an exceedingly foolish idea, seeing as we had twenty acolytes on the walls."

"So, an acolyte did this?"

"Well, that's actually a matter up for debate," Rigar said, then glanced at Droll.

"There was a *sorceress*," Droll said. "I fucking saw her."

"Sorceress?" the recruit asked.

"Yes. The Jaguars had a woman with them when they attacked. She wasn't wearing any armor and she wasn't carrying weapons, but she went charging into the fray all the same. When the first acolyte dropped off the walls, she cast a spell that reduced any man wearing armor into a crumpled ball like the one you just stubbed your toe on. Look around." He gestured across the field. "They're everywhere."

"Why would she cast a spell on her own soldiers?" the recruit asked.

"Well, she obviously fucked it up. But before Fallon's Roost, I heard acolytes were getting their spines ripped out like fish at the morning market." Droll spat. "Nobody's seen her since then, so I'm thinking she killed herself."

The recruit looked at Rigar. "But you didn't see her?"

"I was taking a shit when the attack started. By the time I got up to the walls, all the fun was over. Just a smoking crater and a bunch of dead Jaguars. No sign of a sorceress, alive or otherwise."

"Yeah, but she'd have been pulled straight down to hell by the demons she fucked to get her powers," Droll said, as if this was common and incontrovertible knowledge. "Plus, there was a whole group of Jaguars who retreated into the woods. We went after 'em, but lost the trail at a river."

"What happened to the acolyte?" the recruit asked.

"Huh?"

"That jumped off the wall."

"He was just stunned," said Droll. "The bitch's magic didn't take. A few of those soft-palmed engineers with the dragonskin jackets flew in the next day and brought it back to Floodhaven. We stayed in the Roost for another week, but the Jaguars moved on, so we did too."

"And now we're back," said Rigar. "Whole war's just a horrible circle."

They finished picking through the balled-up wardens and sounded off to the sentries on the wall. Droll sidled up next to Rigar as they headed into the holdfast and spoke to him in a low tone.

"I'll need you with me on double-watch tonight. I want my veterans awake and alert once the sun goes down."

That's what Rigar liked about Droll. He'd pull you for a crap duty as needed, but he was always right there with you, shoveling the shit.

"You smell trouble?"

"They use those totems to mess with us, that's known. Most of the time, when you get an obvious signal like that in the road, whatever savages made them are already two valleys over with no plans to return. But this time . . ." Droll trailed off. Scanned the hills. "Yeah, guess I do smell some trouble."

Rigar made a show of taking a big breath in. "All I smell is this mud and shit and rot."

"They tend to be pretty close traveling partners."

Despite Droll's premonition, Rigar relaxed once they were inside Fallon's Roost.

The Dainwood was swollen with danger at all times, but after a week of patrols in the wild jungle, a decent wall and a big acolyte guarding their crew felt like spending the night in the palace of Burz-al-dun. The men who weren't on duty set up their bedrolls in little groups and started dicing, complaining about the bugs or the dragons or both, and sneaking sips of booze from secret canteens.

There were a few hours before nightfall and Rigar's watch, so he removed his boots and armor, then used a rag to wipe the red face paint from his face. Some Wormwrot men wore that shit day and night, which Rigar would never understand. Not only was it uncomfortable as all hell in the jungle damp, but it brought pimples all over his chin and cheeks.

When that was done, Rigar ran a quick inventory of his rashes. There were three distinct varieties: a black, bumpy one on his left foot, a flaky situation along his neck, and an angry, red flare up on his upper thigh. The upper thigh area itched like a bastard, and given the location, its potential spread made him nervous.

He dug into his pack and found the ointment a surgeon had given him before shipping out from Floodhaven. Applied it liberally to all three areas. It seemed to be working for the black bumps, but the others two were more stubborn. When they rotated back to Floodhaven, he was going to have words with that surgeon.

As he was finishing up, Private Wister came over.

"Any luck?" he asked with a hopeful look on his face.

"Huh?" Rigar asked, distracted by his dissatisfaction with the ointment. "Oh, right. The boots."

He reached into his pack again and came out with Wister's second set of boots, which had taken a rough beating during their last patrol. The men were responsible for keeping their own footwear in order during deployments, and the jungle's dampness had a way of deteriorating them in a hurry. But Rigar had figured out a clever method for waterproofing a few months ago that involved mixing the useless rash ointment with boiled urine. He'd kept the recipe secret and started taking on contract work from fellow soldiers with ruined boots.

"Good as new," he said, tossing them over.

Wister held them like they were decorated with diamonds. "They'll hold up, like Cinder's have?"

"Yep. You have the guarantee of Rigar's Wartime Cobblery."

Wister smiled, then tossed him a canteen. Rigar sniffed it and approved.

"Decent stuff, smells like."

"That's top-shelf juniper liquor outta Burz-al-dun," said Wister. "Enjoy it."

Rigar nodded. He might. Or, he might sell it off in a few more days when the rest of the men had emptied their canteens.

Wormwrot paid well, but price-gouging liquor in the gloom of the jungle paid better.

Rigar ate a quick dinner of half-rotten rice and a scrap of salted pork. The skyships had spent the last year making a concerted effort to deprive the enemy of food and forage, but a side effect was limited rations on their end, too. There were rumors of some major resupply coming in from Dunfar, which between the wars and the famines was the last country in Terra with viable farmland. Rigar liked Dunfarian cuisine. Lots of spices. But he wasn't getting his hopes up until the food was in front of him.

He took a nap after dinner. Droll came through near dark and tapped him for the watch. Rigar grabbed his gear and made his way to the wall where he relieved the current sentry. He scanned the field ahead, keeping an eye out for the enemy as best he could in all the darkness. Moonlight glinted off the balls of dead wardens.

The night passed without incident. By the time the gray-light of early morning arrived, Rigar had succumbed to his baser instincts and been itching at his thigh rash with a purpose.

"Stop jerking off on watch, Rigar."

Rigar turned around to find Droll approaching. "Hey, Lieutenant. I wasn't jerking off, it's these damn rashes."

"Ointment not working?"

"Not really." He forced himself to stop itching. "By Aeternita. Why would anyone ever live in this wretched, rash-inducing place on purpose?"

Droll shrugged. "Probably because the locals aren't afflicted. Their forest gods protect them."

Rigar grunted. "Very funny."

Droll motioned to the field.

"Anything out there?" he asked.

"Just fog and a few Blackjacks in the distance."

When they'd first arrived in Almira, the lizards hadn't returned from the Great Migration yet. Gods, but those were good times, which was saying something because even without dragons, the Dainwood was still a horrific place, full of a thousand different slithering and crawling critters that could kill you with a single bite or sting. Their second day under the canopy, one newbie grunt accidentally set up his bedroll over a nest of giant jungle scorpions who'd stung him dozens of times.

The pain was so bad his nerves went all toxic. He turned delirious and shot himself in the face with a crossbow.

Now, Rigar longed for a time when the scorpions and ants invading your sleeping situation were the primary concern. The dragons of the Dainwood were more common than rats outside a butcher's alley. In the last week alone, the great lizards had eaten five soldiers he knew personally. Three got scooped up while scouting ahead for fresh warrens, which is known to be dangerous work. But the other two got plucked straight out of camp on their way to breakfast.

How are you supposed to protect against that? A man needs breakfast.

"Hmm," Droll said, still looking out in the fog. "I don't like it. The Jaguars could be anywhere."

"Think it's true that the Flawless Bershad is fighting with 'em? You heard about the head thing, right?"

Three patrols in Sector Four went missing without a trace two weeks ago. Five days later, their heads turned up in a pile way down in Sector Twelve. A few days after that, the lone survivor turned up at a random extraction point in Sector Five, face swollen to hell with mosquito bites. He said the Flawless Bershad had massacred the patrols, along with some crazy man in white armor.

"I heard," Droll said. "It's dragonshit. That soldier was delirious."

"But—"

"Vallen Vergun killed the Flawless Bershad back in Taggarstan," Droll interrupted. "I saw that shit myself."

"What, then his ghost killed the emperor of Balaria afterward?"

"Fuck no. But if you were the Horellian guard who let the emperor take the long swim during your shift, wouldn't you make up a dragonshit story about how a legend like the Flawless Bershad was responsible?"

That notion had some merit, but before Rigar had a chance to say so, Acolyte 408 approached and sent a cold, silencing shiver down

Rigar's spine. Droll stiffened as well. They both turned around and saluted the hulking, gray-skinned man behind them.

"Report."

"All clear, sir. Just fog and lizards out there."

The acolyte's void-like gaze shifted out over the tangled wilderness.

"Might be those totems were just a diversion," Rigar said, trying to get the scary bastard to leave.

The acolyte turned to him. "Stay, vigilante. Stop fraternizing."

"I'm patrolling the perimeter and assessing the morale of my men," Droll said. "Not fraternizing."

As far as standing up for your troops, that comment wasn't much. But seeing as the bastard was two heads taller than a normal man and could pop sharpened bones out of his thick arms, Rigar thought that Droll had summoned some real stones to push back a mite.

The lieutenant scratched at his mutton chops with one hand, but he didn't break eye contact or back down.

"Assess morale faster," Acolyte 408 said. Then he hopped off the rampart, landing in the muddy yard below. A jump like that would have sent a normal man's kneecaps on long and independent journeys, but 408 marched back toward the holdfast without a hitch in his step.

"That asshole makes my cock shrink," Rigar muttered.

"That help or hurt the rash situation?" Droll said, smiling.

Rigar scratched at his crotch again. "Nothing helps anything out here."

"Shit, Rigar. That rash has turned you into a dour bastard. Look on the sunny side of this deal. Osyrus Ward's conquered the whole fucking world and we're on his side."

"Not sure I'd call working for Osyrus Ward a sunny situation. I've heard he brings every corpse that comes back from the jungle to the top of that big tower he built. Fucks 'em before filling them with machinery and the like."

"Osyrus is a twisted bastard, all right. But our commander is a known cannibal, so . . ."

"Thought those stories about Vergun were just rumors?"

"Naw. Castor all but confirmed it after he got shit-hammered during a dice game. And Castor would know. He's been Vergun's second-in-command for more than a year."

"But isn't Castor always the one who's saying there's gotta be a line somewhere, too? Eating a few people and fucking corpses are two different things."

Droll shrugged. "There's creepy shit all over this world. Longer you soldier, the longer you realize that trying to gauge the degrees of who's worse is a waste of time. Just follow orders, kill what needs killing, and collect your coin if you survive."

Rigar considered pointing out that Droll's restrained view on soldiering was a minority outlook in Wormwrot. Most of the men had a murder-and-pillage-first, wait-for-orders-second kind of mentality. But he decided against prolonging the debate. It had been a long night and his bedroll was calling.

"I do like collecting coin," Rigar muttered.

"And between normal wages and the cat bounties, we are making an awful lot of coin on this war."

That was a fact. Wormwrot paid well for a mercenary outfit, but Commander Vergun had also issued special bounties on Dainwood Wardens: any man who came back to Floodhaven with one of their Jaguar Masks—and a witness confirming they came by it with violence—was given one-hundred gold on the spot. Rigar had personally been paid six bounties, which was middle-of-the-road compared to others, but the men who pushed hard on the bounties often wound up with their eyeballs decorating mud statues.

"Just hope I get the chance to spend mine," Rigar added.

He had made private plans with himself to use the coin he earned from the war to start up his own cobblery. Given his success with the waterproofing method, he figured that he could have even more success with proper tools and chemicals. And making shoes was a much better long-term vocation than hunting vicious warriors through the jungle.

"If you're scared of dying, you can always bribe some official to give you a better posting," Droll said with a smile. "Buy yourself a nice cushy posting on a cargo skyship."

Rigar sighed. "Those things crash all the time, too."

"Dammit, Rigar, I told you to look on the sunny side of things. That's an order. Read me?"

Rigar sighed. "I read you, Lieutenant."

"Good. Now, I best get back to patrolling before our gray-skinned overlord comes back and—"

Droll's head exploded.

Wet chunks of skull and brain sprayed across Rigar's face. The spatter forced one eye shut.

With the other eye, Rigar saw Droll's body drop to the ground, neck stump pumping a remarkable amount of blood across the stones.

Rigar turned to the forest to find the source of such awesome destruction.

There was a big man in scaled armor the color of fresh snow charging across the field. He had a full helmet covering his face and was cradling one of the balled-up warden corpses under one arm.

"Contact!" Rigar shouted, raising his crossbow.

Rigar pressed down on the loading mechanism as he aimed, which created a metal rumble inside the weapon and arranged a bolt with full tension in the chamber. In the precious seconds that took, the charging man had crossed half the field.

By Aeternita, he's fast, Rigar thought, adjusting his aim for the speed.

When he was a boy, he'd hunted jackals with his father in the badlands of Balaria. This asshole was moving about that pace, despite the armor.

Rigar fired. Plugged him directly in the solar plexus. Kill shot. At least, it should have been.

The bolt shattered across his breastplate as if it was made of Pargossian glass.

Rigar squeezed down on the trigger and held it there, showering the man with bolts.

None of them had a visible impact.

By that time, Wister and Grotto had climbed up to the little stone wall, leveled their own repeating crossbows, and started releasing. They exploded around the charging man in a cloud of chaff. He reared back and threw the balled-up warden. Caught Wister in the chest and whipped him backward. He landed somewhere behind Rigar with a wet smack.

The white-armored man leapt over the wall and grabbed Grotto by the head.

"Morning," he growled.

Then squeezed.

More blood splashed into Rigar's eyes, blinding him and putting him on his ass. There were shouts from below. Then sounds of tearing flesh and joints. When Rigar managed to blink his eyes back into a semblance of vision, the white-armored man was looming over a fallen Wormwrot, beating him to death with his own arms.

Rigar stepped forward, planning to try a close-range crossbow bolt to the base of his neck, which looked like a potential weak spot. But the armored man saw him just as he was raising his crossbow. He swatted Rigar away with one of the arms.

Rigar was airborne for a few seconds, then he crashed through a wooden wall. Scraped the shit out of his face on something rough and sharp.

He tried to breathe. Couldn't. Tried to stand up. Couldn't. For the third time in as many minutes, he was blinded. All kinds of sharp, scratchy shit in his eyes. His boots were gone, and it took Rigar a second to realize that the white-armored man had hit him so hard that he'd been separated from his footwear.

He blinked until he could make out the blurry outlines of his surroundings. He'd been thrown into an old gardening shed. A bunch of rusted hoes were in one corner.

Still gasping for air, Rigar crawled through the hay, reaching the door and poking his head through.

The whole unit was rushing across the yard, blades drawn. Shouting.

The man in white armor jumped into the muddy fray. He'd dropped the arms and was swinging his fists left and right. He took no discernible damage from the swords and spears clattering against him, but dealt out killing blows each time his fist connected with a man, often jamming his whole arm straight through their armored bodies, then scooping out a bunch of organs as he pulled it back through.

He fought like an acolyte, which made Rigar wonder where Acolyte 408 was.

Less than a minute later, the man in white armor had slaughtered the whole platoon except for Westley, who had the new kind of dragon-bone shield Osyrus Ward had designed. The man in white armor beat him back against the wall of the holdfast with a series of brutal punches and shoves and charges that dented the shields, but didn't break them.

Before he could finish Westley off, Acolyte 408 came around the corner at a full run. Dragon-bone barbs popped out of his arm as he ran, turning the limb into the equivalent of a morning star. He slammed his arm into the man in white armor, which sent him flying into the outer wall about thirty strides away, where he shattered two granite blocks and settled into a heap. Alive, but not in a rush to get up.

The acolyte crossed the yard. Stopped a few strides away.

"Master Ward said that we might encounter one of his older models in the field," he hissed. "Such a primitive application."

"Did its job, though."

"Please. A relic like you could never defeat me."

"Wasn't trying to. Just wanted to clear the field and soak up the balance of your attention. Wouldn't want none of it wandering to the top o' that holdfast."

The acolyte cocked his head. Looked to the holdfast.

Rigar looked up, too. Squinted. There was another man up there. He wasn't wearing armor or a shirt or boots, but he was holding a long, queer-looking spear. His dark hair was whipping around in the strong wind.

The man jumped off the holdfast. Collided with Acolyte 408 and jammed the spear straight into his right eye, pinning him to the ground. Acolyte 408 tried to grab the spear shaft, but the man gave his weapon a hard twist.

Acolyte 408 went still.

The spearman was tall. Lean. His black hair was shorter than most Almirans kept it, but unruly and wild all the same. He also had a blue bar on each cheek and about sixty dragon tattoos running down his left arm.

The Flawless Bershad. Had to be.

For unclear reasons, Westley decided this was a good time to charge forward with a war howl and raised sword and braced shield.

Bershad whipped his spear around, shearing the shield apart and slicing Westley's throat open—his larynx flew into the mud like a chucked stone. Westley fell over, clutching his throat.

Bershad turned back to acolyte 408. Peered into the wound in his eye like a man studying an animal burrow.

The armored man removed his helmet, revealing a long shock of greasy red hair.

"Clean?" he asked.

"Clean enough," Bershad said. He looked around at the yard of corpses. "Whole thing went pretty smooth, all things considered."

"Speak for yourself." The red-haired man got up with a groan. Gave his body a gentle once-over. "Bastard broke a few o' my scales. Cracked a rib, maybe. And I don't repair the bastards all quick like you."

Bershad shrugged. "You're the one who wanted to go in strong."

"Yeah." The redhead smiled. Looked around. "Last time you had all the fun by yourself."

"I wouldn't call this fun, Simeon."

"That's 'cause you're a morose bastard. You gotta see the joy in this. The beauty."

Simeon went over to Westley and tore his head off.

"Again with that shit?" Bershad asked.

"Simple but effective war tactic." Simeon moved to the next corpse. Pulled his head off, too. "The next Balarian patrol that comes through is gonna find all the bodies but no heads, and they're gonna be wondering where they went. And when they don't find 'em, they're gonna keep wondering. 'What happened to all those fucking heads?' they'll ask. Are the Jaguars eating them? Casting spells? Making bone fences? Who's to say."

He tore another man's head off.

"And when the next battle comes, we'll have the edge. 'Cause we know what happened to the heads, and they don't."

"Do you know how insane that sounds?"

"You lowlanders just don't understand this type of war. Outnumbered like this—with limited territory and resources—killing the enemy ain't enough." He tapped his temple, leaving a bloody mark. "You gotta make war on their minds, too. On their *dreams*."

"And tearing the heads off dead men will accomplish that?"

"Exactly. Doubt's what kills a man, Silas! Doubt, and poor physical conditioning."

"No. Sharp objects kill people. Doubt just bothers them when *they're* trying to sleep at night."

"Easier to kill a man who's sleep deprived, too."

Bershad shrugged. Then he shoved acolyte 408 onto his stomach, drew a meat cleaver from his belt, and started hacking into his spine. Not too hard—more like a butcher making careful quarters of a quality carcass he could sell for a premium.

"You give me shit for taking heads, but you're the one mutilating all the grayskin creatures."

"This serves a purpose. Those heads are just extra weight, and I'm not helping you carry them back."

"Fine. I can always use the exercise. Because poor—"

"Physical conditioning kills men. Yeah. Got it."

Simeon tore another man's head off. Then stood up and took a long, deep breath.

"Smell that? Ghalamarian blood. I can always tell the difference. Smells kinda musty. Like bad wheat."

Bershad sniffed the air.

"I smell it." Another sniff. "Some of it hasn't gone cold quite yet."

Simeon smiled. "Interesting."

Bershad turned and looked directly at Rigar—wild, green eyes narrowing. "I'll get him."

Before Rigar could even think about running away, Bershad had crossed the yard and yanked him out of the shed by his wrists, pulling so hard it felt like they'd come out of the sockets. He hauled him through the mud and left him in a heap. Glared down at him.

"Name."

"R–Rigar. Private Rigar."

"Where are you from?" Simeon asked.

"Pargos," he said quickly.

Rigar was really from Cornish—one of the Ghalamarian cities that bordered the Skojit territory of the Razorback Mountains. But that seemed like an unwise origin to share.

"That right?" Simeon asked. "'Cause Rigar doesn't sound particularly Pargossian. Their names always have a shitload of *Ls* in them. Calluckstan. Ackllemel. Mollevan. Like that."

"Uh, I guess I'm an exception?"

Simeon gave him a long look, then crouched down. Up close, Rigar could see that his white armor was made from dragon scales that were battered with nicks and scars and dents. Beneath the scales, there were scores of small moving parts that fit to his muscular body like a snake's skin.

"What do you think, Silas?"

"Pargossians all smell like those jasmine spices they trade," Bershad said. "He smells like wheat and fear."

"Wheat. Ghalamarians and their fucking wheat." Simeon stood up. "Welp, it's settled. Gonna use Rigar's skull as my new piss pot."

He raised his bloody fist. Rigar dug around in his pockets for his shell, but his fingers were jelly.

"Wait." Bershad stopped him. "Might be he does smell like jasmine after all. Yeah. I'm getting some whiffs of it—just traces on his breath, though. Could be my imagination."

"Quite the conundrum," Simeon said. "What'll sway the balance, you think?"

"Oh, I'd say the value of the words his breath can form will have a direct impact."

"I can be valuable!" Rigar said quickly, trying to think. "We're under contract with Osyrus Ward. Wormwrot is supposed to find and map every dragon warren in the Dainwood. There's something inside of them that the Madman wants. We find the warrens, and the acolytes come take it out."

"I already know that," Bershad said. "Gonna have to do better."

Rigar tried to think of something else, but his mind was blank with fear.

"How long have you been soldiering for Wormwrot?" Bershad pressed.

"A month," Rigar lied, figuring they'd have less sympathy for a veteran.

"Before that?"

"I was a hired blade for merchant galleys in and out of Taggarstan."

"Why the change of vocation?"

Rigar shrugged. "Commander Vergun was hiring up pretty much any man who knew his way around a sword. And he pays better than anyone. Ten gold pieces a week." Rigar swallowed. "We get an extra hundred for each Jaguar we kill."

"Bounties, is it?"

Rigar nodded.

Bershad's face darkened. "Where is Vallen Vergun?"

Rigar hesitated. "He moves around. Same as you. I . . . I don't know where he is."

"Ghalamarians are known for their lack of specific knowledge." Simeon growled. He raised his blood-soaked fist again.

"Wait! Just wait!"

Simeon's fist stayed where it was, poised over Rigar's face and dripping blood onto his forehead. Rigar tried to think of something useful they wouldn't already know.

"We use a secret code to rank the warrens. There's a rating system based on the amount of vines and overgrowth coming out the entrance." Rigar drew a series of symbols in the dirt beside him. "This is for a small one. This is medium. And these are for the largest. My crew's never found a big one, but I heard from another private that Commander Vergun joins the escort crew personally to harvest them. Doesn't want anything going wrong."

Bershad squatted. Studied the symbols.

Simeon scratched his head, which led to a streak of brain and blood through his hair. "So, this one a Ghalamarian or not?"

Bershad looked back at Rigar. Scanned his wounds. "You're bleeding pretty bad, and you got a lot of jungle between here and home. If you brave the wilds, chances are you'll wind up taking an ugly and painful trip down the river. You want it done clean, instead?"

He lifted his spear a little. Not in a threatening way, just to make it clear what was on offer.

Rigar looked at the spear point, then the clean hole in Acolyte 408's head. Then he looked at the torn and shredded corpses that Simeon had created. Between the two, a clean death seemed preferable, but their next skyship extraction point was only ten leagues away. He could make it.

"I'll take my chances with the jungle, if you're offering the option."

Bershad nodded. "I think this one's Pargossian after all. They're known for being stubborn bastards."

Simeon sighed. "Your merciful nature is the most irritating thing about you, Silas."

"Nobody's ever told me that before," said Bershad. "You sure you aren't just a murderous bastard?"

"Might be a factor as well." Simeon spat. Gave Rigar a long, hard look. Then he pointed east. "Go."

Rigar crab-walked backward—hoping to get some space in case it was a trick—then got to his feet and started a stumbling walk. His ribs were screaming and his face was bleeding and he didn't have any boots, but he didn't care. He could make it.

"And Rigar?" Bershad called.

He turned around, sinking his shoulders and preparing for a spear to be hucked through his heart. But Bershad was still squatting on the ground—his blue tattoos a stark contrast against his skin in the morning light. He pointed up with one finger.

"Keep an eye on the skies. The dragons rule this jungle."

2

VERA
Ghalamar, City of Argel

Vera's left pauldron pinched her armpit as she climbed the tower of Argel's keep. Garret was a stride below her. The sun had set three minutes ago.

They were heading for the private chambers of Argel's ruler, a man named Garwin. He'd been a lowly baron the last time Vera passed through Argel, and she'd watched his city ravaged by a Red Skull. But his prospects seemed to have improved since then.

First, he wasn't a baron anymore, but a count.

The promotion seemed to have come with more resources. His keep had been rebuilt twice as tall, and in the latest Balarian design— all steel beams and decorative clockwork gears. A lingering reward for Garwin's loyalty to the murdered emperor, Mercer Domitian.

But Garwin's time basking in the wealthy, kind sun of the empire was over. Osyrus Ward had requested a full garrison of Garwin's troops delivered to Floodhaven to fuel the war effort in the Dainwood, and Garwin was dragging his feet on the delivery. He knew that Ward needed soldiers badly, so he was trying to delay his way into a better deal.

Instead of sending more favorable terms, Osyrus had sent Vera and Garret.

They reached the upper chambers, which had their windows cracked open to let in the cool sea breeze. Garwin was lying facedown on a table, getting massaged by two yellow-haired Ghalamarians. There were candles and incense. The women were chanting and running oiled hands across his body in a synchronized pattern that would have been beautiful if Garwin wasn't so hairy. The rough sound of his oiled hair being swished around made Vera's skin crawl.

She waited. A few minutes later, one of the women tapped Garwin on his ass, and he flipped over onto his back. Kept his eyes closed. They continued massaging—one starting at his feet and the other at his chest. Eventually, the two of them met at his cock. One started rubbing his balls while the other began jerking his cock into a stiff erection. His moans were loud enough to cover her entrance.

Vera glanced down at Garret, who gave her a single nod.

She opened the window a little wider. Slipped through.

Both women were focused on their work, so they didn't notice her presence until she took a chair from the corner of the room, thumped it down in the middle of the room, and sat.

The girl who'd been jerking Garwin off yelped and brought both hands to her mouth, which caused Garwin's cock to slap against his ample belly. He shot up with a Ghalamarian curse, but froze when he saw Vera.

"Both of you, back up against the far wall," Vera said in Ghalamarian. "Make no sound, make no fuss, and you will both live."

The women did as they were told. By the time their palms were pressed against the stone wall, Garwin's cock had completely retreated into his mound of wild pubic hair. Vera motioned to it with one of her daggers and smiled.

"Not sure I've ever seen a cock shrink that fast." She motioned to her dark hair. "Guess I'm not your type?"

"Who the fuck are you?" Garwin growled.

"You know who I am, Garwin. And you know why I'm here."

"The Madman wants his soldiers."

"You promised them a fortnight ago. Yet the barracks of Floodhaven sit empty."

"As does my skyline," Garwin responded, then smiled. "What's the matter, is Osyrus Ward a little short on spare skyships to come cajole me into submission?"

He was, but there was no reason to confirm that truth for Garwin.

"Ward wasn't in a rush to firebomb a city full of perfectly capable soldiers until he learned the reason for the delay."

Garwin smiled. "The Almiran savages are tearing apart any soldiers who get dropped into that jungle. If Ward wants my men to face a similar carnage, I need more coin."

Ah. Simple greed.

"No. You will honor the agreement, or I will kill you in this room."

Vera knew that Garwin was going to attack her because his pupils dilated and his shoulder muscles tensed. But all he managed was half a lunge before Garret's noose slipped around his throat and tightened, then hauled him up through the air like a bundle of hay being lifted to the top rafters of a barn. Vera leaned back in the chair and kicked the massage table backward, but not too far. Garwin's legs flailed as they sought purchase.

He gurgled. His face was beginning to turn purple. But eventually he found the table again with his toes and managed to balance himself on it by pushing his naked belly forward.

Fully exposed and vulnerable. Good.

"Garwin, Garwin, Garwin." Vera tapped her dagger against her palm in time with the name. "That wasn't a very smart negotiating tactic."

"Fucking bitch," he rasped.

She shrugged. "There is a new deal on offer now. You will deliver your troops on the next tide. All of them. You will receive no remuneration for your contribution to the war effort, other than the chance to continue drawing breath through your greedy lungs. If you do not adhere to these instructions, I will come back here and I will kill you."

Vera stood up from the chair. Stepped forward. She used her dagger to lift the stubby head of Garwin's cock slightly. Balanced it on the flat of the blade.

"You will not get a soldier's death from me. It will not be clean, and it will not be fast. And while the skyships of Kira's empire are currently occupied, they will arrive at their earliest convenience, and kill every man, woman, and child of Argel. Do you understand?"

The veins in his forehead were bulging with a mixture of strain and fury. But he nodded.

"Are you going to be a more obedient count from here forward?"

"Yes."

"Good."

Vera retracted the dagger, then motioned to Garret, who released the noose and let Garwin collapse on the lush, Pargossian carpet covering the floor. He rubbed his throat while he heaved in some ragged breaths.

Vera glanced at the two women, one of whom was crying. The other was shivering, despite the sticky, humid night. "Neither of you will breathe a word of this to anyone," she said. "Or it will be your bedrooms that I visit. Clear?"

They both nodded. Eyes full of fear.

"Good." She crouched down so Garwin could see her eyes and hear her better. "I wish you calm seas and clear skies on your journey to Almira."

Vera moved to the window.

"Should have known the widows would throw in with the Madman after Okinu died. Your order plays solemn and loyal bodyguards, but you're all just lackeys to whomever holds the most power." He spat. "Call me greedy if you want. Intimidate me into obedience. But you're not better than me. None of the widows are."

Vera looked back at him. "My order is destroyed, Garwin. I am the last Papyrian widow. And I've never pretended to be better than anyone."

———

She and Garret left Argel the same way they came in—climbing down the tower and sneaking through the shadows and alleys.

Vera would have preferred to fly the *Blue Sparrow* directly above Garwin's tower and drop in by rope. Moving through the city on foot was the most dangerous part of this mission. But Osyrus had wanted to show Garwin that it wasn't just the skyships that could get to him. It was also a regular blade, brought to him by a human hand in the night.

The logic made sense, but Osyrus Ward wasn't the one sneaking in and out of a fortified city. They'd used a drainage tunnel with a rusted-out grate to get in, and the plan had been to use the same method for getting out.

That would have worked just fine if there weren't four spearmen guarding the mouth of the drain when they returned to it.

Garret and Vera both squatted in the shadows of an alley that ended about two hundred paces from the grate.

"I thought Ward's spies said they never guarded the drain," Garret whispered.

"Either the spy was wrong, or he lied. Either way, we have a problem."

"Secondary exit?"

That involved climbing up one of the dragon watchtowers on the opposite side of the city, which was manned by two sentries who—according to their intelligence—emptied an entire bag of wine into their stomachs before night watch, and worked their way through a second one before their shift ended.

Vera checked the watch on the inside of her wrist. Shook her head.

"Too far away. The sun will be up by the time we return to the *Blue Sparrow*. Ward wants us to be invisible on this one."

Garret nodded. Turned back to the spearmen. "Then this needs to be silent."

"Yes."

They both studied the terrain. There was a long shadow stretching from where they were positioned to a clump of ferns about twenty strides from the left side of the grate. A big stack of replacement shingles gave good cover on the ride side, but it was farther away.

"I'm left," Vera said. "You're right."

"Got it."

They split up and moved into position, both moving slowly and carefully to avoid attracting the attention of the four spearmen, who were relaxed but generally alert. Every few minutes one of them spat or muttered something, but otherwise they kept their eyes on their sectors.

When Vera reached the stack of shingles, she loaded a shot into her close-range sling, then took a spare shot out and tapped it against a crooked nail that was hammered into one of the shingles. It wasn't a loud or suspicious sound, but Vera had been working with Garret long enough to know that it would work as a signal.

She got a good grip on her sling with her right hand, then pulled it taut with her left, which would save her half a second when it came time to swing it.

Silence. One of the guards farted. Then spat again. Tamped the spittle into the dirt with his boot.

Then a hemp rope wrapped around his throat and yanked him into the shadows.

Vera waited for the remaining three to turn away from her. When they did, she stood and whipped her sling in a tight circle. Released. Her shot buried into the back of the nearest spearmen's skull. She followed her shot at a full sprint, drawing *Owaru* as she ran. The spearman tottered and fell before she'd covered half the distance. The sound of their comrade falling over got the two remaining spearmen to turn around again and face her. They dropped their spears into a defensive position. Well-trained bastards.

Vera reared back with *Owaru* like she was poised to strike, but at the last minute she drew *Kaisha* off her left hip and threw her into the nearest spearman's throat. It was a good way to kill him without a sound, but it left her completely vulnerable to a spear strike from the last man, who reared back and prepared to skewer her.

Garret appeared from the shadows and stabbed him through the back of the neck. Held his hand over his mouth while he died. Lowered him to the ground slowly. Pulled his knife out of the back of his neck, cleaned the blood off with three quick strokes across the dead man's cloak, and sheathed it again. He looked at Vera.

"We'll string them together, then pull them through the drainage pipe after us," Vera said. "Nobody will find them until the smell gives them away."

Garret nodded, then starting tying the corpses together.

———

There was an open field on the far side of the sewer tunnel that led to a riverbank with good cover. She and Garret crossed the field in silence, sticking to whatever shadows they could find. Neither spoke until they'd dropped down into the riverbank, and tucked themselves beneath an overhang.

Vera remembered when the Red Skull had attacked Argel during her first visit. This was where the people of the city had taken cover. Now she was doing the same. Strange to have the motions of her life running in circles like this.

Vera pressed two fingers against the watch in her bracer, which caused it to give her the time in four quick pulses. A recent improvement from Osyrus Ward that allowed her to tell time in pure darkness.

"Seventeen minutes," she said.

"Got it."

Vera was tempted to pass the time by smoking her pipe, but that was a really good way to attract the attention of a dragon or a passing human or both. Sharpening her blades wasn't a great idea, either. So, she tried to readjust that left pauldron that had been digging into her armpit during the climb.

Garret produced a small vial of oil wrapped in black cloth from his satchel and started rubbing oil along the length of that rope he liked so much.

For a while, they worked on their respective equipment in silence. The problematic pauldron was the same piece of armor that a Skojit had sheared off during Vera's first trip over the Razorback Mountains, and despite visiting half the armories in Burz-al-dun, nobody had been able to restore the damaged piece to its former functionality. Sharkskin armor was an obstinate material that required years to master.

A widow's armorer in Himeja might have been able to repair it properly. But they were dead, along with everyone else in the capital. At this point, she just had to accept the damage as permanent.

"You told Garwin that you were the last Papyrian widow," Garret said, breaking her out of her thoughts. "Are you sure about that?"

This was the seventh job they'd done together, but the first time he'd asked a question that wasn't required to complete their work.

"Most of my order was killed in the bombing of Himeja," Vera said. "A few were scattered across Almira. Remnants of the aid that Okinu sent to Ashlyn before she was deposed. But I killed the last of those myself."

"Why?"

"She betrayed Kira."

"But there could be other widows. Hiding out in some dark corner of the world."

"No."

"How can you be sure?"

Vera took a breath. "Because I serve the man who destroyed Papyria. If there were any other widows alive, they would have come to try and kill me by now."

"Fair point."

He worked a fresh glob of oil into his noose. Seemed done with the conversation, which was fine with her. But he spoke again a few minutes later.

"I enjoy working with you," he said.

Vera scoffed. Thought he was joking at first, then saw his serious face and was just confused.

"Why's that?" she asked.

"Garwin never gained a modicum of control over his situation. And on the way out when those four guards could have made things messy, you kept calm and kept it clean." He looked at her. "You should be proud of your skills. They're impressive."

"There's nothing impressive about extorting a naked lord."

"No, not the actual job. I don't care about that." He returned his attention to the rope. Tested a braid of his noose with two fingers. "But the skills required to complete the job—and to do it clean—those are different. There is a beauty in your proficiency."

She let that comment linger on its own for a moment, unsure of how to respond. She doubted that Garret offered compliments to people on a regular basis. This was a chance to learn more about the enigmatic man she'd been traveling with for almost two moon turns, but barely knew.

"You don't care about the work that we do?" she asked.

"The outcome is inconsequential."

"Not sure the dead spearmen going to rot in that drain would agree."

He blinked. "What I mean is that *all* outcomes are inconsequential. Someone will win this war eventually. Probably Osyrus Ward, but you never know. Jungle warfare is messy. Unpredictable." He used a knife to slice away a few frayed strands of his rope. "But regardless, the outcome will be the same. There'll be a period of peace. Terra will lick her wounds. A fresh crop of soldiers will be born, and trained for the thresher. And then—a decade or two from now—a new war will start. And another after that, and another after that. The loop is endless and pointless. The best you can do is find beauty in the minutiae."

"I disagree," said Vera. "You can also find people that mean something to you and protect them."

"Ah, right," said Garret. "Your wounded empress. Kira. How long since you last saw her?"

"Forty-seven days." She glanced at the watch embedded in her bracer. "Six hours. Fifteen minutes."

"Are you counting the seconds, too?"

Vera gave him a look, but didn't say anything.

"I suppose that is why you're fighting on the wrong side of this war," Garret continued.

"I thought you said that you didn't believe in right and wrong."

"I don't *care* about right and wrong. But you do. Don't tell me that you believe Terra is a better place with Osyrus Ward lording over her skies."

"Ward is the only person keeping Kira alive. The only one who can heal her."

"We've been working together for months. Been to almost every country in Terra doing the Madman's work. If he can heal her, he is certainly taking his time."

Vera shook her head. "Kira is to come off the machines upon my return. She'll be ready. I have his word."

"And you trust it?"

"I don't trust anyone."

"Then why did you agree to be gone for so long?" he asked.

Vera picked at a cut near one fingernail that had been opened during their climb up the Argel tower. Winced. "Because I don't serve her by moping by her side."

"But you serve her by serving Osyrus Ward?"

She picked a scab off her knuckles. Flicked it away.

"Something like that."

The real reason that Vera had agreed to crisscross Terra on behalf of Osyrus Ward was more complicated, but she wasn't going to share that with Garret the Hangman. The man had an empty, black pit where his soul should have been.

Garret coiled his noose into a neat circle and hooked it to his hip. "I supposed you'll be done with these missions, then. Once your empress is recovered."

"That's right."

"Too bad. We make a good team."

Garret was right. Not only had they helped Osyrus Ward shore up influence all over Terra, but they'd been extremely successful at it. The closest they'd come to a mistake was that hiccup leaving Argel. Somehow, being good at helping Osyrus Ward made her feel even worse about it. The opposite of Garret, apparently.

There was a rumble in the distance. The familiar churn of the *Blue Sparrow*'s engines. A moment later, the skyship rose over a southern cliff and moved toward their position.

Since the *Sparrow* had no weapons and light armor, it was the only skyship that Osyrus was willing to spare for missions like this one. All of the others were on endless patrols and combat drops in the Dainwood, or hovering eternally over a city of Terra, threatening them into good behavior.

Garret headed to the skyship. Vera followed, realizing that this was the first time she'd ever seen the man's back.

"Success?" Decimar asked when they came aboard.

"He'll deliver."

Decimar nodded, then started rattling off orders to his men. They were airborne and heading back to Floodhaven two minutes later.

The sun still hadn't risen, and darkness covered their escape.

3

BERSHAD
City of Deepdale

The heads that Simeon insisted on bringing with him had begun to fester during the journey back to Deepdale. The hulking Skojit approached the city amidst a horde of black flies. The pests didn't seem to bother Simeon, but they attracted the attention and ire of the wardens camped outside the city as they walked through.

Kerrigan was due back with another shipment of food from Dunfar, so most of the disparate warden crews that comprised the Jaguar Army had returned to Deepdale to get their rations, then scatter back into the forest and continue the war. It was dangerous to gather in one place, but there were so many Blackjacks in the area surrounding Deepdale that the skyships couldn't reach the city. Even getting through on foot was dangerous. The Jaguars used secret pathways that were lined with choke weed, which Blackjacks naturally avoided if it grew in high concentrations.

For the time being, Deepdale was the safest place in the realm of Terra. But when the Blackjacks moved on in a few months, that would all change.

Bershad saw Willem, who was playing dice with his men while a caiman cooked over a spit, and headed over. There were seven mud totems arranged around the fire with steel scraps in their hands, looking out at the forest.

"Again with the fucking heads?" Willem asked, frowning at Simeon.

"Just making war on the Balarians' minds," Simeon said.

"Ever considered that the dragonscale armor you wear is war enough?" Willem asked.

Simeon seemed to give that real consideration.

"No. The heads are important."

"Why?" Willem asked.

"Don't get him started," Bershad said.

Willem swatted at some flies that zipped over to the caiman. "Well, do you think you can take your attack on dreams away from our cook fire, at least?"

Simeon grunted. "You lowlanders have squirrel piss for blood. All of you."

The group of veteran soldiers—who'd probably sent a hundred men down the river between them—took the insult in stride. When Simeon saw he couldn't rile any of them up, he headed off to the outer reaches of the camp with his cargo. His plans for the heads was unclear.

"Why do you let him do that?" Willem asked.

"I let you press dead men's eyes into your mud totems," Bershad said. "Can't abide a double standard."

"There's a difference between popping eyes out of dead men and pulling their entire head off, then traveling around with it."

"There is," Bershad agreed. "Simeon would argue that stopping at the eyes isn't far enough."

"Gods, everyone who set foot on that island up north went fucking insane. You should have your brains checked for mushroom rot or something."

"Who told you about the mushrooms?"

"Felgor," said three wardens at once.

"Figures."

Bershad didn't know Willem that well, but he knew the man who'd brought him up. Jon Cumberland. He was a veteran who'd served Bershad's father and carried a strong reputation. Cumberland had been killed by Wormwrot, and from what Bershad could see, Willem was doing his best to fill his shoes. He was the closest thing the Jaguar Army had to a leader.

Willem rolled the dice. Cursed at the result.

"Looks like you came back with a haul of your own," Willem said, pointing at the sack over Bershad's shoulder, which was full of the lodestones and machinery he'd cut out of the grayskin.

"Yeah. I'm on my way to Ashlyn now."

"She's been cooped up in the castle with Jolan all morning," Willem said. "Running experiments."

After Fallon's Roost, Ashlyn and Jolan had retreated from the front lines to try and figure out what had gone wrong. The Deepdale Castle had been the best space for a laboratory.

"Performing *demoncraft,* you mean," muttered a red-haired warden named Sem.

Willem shrugged. "Experiments. Alchemy. Demoncraft. They're all just labels for complex systems that require esoteric knowledge to understand."

"Sounds to me like you're spewing back the chewed-up words of your gray-robed friend again."

"Repeating Jolan's words doesn't make them wrong."

"Why're you so fond of that kid, anyway?" Sem asked.

"He was with me during the skyship thing last winter."

"How'd an alchemist get roped into that goatfuck?"

"Long story," Willem said. "And I'm not drunk or depressed enough to tell it."

Bershad looked up the hill toward the castle. Frowned. One of the towers was missing.

"What happened to the northern tower?" he asked.

"That? Uh, word is something went awry with Ashlyn's work a few weeks ago. Nobody got hurt, though. Aside from your ancestors' masonry."

"See, that's what I'm talking about," said Sem. "In my book, anything that can destroy a castle tower is demoncraft."

They continued bickering. Bershad eyed the caiman as it cooked on the spit, his mouth watering. They'd pushed hard getting back to Deepdale, and hadn't eaten in two days.

He dropped the sack, went over to the caiman, and drew his dagger.

"That ain't done yet," Willem said.

Bershad ignored him. Shaved off a long slice of meat and ate it in two big bites. A flood of tender, fishy flavor filled his mouth.

Eating food always strengthened his connection to the Nomad. He could feel her up in the rafters of the sky, like there was a long string running between them that someone had just thrummed. And he knew she could taste the caiman in her mouth, too. She careened down from the clouds in a tight dive. When she was about two hundred strides from the ground, she opened her wings to kill the descent. Took roost in a massive Daintree that overlooked the camp.

Some of the nearby wardens dropped their food or drink and scrambled for cover. But most of the men in camp had fought alongside

Bershad at one point or another during this war, so they knew about him and the Nomad. A few of them even lifted their drinks in her direction.

Bershad gave her a look, and she craned her head in response.

"Don't even think about giving your pet lizard a share of that caiman," Willem warned. "I can afford to give the lord of Deepdale a slice of meat, but the dragon's gotta procure her own meals."

"She's not my pet," said Bershad.

"Felgor said otherwise."

"Look, as a general rule, just ignore anything that Balarian thief says."

"So, her name isn't Smokey?" Sem asked.

"She's a dragon," Bershad said. "She doesn't have a name."

While they'd been talking, a group of fifteen wardens had come out of the forest. All of them were wearing black Jaguar Masks. The man leading them had long, wild hair that was streaked with mud.

"Oromir the Black, scourge upon the Balarians!" shouted a visibly drunk warden. "How many Wormwrot this month?"

Oromir didn't respond, but he did take off his mask. His left cheek and throat were covered in scars. The top of his left ear was missing.

"Hey, Oro," said Willem. "Got a caiman that's almost ready, if you're hungry."

Willem and Oromir had been with Jolan during the skyship theft gone wrong last winter. From what Bershad had seen, the two wardens had maintained a distant but friendly relationship. But Oromir and Jolan never spoke. Bershad didn't know exactly why, but knew it had something to do with how Jon Cumberland had died.

Oromir gave Bershad a cursory glance as he approached the fire, then took a spot across from Willem and produced a bottle of what smelled like brandy mixed with acid. Took a long drink.

"How've you fared?" Willem asked him.

"Me and my crew tracked three score of Wormwrot over the Green Hills," Oromir said. "One score managed to get scooped up by a skyship before we could get at 'em. Sent the rest down the river."

"You killed forty Wormwrot with fifteen men?" Bershad asked.

Oromir looked at him. "That's right."

"Any losses on your side?" asked Willem.

"The skyship that picked up the survivors dropped a grayskin on us." Oromir took another long sip. "Gunnar wasn't quick enough melting into the jungle. Got torn apart."

Everyone went quiet. Sem started pinching out a mud totem. It could have been for Gunnar's soul, but it could have been in the hopes of conjuring a similar outcome for his crew in the future.

Against a grayskin, only losing one man was an excellent result.

"Any word on the gray-eyed Balarian who killed Cumberland?" Willem asked.

"His name is Garret," said Oromir. "And no. Nothing since those men we captured in Salt Marsh said he's abroad, working for the Madman."

"Too bad."

"I'll get him," Oromir said, with a tone of finality that made Bershad think if this Garret didn't return to Almira, Oromir would cross the whole realm of Terra to find him.

"How'd you do?" Oromir asked Willem.

"Mixed bag. Ran a river-split ambush up north that left more dead on their side than ours, but the margin was thin. We had better luck in the east. Lured a bunch of idiots toward a nest of Blackjacks with the mud totems. They thought they were tracking us down. Got themselves eaten instead."

"Morons don't know the jungle at all," Sem muttered. "What kind of fools don't notice they're walking into a Blackjack nest?"

"Ghalamarians, judging from their armor." Willem looked around. "Don't tell Simeon, though. He'll go charging off in an attempt to collect more heads."

"What's his problem with Ghalamarians, exactly?" asked Sem.

"He's Skojit."

"I know he's Skojit. But what's his problem?"

Willem blinked at him. "You're not really a student of history, are you?"

"I'm a warden of the Dainwood. Last I checked, history doesn't help much when you're sneaking up on assholes in the jungle and stabbing them."

"Carlyle Llayawin would have disagreed, then given you a two-hour lecture on crossbows, but seeing as he's dead and I ain't no high-warden, let's just say that any man with Skojit blood in his veins has good cause to hate Ghalamarians and leave it at that. Bastards have spent two hundred years encroaching on their lands."

"Oh yeah?" Sem crossed his arms. "In that case, I feel that I've got cause to hate the bastards, too. Especially seeing as they drop fresh assholes into the jungle faster than we can kill them. Whole war's like one man standing beneath a wasp nest, swatting at the bastards one at a time, thinking that'll eliminate the problem."

Willem narrowed his eyes. "Did you just make that up?"

"Maybe."

"I've never heard you use a metaphor once in your whole fucking life."

"Fine, fine. I heard it from that big Lysterian pirate, Goll." Sem gave a sly smile. "But regurgitating other people's words don't make them wrong."

Willem waved him off. "Yeah, yeah."

Bershad looked around the camp. A lot of familiar faces were missing.

"What happened to Senlin's crew?" Bershad asked. "And Uppum?"

They were both veteran wardens who'd fought with him at Glenlock. Good men.

Willem winced. "They got tangled up with a grayskin. We found their remains smeared across a whole swath of forest."

"Fucking grayskins," Sem muttered.

"It's not just grayskins. Longbowmen did a number on Newt's and Grant's crews, too," Willem muttered. "They got caught trying to cross an open field. Half died, the other half are at the surgery tents up by the castle. For most, those tents are just a waystation before they head down the river. And almost none of 'em recover enough to rejoin the fight."

He looked at Bershad, expecting him to say something. But he couldn't think of anything helpful to say about that news.

He picked up his sack of grayskin parts. "I need to get these to Ashlyn."

"Why're you even bothering to haul that crap to her anymore?" Oromir asked. "She had her chance with metal and magic last spring, and it went to shit in a real big hurry at Fallon's Roost."

He motioned to the scars on his face, which he'd gotten at Fallon's Roost.

"Because things are still going to shit," Bershad said. "They're just doing it slower."

Bershad headed toward the city. The Nomad moved with him, hopping onto a large Daintree that grew near the city walls.

There was a group of hawkers bringing wares to the camp. Deepdale folk were used to Blackjacks in the general area, but not enormous Gray-Winged Nomads at their walls. They dropped their wares and scattered. One man with a loud voice sprinted back through the city gates, screaming for them to be closed.

"Think you better give me some distance," Bershad said to the Nomad.

She snorted from her spot on the branches. Looked to the castle, then back at him.

"I'm sure Ashlyn wants to see you, too. She's only got seventy sketches of you, so hitting seventy-one is most definitely a high priority. But there's the issue of widespread panic and alarm if you follow me into the city."

The Nomad licked her jowls. Sniffed at the fruit of a mango tree that was growing alongside the Dainwood.

"Yeah, eat some fruit while you wait." He paused. The fruity scent of the mango was filling his own nose, along with the Nomad's. "Smells ripe."

She gave him an irritated look.

"Okay, okay. That one's not quite ripe. But just wait here and don't eat any people."

The dragon let out one final, irritated snort, then settled herself into the canopy.

"Good enough."

———

As soon as Bershad was behind Deepdale's walls, he felt an itchy discomfort sprawl across his skin like the first sign of a bad rash coming on. Cities always did that to him, even ones that had been built and ruled by his ancestors.

He headed up Canal Street, toward the castle. The street was named after the canal that ran alongside it, which was fed by a deep lake in the middle of the city. The water smelled of moss and algae and fresh rain.

Armorers and craftsmen were waiting outside their shops along Canal Street, trying to drum up business from anyone passing by. They recognized him as he passed.

"Lord Bershad, is today the day I can finally convince you to try my wares?" said the cobbler with a smile, eyeing Bershad's bare feet.

"Maybe next time."

"Ah." He waved the notion away. "Sometimes I fear you'll start a trend and put me out of business. I make a totem every night to honor the thornbushes and scorpions to keep my trade going."

"Not a bad idea."

The armorer asked for another look at his dragon-bone shield and Naga spear. Praised the craftsmanship, as always.

"Who made it?" he asked for the fiftieth time.

Bershad shook his head. "That's a long story, and I'm already late."

He continued uphill until he reached the lake. There was a girl fishing along one bank.

"Catch anything?" he asked.

The girl looked up, then quickly stiffened when she saw who'd come up behind her.

"Lord Silas," she said, starting to dip into a bow.

"Better focus on your fishing," he said, halting the formalities. When he was younger, Bershad had never liked the ass-kissing that came with being a lord. But now—after all his years outside, without a roof or a kind eye for leagues—he hated it. Felt like someone was selling him a lump of crap and calling it sugar.

"Right," the girl said, turning her attention back to the rod and resuming her slow reel. "My sister saw the paku trawling the shallows of this bank last night. I'm hoping he's still nearby, so I can catch him for my customers."

The paku was actually lurking in some heavy reeds around the little island in the middle of the lake, his fishy pulse slow and relaxed. But Bershad figured that if the girl wanted that fish, she'd need to find it on her own. Only fair.

"Customers?" Bershad asked. "You a fishmonger?"

"Please," said the girl. "I run the Cat's Eye tavern, up on the shady side of the canal."

"You're a little young to be running taverns, aren't you?" Bershad asked. The girl looked like she'd seen about ten summers.

"Well, I don't run it by myself, obviously."

"Obviously," Bershad agreed. "What's your name?"

"Grittle."

"Grittle? That short for something?"

"No." She gave him a look. "My sister says us simple folk don't need to bother with bulky names."

"I see."

Grittle sighed, and started reeling her line in with a purpose. "I don't think that fish is in my future. Not today, anyway. But I have a fresh batch of rain ale back at the tavern if you're interested."

Bershad shrugged. Ashlyn and Jolan weren't going anywhere, and he was thirsty. "Sure. Lead the way."

They walked up Canal Street together, making a strange pair that drew a lot of confused glances. Bershad could hear people stop and murmur after they'd passed.

To their left, where the hills of the Dainwood rose over the city, a trio of Blackjacks popped out of the canopy and chased each other in a loop across a streak of Daintrees with yellow flowers blooming off the top. One of the dragons raked his claws along the canopy, causing a shower of shredded petals.

In any other city in Terra, three fully grown dragons that close to the city would have gotten the alarm bells booming and turned the people into a panicked mob, running for basements and root cellars. But Deepdale was different. This time of year, hundreds of Blackjacks swarmed the forests around the city, gorging themselves on mango and monkey and deer after their long flight back from the Great Migration.

"Trotsky says that you talk to the dragons," Grittle said. "Tell them to protect Deepdale from the skyships, but also to stay outside the city."

"Who's Trotsky?"

"One of my regulars. He fought in the Balarian War."

"Old-timer, is it?"

"Yeah." They crossed a narrow bridge over the canal that was made from two sagging planks, the underside festooned with thick moss that smelled flowery and thick, like basil. "So, did you?"

"Did I what?"

"Tame the dragons and tell them to protect the city?"

Bershad glanced at the Blackjacks, who were still doing loops in the sky and skimming across the canopy.

"Those dragons aren't tame," Bershad said.

"But why don't they attack the city?"

"Years of experience." Bershad pointed to one of the dragon lookouts above them. "Why fuss with a city of troublesome humans who'll shoot arrows at you when you have a canopy full of ripe mangos and fat monkeys?"

"Oh."

"You sound disappointed."

She shrugged. "I liked the idea of you talking to the dragons, that's all."

Bershad gave her a look. "Those Blackjacks *are* protecting Deepdale from the skyships. They just aren't doing it because of me."

Bershad left the last part unsaid, which was that the Blackjacks would be scattering across the jungle within the next few moons, once the mangoes and monkeys started to thin. When that happened, the wall of impenetrable and aggressive dragons would be gone, and the skyships would have a clear route into Deepdale.

"I should have known it wasn't true," Grittle said. "Trotsky is always telling me lies because I'm little. He also said the big gray one follows you around everywhere and gives you magical powers."

Bershad grunted. Didn't say anything.

Grittle pointed down a narrow tract ringed by sagging buildings. "The Cat's Eye is just down there."

————

The tavern was locked up when they got there. Grittle took out a set of keys and opened the place up. Once they were inside, she hopped over the counter and lined up a bunch of ceramic mugs. Inspected them carefully, and cleaned a few that needed it.

"My regulars will be coming in for their breakfast beers soon," she explained. "Got to be ready for the rush."

"Your parents around to help?" he asked.

"My parents are dead."

"Then who runs the tavern with you?"

"I do," said another girl's voice as she came up from a downstairs cellar, carrying a cheese wheel in one hand and a stale loaf of bread in the other.

When Grittle had said that she ran the Cat's Eye tavern, Bershad had figured that her mother or father owned it and let her sweep the floors or something. But this girl—a sister, judging from the similar shape of their nose and mouth—wasn't much older than Grittle.

"Just you and her?"

"That's right."

"What are you, fourteen?"

"Fifteen," she corrected. "And if wardens can go to war at sixteen, I think I'm old enough to run a tavern."

"Fair point. What's your name?"

"Nola."

"Nola," Bershad repeated. "It's good to meet you."

She glanced at him, lingering on his tattoos a little longer than she probably meant to. Most people did.

"Likewise, Lord Silas."

"Just call me Bershad."

She scoffed. "Not likely, Lord Silas."

"I could have you beheaded for addressing me in a way I don't like," he warned.

"I find that even less likely, Lord Silas."

Bershad smiled.

"I promised him a beer," Grittle said from behind the counter.

Nola sighed. "Of course you did."

She came around the counter, too. Grabbed one of the mugs Grittle had cleaned and started filling it from an oak keg.

"I brew the rain ale myself. Since the war started, I've been watering down my pours so things last a little longer, but seeing as you're our first customer of the day, and lord of the city, I'll serve you straight."

Bershad gave a little grunt. The girl was funny. "Appreciated."

He took a sip. Savored the flavor of flower and hops and strong alcohol. "Not bad."

"Not bad?" Nola repeated, frowning. "That's the best rain ale on the shady side."

"You're pretty confident."

"Easy to be the best when you're the only tavern still brewing it."

"Hops hard to come by, these days?"

"They are. And the fact that all the lords are hoarding ingredients for their homebrew doesn't help. Such a tragedy. Rich folks always screw up the floral notes."

"If the lords are hoarding hops, how is it you have a full cask?"

She smiled. "Got my ways."

"Uh-huh." Bershad took another sip. "And how is it that two girls with barely a score of years between them wound up with the run of the best tavern on the shady side?"

The girls' faces both changed. Nola took a rag out from behind the bar and started wiping down the counter, which was already clean.

"Our mother died having Grittle," said Nola. "Our father got eaten by a Blackjack that same summer. But we had three older brothers to raise us. They were Jaguars, but they hung up their masks when the Grealors took over the Dainwood. Said that dying on behalf of an Atlas Coast asshole was its own kind of crime. So, they started this place up. We ran it together as a family for years. That's how I learned everything. But when Grealor got killed and the Jaguars rebelled, my brothers picked up their masks again. Joined the fight." She picked at the rag with dirty fingernails. "They went down the river last summer."

"High-Warden Carlyle came here himself to tell us," said Grittle. "He said they died bravely, protecting a very important bridge."

"They always tell you that," said Nola, a barb in her voice. "Even if you die screaming and crying for no good reason at all."

"You don't varnish the truth of things for her much," Bershad said.

"Most of the varnish that exists in this world is made from drag-onshit." She looked at him. "Do you tell people the truth of how their sons and husbands and brothers die?"

"No," Bershad admitted. He turned to Grittle. "But your brothers don't sound like cowards to me."

"You've heard four sentences about them," said Nola.

"They stood up against Grealor. A lot of others didn't."

"Since when is hanging up your mask a brave thing to do?" Nola asked.

"For a soldier, fighting for the man in charge is easy," said Bershad. "Standing up to him isn't."

"I guess."

Bershad drank more of his beer. Nola gave him a long look.

"You're not like the other lords I know."

"You familiar with a lot of nobility, are you?"

"Familiar enough to know they don't generally praise people for standing up to them. And they *do* generally wear shoes." She mo-tioned to his bare, dirty feet. "Lord Cuspar's got a different pair on every time he shows up to collect his take."

"Thought you owned the place."

"We do. Most of it anyway." She looked down, a little ashamed. "I kept us independent for as long as I could, knowing it's what my brothers would have wanted. And I was managing until the skyships started salting the farms and everything turned twice as expensive. The supplies that come in from Dunfar help, but I couldn't afford the up-front cost on my own. So, I went to see Cuspar. I tried for a straight loan—even if he was gonna rake me over the coals on interest—but you know how lords are, always trying to dig their fin-gers deep into your skin and keep them buried there." She looked at him. "Uh, sorry. Wasn't talking about you. The lords who wear shoes, I mean."

"Don't apologize," said Bershad. He remembered Cuspar from when he was a kid. The man had stakes in businesses all over Deep-dale. And Bershad knew that he'd thrown in with Grealor faster than most after his father was executed and he was exiled. "How much of a stake does he have?"

"Thirty percent," said Nola. "But he insisted on a minimum threshold of a hundred silvers a moon's turn, whether I've got a profit to show or not. I was short last month, that's why I've been sending Grittle out to try and catch the paku. Help us scrounge a little extra until the next shipment from Dunfar gets here. Assuming the lords and gangs don't take it all, first."

Bershad tightened his grip on the ceramic mug. Took another long gulp. He'd gotten the blue bars before he'd had to deal with the realities of being a high lord. Running a city. Running a whole province. He was back now, but with the war on, he hadn't needed to face that life. Being honest, he wasn't in a big rush to. The whole thing was a big web of shit and lies, strung together by unfair laws and vile traditions.

"When I came back and saw what Deepdale had become, I wanted to kill them all," Bershad said quietly.

"Kill who?" Grit asked.

"The lords who stood with Grealor."

"Oh." Nola seemed to think on that for a moment. "The queen stopped you, didn't she?"

Bershad raised an eyebrow. "How'd you know that?"

Nola shrugged. "Cuspar turned over most of his wardens for the war effort. If you took his head, might be they'd keep fighting for the Dainwood. Might be they wouldn't. Hard thing to risk right now."

That was almost exactly what Ashlyn had said.

"You're pretty clever."

She shrugged again. "You don't have to be that clever to see the right choices with a war on. It's the Balarians who need dealing with first. Everything else has to wait."

"Yeah," Bershad said.

He finished his beer. Savored the last swallow with a purpose. Then he dug some coins out of his pocket—far more than one rain ale was worth, and far less than the girls needed—and slid it across the table.

"Thanks for the beer."

"Thanks for paying. You didn't have to."

"Yeah. I did."

He headed for the door, but when he reached the frame he turned around. Nola had already gone back to her duties, but Grittle was still looking at him.

"The paku is hiding in the reeds on the southern side of the island in the lake. Swim out in the afternoon and wait there till dusk, until he forgets about you and the bugs lure him out. And they like fruit more than the worm you were using. Try a Daintree berry."

Grittle smiled. "I will. Thanks, Lord Silas."

Bershad left the tavern. Made his way back uphill to the castle.

The old fort looked the same as it did when he was a kid. It was built from gray stone, but the walls were mostly covered by flowering vines sprawled across the different sections, their white petals busy with hummingbirds and bees zipping around. Thirty-two stone jaguars lounged along the ramparts, one for each Bershad lord who had ruled from those halls.

The only two lords who didn't have a jaguar were him and his father. Leon's had been torn down on orders from the king. His had never been built at all.

The main difference between the current situation and Bershad's memories was that they'd set up the infirmary in the main castle yard—erected tents and filled them with cots where the wounded could be cared for. The air smelled like pus and bile and shit and vomit. Men were groaning and muttering in pain. Others were screaming as they endured their surgeries.

Even from across the city, he felt the Nomad rile as the rotten smells of the infirmary filled her nose, too. Bershad hoped she wasn't causing a scene by the city gates.

He spotted Cormo as he was leaving one of the surgery tents. Despite the fact that he was a pirate, not an alchemist, he was wearing the gray robes of the order. Said it made his patients more confident in the outcomes. His sealskin gloves were slick with blood, and he was in the process of wiping them with a goatskin cloth.

"Silas. Hey."

"How are things going here?" Bershad asked.

"A lot of amputations this time," Cormo admitted.

"You sure they're all required?" Bershad asked. "As I recall, unnecessary amputations is what got those bars drawn down your cheeks."

"Almost wish I could blame booze and bad decisions on my part—those problems have clear solutions. But no. Those Balarian longbows come in with such speed the arrowheads break bones like eggshells. Nothing to do but take the limb. But we're having good success with Master Jolan's latest anti-infection tonics after the surgery. People lose the limbs, but they keep their lives."

Bershad nodded.

"You want me to try pulling those last few crossbow bolts outta your back one more time?" Cormo asked. "I don't like leaving jobs half finished."

Cormo and Silas had met after a band of pirates had porcupined him with crossbow bolts. Cormo had pulled most of them out, but two remained, stuck deep in the bone.

"You nearly ripped my spine out last time you tried," Bershad said.

"But I got some new pincers that might do the trick."

Bershad waved the notion off. "Sometimes you just have to let old wounds be. Trust me on that."

Cormo shrugged. "Guess you're the expert on that front."

"Do you know where Ashlyn and Jolan set up shop this time?"

"Last ruckus I heard sounded like it was coming from the grain pantries toward the back."

Made sense. Ashlyn and Jolan used a lot of equipment for their work, and given all the food shortages, the pantries were available.

"Thanks, Cormo. I'll see you later."

———

Bershad moved through the empty halls of the castle, thinking back to his childhood when the castle was always bustling with people, and then actively trying to forget it because he felt his mood sliding toward darkness.

He reached the grain pantry. The door was closed, but not locked. He went inside.

Ashlyn was sitting in a chair in the middle of the room with her left arm stretched out, palm facing the ceiling. Her eyes were closed and there were four orbs the size of coconuts hovering above her head. There was a fresh cut above her left eyebrow.

Her outstretched arm was wreathed in banded, black metal from elbow to fingertips. The bands near her elbow were three fingers thick. The ones along her fingers were as thin as rings. All of them were studded with gray lodestones of various sizes that Bershad had salvaged from the spines of murdered grayskins. The bands were spinning in a complicated but orchestrated sequence, powered by the Ghost Moth nerve that was bound to Ashlyn's forearm.

"Careful with the upward polarity on number three," Jolan warned from his place behind a massive dragon scale that he was using as a shield. "It's starting to lilt downward on the vertical axis."

Bershad took a step forward, but Jolan motioned for him to stay where he was.

"I'm aware," said Ashlyn, keeping her eyes closed and stretching her fingers a little farther apart. The bands on her index and pinky fingers spun a little faster for several heartbeats, and one of the hovering orbs rose in the air so that it was aligned with the other three.

"That's it," said Jolan. "Okay, that's corrected. Ready for the fifth?"

"Ready."

Jolan took another lodestone out of a cloth sack and checked the complicated script that was etched into the side of it.

"How fast?" he asked.

"Full speed."

"You sure? After last time, I feel like—"

"Just throw it, Jolan. Another bruised eye isn't going to kill me."

The kid shrugged, then threw the stone at Ashlyn's face as hard as he could, grunting from the effort.

Three bands near Ashlyn's wrist whirred. The lodestone stopped an inch from her nose. Hung there as if it was attached to an invisible string.

A series of finger bands turned in a slow cascade, and the fifth lodestone rose above her head and joined the others in a line.

"Full control?" said Jolan.

Ashlyn nodded. "Give me something to break into."

Jolan moved over to a table that was covered with an assortment of different-sized lodestones and started moving some of them into a wooden tray.

Bershad didn't pretend to understand the inner workings of Ashlyn and Jolan's work. They'd tried to fully explain it to him once, but the conversation had ended with Bershad extremely confused and Ashlyn so frustrated that she'd stormed out of the room.

Eventually, Jolan had managed to describe the basics.

Ashlyn's arm and Osyrus Ward's grayskins were both built on the foundation of lodestones. A single lodestone wasn't much different than a regular rock. A pair of them could be made to either repel or attract to one another. But a larger group—which they called loops—could do far more complex things. That's how Ashlyn was controlling the lodestones hovering over her head, and how Osryus created his nearly indestructible creatures—their artificial organs and spines were powered by lodestones.

Because they shared the same foundation, Ashlyn had spent the first few weeks of the war tearing out grayskin spines as easily as a farmer pulls weeds from the earth.

She said it was like sewing: she wove an invisible, magnetic strand around each lodestone in the loop along the grayskin's spine. When she ripped the strand free, Ward's system was erased, giving Ashlyn control of the lodestones.

For weeks, it seemed like winning the war was just a matter of getting Ashlyn to the right place at the right time so she could tear the grayskins apart, then use the lodestones to forge another band on her arm.

But everything had changed at Fallon's Roost.

After that disaster, Ashlyn and Jolan had retreated to the Deepdale castle to figure out what went wrong, and how to prevent it in the future. That was three months ago.

Bershad was hoping they'd finally made some progress.

Jolan had filled the tray with twenty grape-sized lodestones. They were all white except for one in the middle, which was black. He placed the tray on the ground in front of Ashlyn.

"Let me connect the diagnostic tool," he said.

Jolan went back to the table and grabbed a machine Bershad had never seen before. It was about the size of a dinner plate and looked like about fourteen different clocks all rammed together with screws, gears, and springs. There was a crank on one side, and two copper nubs protruding from the top like the horns of a goat.

Jolan produced a bundle of wires from inside his robe, and quickly twisted a wire around each of the nubs. He wrapped one wire around the black lodestone in the center of the tray, and plugged the other into a little socket on one of Ashlyn's thicker bands.

He wound the crank three times, then released. The machinery of the diagnostic churned and spun as the crank slowly unwound.

"I recognize this loop," Ashlyn said. "It's from the spine of the grayskin Silas killed in Vermonth, right?"

"That's the one."

Ashlyn nodded, still frowning with focus as the diagnostic finished unwinding.

"Okay, I have it. I'm ready."

Jolan disconnected the machine from both Ashlyn and the lodestone, then returned to cover behind the dragon scale. He motioned for Bershad to move behind a stone pillar for protection.

"Go ahead," he said.

Ashlyn's bands started rotating, which caused her five lodestones to move into positions above the tray. When they were all in place, she started increasing the speed with which her bands rotated, until they began to make a high-pitched whine, similar to a mosquito buzzing near your ear.

The black lodestone didn't move.

"Not getting anywhere with brute force," she muttered. "This is like trying to sew a quilt without a needle."

"Try the cascade again?" Jolan asked.

"Yeah."

Her bands froze, then started rotating in a measured pattern that rolled down her arm, then back up again. Ashlyn increased the speed of her bands with each cycle, until instead of a steady mosquito's whine, there was an erratic and piercing roar that sounded like a forest demon's wild shriek.

No wonder nobody went into the castle anymore.

But despite the spinning bands and horrific noise, the black lodestone still didn't move.

Ashlyn licked her dry lips. Sweat droplets were pouring off her forehead. Steam rose from her damp hair and Bershad could smell the acrid scent of her fatigue filling the room. The bands of her arm continued the rolling cascade, but the pattern turned more complex and rapid.

Finally, the black lodestone started to spin. A little plume of smoke arose from beneath it as the wood of the tray began to singe.

"Progress," Jolan said.

The white lodestones started to shake. More smoke arose from the black one as it spun faster and faster.

"Come on, you little bastard," Ashlyn muttered. "Let me in."

The white lodestones were rattling around so much they threatened to spill out of the tray.

Then the black lodestone froze.

"Wait. Shit."

Without warning, Ashlyn's lodestones were sucked toward each other with a loud crunch.

"I've lost control," Ashlyn said. "Trying to back out gradually."

She gritted her teeth. Her lodestones started to crack from the pressure. Metal instruments on the desk started to twitch and move. Bershad felt a rising pain in his back where the iron crossbow bolts were embedded.

"It's no good!" Jolan shouted. "Use the kill switch!"

Ashlyn cursed, then, with what seemed like considerable effort, she pulled her arm in front of her chest and tightened her hand into a fist. Her bands froze. Her lodestones dropped to the floor and scattered. The pain in Bershad's back disappeared.

Ashlyn puked on her own feet. Then she picked up the tray of lodestones and threw it into the corner.

"Black fucking skies!" Ashlyn snarled. "Fuck those stubborn fucking bastard spinal cords and fuck Osyrus Ward and his opaque security measures."

She spat some vomit onto the floor, then she stood up, grabbed the chair she'd been sitting on, and threw it against the far wall, breaking two of the legs. With that done, she took a long breath in and out.

"Catch you two at a bad time?" Bershad asked, coming around from behind the pillar.

Ashlyn turned around, the frustration disappearing from her face.

"Silas. You're back."

"Brought another stubborn bastard with me, too," he said, lifting the sack.

Ashlyn glared at the sack as if it was full of snakes, then moved to a big table that was littered with scraps of papers and spools of wire. She picked up a waterskin and drank deeply.

"Are all the lodestones from the spinal column intact on this one?" Jolan asked.

"Yeah," Bershad said. "That's not easy to do, by the way."

"Maybe not, but the last one you brought back was so chewed up we couldn't even *try* to break into it."

"That asshole tore every muscle off my left leg. Keeping the corpse pristine wasn't really a priority."

Jolan opened the bag and started rummaging around. Taking out metal orbs and shafts and casings—all the crap that Osyrus Ward put into the grayskins to make them so difficult to kill.

"If you hadn't stopped, felt like you'd have ripped the crossbow bolts straight out of my back," Bershad said, rubbing one shoulder.

"Cormo still hasn't gotten them all out?" Ashlyn asked.

"Nope. The last two are wedged deep in the bone."

Ashlyn swallowed a big gulp of water. Raised her arm. "You know, I could pull them out anytime. Little scraps of iron like that are easy to manipulate if I'm close to them."

"No need."

"Why not?"

Bershad shrugged. "They don't hurt."

Ashlyn raised an eyebrow and gave him the face that said she knew he was lying, but didn't push the issue further.

She was right, though. The real reason he didn't want the bolts out was because they *did* hurt him. Always. And he'd committed enough crimes in his life that being saddled with a scrap of constant pain seemed like fair punishment.

Jolan finished arranging the lodestones into little groups on the table.

"This gives us more to work with," he said, although he didn't sound excited by the prospect.

"Glad to be of service," said Bershad.

"Were you injured collecting them?" Ashlyn asked.

"Nothing permanent."

"How much moss did you use?" Jolan asked.

"Not much."

"A pinch? Ten pinches?"

"Enough so I could jump off a holdfast tower without dying."

"Silas, don't be obtuse. Jolan needs to know the exact amount so he knows how strong the tonic needs to be."

Bershad grunted. "Four pinches."

Ashlyn raised her eyebrow.

"Fine. Seven."

She turned to Jolan. "Go ahead and get started on the suppression tonic."

Jolan moved to an alchemical station in the corner and lit a few of the burners. Within moments, the entire room smelled of acid and tar. Bershad's stomach turned.

"I hate this shit," he muttered. "And every time we use it, the Nomad disappears for days. Last time, she was gone for a full week. I need her with me to win this war."

"You can't win this war if you turn into a tree," said Ashlyn.

"That's going to happen eventually anyway."

Ashlyn tossed the waterskin back onto the table. "Are we going to have this fight in front of Jolan, or do you want to find a private chamber? Or, better yet, do you want to just skip the argument entirely and take the shot?"

Bershad sighed. "We can skip it."

"Good." She wiped some sweat off her forehead. "Was Simeon hurt?"

"Just a few cracked ribs. He'll be fine."

"Did he bring back a bunch of heads again?" Jolan asked without looking up from his work.

"Yeah."

Jolan shook his head. "It's a very unsanitary practice."

"You're welcome to try talking him out of it. I haven't had much luck."

"No, thanks," said Jolan, scooping a spoonful of thick, black sludge into the mixture he was brewing.

Ashlyn was still looking at him, studying his face. "Did something else happen?"

"I might have found a way to get to Vergun," Bershad said, re-membering what Rigar had told him about the warren symbols. "But it'll have to wait until the army's in a better spot."

"Am I hearing a level of restraint coming from the famously wild dragonslayer?"

"Just a little."

Ashlyn smiled. Moved to the table and started scratching a few notes on a piece of paper.

"So, couldn't help but notice there's one less tower on this castle than when I left," Bershad said.

"Yeah. I passed out during an experiment. Sorry about that."

"You know, Ashlyn, you have a pretty clear pattern of destructive tendencies when it comes to castles. Maybe you should do this outside?"

"Wind and humidity add more external factors and complexity. Anyway, we installed countermeasures."

"That kill switch?"

"Yes. Which I need to unlock."

She started twisting different bands in what seemed to be a very specific sequence. Bershad was going to wait until she was done to keep talking, but the process went on for over a minute.

"How many turns does it take to unlock it?" he asked.

"Thirty-seven," Ashlyn said, continuing to turn the bands. "It took two sleepless weeks to build, but testing goes much faster this way. And I'm destroying fewer rooms in your castle."

She turned a final band, and then everything came to life again for a moment before settling down.

"I can lock the system myself, like I just did, but the entire system locks down automatically if I lose consciousness. When that happens, nobody can turn it back on except me or Jolan."

"No offense to Jolan, but why's he get the codes, too?"

The two of them exchanged a quick glance. Ashlyn answered.

"The line between temporary unconsciousness and a permanent coma is pretty thin. If that were to happen, Jolan needs a way to keep going."

"Fuck, Ashlyn."

"It's just a precaution. I haven't passed out in weeks."

"You're taking too many risks."

"And you're jumping off too many towers."

"Doesn't make me wrong."

"Just hypocritical."

Bershad sighed. Decided to drop it. "How's progress, generally?"

Ashlyn stopped writing. Then scratched at her hair with the same hand that was holding the quill, which left a smear of ink across her cheek.

"You saw how it's going."

"Maybe you should try it out in the field again. Could work differently."

"Sure. Seeing as I can't conquer a set of lodestones sitting in a tray without causing a massive backfire, I'm definitely ready to take on a horde of grayskins again. That's brilliant, Silas. Thank you."

"Ashe. I know that you're afraid of repeating Fallon's Roost, but—"

"Can you please stop referring to it like that?"

"Like what?"

"Like the whole incident is just a fortress on a map." She paused. "I was reckless and arrogant and I got eighty-seven wardens killed because of it."

Ashlyn had been having so much success killing grayskins that when their scouts reported fifty of them gathered at Fallon's Roost, they hadn't hesitated to launch a full attack, thinking that this was their chance to turn the tide of war.

But it had been a trap.

The grayskins at Fallon's Roost were the first to have security systems installed in their spines. When Ashlyn tried to break through them, the same thing that had just happened in the pantry happened on the field, but there wasn't a kill switch to stop it from getting out of control.

The wardens closest to her were crushed by their own armor. Bershad had needed a pound of Gods Moss to recover from his wounds. Hundreds of others survived, but had been peppered with shrapnel like Oromir.

Bershad swallowed. "Simeon and I went back. That's where we killed the grayskin."

"Why?" Ashlyn asked.

"It was vulnerable. They moved most of the soldiers down south, chasing Willem's crews." He paused. "And the men were still out there on the field. They needed shells."

Ashlyn nodded. "A proper burial doesn't change the fact that I killed them."

"You're right, Ashe. But we're losing hundreds of wardens every moon turn. You understand? We're not winning this war. We're just losing it as slowly as possible. And we're going to run out of soldiers a long time before Osyrus Ward does."

"If I go back out there now, the only thing I'll do is get more men killed."

Bershad looked around the workshop. Then he thought of the half-filled war camp outside the city, and all the wardens who should have been there but weren't. He felt a rage rise in this throat.

"Are you getting *any* closer?" he pressed.

"It's not like chopping down a tree," Ashlyn said. "There's no easy way to gauge progress. It's more like digging a well blind. There might be water a stride down, there might be nothing at all. There's just no—"

"Don't hide behind some metaphor. Just tell it to me straight. Are the spines that I'm bringing back even helpful?"

Ashlyn glanced at the sack he'd brought. "I've tried to break into every acolyte spine you've brought back. I've tried it a dozen different ways. The result is always the same. I don't know what Osyrus changed, but I can't get through it. We thought the diagnostic was the key, but that turned out to just be a way to get a better look at the problem, not solve it. To make things even worse, we can't add more bands to my arm until we find a way through Ward's system, so I'm stuck at only being able to balance five lodestones in the air."

"Then what's the point of me even bringing this shit anymore?" Bershad asked.

There was a silence.

"I've started disassembling the pieces that Ashlyn can't break through." Jolan motioned to one corner of the room, where a mess of cleaved lodestones, copper orbs, gears, wires, powders, and scraps of metal were arranged on a table. "I'm trying to rebuild them into something we can use."

"Use how?"

He shrugged. "I'm not sure yet. But we have so many raw materials at this point, I have to believe there's something we can use them for."

Jolan moved his tonic off the burner, then drew the liquid into a long syringe.

"This is ready," he said.

Bershad stayed where he was. Arms crossed.

"Can you sit down so that I can give you the injection?" Jolan pressed.

"Well, I'd use that chair over there if our even-keeled queen hadn't shattered it."

Ashlyn gave him a look, and Bershad gave in. He muttered a curse to himself and sat down on the cold floor next to Jolan, who rolled back the sleeve on his left arm and tapped a finger against the syringe, forcing the liquid to congeal. He moved it toward Bershad's skin, but he stopped him with an open hand.

"Just give me one second, kid."

Jolan nodded. Bershad closed his eyes.

He reached out, across the city, and focused on his connection to the Nomad. She was still in that Daintree.

"Sorry about this, girl," he muttered. "I'll meet up with you down the line a ways, when you decide to forgive me."

He gave Jolan a nod, and the boy pressed the metal needle into his flesh and filled his veins with fire that spread from his arm to his lungs and eventually into his heart. His connection to the Nomad snapped. The thousands of sounds and sensations she funneled into his body went quiet. Far off, she released a bone-chilling howl. The Daintree shook and shuddered as she took to the sky and flew away.

Bershad rolled down his sleeve. He felt hollow and dead inside.

"Kerrigan is due back from Dunfar tonight," Ashlyn said, moving to a trunk in the corner and removing a yellow poncho, which she threw over her head and adjusted until it completely covered her left arm.

Early on, Ashlyn had tried explaining to the people of Deepdale that her abilities came from technology and magnetism, not sorcery. That little campaign hadn't panned out, so she resigned herself to wearing the poncho in public.

It was easier to conceal something people feared than help them understand it.

"We'll inventory her shipment, distribute everything to the army, and then we'll see where things stand," she continued. "We might be losing this war slowly, but so long as we have a steady stream of supplies, we have time." She motioned to the materials strewn across the tables. "And time gives Jolan and me a chance to find a path forward."

4

ASHLYN
Jaguar Army War Camp

"What do you mean, you lost four supply carracks?" Simeon growled, leaning forward on the table so hard that the legs squeaked. "You left with five. That's not a good ratio of return, Kerrigan."

Ashlyn, Bershad, and Jolan had gathered with the leaders of the Jaguar Army crews in a tent outside the city to meet with Kerrigan and distribute supplies. Simeon hadn't been officially invited, but he'd shown up anyway.

"Back off, Simeon," said Kerrigan. She had a bandage around her head and was sipping from a mug of hot tea. "I'm not some pirate lackey who just fucked up a reeving for you. And take your weight off the table before you break it."

Simeon held her with a long glare, but eventually stepped back. The damage was done, though. The table now stood so lopsided, no drink would be safe on the surface.

"Thank you," Kerrigan said, then turned back to Ashlyn. "As I was saying, there was some trouble on the way back from Dunfar."

Trouble. Trouble didn't begin to describe the situation they were currently in. The whole war effort depended on Kerrigan's open smuggling lines with Dunfar. Without them, they had no way to keep the army and the people of the Dainwood fed.

"What was on the ship that you *did* bring back?" she asked.

"Well, I was on it, for one thing. Glad to see you're all falling down with relief on that front." She glared around the room. "Nor am I detecting much sympathy for the hundred men I lost on the carracks that sank."

"Feeling shitty about people dying doesn't bring them back to life," Simeon said.

"Maybe not, but they were my crew. Under my charge. And they died trying to keep your belly from going empty, you cold bastard."

"Enough," Ashlyn cut in. "I agree that the loss of a hundred men should be met with a little more sensitivity than Simeon seems to possess. But right now, I'm more concerned with the thousands of men those ships were supposed to feed. What do we have?"

Kerrigan licked her lips. "One hundred Pargossian crates of flour.

One hundred Pargossian crates of rice. One hundred and forty-three Dunfarian swine."

Kerrigan sipped her tea. There was a pause while everyone waited for her to continue the list after she'd swallowed, but she just stared back at Ashlyn.

"That's it?" Ashlyn asked.

Kerrigan hesitated. "I dropped most of my cargo when we were spotted by the skyship. Made for a bank of fog that was nearby. That's why my ship made it and the others perished. They held onto their pigs like softhearted theatre singers."

"That isn't enough," Ashlyn said. "That'll only last us . . ."

She trailed off, thinking.

"I already ran the calculation, Queen," said Kerrigan. "Assuming our casualty rate has been consistent since my last supply run, we have enough to feed the army for a little less than a moon's turn."

"Our casualty rate grew by ten percent," said Ashlyn.

"Call it an even month, then."

"I don't think that's right," Jolan said. "It seems high, considering the rice will only cover—"

"You're shorting the swine," Kerrigan interrupted. "They're Dunfarian pigs. Twice the size of those runts you raise in the jungle."

"Oh." Jolan chewed on his lip for a moment. "Yeah, then. One month."

"There's a bigger problem," said Kerrigan. "That was the last clean route to Dunfar. The skyships will be patrolling it now." She paused. "I can't bring any more food into the Dainwood, Ashlyn."

That news created a long silence. Willem scratched his nose. Opened and closed his mouth a few times before finally speaking.

"The only way to end this war in a month is to stand against the grayskins and the skyships in the open," he said. "Ashlyn, we all remember Fallon's Roost, but you and Jolan have been working in that castle for months. Are you any closer to a solution?"

Everyone turned to Ashlyn, expectant and hopeful.

"That's a complicated question to answer. We have much better understanding of how Osyrus Ward's technology functions than we did at the beginning of summer."

"If a grayskin dropped into this tent right now, could you kill it?" Oromir asked from his place in the corner of the room.

Lying wouldn't do any good.

"No."

"And if you tried, would you wind up killing all of us instead?"

"Simeon and I would be fine," Bershad cut in.

"Is this a joke to you?" Oromir asked him.

"I thought that was pretty funny, yeah."

"Good for you. Do you also think it'll be funny when the men start deserting their crews and taking shelter in the gloom because they haven't been fed in weeks?"

"Taking shelter in the gloom isn't the worst that'll happen," Bershad said, voice turning serious. "There's a thin line between warden and bandit when you're starving. Pretty soon, we're not gonna be an army. We're gonna be a group of desperate men. And we're all carrying sharp objects."

"Then why are you making jokes?"

"Because we aren't out of options yet. Felgor and Cabbage are due back from Floodhaven soon. I'm gonna meet them in Dampmire."

Willem grunted. "No offense, Silas, but how are the two Balarian spies going to get us out of this big of a fix?"

"Because I sent them to Floodhaven for that specific purpose," Ashlyn said. "We weren't learning enough about Osyrus Ward's technology from scavenging parts, so Felgor went in to steal as much information about them as he could directly."

"He might have done that," Willem muttered. "Or he'll have spent the last moon drinking a hole in his belly and fucking his cock raw."

"Might not seem like it, but we can rely on Felgor," said Bershad. "He's hasn't let me down yet."

"That's true of everyone until they let you down," said Kerrigan.

"You gonna turn sour on me, too?" Bershad asked. "Thought that was Oromir's vocation."

"Hey, if you get to be all sarcastic during tense conversations, so do I."

"Fair enough."

Jolan cleared his throat. "Um. I think we're forgetting something. The shipment from Dunfar was also supposed to feed the people of Deepdale for the whole summer. The army might have a moon turn's worth of food, but what are they going to eat?"

Everyone looked to Ashlyn again. She cleared her throat.

"One way or another, we need to push this war forward. That means leaving Deepdale, and not returning until the war is over. The people here are young or old or crippled or sick." She paused. "They get the food. All of it."

"And we're gonna eat hopes and dreams and promises?" asked Oromir.

"We'll scavenge and forage as best we can," said Bershad.

"Foraging in the Dainwood this time of year is almost as dangerous as fighting a grayskin," Willem warned. "You're gonna start losing men."

"Not if the whole army marches with us to Dampmire," said Bershad. "We'll tell them it's so we can coordinate a fast response to whatever Felgor brings us."

"Why are we actually doing it?"

"Because they'll be less likely to desert, or otherwise cause trouble, if they know I'm nearby to run them down," said Simeon.

Bershad shrugged. "Pretty much."

Kerrigan sighed. "Also, leaving Floodhaven full of food and devoid of wardens to keep order might cause some problems, too. It might cause pure chaos."

"They're gonna have to figure that out for themselves," said Bershad.

"Well, we're turning into a beacon of moral superiority here, aren't we?" said Kerrigan.

"Moral superiority doesn't win wars," said Ashlyn. "We go to Dampmire. *All* of us."

Kerrigan shook her head. "Let's just hope Felgor doesn't fuck this up."

5

CABBAGE
Floodhaven, Wicked Raven Coffeehouse

"Stop playing with your ears," Felgor said, taking a sip of coffee.

Cabbage hadn't even realized he'd been touching them. He pressed his hands flat on the coffeehouse table. "Sorry. They just feel wrong, somehow. I'm afraid people'll notice."

"Only way they'll notice is if you keep screwing with them like a kid who's just discovered his cock." Felgor burped. "Relax."

"Relax?" Cabbage repeated. "Are you joking?"

He gestured around the café, which was full of Balarian naval officers in formal uniforms. Most of them were sipping coffee like him and Felgor. Others were drinking imported tea or juniper liquor. All of them had swords on their hips.

He and Felgor were wearing uniforms, too. But they were stolen.

"Yeah, no reason to be worried." Felgor pulled out an empty chair from the table and put his freshly polished boots on it. "You got yourself a pair of Malgrave-made prosthetics covering those earholes and barred cheeks. Nobody's gonna see through her work. Did I ever tell you that I saw her explode the bone wall in Ghost Moth with nothing but—"

"You told me," Cabbage interrupted. If he had to hear Felgor tell the story about Ashlyn Malgrave blowing up the bone wall, or—worse yet—him and the Flawless Bershad crawling up a shitpipe in the palace of Burz-al-dun, he was going to tear his fake ears off and cram them down the Balarian thief's throat. "And I got it. No ear touching."

Cabbage looked around the room again.

"Where is Brutus, anyway?"

"Late."

"Forty-three minutes late, by my watch."

"In all fairness, I nicked his timepiece on our last meet."

"What?" Cabbage hissed. "Why?"

Felgor shrugged. "Seemed like a good idea at the time."

Cabbage moved to touch his ears again, but detoured his limbs to a stern arm-crossing. By Aeternita, his partner in this madness was a liability.

"Don't even see why I'm here," he muttered to himself.

"You're here," said Felgor, "because despite the quaint diversity of our little army, you're the only other asshole with a natural Clockwork accent."

"Cormo's accent is just as good as mine."

"Eh. It's close I'll admit. But Cormo is too fat to be an officer. He's also got brown eyes and a button nose. That'd never work."

Cabbage crossed his arms a little tighter. "Whatever."

"Drink some of your coffee."

"No," Cabbage said, eyeing the warm drink. "Stuff makes me have to . . . you know."

"Aye. I do. And from the amount of stress you appear to be under, a proper bowel movement seems like it could do you some good."

"I'm fine."

"Eh, probably best. Looks like our friend has finally arrived, so you don't have time for a shit break." Felgor motioned to the entrance of the coffeehouse, which Corporal Brutus was walking through. His hair was wet from the afternoon rains and he was carrying a supple leather traveling bag. He had an expression on his face that was half excitement, half abject terror.

"Brutus!" Felgor yelled, kicking out the chair he'd been resting his legs on and waving to the corporal. "Saved you a seat!"

Brutus looked around sheepishly before walking over, shoulders hunched as if that would hide his identity from the other patrons of the coffeehouse.

"Could you have yelled my name any louder?" he hissed at Felgor, taking the seat.

"I'm a vice-commander," Felgor said. "I can say people's names as loudly as I please."

Brutus glanced at the golden clocks adorning Felgor's shoulders, as if to re-convince himself that Felgor was in fact a high-ranking officer on the skyship called *A Moment's Value,* which transported minerals from the kilns of Balaria to Ward's big tower. Very light duty.

A woman with a skintight black gown approached their table. She had the dark hair of an Almiran, and the cold look that was carried by the few natives who'd managed to thrive despite their city being occupied by foreigners.

"May I offer refreshment?" she asked Brutus.

"Juniper liquor," he said.

"Would you like a lemon or lime added? I can also cut it with freshly imported bubbled—"

"Just fill a cup to the fucking brim with booze," Brutus snapped.

The woman raised an eyebrow, but otherwise didn't react. She left to fill their orders.

"Come now, Brutus, where are your manners?" Felgor asked when she was out of earshot. "If you behave that way, the Almirans will begin to think that we men of the Clock are barbaric and cruel."

"I don't care what that muddy-haired savage thinks of me," Brutus said. His brow was clammy with sweat.

"Hmm," Felgor said, watching the woman weave between a set of tables to see about some other customers. "*Savage* is not the word I would use for her. Definitely not."

Brutus sat in nervous silence until the woman returned with his order, which he drank from immediately, holding the cup with both hands and taking three large gulps.

"You're sure that you can manage my transfer?" Brutus asked, putting his half-empty cup down.

Felgor turned back to the table. Sighed.

"Brutus, enough with the suspicion and second-guessing. I pull mid-ranking officers out of combat all the time. Nobody gives a shit."

Brutus blew out a sigh. "Good. I simply can't take another combat mission over that wretched jungle. Last week, two skyships got taken down by dragons. And we had to go back and *bomb* one of them to make sure the rebels didn't get ahold of the wreckage. Can you imagine that? One ship gets destroyed by dragons, and we fly back to the *same fucking spot*."

"Yeah, it's real shitty. There's none of that nonsense on the kiln routes," Felgor said. "But I don't pull men onto my detail for free."

"I know. But I brought it. Every last coin."

"Coin's great," Felgor said. "Real great. But it was only half of our agreement."

"Right," Brutus said. "The information. What do you want this stuff for, anyway? It wasn't easy to get. I had to bribe one of Ward's engineer cronies."

"That is not your concern, *Corporal,*" said Cabbage, cutting in at the agreed-upon time. It wasn't proper for a vice-commander to answer those questions. His second was meant to do the pushy work on his behalf. Felgor had made that *very* clear before they'd started, and even forced Cabbage to practice for hours. "Your only concern is giving us what we asked for. If you don't have it, this conversation is over."

Brutus swallowed. He was so desperate to get out of this war that he drank up Cabbage's deception as desperately as he'd drunk that juniper liquor.

"I have it."

"Fantastic." Felgor opened his palms. "Let's see it."

Brutus took one more gulp of his drink, then he leaned down and opened his satchel just enough for them to see a thick sheaf of carefully folded papers.

Felgor took the papers and leafed through them quickly. Smiled.

"Very good, Brutus. This is very good."

"It's only good if the information is accurate," Cabbage added. "Should we find any fabrications, you will be arrested for treason and turned over to Osyrus Ward for experimentation."

Men who disobeyed orders or took bad injuries in the field were apt to disappear into the upper workshops of the castle. Nobody knew for sure if Ward was transforming normal men into the hulking, deformed monstrosities that were the acolytes, but nobody wanted to find out the hard way, either.

"No, that won't be a problem," Brutus said quickly. "The engineer took them directly from Ward's vault."

The threat of becoming one of Osyrus Ward's playthings was so intimidating that Brutus didn't seem to realize Felgor was threatening punishment from the same man he was stealing from, but that was fear for you. Turned men into idiots.

"Of course I trust you, Brutus," said Felgor. "And now that we've concluded our business, you need not worry anymore. I will get to work on your transfer right away. You should receive confirmation soon."

"But how soon?" Brutus asked. "We're due for another combat deployment in three days."

"Oh, long before that," Felgor said, standing up.

Cabbage followed suit—pulling his uniform tight. It was important to keep up his persona as the second-in-command with a pole up his ass.

Felgor dropped some coins on the table, which was more than enough to pay for their drinks.

"Stay a while," he continued. "Have a few rounds on me, Corporal. Soon, it'll be nothing but clear skies and boring grain transports in your future. I promise."

———

"That guy's fucked," Felgor said as soon as they were out of the coffeehouse.

"Properly fucked," Cabbage agreed.

Felgor guided them east, down the main avenue and deeper into the city.

"Shouldn't we be making our way to the main gate? Between these documents and the maps you stole last week, we're good to return to the Dainwood."

"Not quite yet, Cabbage."

"What's left?"

"We need to spend Brutus's coin. Once we're back in the jungle, that money won't buy anything besides rotten rice and cooked insects. But in this city, that same coin can buy all manner of delights, especially for two Balarian officers."

Cabbage realized they were heading to Foggy Side, where Felgor's favorite brothel was located.

"No, Felgor. We can't go back to the Eagle's Roost."

"Sure we can. It's just around the next corner."

They moved down the street, passing soldiers and engineers, mostly. It was rare to see an Almiran face in the capital, these days. Most of them had fled to wilds of the Gorgon River or the Dainwood, if they could get that far.

The reason for the exodus was just ahead of them. One of Osyrus Ward's acolytes was posted in the middle of the intersection.

Cabbage felt his cock shrivel. The hulking creatures were terrifying. This one was three heads taller than a normal man. He had spiraling horns made from dragon bone protruding from his forehead. While he wasn't visibly armed, everyone knew that at the first sign of a threat, razor-sharp spikes made from dragon bone would pop out from between his knuckles and along his back and arms. Those spikes could cut through bone like butter. Cabbage had seen it happen.

There was an acolyte like that guarding every major intersection in Floodhaven, along with all the other conquered cities of Terra. They never switched guard. Never slept. Never ate. Just scanned the crowd with cold, ceaseless vigilance. Killed anyone who caused problems.

No wonder most of the Floodhaven natives had abandoned their own city.

Once they were out of the acolyte's sight, Cabbage stopped focusing on not shitting himself, and turned his attention back to the task at hand.

"Please, Felgor. Last time you went on a three-day bender."

"Bender? That was research. And it worked splendidly, seeing as that is how we found Brutus, our perfect little honey-pot of classified information, crying into a companion's tits about his scary combat missions."

"What if we run into him there?"

"Seeing as you're holding his life's savings in your hand, I find that unlikely."

Cabbage swallowed. Before Queen Ashlyn had dispatched him to Floodhaven with Felgor, she had specifically told him to keep the thief out of trouble, which he was prone to wading into neck deep. Cabbage hadn't thought it would be that difficult, seeing as he'd spent ten years trying to keep a lid on the pirate scum of Ghost Moth Island.

Oh, how wrong he had been.

"We can have dinner and a few drinks," Cabbage said, knowing it was easier to bargain with Felgor than flat-out refuse him. "Then we'll start back to the Dainwood."

"Definitely," said Felgor. "One good meal, then we'll fly home like Balarian arrows—straight and true."

6

VERA
Floodhaven

As soon as the *Blue Sparrow* was hovering above the skyship platform, Vera dropped a rope and slid down it. She had no patience for the three-minute landing sequence.

She headed straight to Kira, which was a journey all its own after Osyrus Ward's expansions.

The skyship platform was attached to the middle levels of the Queen's Tower and sprawled out over the city like a fan. Below her, seven city blocks were eternally cast in shadow beneath the heavy beams and wide planks.

Osyrus had ordered the platform constructed the morning that he took control of the armada, and his acolytes had finished within several weeks, despite the massive scale of the project. They worked tirelessly among the maze of construction rafters that encircled the towers.

Once the platform was finished, the acolytes turned their industry to the castle itself, which was hardly recognizable as Castle Malgrave.

The western tower was now a massive barrack for Wormwrot Company. The eastern tower—which had been nearly destroyed in a strange fire—had been retrofitted to be a massive silo for dragon oil. Its windowless walls were made from sleek, dark stone. There was a hunting ship hovering above it with a massive rubber hose connected to the tip, pouring oil from slain dragons into the basin.

Then there was the King's Tower.

Osyrus had built scores of new workshops into the guts of the tower, then added more around the exterior that bulged from the walls like blisters on burned flesh. When he ran out of room there, he began adding extra levels to the tower. Its shadow now extended past the outer walls of the city.

The top of the tower was capped by a massive, black dome. Nobody knew what Ward did up there, but there was a near constant stream of valuable materials being delivered from abroad. Nickel, lead, and copper were mined from Lysteria and refined in the kilns of northern Balaria. Dragons were shot from the skies above Ghalamar and Dunfar for their bones. Rubber was siphoned from the trees along the northern rim of the Dainwood, and some unknown material was harvested from the dragon warrens in the south.

All of it was brought to Floodhaven. All of it ended up in that tower.

Whatever Ward was building, he'd conquered the entire realm to amass the materials for it.

Kira was being held several levels below that, in the garden room. As she crossed the platform, she glanced at the garden room's tall, narrow window. Vera had to resist the urge to break into a sprint to reach Kira faster.

Vera entered the Queen's Tower through a wide circular door that had been cut directly from the stone. Jogged up stairwells and trotted across long hallways until she reached the bridge that connected it to the King's Tower. More stairs and hallways. More doors locked by Balarian seals and guarded by acolytes, who let her through amidst wheezing grunts and mechanical groans.

By the time Vera reached the floor beneath the garden room, she was breathing hard and her forehead had a sheen of sweat across it. As she climbed the final stairwell to the garden room, she took out her personal seal, which could open Kira's private recovery chamber.

She froze when she saw an unfamiliar and enormous acolyte standing guard in front of it.

He was so tall that he would have never fit inside a normal castle room. But the garden room actually comprised three castle floors, which had been gutted long ago so that peach and orange trees could be planted on the loam-covered floor and grown in the high space.

It had once been a favorite meeting place for Ashlyn Malgrave. Now, it housed a domed healing chamber for Kira that was two stories tall and filled half the space. The massive acolyte filled the rest. The top of his gray pate was nearly at an even height with the top of the dome.

"What are you doing here?" Vera asked, moving toward the acolyte.

"Protect. Empress."

Vera studied the acolyte. His arms were as thick as tree trunks. Fingers like carrots. A true giant.

"Get out of my way."

"Protect. Empress."

"I'm *Vera*," she said. "Her widow."

The acolyte's muscles rippled with a coiled strength, but otherwise gave no acknowledgment that he understood her words.

"Ah, I see you have met Seven-Zero-Nine!" came a familiar voice from behind her.

She turned to find Osyrus Ward. He was wearing a new dragonskin jacket—this one went down past his knees and was made from a Ghost Moth dragon's pale white hide. There were three engineers behind him, all of them wearing similar garments.

"What the fuck is going on here?" Vera hissed.

Osyrus frowned, puzzled. "With you abroad, I assumed that you would want Empress Kira guarded." He motioned to the enormous acolyte. "Seven-Zero-Nine is one of my latest successes. I used a new slurry for the growth and strength hormones that have tripled his—"

"I don't care, Osyrus. I want him out of my way and out of this room. Now."

Osyrus bowed his head. "Of course, of course."

Ward snapped his fingers and gave a firm command. "Sleep, Seven-Zero-Nine."

The acolyte stiffened. "Acknowledged, master."

He lumbered to the side of the room and squatted beneath a gnarled orange tree. Closed his eyes. Within a few moments, he was snoring.

"I said that I want him *out*."

Osyrus winced. "Getting him in here to begin with was quite a challenge. Given his size, removing him would require either that Seven-Zero-Nine destroy a part of the castle, or I destroy part of Seven-Zero-Nine. I will do so, if you wish. But there is a value to a tireless protector outside our precious Kira's door, yes?"

Vera chewed on her lip. She could deal with this problem later.

"That's fine for now. I want to see Kira."

"Of course." Osyrus motioned to the men behind him. "When we saw the *Sparrow* on our horizon, we began all the preparations for removing Kira from the respirator. Let us all go inside."

The interior of the healing chamber was humid and hot. Vera started sweating immediately.

Kira was laid out on a pallet in the middle of the room, the same place where Vera had left her.

Everything else about her was different.

When Vera had left, Kira had been in a coma, but her skin was pink and healthy. Now her lips were the color of raw clam meat. Her cheeks sunken. The circles under her eyes so dark, they seemed like bruises. She was covered in thin bandages that crisscrossed her torso and hips, allowing access for two black tubes that were connected to either side of her chest and pumped her lungs full of air in steady increments. Other than their steady pumps, she was so still—almost like someone had carved her likeness from wax, and the real, vibrant Kira was hidden away in some secret room.

"Why have you let her deteriorate like this?" Vera snarled.

"What are you talking about?" Osyrus asked, squinting at one of his dials. "Her blood pressure is perfect. All of her organs are functioning at full capacity. The new respirator model is working wonders for the health of her throat and mouth, as well."

In contrast to Kira's horrific physical appearance, all of the machines and contraptions around her were brimming with movement and bright colors. Vats the size of ale casks hung suspended from the ceiling. They were filled with green fluid that pumped and churned with the cadence of a heartbeat, but the metallic clang of artificial invention. The floor and walls were dominated by copper and steel pipes that powered the vats' ceaseless mixing and churning. The fluid was siphoned from the vats, through a series of rubber tubes, and into Kira's broken body.

"Full capacity? She looks like she's on the brink of *death*."

For the first time since they'd entered the room, Osyrus looked up from his machines, giving Kira the shortest of glances. "Physical appearances are poor indicators of specimen health."

"Do not call her a specimen."

Osyrus bowed his head slightly. "I assure you, she is quite healthy."

Vera moved to Kira. She removed one glove and put a bare hand on Kira's cheek. Winced at how cold her skin felt, despite the heat of the room.

"Why is she so cold?"

"It's necessary to lower her body temperature before attempting to rebind the nerves," Osyrus responded. "Which we are ready to do, if you'd like."

She gave Kira's hand one more squeeze, then backed away. "Yes."

"Excellent." Osyrus signaled his engineers, who moved to various consoles and machines around the room, adjusting dials and writing down different readings.

"If you'll wait over there," Osyrus said, pointing to the only place in the dome that wasn't dominated by machinery.

"I think you'll find the new visualization matrix I've created to observe the process quite useful," Osyrus continued. "A product of my latest filament designs."

Vera didn't say anything. She'd learned to ignore Ward's esoteric descriptions of his work, and to stop attempting to understand how he made his strange creations and machines function.

She didn't care how they worked, she just needed Kira to be free from them.

But when a series of black threads descended from the dome's ceiling—connected and hung by some unseen force—and then braided themselves into the shape of a spinal cord, Vera became more interested.

"Is that . . . Ki's spine?"

"A representation of it, yes," said Osyrus, admiring his own work. "See those smaller filaments?" He pointed to a series of thinner wires that were wrapping around the spine like root tendrils. "Those are the nerves. And you can see where they've been severed. There. There. There."

Osyrus moved to a rectangular panel console that was covered in hundreds of dials, buttons, switches, and pressure gauges.

"The fermentation of the latest healing steroid is complete," he said, flipping switches in rapid succession. "Let's see if those frayed nerves will connect with each other."

He adjusted a few dials on his machine, then flipped a switch made from red metal. The vats bubbled with pressure. Liquid started flowing into the rubber tubes that connected Kira to the machines.

"I'm seeing a small activity increase in the Empress's receptors," said one of the engineers. "Look."

Vera looked up at the strange filament model. Some of the thinner root tendrils did seem to be writhing around with a little more strength than before.

"But they aren't attaching," Vera said.

"We just need to coax things along a bit," Osyrus responded as he flipped a few more switches on his console. He turned to his engineers. "Remove the lung apparatus."

The two men moved to either side of Kira. Put their gloved hands on the tubes that connected to her chest. Vera winced at the metal click as they twisted each tube in unison and removed them from her chest, then placed them carefully in nearby holsters. They hustled back to their positions.

"Mark the time," said Osyrus.

"Marked," the engineer replied. "We have two minutes."

Vera stared at Kira and dug her fingers deep into the inside of her palms. She said a silent prayer to the skies above, asking the stars that Kira's lungs would work and her chest would lift.

"All receptors are spiking," an engineer reported. "Her body is reacting."

Osyrus didn't respond. He just kept adjusting different dials and controls. Every machine in the room was whirring and pumping with activity now. The churn and the motion made Vera's teeth hurt.

"I think I see a braid!" one engineer said, his voice cracking a little. "Right there."

He pointed to a place in the model where two tendrils were twisting around each other, forming a bond. The filaments started to glow a deep, healthy green.

"Confirmed," said the other engineer. "I have a few on my side as well."

"It's working?" Vera asked.

"Just an initial positive response to the latest steroid therapy," said Osyrus. "We're a long way from a full breath."

Vera glanced at the clock. They had less than a minute remaining. But when she turned back to the filaments, there were seven or eight glowing. Color was returning to Kira's cheeks and lips.

Please. Please.

She searched for more green tendrils, but didn't see any.

"We have a healthy baseline," one engineer said. Paused. "But I'm not seeing further growth."

Osyrus frowned. "Begin the manual stimulus. Level two."

"Level two," the engineer repeated. "Charging."

Vera looked away. She couldn't stand this part.

There was a high-pitched whine when the stimulus machine was charged, kind of like a mosquito buzzing next to your ear.

"Primed," said the engineer.

"Execute."

There was a pop. Ki's fingers started twitching, erratic and wild.

"Again."

Another pop. More twitching.

"That's enough."

Her fingers stopped moving. Everyone in the room looked at the filaments. For ten long seconds, nothing happened.

Then they began to ignite. One after the next. Soon, the entire spinal column was aglow.

"Yes," Vera whispered to herself.

But the filaments started to turn black again a moment later.

"What does that mean?" Vera asked.

Osyrus didn't respond. Just concentrated on his console, furiously adjusting dials. Then he ran to another machine and worked a hand crank up and down. Crossed the room again to depress a series of pedals.

"We're losing receptors!" an engineer called.

"I know we're losing receptors," Osyrus snapped. He dipped his finger into one of the vats and sucked the contents into his mouth. Made a weird chewing noise before spitting it on the floor. "Her body is rejecting the nerve growth."

"Why?" Vera asked.

"Unknown." He looked around the room. "We could try reinvigorating with a norishroot mixture . . ."

"We're losing them faster," said one engineer.

"It's a full toxicity waterfall," said the other.

The filaments were all black now. The tendrils withered like dying eels.

"We've passed the two-minute mark," the engineer added.

"I'm aware," Ward said, voice tight. "Kill all therapeutics. Put her back on the breathing apparatus. Now."

The engineers scuttled to work, adjusting some of the machines and then plugging Kira back into the machine with two metallic snaps.

"Turn off the filament model and leave the room," Osyrus said.

The visualization model retracted into the ceiling. Vera and Osyrus both remained silent until they were alone.

"What happened?" Vera hissed.

"There was probably an impurity in the regeneration tonic." He motioned to one of the many vats that hung from the ceiling, surrounding them. "Despite all of this machinery, a truly pure sample has remained elusive."

"Pure? I wiped a bunch of muddy river moss across Silas Bershad's bones and they healed in weeks."

"Different injury. Different sp—" He stopped himself. "Person."

"Different *how*?"

"You break a bone, all you need to do is put it in a splint and wait. Have you ever seen a paralyzed person start walking again all on their own?"

"No," Vera said. "But I've heard of it happening."

"What are you talking about?" Osyrus asked, screwing up his face.

"When I was last in Lysteria, I was told the same story by three different people. A child fell off a roof and had no feeling in his legs for three days. An old woman appeared from the hinterlands and gave him a tonic. He was walking half a day later."

That was what two people had told her, anyway. The third had insisted that the woman was a witch who'd cast black magic on the boy, and that he was now a half-demon who talked to Milk Dragons in the night.

"Did I send you to Lysteria to interview peasants about the injuries of children?"

Vera tightened her jaw. Osyrus liked to change the subject of conversations he didn't enjoy.

"No, you sent me to kill the governor of Kushal-Kin after he revolted. I did that, then I interviewed the peasants."

"Did the governor put up much of a fuss?"

The governor had never known that Vera was in his room before she killed him.

"Forget the governor of Kushal-Kin. The story. The woman."

Osyrus waved a hand in the air. "She gave the child a tincture to reduce the inflammation. He'd have been walking inside of a week without it, all she did was speed things up a little. That happens all the time. It's not the same situation we're dealing with right now."

"I want Kira off these machines. I want it done *now*."

"You are forgetting that the risks of rushing are extremely high. Kira could transform at any time."

Ward had explained the affliction of people like Kira and Silas to her several days after her injury. Vera suspected that he was making the entire thing up—a person turning into a tree seemed impossible—but these days the world was full of things that seemed impossible but weren't.

Vera couldn't risk Kira's life if Ward was telling the truth.

"Silas took thousands of injuries and never transformed," Vera said.

"Again with this? Kira is not the same person as her brother. Silas Bershad was born with an innate resilience to the change, and he showed a remarkably positive reaction to my suppression tonic. When he was under my care in Burz-al-dun, I gave him a single injection, which allowed me to perform several extremely aggressive treatments without a whiff of the change. Kira does not share her brother's resilience. Even with the tiny, iterative steps I am currently taking, she requires an extremely strong suppression cocktail to be in her bloodstream at all times to avoid the change." He pointed to a tube that was connected to Kira's left wrist. "If I stop that drip, mark my words, Kira will turn into a tree. The only way forward is with slow, careful work."

Osyrus had made the same threat about Kira—and the same irritating declaration about a path forward—six months ago. The reason that Vera had agreed to fly across the realm on his behalf was because she did not believe him, but needed proof.

There had to be a faster way. Ward just had no incentive to try it. He maintained too much power while she was incapacitated.

"If you cannot heal her quickly, I will find someone who can," Vera said.

Ward's eyebrows rose. "Oh? And who might this unimaginably qualified person be? That old woman from the hinterlands?"

"I've been making other inquiries," Vera said. "Talking to alchemists."

"Alchemists," Osyrus repeated with disdain. "All they have done is waste the last few centuries mixing herbs that compel coin from people's pockets in exchange for a stronger erection. Trust me, there is no herb poultice that can regrow a spinal column. The alchemists cannot help us."

"What about Gods Moss?" Vera asked.

Osyrus stopped fiddling with the machines and looked at her.

"Where did you hear about that?" he asked, voice flat.

"As I said, I have been making inquiries."

"Inquiries," Ward repeated. "What kind of inquiries?"

Vera had questioned five alchemists about Seeds before one of them finally told her about the existence of Gods Moss, and that was only because she'd put *Kaisha* into his mouth, and threatened to fillet his cheek.

"The kind that gets answers."

She hadn't learned much from him, just that Gods Moss triggered an extremely powerful reaction in Seeds, and that it was incredibly rare. The alchemist had never seen any himself.

"Now, I repeat, what would happen if we used Gods Moss on Kira?"

Ward gave that some thought, twisting a strand of beard into a braid and releasing it. "There would be a reaction, of course. If the moss was administered orally, Kira would most likely regain the ability to speak and breathe on her own. But given the amount of suppression fluid that was required to keep Kira in her human state, the result would be temporary. Five, ten minutes at most. Then we would be right back where we are now."

When he saw Vera's skepticism, he softened his tone.

"You see, Gods Moss is a potent but blunt instrument. Kira's injury—and her condition in general—is far more complex. Thus, it requires a complex and slow solution."

"I would like to keep searching for something that works faster."

He shrugged. "If you must."

"Good. I'll return to Pargos first."

"Again? Why? You didn't find anything the first time."

After Kira had remained on Ward's machine for the first month, Vera had insisted on traveling to the Alchemist Archives in Pargos to look for a faster method of healing her. All that she'd found was a massive building filled with plant identifications, soil samples, and insect categorizations.

"I do not believe that those archives are the only place where the alchemists keep records. There was nothing about dragons or Seeds. Nothing about moss. The main archive in the capital is famous, but I've heard rumors of more secret enclaves that are hidden in smaller villages throughout the country. I plan to find them. There might be some Gods Moss there."

"As I said, a temporary solution."

"Temporary is still valuable. I'm going to Pargos."

"Not possible," Osyrus said quickly. "I sent you to Lysteria because there was unrest. Pargos has put up no real resistance to us, so there is no reason for you to go there. However, there are reports of unrest in the northern mining towns of Balaria. A very delicate situation, seeing as those mines produce all our silver and nickel. Things are a mess, Vera! I simply cannot afford to have you wandering around Pargos looking for imaginary enclaves while Kira's empire endures such strain. You can go back to Pargos the moment another one of *their* governors decides to rebel."

Osyrus hadn't mentioned any unrest until she mentioned Pargos. Now, suddenly, she was needed everywhere else except there. He did not want her going to Pargos. Good to know.

Vera decided that she'd pushed him enough for now. She got what she needed.

She forced her lip to quiver and her face to turn red. Drew a breath and made a show of slowly letting it out, then spoke with a weak voice.

"I just want her back. I . . . miss her so much. If we keep on going as we have, with the cultures and tonics and therapies . . ." Vera said, putting a little strain and pitiful hope in her voice, "do you truly believe that Ki will recover with time, and breathe on her own?"

Osyrus gave his best attempt at a comforting smile, and patted her hand with his own. It took a large amount of Vera's self-control to avoid shuddering at the feeling of his bony knuckles against her skin.

"I do," he said. *"Truly."*

Vera could tell that Ward was doing his best to make that last word sound sincere. He did a decent job.

"Then we'll continue this way," Vera whispered.

"A wise choice," said Ward. He looked at the clock. "Now, if you'll excuse me, there is an injured Wormwrot private who I must prep for the acolyte surgery. He is the only surviving member of a vanquished patrol in which another one of my war acolytes was killed. I am interested to discover how the Jaguars are continuing to destroy my creations, despite the countermeasures I installed last spring. Perhaps they've found a loophole."

Vera nodded. "Would it be all right if I stayed with Kira a bit longer? I have missed her."

"Of course, Vera. Of course."

———

As soon as Vera was alone with Kira, she reached behind her breast-plate and removed an egg-sized lump of cloth. She pulled the cloth back to reveal a chunk of moss with deep green tendrils and blue flowers that smelled of honey and loam.

Gods Moss.

She'd put a blade in some grayrobe's mouth to learn what the moss did to Seeds. To actually get some, she had done something far worse, but she didn't care. A blackened conscience was a small price to pay if it saved Kira's life.

Vera knelt by Kira and carefully placed the clump of moss in her mouth. Some of the reflexes in her throat still worked, so Vera only had to massage her throat to make her swallow.

The speed with which her skin changed tones surprised Vera. A few breaths was all it took for the clammy, pale skin to turn pink with healthy color. Kira's turquoise eyes opened a moment later, pupils adjusting to the light in the room.

"Kira?" Vera asked, her body flooding with relief. "Ki. Can you hear me?"

Kira swallowed with a great deal of effort. "Where am I? What's . . ." Her hand moved to her stomach. Running along the scar there. "Am I dead?"

"No, You're safe, Ki. Osyrus saved your life. But you're very badly hurt. We're trying to heal you, but there have been complications. We may only have a few minutes to speak before you have to go back to sleep."

Vera looked at the tubes in her chest. Part of her was tempted to unhook them and make a run for it, but that enormous acolyte was still outside, and if Osyrus was telling the truth about the effect only being temporary, she needed to leave her on the machine for now.

"I can't move my legs," Kira said. "I can't feel them at all."

"That won't be permanent," Vera said quickly, needing to convince herself just as much as she wanted to convince Kira.

"I remember the blade," Ki said. "The woman who attacked me . . . she was a Papyrian."

"Empress Okinu betrayed us," Vera said. "She sent a widow named Shoshone to assassinate you."

"What happened to her?"

"I killed her."

Kira nodded. "How long have I been asleep?"

Vera swallowed. Given all the information she was about to absorb, Vera's instinct was to lie to Kira, but she couldn't bring herself to do it. "Six months."

Kira's eyes widened with panic, but she regained her composure with a quickness that both surprised and impressed Vera. "And what's happened since then?"

Vera did her best to explain the situation. Told her how Osyrus had conquered almost all of Terra within a fortnight. Mostly without violence, but that he'd used his acolytes when it was required. She glossed over the bombing of Papyria, saying only that the empress had paid for her betrayal.

"The Dainwood are the last unconquered province in Terra," she said. "Between the jungle canopy and the dragons, the Jaguar wardens are protected from the skyships."

"Is Carlyle Llayawin leading them?" Kira asked.

Kira had just made peace with Carlyle before the assassination attempt turned everything sour. Carlyle had been killed, but Vera didn't have the heart to tell Kira that. She had enough to absorb.

"I'm not sure," said Vera. "Reliable information is hard to pluck from the Dainwood."

"I see." Ki paused, thinking. Then her nose scrunched up and she gave Vera a little scowl. "Oh. Vera. You smell *really* bad."

"Oh, sorry." She leaned back a little. Realized that she couldn't remember the last time she'd had a proper bath. "I've been busy. Haven't bathed in a while."

"The only thing more powerful than your body odor is the smell of that pipe. Ugh."

"Smoking helps me relax."

"You only need to relax after a fight."

Vera shrugged.

"What does Osyrus Ward have you doing? Tell me the truth."

Vera let out a slow breath before answering. "I have been traveling on behalf of your empire."

"My sister told me once that there is only one reason for a widow to travel."

"That's . . . not the only thing that I'm doing. I've been looking for a way to heal you myself. The only reason we're speaking now is because of something I brought back."

"But what have you *done*?" Kira asked, struggling to put emphasis on the final word. The Gods Moss must be wearing off.

"That doesn't matter."

"Yes, it does, Vera. I don't want you to darken your honor because of me."

"I don't care about my honor anymore."

"Don't say that. Don't abandon yourself for me. If the war is as terrible as you say, there must be people suffering all over Terra. You must try to find a way to help them. Keep them safe."

"The only way for me to help them is to kill Osyrus Ward. And I can't do that until you're off this machine and safe."

"Yes, you can. I'm just one person."

"Not to me," Vera said. She swallowed. Felt her emotions finally overwhelm her. "To me, you're the only person who matters. Do you understand, Kira? I . . . I . . ."

She trailed off, still unable to get the words out, after all this time.

"I understand, Vera." Her voice was weak. Strained. "I feel the same."

Vera wiped a tear away from her cheek. Nodded.

"I've caused so much trouble. For my family. For the people of Terra."

"There was always going to be trouble."

"Still," Kira said. "I have so many regrets."

"Do you know what I regret most, Ki?"

She shook her head.

"Last winter, when you asked me to go for a ride with you alone on the *Sparrow,* I wish that I'd said yes. And I wish we had left the feasting hall that moment and gone. Just us, away from all this mess." Vera touched Kira's cheek, moved her hand around to the base of her neck and rubbed it a little. She felt a swelling of emotion in her throat and her chest and belly that threatened to overwhelm her even more than she already was. "We're trapped in the mess now, but I *am* going to get us out of it. You will walk out of this room on your own feet, I promise you."

Kira nodded. "I can feel my lungs going weak. There isn't much time left." She swallowed with great effort. "So I have to ask you a very important question."

"Anything."

"What did you eat for breakfast this morning?"

"That's your important question?"

"I want to hear about you. Just regular things about you."

Vera hesitated. The last thing she'd eaten was a cold meat bun hastily stuffed in her mouth before she and Garret had left the *Blue Sparrow* to coerce Garwin. The bread had been old and hard, the meat gray and lacking flavor. But she understood what Kira needed.

"A steamed pork bun," Vera said. "Made fresh from the Floodhaven kitchen and brought to me in bed by one of your servants."

Kira gave a weak smile. "You're a terrible liar."

"No, it's true," Vera said, smiling back. "With you having been indisposed for so long, I've moved into your chambers and taken over your staff. I insist on a pork bun brought in on a silver platter to start my day. From there, it's a pudding and fish course, followed by a fresh soup. Then two women rub my feet for twenty minutes before I dress and start my day of leisure."

Kira smiled a little wider, but it soon faded. Her breaths turned ragged and hoarse. The color in her cheeks started to fade.

Vera looked into her eyes, trying to burn the color and the shape into her memory.

"Close your eyes," she said. "The machine will take over."

Kira did as she was told. Drifted away, back to darkness.

Vera stayed in the room until her body stopped trembling, which took a very long time.

On her way down the tower, Vera tried to think about how she was going to get back to Pargos. It wouldn't be easy, but there had to be a way.

7

PRIVATE RIGAR
Location Unknown

Rigar awoke in darkness. It was cold. His body felt bloated, but also tight. Muscles rigid and unmoving.

"Specimen Seven-Nine-Nine is conscious," someone said in Balarian. He had a nasally voice.

"Excellent," came another voice. This one was deeper. "We'll perform baseline conditioning, then move to the debrief."

The sound of movement. Footsteps. Moving closer.

"What is your name?" asked the man with the deeper voice.

Rigar's face muscles warmed, then slackened. Fell into his control.

"Ri-Rigar."

"False."

There was a click, followed by a buzz, then a massive surge of pain through his body. The worst pain Rigar had ever felt—like his whole body was a tooth and someone was jamming an ice pick into it. He howled. Tried to thrash, but his body was locked down. Not his own.

"What is your name?" the voice repeated.

"Please. I don't understand."

The last thing he remembered was falling down a muddy slope in the jungle. He'd been so thirsty. So tired. And then a shadow had fallen over him.

"The question is very simple. What is your name? A name is an identifier. In your case, it is a sequence of numbers. What are those numbers?"

"I don't have a number. My name is R—"

"False."

Another shock. Worse than before. Longer.

"Think. *Remember.* What is your number?"

Rigar wracked his brain. Tried to remember.

"Does it start with a seven?"

"True. The rest, please."

"Seven." He hesitated. "Eight."

"False."

More pain.

"Try again, please.

"Seven. Nine?"

Rigar waited for the pain. When he did not feel any, he prayed to Aeternita, then continued.

"Nine."

"True," came the voice.

Rigar had never felt more relieved in his life. But that relief was short-lived, because if he had a number, there was only one thing that could have happened.

"Wait," he said. "Wait. Wait. Wait. Am I . . . what have you turned me into?"

"Please refrain from inquiries during your conditioning process. Now. Who is your master?"

"Master?"

"Yes. Identify your master."

"Uh, Sergeant Droll?"

"False."

Pain. Such deep, terrible pain.

"Who is your master?" the voice repeated.

"C-Commander Vergun."

"False."

More pain. Why didn't it kill him? Why wasn't he turned to ash?

"Who is your master?"

Rigar swallowed. Throat aflame. But finally, the answer dawned on him.

"Osyrus Ward."

"True."

Another flood of relief. It felt almost chemical—like the wave of pleasure after the first drag on an opium pipe. He loved his master. If his master brought that feeling, then he was the only master that he would ever need.

"You're doing well, Seven-Nine-Nine. We will now move to your mission debrief before applying the full barrage of chemicals. Wouldn't want to foggy that memory up before we learned what happened at Fallon's Roost."

8

CABBAGE
Dainwood Jungle

Three days after leaving Floodhaven, Cabbage was still slightly hungover from their antics at the brothel. This was the first morning that he hadn't begun by puking in the bushes.

"Pretty sure this is the worst hangover of my life," Cabbage complained, finally able to choke down a few strips of burned bacon as his breakfast. "And given how deep I stayed in the potato liquor on Ghost Moth Island, that is saying something."

"If I was stuck on the horrible island for years, I'd develop a bit of a drinking problem, too," said Felgor, munching on his own bacon.

"You drank an entire cask of Atlas Coast cider by yourself," said Cabbage. "I'd say that constitutes a bit of a drinking problem right there."

"I bought the entire cask, but I had help drinking it from both you and the girl from the Gorgon River Valley. Yesmana or Yasamu or something."

"Yesmine," Cabbage corrected. He remembered her because she'd run a hand down his cheek and felt the slivers of artificial flesh that hid his blue bars. Cabbage had tensed up, thinking they had a problem, but Yesmine had just smiled and whispered in his ear that it would be their little secret.

"Yesmine," Felgor said. "Right."

They reached a high bluff, where Cabbage looked behind them. He could just barely make out the Gorgon Bridge, and the massive skyship that hovered over it at all times.

"I still can't believe you talked your way across that without the proper seals," Cabbage said.

When they'd reached the bridge checkpoint, Felgor had babbled on about being reassigned to one of the rubber plantations on the outskirts of the jungle at the last minute, and explained that they didn't have seals because the Balarians who'd carried the official seals had been eaten by a dragon, his body snatched into the sky. There'd been no time to make replacements. He talked so quickly and in such great quantities that the border guards eventually let them through to avoid causing a traffic delay, which came with severe penalties from the higher-ups because rubber was in extremely high demand by Osyrus Ward.

"It's not the fast talking and flimsy excuse that does it," Felgor explained. "It's the talking *and* the uniforms *and* our gray eyes *and* our long noses, all working together to form a picture that feels natural. Most people in this world will believe a lie if it's shown to them in the shape of a convenient truth."

"I guess so," said Cabbage. "Being honest, I was never very good with words."

"Nonsense. You did great back there in Floodhaven. The perfect straight-man to cover my antics. No way would Brutus have bought the con without you. No way at all."

"Any chance that's just the shape of a truth instead of a real one?" Cabbage asked.

Felgor sighed. "Okay, fine. The truth is, I mostly took you because of your accent. You got that middle-class ring to it that's hard to fake, like you spent years apprenticed to some grunt of a workman in the Fifth District of Burz-al-dun."

"I did apprentice to a clockmaker in the Fifth District. I told you that."

"Makes sense, then."

They hiked through the jungle for the rest of the day. Dampmire village—the place they were meeting Bershad—was famously difficult to find, so they followed a trail of mud totems that the Jaguars had left for them. The totems were all over, but the ones with blue stones for eyes each had an arm made from sticks that pointed them in the direction of Dampmire.

Around late afternoon, they summited a hill that looked over a valley of heavy canopy. There was a Gray-Winged Nomad circling the valley from among the high clouds above.

"Guess the village is down there," said Felgor. "Looks like Bershad got here ahead of us."

"I'll never get used to that dragon following him around."

"Smokey? She's harmless."

"No," Cabbage said, remembering what she'd done on Ghost Moth Island. "She is not."

"Well, harmless so long as you stay on Silas's good side." Felgor smiled. "C'mon. Let's get down there."

———

They'd barely made it halfway down the hill when two stumpy little trees came alive and pointed blades at their throats. Not trees. Jaguar wardens. This lot were all wearing black cat masks.

"Peace!" Cabbage squeaked, arms up. But he was so surprised that he said it in Balarian, which caused the two wardens to jerk their blades closer with a clear intention of ramming them straight through Cabbage's chest.

"Stop." A third warden melted out of the undergrowth. "Those are Ashlyn's little spies. They're expected."

The other wardens relaxed their blades. "Aye, Oromir. Whatever you say."

The warden removed his mask, revealing a surprisingly young face. Cabbage figured he was seventeen or eighteen. But he had the scars of a warden who'd been fighting much longer.

"I'll take them in."

Oromir led them down the hill without a word. His icy demeanor was even enough to silence Felgor, who was the most talkative person that Cabbage had ever met.

Dampmire was one of the canopy villages in the Dainwood—strung up between massive Daintrees in such a way that it was practically invisible from both the sky above and the ground below. These were the last safe havens for anyone living outside of Deepdale.

Oromir took them to a hidden walkway that wound around an especially large Daintree to form a ladder.

"Up," he ordered.

Cabbage was winded by the time he'd ascended to the village, which spread out in all directions along the canopy. The little huts were made from clay and thatch, all of them nestled perfectly into the nooks and branches of the massive trees.

Oromir guided Felgor and Cabbage along the platforms and past the small, acorn-shaped huts until they reached a larger building hanging from the limbs of an ancient Daintree. He stopped at the door—which was just a woven flap—and motioned for them to wait outside. Then he ducked inside.

"Found the Balarians," he said to whoever was in the hut.

"Good," came Ashlyn's familiar voice. "They can come in."

"Course we can fucking come in," said Felgor as he barged through the flap with a purpose. Cabbage followed. Oromir stayed by the door.

Inside, six people were sitting around a fire that had burned down to smoldering coals: Ashlyn Malgrave, Silas Bershad, Simeon, Kerrigan, Willem, and the boy alchemist who worked with the queen. Julan or Jorro or something.

"Did you assholes miss me?" Felgor said, spreading his arms as if he was planning to hug them all in one big embrace.

"Sure," growled Simeon. "'Bout as much as I miss the cock rot after it's cured."

Ashlyn and Kerrigan gave little smiles, but Bershad kept his face unreadable as he appraised Felgor for a long moment, before finally breaking into a massive grin, standing up, and scooping Felgor into a strong embrace.

"Glad you made it back in one piece, you fucking thief."

"Of course I made it back. I'm a professional."

"My earless Balarian didn't get in the way?" Simeon asked.

"Nope. Cabbage was instrumental to our success, actually."

"Success?" Ashlyn asked. "I like the sound of that."

She motioned for them to sit with her right hand, careful to keep the left hidden beneath her yellow poncho. Cabbage knew why, and he was glad for it. Ashlyn seemed like a nice person, but after the things he'd seen her do with that metal arm, he was terrified of her.

Felgor took a seat around the fire. Looked at everyone with a huge grin.

"Well, what did you get?" Bershad asked.

"All kinds of shit," Felgor said happily, motioning for Cabbage to hand him their first saddle bag of documents.

"First up . . . what is this one again?" He squinted at the maps. "Oh, right. These are the skyship drop-off and extraction locations for their combat teams, scattered all over the Dainwood. Each one's clearly marked and ranked according to lizard safety and strategic value."

"What?" Willem asked. "That's a hell of a . . . let me see those."

Willem took the maps and riffled through them for a few moments. "I've seen them use some of these before, but a lot are new. Places we don't usually patrol."

"Pretty sure that is the point," said Felgor. "Clean exit and all that."

"Where did you get this from?" Willem asked, moving to another map.

"They got all their cartographers holed up in a basement of a manse near Castle Malgrave, which I'd actually robbed before. Twice. So nicking those from their vault was pretty straightforward."

Willem licked his lips. Looked up at Felgor. "I could kiss you right now."

Felgor shrugged. "Your beard looks kinda scratchy, but maybe if you oil it down a bit?"

"Was there any news of my sister?" Ashlyn asked.

"Well, there's a shitload of unsubstantiated stories floating around the city. Everyone's firm on the fact that she's alive, but things get pretty wild from there. Some people are convinced that Ward's using her blood to make the grayskins. Others say he's turning her into a goddess from some workshop in the top of the tower where all kinds of weird shit gets delivered. And others still say that she *is* Osyrus Ward, just wearing a disguise. I've seen Osyrus Ward before, and that is pretty far-fetched."

"What else?" Ashlyn asked, motioning to the bag.

"Ah, don't you worry, Ashe. I know you're hungry for information on the grayskins, and once again, I have delivered. The schematics, Cabbage."

Cabbage dug through the pack again—a little annoyed to be playing the part of paper jockey, but he had to admit that it was better than being Simeon's murderous helper. He handed over the documents that Brutus had given them.

"Those are detailed material requirements, diagrams, and capabilities of all the Madman's different grayskin creatures," said Felgor. "Personally, I found the arachnid models to be especially unsettling."

Ashlyn looked at the pages. "Oh, Felgor. I could kiss you, too."

"Gonna have to make a hard pass on that one, Queen." He glanced at Silas. "Don't wanna have my head torn off. No, our agreed-upon fee is plenty of thanks for me. Fifty thousand gold pieces per each piece of valuable intelligence."

"Of course," Ashlyn said, already turning her attention back to the pages. "You'll be paid when the war is done."

Felgor frowned. "The cavalier nature with which you are referring to one hundred and fifty thousand gold pieces makes me nervous. As if you do not expect to actually pay it."

"I am trying to deal with one problem at a time, Felgor. My debt to you is not very high on the list. Jolan, look at these." She pointed. "See this model? Ballast acolytes. They're some kind of stabilization unit to prevent skyship cores from overheating during long journeys."

Jolan came over. "Huh. Yeah. But how is he getting around the heat cascades at high rotations?"

"I'm not sure. These pins that are inserted into the cores could do it, but he doesn't offer detail on them."

Those two descended into a prattle of esoteric conversation that Cabbage couldn't understand. Willem and Oromir started poring over their sets of maps, mumbling to each other as well.

Felgor kicked his feet up on the table.

"It was difficult work, I'll admit, but there were advantages of infiltrating our way into a bit of civilization. My favorite spot is the Eagle's Roost brothel and restaurant. They have a *real* nice setup there. And the men from Clockwork love it because their cook uses Balarian spices, so that's where we set up to find a mark. First few nights me and Cabbage were just doing field research. You would not believe the pork roast and scallops they were turning out for dinners. Perfectly cooked in butter and covered in fresh pepper and turmeric that must have been imported from beyond Taggarstan, but *real* fresh, you know? I wonder if there's a spice skyship, because the way it blended with the pork was just—"

"Felgor, if you mention one more detail about food, I'll murder you," growled Simeon.

"What? What's the problem?"

"We lost our supply line to Dunfar," Ashlyn explained.

"Lost? Well, where'd you last see it?"

"Not funny," said Kerrigan. "I watched four ships and a lot of good crew get incinerated. And seeing as the Balarians have made a point to burn and salt all the Dainwood's farms over the last year, we're currently in a bad way when it comes to rations."

"How bad, exactly?" asked Cabbage. He'd been looking forward to a proper meal, now that they were back on allied ground. The long walk and horrific hangover had left him feeling thin. The only food he had left was a lump of salted pork that had been stewing in his pocket for the whole walk home.

"The men's last proper meal was two weeks ago, when we left Deepdale," Bershad said. "Since then, we've had to scrounge what we can from the jungle, but that's dangerous with so many dragons about. Three wardens got eaten yesterday chasing after a fucking rabbit."

"Wasn't even a big rabbit," Simeon added.

"Those deaths are a problem, but they're not our biggest concern," Ashlyn said. "It's the crews who've taken to raiding and robbing the villages that we move through."

"I dealt with the men who did that," Simeon growled. "Won't happen again."

"Beating a few men to death with their own arms isn't a permanent solution," Ashlyn said.

Cabbage swallowed, glad he wasn't around to see that happen. He'd gotten enough of that on Ghost Moth Island.

"You sure? Anyone turn to thieving since I dismembered those assholes?" he asked.

"No," Kerrigan said. "But desertions have tripled since then."

"Well, you should have said something, Kerri. I'll track 'em down and deal with them, too."

"No," said Bershad. "You won't."

"Why not?"

"Because we can't win this war if you keep ripping our warriors' arms out of their sockets."

"Can't win it if our warriors all fuck off into the jungle, either. Doesn't matter how many scraps of paper the two Balarians have brought us."

Everyone started talking at once—muttering and arguing and throwing out unhelpful suggestions.

But an idea occurred to Cabbage. Something he'd heard a few skyship captains talking about in that brothel on their last night in Floodhaven.

"Hey, wait, I might have a solution."

Everyone ignored him. Cabbage took a breath and embraced the pirate inside of him.

"Hey, assholes! Shut up."

That got their attention.

"On our last day in Floodhaven, I heard some captains talking about a skyship crash in the Dainwood. One of their big cargo models that was carrying a bunch of food. We could try to salvage it."

"Ha!" Felgor shouted. "I told you one more visit to the brothel would be worth it, Cabbage."

"How much food?" Kerrigan asked.

"They said it was meant to resupply all of Wormwrot for a month. Given how outnumbered we are, that'll be enough to feed our wardens for . . . I dunno, exactly."

"Through summer, at least," Kerrigan said. "Longer, if we keep our rations strict."

"And manage to live that long," Willem muttered.

"If there's that much food, why haven't they gone in to retrieve it?"

"That's what the captains were talking about," said Cabbage. "They said the skyship went down near some big dragon nest, so they're afraid to go in. They've had ships circling for weeks, but nobody can get through."

"Which nest?" Ashlyn asked.

"Um . . . one of the captains had just come back from patrolling around it." Cabbage tried to remember. He didn't want to admit that he'd been extremely drunk while talking to them. "Southwest of Glenlock, he said. Due directly south of the ninth bend in the Gorgon."

"That isn't near a nest of dragons," Bershad said. "That's in the middle of the largest population of Blackjacks in the realm of Terra."

"Like the ones around Deepdale?" Felgor asked.

Bershad shook his head. "More. A lot more. Leave it to the idiot Balarians to fly through there."

"But we can sneak underneath, right?" said Felgor. "Same way the wardens get in and out of Deepdale?"

"No, it took hundreds of years to make those choke weed trails," said Bershad.

There was a silence.

"There *is* a way through," Bershad said eventually. "The Blackjacks will give the Nomad some distance if we come through underneath her shadow. We couldn't take more than a score or so of men, but it could work."

"Hold on," said Kerrigan. "Am I to understand that we're gonna hike through a dragon-infested jungle that Balarian skyships are afraid to even *fly* over?"

"Well, if you hadn't gotten caught on the supply run we wouldn't have to risk it," said Simeon.

"Oh, you can fuck all the way off with that dragonshit. If you'd tried that run, you'd have turned yourself to flotsam on the very first voyage. You were always a shit sailor."

"I'm a fantastic sailor."

"It doesn't matter how we got here," said Ashlyn. "This is our current reality, and we have to decide how to handle it." She paused. "I'll go with Silas. Who else is willing?"

"I think it's suicide," said Kerrigan. "But seeing as I'm partially responsible for our current predicament, I suppose getting killed trying to rectify it isn't all bad. I'm in."

"I'll go, too," said Jolan. "From what these documents show, there could be technology in the skyship that we can salvage. That's worth just as much as the food."

"Simeon?"

He shrugged. "Screw it. I'd rather get eaten by a dragon than keep eating bugs and worms for every meal."

"Says the asshole wearing a suit of dragon-scale armor," Kerrigan mumbled. Simeon ignored her.

"I'll go, too," said Willem.

"No," said Bershad. "Someone needs to keep the pressure on the Balarians while we're getting this done. Put those maps Felgor stole to good use, and make the enemy hurt."

"There are plenty of wardens who can do that."

"There are," Bershad agreed. "But you're the closest thing the Jaguar Army has to a commander. You need to stay with the men."

"Meaning, I need to lead the men if you all get yourselves eaten?"

"Yes."

Willem gave a slow nod. "Yeah. All right."

"Cabbage and I will obviously go as well," said Felgor.

"What?" Cabbage hissed.

"You're coming, Cabbage," said Simeon, in a tone that made it clear the issue wasn't up for debate. Cabbage just sighed and waved his hand in a vague gesture of both acceptance and defeat.

Everyone was quiet for a few moments.

"Seven of us isn't enough," said Bershad. "I'll walk the camp and ask for volunteers."

"No need," said Oromir. "Me and my crew will go, too."

"You sure?" Bershad asked.

"I don't put stock in sorcery or dragonslayers or stacks of paper. But we need food to fight this war. So yeah, I'm sure. Twenty more men. That enough?"

"About all we should risk, I'd say."

"Good."

Jolan cleared his throat. "If we're only taking twenty-seven people, how are we going to haul the food back out of the jungle once we get there?"

Another long silence.

"Am I really the one who's gotta solve this problem for you idiots?" Kerrigan asked.

They all looked at her. She sighed.

"We'll use the donkeys," she said. "The ones we took down from Naga Rock. Wendell's still looking out for them with his asshole father down south, right?"

"Yeah," said Bershad. He wanted the boy and his father kept

out of the war, and kept safe. "It's actually on the way to the sky-ship."

"Good," said Ashlyn. "We leave in thirty minutes."

———————

On Cabbage's way out of the hut, he noticed a small black dog napping in the shade of a big Daintree leaf. There were flies buzzing around his dry nose and Cabbage could see the lines of his ribs underneath his hide. Seeing that made his heart hurt.

Cabbage reached into his pocket for his final scrap of salt pork.

He knew it was stupid and softhearted to give his last bit of meat to a dog he didn't even know. Simeon would have slapped him and told him for the thousandth time he had the wrong blood for this work. But Simeon wasn't around and Cabbage couldn't bear the idea of eating it himself. He walked over to the dog.

"Hey, buddy. I got something for you," Cabbage said, taking the cloth out of his pocket.

The dog continued sleeping.

"You hungry?" Cabbage asked.

Still nothing.

"Hey. I've got some pork for you if you'll wake up."

Cabbage gave the sleeping dog the gentlest of taps with his boot. The dog responded by jumping up with a yelp and careening down the forest path at speed, howling the entire way as if Cabbage had just put a thumb up his ass instead of trying to give him a scrap of swine meat.

"What the hell?" Cabbage muttered.

"You know there's an old Dunfarian saying about sleeping dogs," said Kerrigan, coming up behind him and crossing her arms.

"What is it?"

"Difficult to translate. But kicking them isn't part of it."

"I didn't kick him!" Cabbage said. "I was just trying to . . ." He tightened his hand around the scrap of pork. Kerrigan was nicer than Simeon, but that wasn't a hard thing to be. She probably wouldn't approve of wasted pork, either. "Never mind."

Kerrigan shrugged. Flicked a spider off her wrist, then wandered off down the plank road.

Cabbage went after the dog.

At this point he was just being stubborn, but if Cabbage was willing to part with his pork for the good of an unknown dog, then by Aeternita the dog was gonna eat it.

He moved past a series of tree huts, searching for the dog and giving awkward waves to the people of Dampmire that he passed.

He found the dog huddled up in a tomato garden that was next to a small hut. The dog was glaring at him. When he got closer, he bared his teeth and released a low growl.

"I'm trying to *feed* you, you little asshole." And by that point, he had no idea why he was still trying. But he'd gone this far and refused to give up. He took one step into the garden, bending a plant. The dog barked, and a moment later the door to the hut opened. A woman with a half-woven basket in her hand came out. Frowned.

"You bothering my dog?" she asked.

"Huh?"

"That's my dog," she said. "Why are you screwing with him?"

"Well, I was trying to do the opposite of that." Cabbage held up the pork. "But for such a skinny creature he's being awfully stubborn about a free snack."

The woman snorted. "He ain't nearly as starved as he looks. Little troublemaker was always skinny, even before the skyships torched all the farms. Probably because he's willing to eat dragonshit."

Cabbage shrugged.

The woman eyed the meat. "That pork?"

"Yeah."

"What forest god did you fuck to get it?"

"Uh . . ."

"Never mind. I don't really care. How about you make up for molesting my dog by letting me drop that in the stew I've got going. I haven't had a scrap of meat in three moon turns."

Cabbage had to admit that giving the pork to a woman made a lot more sense than forcing it up some asshole dog who was perfectly happy subsisting on dragonshit.

"Sure."

———

The hut was just a one-room affair with dirt floors, a lofted sleeping area, and a cookpot situation in the middle, which was bubbling with a delicious-smelling broth. The woman took the pork, then motioned him to a wicker chair next to the cook fire.

"My name's Jovita. What's yours?"

"Cabbage."

"Cabbage?" She frowned. "That a Balarian name?"

"Pirate name," he said.

"What's your non-pirate name, then?"

"My what?"

A strand of Jovita's hair—which was black, but streaked with gray—fell in front of her face. She tucked it behind an ear. "Your mother didn't name you Cabbage, did she?"

"Oh, yeah. I mean no. It's Cabargato. An old Balarian name."

"I think I can intuit the origin of the pirate version."

"Yeah."

Jovita took a knife from the wall and cut the pork into thin slices—clearly trying to make the handful of meat stretch further than it naturally would. She cut up a few gnarled roots, too, and dropped the entire balance into the pot.

"Needs to simmer for a little while," she said.

Cabbage nodded.

"You got some nastiness going on with your ears," she said, pointing at his face with the knife.

Cabbage touched his right ear. Came back with a blackened mush.

"Uh, they're fake, actually," he explained. "The queen made them for me, but the jungle wet rots them out eventually. It's hard to get them off, though, 'cause of the glue she used."

The woman nodded with understanding, as if she encountered earless men with prosthetics made by a queen on a regular basis.

"I can help you get them off, if you want."

"You're not gonna use that, are you?" Cabbage asked, pointing at the knife.

"No." She grabbed a roughspun cloth, then turned to a line of glass jars filled with various liquids. "A little hot water and vinegar is all we need here."

"Vinegar," Cabbage repeated. "Right."

Jovita dampened the rag, then squatted and started dabbing the edges with it. The sharp smell of vinegar filled his nose.

"Um, I should warn you that what's underneath isn't . . . pleasant to look at."

"Please. I was married to an Almiran warden for fifteen years. Scars don't bother me."

"Oh." He paused. "What happened to him? Your husband."

"He died in a skirmish against Linkon Pommol's men last fall."

"Sorry."

"His crew all came to Dampmire to give me the news. They said that he died bravely, and that it was fast. Painless."

Cabbage swallowed. Thought of all the men he'd watched die. Very few of them had done so quickly.

"I'm sure it was."

Jovita dabbed for a while longer. Cabbage could feel the warm vinegar dripping down his neck.

"Ready?" she asked.

"Yes."

She peeled away his left ear, slowing when she saw Cabbage wince, so that it didn't hurt much. But Cabbage winced again once it was totally off, knowing that Jovita was staring at a hole in his head surrounded by rough scar tissue.

"Sorry," he said. "I know it's—"

"Stow the apologies," Jovita said, moving to his left ear and beginning to dab.

She peeled his left ear off without incident. Held the two appendages in her palm, studying them.

"The witch queen really made these?"

"Yes."

"They look so real. I suppose it makes sense they're sorcery-forged."

"She's told me on a number of occasions that there's no such thing as sorcery, but some of the things that I have seen her do . . . there's no other explanation."

"Do you want to keep them?" Jovita asked.

"No, it's okay."

She threw them in the fire. "Well, that's done."

Cabbage hesitated. "Not quite, actually."

Jovita turned to him, a question in her eyes. But then she studied his face a little closer. His cheeks.

"Oh. Of course. I can do those, too."

"Might as well."

Jovita squatted in front of him this time, her brown eyes focused on his face as she started rubbing off the layer that hid his blue bars.

She didn't speak for a while. When she was halfway through removing the second bar, Cabbage couldn't take it anymore.

"Do you want to know how I got them?"

"Not really. Do you want to tell me?"

It had been a long time since Cabbage had told anyone how he got the bars. Up in the Proving Ground, where everyone had bars, nobody really cared.

"Afraid if I tell you, I'll miss out on the stew."

Jovita smiled. "Save it then. Because the stew's ready."

Cabbage served himself, and made a point to ensure only one thin slice of pork made its way into his bowl. He took slow sips, savoring the flavor, which was plain but rich. Lots of roots and a little onion.

"It's better with corn," Jovita said, taking a spoonful. "And salt. Gods, I would murder someone for a pinch of salt."

"Maybe I can bring some back for you, if we come through this way again."

Jovita gave him a look. "Would you kill someone for it?"

Cabbage cocked his head. Wasn't sure what to say. "Being honest, I've killed men for less."

"That so?" Jovita said, dipping her bowl back into the pot. Picking out a pork slice and taking a bite. "Because despite a pretty screwed-up face, you seem a little softhearted to me, trying to feed extra scraps to my dog and all."

Cabbage finished the last sip of his stew. "My boss is the one who wears the dragon-bone armor," he said, staring at the dregs in the bottom of the bowl. "Do you know him?"

"Everyone in the Dainwood knows Simeon the Skojit by now."

"Yeah. I guess he stands out." Cabbage swallowed. "He likes to tell me that I've got the wrong blood for this kind of work. I took offense to it at first, especially seeing as offense is what was intended. But lately, I'm starting to think he's right, and that it's a good thing. Not being right for this life. Problem is, just because a set of boots don't fit doesn't mean a replacement's readily available."

"Dunno about boots, but it seems to me you could use your feet to walk away from this war anytime."

"No." Cabbage shook his head.

He thought of Ashlyn and Silas and the Jaguar wardens. They were all fighting this war with such conviction. Even Felgor, in his own way. He joked around constantly, but the things they'd done in Floodhaven had been incredibly dangerous.

"The people fighting in this war are my friends," Cabbage said. "I can't abandon them."

He might not have felt the same courage as the others, but he could help them. That was one thing he could do. And when it was done, maybe that would form some kind of penance for all the years of murder and mayhem he'd wrought from Ghost Moth Island.

"Well, seeing as how a dog you've never met turned your heart to mush, I can see where the whole war camaraderie thing would have deep hooks in you," Jovita said.

Cabbage opened his mouth to say something else, but was stopped by the thump of heavy boots outside as wardens moved past Jovita's hut. They were muttering about orders and locations and skyship drops.

"I need to be moving," he said, standing up.

"Yeah," Jovita agreed. She lifted her bowl. "Thanks for the stew, Cabbage."

He nodded. "I'll keep an eye out for some salt. And if we come through this way again, I'll make sure you get some."

Jovita smiled, but sadly. Cabbage could read on her face that she was figuring the odds she'd ever see him again, and coming up with narrow figures.

"Well, you know where to find me."

9

CASTOR
Castle Malgrave, Level 62

"You seem nervous, Castor," said Commander Vergun, as they made their way toward the upper chambers of the King's Tower.

"No, Commander. Just a little tired of these meetings, is all."

Castor figured that—all in—he'd spent about half his waking life split between training for a fight and standing around in different rooms doing nothing. The charming and glorious existence of a Horellian guard turned mercenary.

There was, of course, that little sliver of actual combat, which had widened considerably since Castor had left the Horellians and started working for Commander Vergun. Some Wormwrot men loved the thrill of a battle even more than the coin they were paid for it, but Castor never understood the emotional fixation men had with mercenary work. It was just a trade, like any other. Glorifying it to such an extreme seemed to Castor like a blacksmith who pounded out steel all day with a throbbing erection threatening to burst through his pants.

It was unprofessional, and it interfered with the work.

"You would prefer to be back in the jungle, where any tree could be a warden in disguise, waiting to gut you?"

Castor shrugged. "I understand the jungle, and I understand ambushes. The shit that goes on in this castle makes no fucking sense."

They reached the large chamber where the meeting was to take place and went inside. Castor's mouth went dry at the sight of the interior.

Hundreds of vivisected insects and rodents were splayed out inside glass cases that ringed the walls. Their organs and nervous systems pinned in odd, whirling patterns. An autonomous spider made from copper and gold clacked around the room, hunting roaches and rats that Ward had deliberately released across the upper levels. He said that the hunt helped Bartholomew—the only one of his creations with a normal name—hone his coordination. It also led to the secondary creation of little piles of gnawed rat bones in most corners.

Castor had worked for unsettling men. And he had seen his share of unsettling things. Vallen Vergun was known for keeping impaled enemies in his tent, which was made from human skin. That was horrific, but it served a purpose: intimidating the living shit out of everyone in Taggarstan.

Castor wasn't sure what the point of a metallic, rat-hunting spider was, especially when Ward had all the intimidation he needed standing in each corner.

The four war acolytes in the room each had ram horns implanted into their skulls. Their breath was ragged and their gaze unknowable.

The Wormwrot grunts often lamented their frustration with taking orders from a skinny—and very likely insane—old man. They wondered why Vergun didn't just kill him, and take the armada of skyships for themselves. Truth was, it had been considered and even tried by a few ambitious captains, early in the war. They'd been torn to shreds for their trouble. So, Castor always told his men the same thing when they seemed to be getting ambitious, too.

Soon as you come up with a way to cut through four of his acolytes, you're welcome to take the whole empire for yourself. Till then, shut up and do your job.

Castor followed Vergun into the room. The air smelled like burning hair and melting rubber.

"Ah, our illustrious Wormwrot officers have finally arrived," said Osyrus Ward from his place at a large rectangular table, which was littered with bloody tools and dragon bones. "You're the last ones."

The rest of his council was a strange mixture of people. There were Ward's engineers—ten soft-palmed men with soot-coated cheeks who wore the same kind of white dragonskin jacket as Ward. Osyrus seemed to have collected that lot from the kilns, factories, and workshops of Balaria, then charmed them into service with the wonders of his inventions. They were murmuring to themselves and going over a complicated set of charts, pointing to various areas with clear frustration.

On the far side of the table was Decimar, who commanded the Balarian longbowmen. Castor hadn't thought much of his unit at first, probably because they almost never actually dropped into the jungle with Wormwrot, but instead enjoyed the luxury of remaining in the skyships all day and sleeping in their own bunks each night. But his opinion of them changed when he saw Decimar and his men in action. They'd been salting rice paddies from the air, and were lucky enough to catch three scores of Jaguars in the open. Decimar and his archers had sent them all down the river with three volleys.

None of them had missed. Not even once.

Then there was Garret the Hangman—the gray-eyed assassin Osyrus Ward kept in private employ—who was standing to the side with his arms crossed. Castor was unclear on why Garret attended these meetings, seeing as he never said anything in them, but so long as the Hangman stayed out of his way, he didn't really care.

And, lastly, there was the Papyrian widow. Vera.

She was lounging in a windowsill, apart from the rest, which Castor imagined the others were grateful for. Everyone was afraid of Vera because she and that gray-eyed Balarian had been crisscrossing the realm of Terra, intimidating and torturing and killing any lord or governor or general who seemed to have even the kernel of an idea about bucking Ward's authority. Every man in that room knew that if their minds sprouted similar ideas, it would be Vera's face and Vera's blade that came for them in the night.

"We'll begin," said Osyrus. He picked up a preserved dragon bone that was fit with a kind of ratchet gear, which he twisted a few times, as if he'd forgotten what purpose it served and was trying to remember. Placed it back amongst the pile. "Commander Vergun, how is our little jungle war going?"

Vergun sucked a pink scrap of gristle from between his teeth and spat it away.

"We ran ten drops last month. The eight patrols with an acolyte attached didn't encounter the enemy at all, other than those fucking mud totems they leave everywhere. One patrol wandered into a dragon nest like morons and got themselves eaten. My drop didn't have an acolyte attached, so we naturally saw contact."

"Combat report."

"They waited until we were halfway done crossing a river, then attacked from both sides. I annihilated the war bands that attacked my side, then crossed to assist the others. We prevented the unit from being destroyed, but they still suffered heavy losses. Two score dead. Twice wounded."

"Losses to the enemy?"

"They carried away their dead. Pretty sure they know about the bounties Wormwrot collects for masks."

"Give me your best guess."

Vergun muttered a curse under his breath. Gave Castor a look, silently asking him to take over.

Castor shrugged. "I'd say about a score."

"A score," Ward repeated.

"Give or take."

Ward returned his attention to Vergun.

"You lost twice as many men as our enemy. How did you muck that up so badly? No, forget some ambush by the river. Let's back up. How is it that despite the fact that I have allocated immeasurable resources to your war effort—resources that quite literally did not exist until I built them—along with a domineering advantage of troop numbers, equipment, and rations, all you've managed to accomplish in the last six months is a protracted stalemate?"

Vergun stood up. "Fuck your supply lines, Ward. You're not a soldier. You're not a tactician. You're just an old man in a tower with a bunch of metal toys."

"But *you* are a soldier. *You* are a tactician. Explain to me why you're failing to win this war. The Jaguars are hamstringing our ability to extract vital resources from the jungle, and it is putting my work behind schedule."

Vallen seethed. Castor realized that if he didn't answer, nobody would.

He cleared his throat.

"We're doing everything that needs doing to root a native force from their homeland, but the Jaguars are doing everything they can to stop us," Castor began. "The skyships help us dump men deep into the jungle, but once we're down there in the gloom and the mud, that advantage is gone. And if I'm being honest, the Dainwood wardens are the best warriors in Terra. Especially when the fighting's in their own jungle."

"Elaborate," said Osyrus.

"A hundred wardens can camouflage themselves a stride back from some muddy tract, and Wormwrot will march right past them being none the wiser. When they do strike, they do it fast and almost always at our most vulnerable-but-important point. Then they disappear before we can counterattack. Far as we can tell, they have no central command. No rigid battle structures. Each band of wardens sets out on their own and adapts to the situation as they see fit. And they are *always* adapting. They never fight the same way twice. Conquering the villages along the northern rim of the Dainwood was easy enough at the start of this war, but the men we left behind to hold the villages were slaughtered. Any ground we gain is impermanent. These days, we can't seem to find any villages at all. It's like the people just . . . disappeared. Some of my men think they built new villages in the trees, but there's no evidence of that."

Castor paused. Seemed to realize that he'd rambled off course.

"Anyway, that's what's giving us trouble from a, uh, tactical perspective."

"I am not hearing much about how my acolytes are being used to forge a tactical advantage from *your* perspective, Castor."

Castor put up his hands. "The acolytes are an undeniable asset. Whatever you did a few months back to stop their spines from getting ripped out has certainly stuck. But the Jaguars have learned to avoid 'em, mostly. And there are still occasional losses, like Lieutenant Droll's unit." He paused, not sure if he should proceed. "There's rumors amongst the men that the Jaguars have a sorceress in their midst. Some say it's Ashlyn Malgrave."

"Ashlyn Malgrave is dead," said Osyrus. "And sorcery does not exist."

"Then what's killing the acolytes?"

"According to Private Rigar, the lone survivor of Lieutenant Droll's unit, it was Silas Bershad and a rather vulgar Skojit man wearing an old prototype of mine."

"Oh," Castor said, surprised. "I thought Silas Bershad was dead, too."

"Not yet. But I would like to rectify that issue. Double the bounties on Jaguar wardens in general. Let's also put a special bounty on Silas Bershad and his Skojit friend. Ten thousand gold per head."

"Might help," Castor said.

"It better. You cannot fathom the rarity of the materials that go into my acolytes. I want their destruction completely *stopped*."

"Why not just firebomb the whole jungle, then?" Castor asked without thinking.

Ward's stare made him regret the comment immediately.

"Well, that's a good question, Castor," Ward said in a tone that made it sound like the exact opposite. "The reason we don't fire-bomb the Dainwood is because that jungle contains the highest density of the rarest resources in this realm. Conquering the jungle has no value if those resources are destroyed in the process."

"What are you doing with those resources?" Vera asked from the window.

They were the first words she'd spoken during the meeting—each rough Balarian word pronounced in that smooth Papyrian accent of hers. Despite Vera's cold and threatening exterior, Castor found himself oddly soothed by her words.

"Pardon me?" Osyrus asked.

"We're fighting this war to preserve and extract those resources, which you are hoarding in the King's Tower. What are you doing up there?"

Osyrus smiled. "The same thing that I am always doing. Trying to forge a better world."

Vera stared at him, clearly unsatisfied with that answer. But she knew as well as everyone else that there was no way to compel extra information from Ward so long as he had his acolytes in the room.

And they were always in the room.

"Perhaps you would be willing to update everyone else on what *you* have been doing on the far side of the Soul Sea?" Ward continued. "You were gone for a long time."

She sighed, then spoke again in that silky, beautiful voice. "The Lysterian governor of Kushal-kin was indeed fomenting rebellion, so I killed him and his three coconspirators. There were also some Lysterian natives in the southern reaches who had overwhelmed the local garrison. I defeated their war chieftain in single combat and they have sworn loyalty to Kira's empire anew. Five ministers in Burz-al-dun were skimming profits from their kilns, but a nocturnal visit set each of them straight." She paused. "And lastly, the count of Argel has seen the error of his dawdling ways. He arrived this morning on the first carrack from Ghalamar with fresh troops. More are on the way."

Castor had never heard Vera speak so many words at once. It made his head go fuzzy.

"You see, Vergun, *this* is the type of successful mission report I would like to hear from Wormwrot," said Osyrus.

"Murdering some milk-drinking savages and intimidating corrupt government pawns is not difficult," Vergun said, then slid his eyes over to Vera. "Come into the jungle with me, and we'll see how fearsome you truly are, widow."

Vera returned his gaze, but didn't say anything.

Osyrus turned to Decimar next. "Lieutenant."

The longbowman straightened his posture, ever the good soldier.

"While I was in Ghalamar, my longbowmen split their forces across three ships and had success on their strafing runs of the southern coast. They caught five frigates moving along the coast from Dunfar to Almira on an old pirate route."

"Eradicated?"

Decimar licked his lips. "Nearly. We lost one ship to the fog."

"That's disappointing."

"I agree," said Decimar. "But this is one more supply line of theirs that we've severed. Between that and all the farms that we've already destroyed and salted, we must be getting close to exhausting their ability to feed their army."

"How close?" Garret asked.

That was the first time Garret had ever asked a question in a council meeting. Castor thought the Jaguars' food supply was an odd thing to grab his interest.

"Uh, well, I don't know exactly," Decimar said, sounding equally surprised to get a question from the Hangman. "But we know food's scarce because the people are willing to risk foraging the open fields, even though they know we patrol them."

Garret nodded, but said nothing more.

"What I don't understand is how the bastards are so adept at seafaring smuggling," one of the engineers said. "They're a bunch of jungle savages."

"There are rumors that they're aided by the pirates of Ghost Moth Island," said Decimar.

"Ghost Moth Island is a myth," said another.

"No, it's not. I used to know an old drunken sailor in Burz-al-dun who—"

"Enough," Ward interrupted. "Lieutenant, please send two of your ships to Dunfar."

"Dunfar. Why?"

"They were aiding the Jaguars, and must be penalized. Have your men annihilate, oh, three villages."

"But we don't know which villages were giving them food."

"That isn't the point. Pick three, and eliminate the entire populace. No survivors. That will dissuade the other villages from reopening any supply lines in the future."

Decimar swallowed. "By your orders."

"Good. When that's done, I need you to resume patrols along the northern rim of the Dainwood. There have been attacks upon the rubber farms that are inhibiting production."

Decimar scratched his ear. "We can patrol them, no problem. But what's so important about those damn trees?"

From the outset of the war, Osyrus had been running teams of laborers into the rubber plantations of the Dainwood. They'd been harried and ambushed from the outset, too, and there was good reason to believe that more than a few enemy agents had slipped across the Gorgon due to the open supply line. No security system was perfect, even the seals.

"Huh?" Ward asked. He'd become distracted by the dragon bones on his desk again. "Oh, I need the rubber to make gaskets."

"Gaskets?" Decimar repeated when Osyrus didn't elaborate. "And that's why we're going through so much trouble to conquer the Dainwood? For gaskets?"

"Among other things." Osyrus turned to his engineers. "And now to my illustrious team of engineers. What good news do you have for me?"

A Balarian named Nebbin—the de facto leader of Ward's engineer cronies—stepped forward to speak. He had close-cropped, snow-white hair and eyes the color of sparrow eggs. He was the definition of soft-palmed, but he was also a ruthless bastard in his own way.

All of Ward's engineers were eager to push Ward's insane projects forward to the best of their ability. They brought him new formulas scrawled on scraps of paper. Worked furiously through the night to repair his machines when they broke down. They also cheated and lied—scrambling to take credit for new discoveries and pointing out the mistakes of others. The reason Nebbin had risen to the top of their fucked-up pecking order was because he was simply better at the betrayals than everyone else. Castor was fairly certain he sabotaged his colleagues' work, and Castor knew for a fact that he had hired two Wormwrot men on side contracts to murder his rivals.

Osyrus either did not know about Nebbin's behavior, or did not care.

"Two more warrens have been successfully harvested," Nebbin

said in that nasally voice of his. "Both middle-grade samples, which have been moved to the upper levels for processing."

Ward's face made it clear he wasn't thrilled with that result.

"I know that progress is slower than we'd hoped," Nebbin said carefully. "Perhaps we might try another attempt at harvesting from the Heart of the Soul Sea? Those islands are so riddled with warrens, a single skyship could bring back enough specimens to put us back on schedule."

"No. We've already lost too many skyships to the dragons in that area," Ward said, brushing the idea off. "Speaking of which, give me an update on that latest crash. The *Eternity*."

Nebbin nodded. "We've had ships patrolling the borders of sector thirteen for two weeks now, waiting for an opportunity to salvage the cargo. But they have yet to see an opening in the Blackjack horde."

"Yet the crash site itself remains unharmed?" Ward asked.

"Yes. Our theory is that the Kor was damaged during the crash, and may be emitting some kind of noise or signal that is deterring the lizards."

"That *is* possible. And interesting."

There was a long silence while Ward appeared to be internally exploring the interesting nature of this fact in more depth.

Nebbin cleared his throat. "Shall we continue the patrols, Master Ward?"

"No, we've wasted enough fuel on that errand," said Ward. "At this point, we can declare the *Eternity* unsalvageable and move on. Divert rations from the colonies to feed the soldiers."

"The shipment was our largest to date. The loss of that cargo will put a considerable strain on satellite colony supplies, where unrest remains a problem, even with the acolytes stationed in each city and the, uh . . ." Nebbin glanced at Vera. "Other efforts we've made toward control."

Osyrus thought about it. "No half measures, then. Select four cities and cut off their entire food supply. Preferably ones that have already been deprived of resources for an extended period of time. They will be too weak to revolt as they starve to death. The slums of Burz-al-dun are an obvious choice. Figure out the other three. Now, please."

"Yes, Master Ward." Nebbin turned to the engineers, who quickly huddled together and started rattling off the cities that they were planning to starve out. They seemed to approach the task as if it was a mathematical puzzle rather than a genocidal order.

Vergun's attention wandered back to another piece of meat stuck in his teeth. Osyrus picked up another one of his tools and started messing around with it. But Castor remained on edge. Something had changed in the room.

Staying sensitive to subtle change was one of the first things they teach you as a Horellian. You can be the best there is with a blade or your hands or a bow or any weapon, really, but you couldn't protect anyone for shit if you got surprised. And little changes were the precursor to a surprise. A man in a crowd who'd been standing still for an hour, but starts to move. A gentle draft in a room with closed windows. A doorknob slowly opening. Like that. Once you got used to looking for them, it was the fact something was different that registered before the difference itself. It took Castor a few moments to hone in on what had his hackles up, but he got there.

Vera's posture had changed. Stiffened, just a little. And her eyes were flicking back and forth between Osyrus Ward and the engineers with a calculated kind of wrath. For a moment, Castor wondered if she was about to attack Osyrus. He wondered if he should intervene.

Before he'd arrived at a firm decision, Vera straightened up and slowly put both of her boots on the floor.

"You're going to starve thousands of people to death, just like that?"

"Better to amputate a finger than let the entire hand go to rot." Osyrus motioned to her gloved hand that was missing its little finger. "You of all people should know that."

There were a lot of stories about how that had happened. Some said a drunken Wormwrot bit it off in a tavern brawl, which she repaid by pulling his stomach lining out of his mouth. Others said she bit it off herself to intimidate some local governor.

Castor didn't believe either story.

"Losing a finger is only better when there's no other option," Vera said.

"There isn't. The *Eternity* is unreachable, and we cannot risk more of these troublesome rebellions before the war with the Dainwood is resolved. The acolytes are stretched far too thin as it is."

Osyrus went back to his dragon bones. The engineers continued to murmur.

Vera moved to Decimar and whispered something in his ear. The longbowman leaned back from her, shaking his head. Apparently, he didn't like what she had to say. But they went back and forth with whispers a few more times, and eventually Decimar gave a defeated nod. Vera stepped back from the table.

"Stop looking at those maps," she ordered the engineers. "Right now."

Even though Osyrus commanded the engineers, not Vera, all of them went silent.

"A problem, Vera?" Osyrus asked.

"There is no need to starve these cities. I will salvage the *Eternity*."

Osyrus scoffed. "And how do you propose to accomplish such an ambitious task?"

"Decimar and I will take the *Blue Sparrow* to the crash site."

Osyrus raised his eyebrows. "Is that so?"

"Yes. We'll expand her exterior cargo capacity with nets. We'll bring as much of the food as possible for the army, but we'll resupply the slums of Burz-al-dun first."

"Why are you so fixated on the slums?" Nebbin asked.

Vera glared at him, which made the engineer's face appear very much like a stick of butter that was about to melt.

"We are all working to preserve *Kira's* empire, are we not? To rule the realm of Terra as she would have done?"

"Of course."

"Kira would never allow her people to starve just so you can reduce the risk of *troublesome* rebellions." She paused. "But I also understand the realities of war. So I will take this burden upon myself." She paused. Seemed momentarily filled with emotion. "I can't help Kira by moping at her side and waiting for her to heal. But I can honor the path she would have wanted me to take, no matter how dangerous it might be."

It seemed to Castor that Vera the widow—famous for her cold composure and pragmatism—had finally been broken by her feelings for the empress. It was possible for her to succeed on this mission, but it was far, far more likely she and her ship would be destroyed by Blackjacks before she got anywhere close to the *Eternity*.

"I cannot spare any acolytes for such a mission," Osyrus warned, apparently coming to the same conclusion as Castor. Can't waste such a precious resource on a fool's errand.

"I don't need them," said Vera. "I just need the *Sparrow* and Decimar's crew."

Osyrus gave a helpless gesture. "Fine. Request granted. I will have the ship refitted and fueled."

"Good."

Vera stalked out of the room at speed, with Decimar following quickly behind. The doors closed behind them, and there was a long silence.

"Well, it seems we might finally be rid of that Papyrian cunt," Nebbin said eventually.

The engineers all laughed at that. So did Commander Vergun.

Castor wasn't so sure. Just didn't seem right, the widow making such a stupid decision. And he noticed that neither Garret nor Osyrus Ward were laughing, either. Ward leaned forward in his chair.

"Castor, would you be so kind as to locate our newly arrived count from Ghalamar and bring him up here?"

"Garwin?"

"Yes. I have the perfect task to get him started."

Garwin's face turned increasingly deep shades of red while Osyrus Ward explained his assignment.

"You better be fucking joking," he hissed.

"I am not."

Garwin's hand was gripped tight around his sword, but the war acolyte standing half a stride behind Ward was clearly enough motivation for him to keep it there. "We'll be chewed apart by Blackjacks."

"Possibly. But in the event that you are not, I would like someone aboard the *Blue Sparrow* to provide stringent supervision over Vera the widow."

"You send her to threaten me in the night, now I'm going to police her on a fucking suicide mission?"

"That is correct."

Garwin's face twitched with rage. "What was the point of even cajoling me and my men across the Soul Sea if you were just going to send us to our deaths? I'd have rather died in my own fucking bed."

Osyrus pursed his lips. "You raise a valid concern."

He began twisting his beard into a greasy knot, lost in thought once again.

"So, we don't have to go?" Garwin asked.

"Oh, no you most definitely do. If you refuse, or fail to follow my orders exactly, I will kill you, all of your men, and every last citizen of Argel. But it occurs to me that there is an opportunity for experimentation here. If that crashed ship is repelling dragons by pure chance, there must be a way to reliably re-create the effect."

"Some kind of resonance generator, perhaps?" Nebbin asked.

"Exactly."

"What the fuck are you two talking about?" Garwin asked.

"No time to explain." Osyrus stood. "I will manufacture a prototype with haste. My acolytes will install it onto the *Sparrow* before your departure."

Osyrus disappeared up a stairwell in the back of the room that led to the upper workshops. Everyone else began to disperse, too. Before Castor could do the same, Garwin stopped him with an arm on his wrist.

"You're Horellian, aren't you?"

"Used to be."

Garwin grunted. "This the way shit typically goes under Ward?"

"Pretty much."

"Fuck." Garwin shook his head. "I'm only here 'cause I'd be dead if I wasn't. Why're you?"

Castor shrugged. "'Cause they pay me."

"Gold the only thing you care about?"

At the start of this, Castor had cared about watching the Balarian Empire burn. He'd helped the clock-toting bastards tear apart enough nations, he figured he owed it to the world to put them on the receiving end for once. Problem was, now that the line of Domitian emperors was broken and Actus Thorn was dead, the thing that had risen under Osyrus Ward wasn't any better. Any sane man could see that it was worse.

So, Castor had decided to stop caring. He'd do his work, collect his coin, and once he had enough of it, he'd buy a little island for himself and never work another day in his life.

But he wasn't going to waste breath telling any of that to Garwin. Poor bastard was a dead man.

So Castor just smiled. Slapped him on the shoulder.

"Good luck on your journey, *Count*."

10

VERA
Castle Malgrave, Level 40

"Vera, please reconsider this," Decimar said, following her down the winding stairwell of the King's Tower. "If we go into that sector of the jungle, we're all gonna get turned to dragon shit."

"Relax, Decimar. We're not taking the *Sparrow* to the Dainwood. And we're definitely not going to sector thirteen."

"Oh. Uh, where are we going then?"

"Pargos."

"Again? Why?"

Vera gave him a look. "Just get your men ready. I know what I'm doing."

"Right. On it." They reached a landing and stopped. "Where are you going to be?"

"I need to get ready."

"Any chance a bath is included in your preparations?" Decimar said. "Because, meaning no offense, you're getting kinda ripe again."

"No time," Vera said, already heading toward the next stairwell down.

"It really doesn't take that long!" Decimar called after her.

She ignored him.

First, Vera went down to the castle armory, where she refilled the pouch of shot for her sling from Ward's stockpile. She didn't like admitting it, but the machines he used to produce the shots created perfect orbs that flew far straighter and farther than anything she could carve by hand.

She also used a spare sharpening stone to freshen both of her daggers and Bershad's old sword. None of the blades really needed the work, but Vera didn't feel right leaving Floodhaven without going through the routine.

When that was done, she went to the kitchens, where she found a dozen fresh loaves of bread cooling by the window, and some kind of meat stew bubbling over a stove. She tore one of the loaves apart and started dipping the wedges into the stew, eating directly over the pot as quickly as possible.

A cook walked into the room. "Hey, what do you think you're—"

He stopped talking when he saw who the kitchen intruder was.

"Uh. Sorry, mistress." He paused. Bowed his head. "Um, do you want butter or anything to go with that?"

Vera swallowed her last bite of food. "No. Just get me a canteen of fresh water and a clean cloth."

After the cook delivered those items, Vera went back to see Kira.

The giant acolyte had resumed his imposing protection of the dome, which was currently bathed in the golden light of low evening that streamed in through the tall, narrow windows. The acolyte was so large that the entire door to the dome was blocked by his torso and meaty thighs. When she approached, his attention focused, and his hands formed massive fists, ready for violence. Vera had a momentary image of how easily those hands—which were the size of cook pots—could tear her apart.

All the same, she moved farther into the room, stopping in a beam of light.

"Let me through," she said.

"Area restricted," he rasped. "Offer identity."

"Vera."

The acolyte's head cocked. He sniffed the air curiously, as if he could recognize her by scent and voice alone. Given all the things that Osyrus Ward had managed, that didn't seem impossible.

"Identity confirmed."

The acolyte moved out of the way, extending a welcoming arm toward the door like a butler or servant. Vera found the gesture both out of place and oddly disturbing. Like watching a wolf use a fork and knife.

"You may proceed, Vera Kilara-Sun."

Vera had to walk through the acolyte's enormous shadow to reach the dome. He smelled like burnt hair and moldy hay. The sound of his ragged breathing made her neck hairs tingle.

She released a low sigh of relief when she'd sealed the door again from the far side.

Kira's eyes were closed. Her breathing artificial and steady. All around her, the machines whirred and hummed as if there were a thousand beehives embedded behind the metal and glass and rubber tubes. Vera knelt by her side. For a few moments, she couldn't bring herself to do anything more than hold her hand. Eventually, she pulled the cloth she'd gotten from the kitchen from behind her breastplate, and uncorked the canteen. She dampened the cloth and carefully cleaned up Kira's face—wiping away the sleep and gunk from her eyes.

Vera knew the act was useless and selfish. But she did it anyway. And when Kira's face was clean and looking like some semblance of her old self, Vera felt guilty for feeling better.

"When I come back, I'll have a way to get you out of here, Ki. I promise."

Vera stayed with her for two hours, marking the seconds by her wrist bracer, and silently willing them to pass slower.

Then she headed to the skyship platform.

———

The *Blue Sparrow* was fully prepped. Levitation sack filled. The sides of the ship's hull were decked out with tight netting that could hold the extra food and the engines were humming in a low idle. Good. Vera wanted to be in the sky before Osyrus Ward had a chance to think more about why she'd been so eager to take on such a dangerous task.

The Madman's mind never stopped working.

Decimar saw her from the deck. Waved to her, then climbed down. But when he reached her, his face was stricken with alarm instead of the excitement she usually saw in him before a flight.

"We have a problem," he said.

"Everything seems to be in order with the *Sparrow*."

"Not with the ship. Osyrus Ward has added some passengers."

Vera turned back to the deck. Along with the bowmen she recognized, she now saw a slew of unfamiliar faces. Some of them were wearing the standard skymen uniforms and helping out with the ship.

The rest were wearing Ghalamarian armor.

"How many?" she asked.

"Two score of my best men," came a gruff and familiar voice from behind her.

Count Garwin. He was decked out in a full suit of armor, too. A lord's plume running down from the top of his helmet.

"Seems the Madman doesn't trust you to make this jaunt on your own," he said. "I've got orders to gut you like a fish if this skyship goes even a fraction of a degree off course."

Vera's stomach tightened. Apparently, she hadn't managed to get ahead of Osyrus Ward's machinations after all. But she couldn't solve that problem on the skyship platform.

"Very well, Count." She motioned to the *Sparrow*. "Welcome aboard."

Garwin tromped toward the ship, heavy footfalls echoing loud against the metal platform.

"What are we going to do now?" Decimar whispered when he was out of earshot.

"Improvise," Vera said. "But we'll do it from the air."

"Aye. We'll be . . ." Decimar trailed off. Looked over Vera's shoulder. "Perfect. This is all we need."

Vera turned around to find Garret walking toward them. The noose was on his hip and a traveler's pack was slung over one shoulder.

"Ward ordered you to go with us, too?" Vera asked when he reached them.

"I volunteered."

"Why? Dropping a skyship into a dragon-infested jungle to recover some lost food doesn't offer a lot of opportunities for clean work."

Garret glanced at the skyship, then back at her. "I disagree."

11

BERSHAD
Dainwood Jungle

Bershad, Goll, and Felgor separated from the main army to get the donkeys.

When they'd landed on the western shore of Almira last winter, Vash was one of the only warriors from Ghost Moth Island who didn't join the war. Goll had given him a lot of shit, but Bershad understood. After what they'd been through, Vash wanted to protect his son at all costs. These days, the only way to do that was to get lost in the Gloom.

Bershad picked up the familiar scent of the beasts an hour before they reached Vash and Wendell's home. The smell reminded him of Alfonso and Rowan. Made his throat ache.

The Nomad—who'd returned to him a day before they had reached Dampmire—caught the scent, too. She flew ahead. Started circling.

"Leave those donkeys alone," Bershad warned. "They're not for eating. And you're gonna scare the shit out of them if you drop any lower."

The Nomad gave an irritated yank on their connection. She was always a little twitchy after Bershad got an injection. But she leveled off.

"You know that it makes you seem pretty crazy when you talk to Smokey like that, right?" said Felgor.

"Better than letting her eat all the donkeys," Bershad muttered. "And stop calling her Smokey."

"Put forth a different option and I'll consider it."

Bershad thought of Alfonso again. And again, his throat tightened.

"She doesn't need a name."

"The key is to pick one that suits her. What does she like to eat?"

"Boar. But it gives her the shits."

"Hm. Yeah, that's no good. Anything else?"

Bershad sighed. "I gave her a tuna once, way back. She liked that."

"Tuna . . . hm." Felgor paused. "Tuna the Enormous Gray Dragon. Tuna the Terror. That's not bad."

"I'm not calling her Tuna."

"Why not?"

"Because it's stupid. And she *doesn't* need a name."

———

When they reached the farm—which was nestled into a shallow valley with good cover from the canopy—Wendell was in the pens, feeding the donkeys carrots. Vash was sitting on the porch with a sword across his lap, smoking a pipe.

Goll walked up first. Pulled his axe off his back. "Came here to rob you, I'm afraid. We'll be needing all your valuables in a right hurry, or I've got to take your head."

Vash took a pull from his pipe. Blew the smoke out of his nose. "You want it, come and get it."

The two men broke into smiles. Then came over and embraced each other—slapping each other on the back and laughing.

"It's good to see you, my friend," Vash said. "Glad the war hasn't killed you yet."

"Uncle Goll! Flawless!" Wendell shouted, dropping his pail of carrots and running toward the fence. Behind him, the donkeys swarmed the spilled treat. "You're back! Have we won the war?"

"Not quite," said Bershad. "But we have news."

Vash nodded. "Come on in. I'll get you fed while you tell me."

When Bershad had finished explaining what had happened, and why they needed the donkeys, Vash sat for a few moments smoking his pipe. Eventually, he placed it on the table and cleared his throat.

"You're all fucking crazy, you know that, right?"

Goll shrugged. "Between sneaking into Blackjack territory and crossing through the alchemist's territory back on Ghost Moth, I'd say it's a toss-up in terms of insanity."

"There was a reason to do that, though," said Vash, glancing over at Wendell.

"There's a reason to do this, too," said Bershad. "We can't fight a war without food."

"Yeah. Well, not like I owned the donkeys to begin with. Just been looking after 'em for Kerrigan. So, if you want 'em, take 'em." He paused. "Where is she, by the way?"

"Uh, she had other business to work out."

Vash nodded. "Still raw about the whole loss of her island thing, is it?"

"Yeah."

"Can I come with you?" Wendell asked. "I know all the donkeys' names, and some of them are stubborn bastards who only listen to me. I can help."

"Best way you can help is by staying here and staying safe," said Bershad. "I'll look after them, I promise."

Wendell sighed. "Fine. At least let me show you the biggest assholes before you go."

Bershad nodded. "Sure, kid. That'd be helpful. How about you point them out to Goll and Felgor?"

They left. Bershad and Vash sat in silence for a moment.

"How's the war going, truly?"

"We're losing it. And more food isn't going to change that."

"I can do more than give you the donkeys. I can fight."

Bershad shook his head. "One more sword and one more life to lose isn't going to make a difference. I want you here, raising that boy to be a proper child of the Dainwood." He swallowed. "If we don't make it, promise me that you'll stay in the Gloom as long as you can. Promise me you'll survive."

Vash nodded. "I promise, but you gotta do something for me, too."

"What's that?"

"Carve yourself a mask."

"What?"

"A warden's mask. You're leading the Jaguar Army and you don't have one. It's unseemly."

Bershad waved the notion away. "Willem's their leader more than

I am." He paused. "And some of the things that you lose need to stay lost."

"The Dainwood is your home, Silas. That's something you'll never lose."

Bershad rubbed his throat. Pushed his emotions down as best he could.

"I'll think about it, Vash. I promise."

Vash gave him a sad smile. "Good enough."

12

JOLAN
Dainwood Jungle

After weeks of being cooped up in the castle of Deepdale, Jolan enjoyed the jungle. Even days like this, where it had been raining for nine hours straight. Toucans and motmots were chirping from the canopy. Rare flowers grew from almost every Daintree. To him, it was a paradise.

Everyone was up ahead, setting up camp. But Jolan had lingered in the dense undergrowth, picking around at different clusters of edible mushrooms, which were few and far between in the Dainwood. Most were toxic. He hummed to himself as he picked. His bag was half full.

"You seem to be having a good time."

Jolan jumped. Turned around. Silas Bershad was coming out of the undergrowth. He had a handful of headless snakes in one hand, and there was blood dripping down his beard.

"I like the jungle."

Bershad nodded. "Me too."

Jolan motioned to the snakes. "Did you, uh, bite the heads off?"

"Ate 'em."

"Why would you do that? They're poisonous."

He shrugged. "The venom doesn't bother me. Leaves more meat for everyone else."

They walked past the donkeys, whose rain-wet backs were shimmering in the late-day light like a twisting river. Jolan noticed that while the donkeys all reacted to Bershad with friendly sniffs and ear wiggles, he never touched any of them.

They started passing the men, who'd made small camps tucked into different Daintree nooks. A lot of the Jaguars had managed to scrounge their own meals from the forest—insects and rodents and caches of nuts, mostly. Bershad offered a snake to anyone who'd come up empty. Jolan did the same with his mushrooms.

He also stopped to check a few wardens' wounds for infection. One warden had decided he was going to stop wearing boots like Silas, and now had torn up soles because of it. Jolan worked out a poultice and Bershad told him to put his boots back on.

Eventually, they found Ashlyn. She was huddled up in her yellow poncho, sharing a cook fire with Kerrigan, Simeon, Goll, and Felgor. There was a pot of water over the fire, but it looked like the only thing they had boiling inside of it was a bunch of dilly thistles.

"Flawless!" Goll called. "You bring us something to eat besides weeds?"

Bershad dropped his last snake in front of Goll, which was about a stride long with decent meat.

"It'll do," said Goll. Then he turned to Jolan. "What about you, alchemist? You finally gonna turn my water into something worth drinking?"

Goll frequently offered Jolan suspiciously large sums of gold if he could transmute water into Dunfarian rum.

"I told you before, I'm not that kind of alchemist. That kind of alchemist doesn't exist."

Goll narrowed his eyes. "I have seen you gray robes bring monsters up from the ground and grow enchanted mushrooms the size of trees. You are telling me this these things are possible, but conjuring me a decent drink is not?"

"That's what I'm saying."

"Hm. I think you're in league with Ashlyn to deprive me of my rum."

Goll butchered the snake, cut its meat into cubes, and dropped it into the pot. Felgor produced a sack of salt and pinched in a few good helpings, then started to stir.

"Where'd you get that?" Ashlyn asked.

"Usual place. Won it at dice."

"You know, Felgor, one of these days the wardens are going to realize you're cheating," Bershad said.

"But not today. And we're all benefiting from that fact."

Kerrigan frowned at the boiling pot of snake meat. "Back at Naga

Rock, I used to breakfast on dragon eggs and dine on choice cuts of swine that were fed nothing except the freshest Dunfarian acorns. Gods, those were the fucking days."

Simeon grunted. "Well, if you wanna mentally jerk yourself off about meals past, I'm more than happy to eat your share of the snakes, Kerri."

"No, no. I was just remembering. Nostalgia makes for good seasoning."

While the snake boiled, Ashlyn took a lodestone out of her satchel and went through a few exercises—raising and lowering it across a varied set of heights. Her bands twisted and whirred in slow circles as the orb moved.

"Okay, witch queen, I want you to explain how that arm of yours works," said Kerrigan, watching the orb bob in the air like a fisherman's float on the surface of a lake.

"Sorcery isn't a satisfactory explanation for you?" Ashlyn asked.

"No. And don't give me some vague dragonshit about the mathematics being too complex. If I can run an island economy built on piracy but operating in a hundred different legitimate exchange markets, I can handle the particulars of that floating rock."

Ashlyn gave her a look. "Very well. Do you understand the basics of lodestone attraction?"

"Sure. Some of the gray rocks from Ghost Moth stick to each other. Others do the opposite."

"Right. In their natural state, lodestones have a simple relationship. Attraction or repulsion." Ashlyn held up her arm so that Kerrigan could see the bands rotate. "But these complicate that relationship."

"How?"

"Each of these bands has scores of lodestones implanted inside of it. And each position represents a different kind of relationship to that orb. It's all attraction and repulsion, but coming from hundreds of angles and with hundreds of degrees of strength. By changing those relationships rapidly, I can make the orb move in any direction that I want."

The bands on Ashlyn's arm started turning a little faster, and the orb rose higher, then swooped down through the fire like a suicidal moth and back out again.

"And the scrap of dragon that's burned into your body powers the bands?" Kerrigan asked.

"Yes."

"Doesn't it hurt to use it?"

Ashlyn froze her bands. The lodestone dropped into her waiting palm. "You get used to the pain."

Kerrigan nodded. Went quiet.

Felgor stirred the stew a little. Tasted it. "We're good here."

Between the six of them, there was barely enough for each of them to have more than a few bites, even though Bershad didn't have any.

"You ate the snake heads again?" Ashlyn asked.

"They're filling. Probably won't be hungry for two, three days."

"Their heads are full of poison," said Ashlyn. "Which means I won't be able to come near your mouth for two or three days, either."

"Nonsense," he said. "I'll rinse everything out real good before we tent up for the night. Make sure it doesn't get between the witch queen and her pleasure."

"Ugh, stow the romance," Felgor said, scratching a nasty rash on his neck. "Just 'cause you two have yourselves for company out in this muddy wilderness doesn't mean we all wanna bear witness."

"What's the matter, Balarian?" asked Kerrigan. "You missing your city brothels?"

"Yes, Kerri. I am missing them most severely." He looked up at the canopy, where a team of monkeys was scrambling across the branches. "I'm not built for this wilderness work. Truly."

"You didn't have to come," Bershad pointed out.

Felgor gave him a long, cool look. "Silas Bershad. After all that we've been through, that is an unbelievably insensitive thing to say. My feelings are hurt."

"Uh-huh. That grieves me."

Felgor stood up and cracked his back. "Excuse me, friends. I have personal business with which I must attend. Silas, which stretch of private jungle is safe for a shit?"

Bershad pointed to the left. "Don't go more than fifty paces."

"Why not?"

"You don't want to know."

Felgor muttered something, then disappeared into the jungle.

"What's out there?" Ashlyn asked.

"Nothing dangerous. Just a toucan's nest full of chicks. Don't want Felgor's farts startling the little ones."

Simeon muttered a Skojit curse. "You know, after that scrap of ours on Ghost Moth Island, I took you for a genuine killer. I respected you for it. Hell, that's half the reason I came down here to fight this war with you—aside from the huge number of Ghalamarians available for killing. Thought it'd be a real honor and pleasure to go into battle with such a merciless bastard."

"But?" Bershad asked.

"But the more I see you acting all tenderhearted for tiny birds with massive beaks and communing with lizards like some monk, the more disappointed I am in you."

Bershad shrugged. "You dote on Cabbage an awful lot."

Simeon's face hardened. "I don't dote on Cabbage. He's a moron who needs constant supervision or else he'll get himself killed. Idiot couldn't even maintain a hold on his own ears."

"Speaking of communing with lizards, where's your gray friend?" asked Kerrigan. "Much as that dragon scares me, there's no way that I'm going into that stretch of Blackjack country without her directly overhead."

"Oh, she's around," Bershad said. "Don't worry."

"All Kerri does is worry," said Simeon.

"Fuck off, Simeon. Anyone who doesn't worry is just too stupid to think situations through to their most likely consequences."

"Oh, I'm well aware of consequences," said Simeon. "Most of the time, I just don't care about them."

Kerrigan's response to that was cut short by Felgor coming back out of the bushes, tying up his pants. He flopped down in his spot and stoked the fire a bit.

"Hey, Simeon. Something I've been wondering about. How do you take that armor off?"

"Doesn't come off," said Simeon, running a hand over the scales on his wrist. "Part of the bargain I made with Kasamir."

"Okay, but if it doesn't come off, how do you take a shit?"

Simeon looked up, saw that everyone was looking at him expectantly.

"I was always curious about it, being honest," said Kerrigan.

Simeon hesitated. Sucked on his teeth and spat in their fire.

"There's a mechanism," he muttered eventually.

"A *mechanism*?" Felgor asked. "What kind of mech—"

"It's complex and personal!" Simeon growled, standing up. "How 'bout you all just fuck off with your questions, yeah?"

Simeon stalked off. There was a silence. As usual, Felgor was the first one to break it.

"Guess he's off to clear the mechanism, yeah?"

They all laughed.

Everyone chatted by the fire for a while. Felgor told the story about picking a Balarian seal with a chicken bone, which Jolan had already heard about fifty times, but pretended that he hadn't.

He didn't feel quite like he was part of their crew—they'd all been on so many adventures together, and all Jolan had done was write lodestone orientations with Ashlyn in a pantry of Deepdale's Castle. But he liked spending time with them. It reminded Jolan of his time with Cumberland and the others on their way to Blackrock. Before everything had gone sour and poisoned.

Eventually, everyone began to turn in for the night. Felgor bundled himself up in a blanket by the fire—muttering about wrapping himself tight to keep the bugs and ants out. Bershad and Ashlyn left together with clear plans to test the limits of Silas's poisoned breath. Goll went looking for alcohol.

That just left Kerrigan and Jolan. They stared at the fire in silence for a bit.

"What passed between you and that dour warden in the black mask? Oromir, I think."

Jolan straightened up, surprised. "What did you hear?"

"Nothing. But any time the two of you are in a room together the temperature seems to drop a mite with all those icy stares and glances. I'm curious what's causing them."

"It doesn't matter."

"We're all heading into a nest of dragons tomorrow, with nobody to look out for us besides each other. So, it kind of does matter, Jolan."

He blew out a breath. "Last fall, we traveled together for a time. Things ended badly. Someone who Oromir cared for deeply was killed, and he blames me for it."

"Do you blame yourself?"

Jolan looked at his boots. "Yes."

Kerrigan nodded. "The thing about blame, in my experience, is that there's always plenty to go around and the shit is pretty much useless. Take my last supply run, where a hundred of my men died. Now, the most immediate party to blame there is the Balarian skyships that turned them to splinters. But a thinking person would take it to the next level. Blame the asshole who started the war. Problem there is that it's a bit unclear who that is. Some idiot general named Actus Thorn, maybe. But his role is murky at best, plus he's already dead so who cares? Instead, maybe let's blame the crazy asshole who built those skyships to begin with? That's not bad. No skyships, no dead men. But then there's the notion that those men never would have been on those ships if it weren't for me. And they never would have met me if I hadn't founded Naga Rock. But if I hadn't done that, the men on that ship would have been eaten by dragons a decade ago because of the asshole who wrote the laws of this realm." She leaned forward. Tapped her temple. "See what I mean?"

"You're saying nobody's to blame?"

"I'm saying *everyone's* to blame."

Jolan met her eyes. "Does that help you sleep at night?"

Kerrigan winced. "No. Not really."

"Then it doesn't do me any good."

———

Jolan didn't make a conscious decision to go see Oromir. He just kind of found himself walking to the circle of tents that Oromir and his men had set up apart from the others.

Oromir's crew decorated their tents with the bones of the Worm-wrot they'd killed. A lot of warden crews did the same, they just didn't have nearly as much material to work with. The ribs, femurs, and skulls of slain mercenaries rattled in the wind. Jolan made his way to the center of the circle, where there was a tent with five skulls hung over the entrance.

Oromir's horse was hobbled next to it, munching on some wild grass.

Jolan hesitated. He suddenly had no idea what he was going to say. Maybe he should go back. This was stupid. But before he could slip away, the tent opened and a warden came out.

It wasn't Oromir.

He was about thirty, with long black hair full of rings and a rough beard that glistened with oil in the moonlight. He was tying up his pants with thick, callused fingers.

"You tryna get yourself killed, boy?" he asked in a thick Dainwood accent.

"I, uh. Sorry. I—"

"What's the trouble, Kes?" came Oromir's voice from inside the tent.

"Some skinny kid out here," said Kes, taking a closer look at Jolan. "That healer, looks like. The one who walks in the queen's shadow like a cowed bitch."

Oromir grunted. "He's harmless. Let him through."

Kes shrugged, then shoved past Jolan.

Inside, the air smelled like ale and sweat. Oromir was sitting up on his bedroll in the corner. He was naked and cradling an earthen-ware jug in the crook of his elbow.

Outside, it started raining.

"Kes seems like a pleasant person," Jolan said.

"What do you want, Jolan?"

"I came to talk."

Oromir shrugged. "Talk, then."

Jolan studied Oromir's face. The wounds he'd taken at Fallon's Roost had been stitched together messy and erratic, leaving deeper scars than necessary.

"I wish you'd come to me for those," Jolan said, putting a finger to his own cheek. "I could have limited the scarring."

Oromir scoffed. Took a gulp from the jug. "Nobody ever died from uneven stitches."

"That's true." He swallowed. Sat down on the floor of the tent. "Willem told me that you're still hunting Garret."

"I'll be hunting him until he goes down the river, or I do."

"Do you know where he is?"

Oromir's face twitched. "Did you come down here to talk about Garret?"

"No." Jolan hesitated. "We haven't really spoken since Cumberland died. I wanted to see how you were doing."

"Oh, I'm fantastic. Living the life I've always dreamed about."

Jolan felt a sudden surge of anger rush through him.

"Fine." Jolan stood up. "You wanna drown yourself in alcohol and anger, go right ahead. Sorry I interrupted you. Try not to die tomorrow in the Blackjack nest."

Jolan turned and reached for the tent flap.

"Wait," Oromir said, then sighed. "It's raining, and you walked all the way down here. I'll give you something to drink, at least."

Oromir dug up a ceramic mug and filled it with a brutally powerful and thick alcohol.

"What did you ferment to make this?" Jolan asked, eyes watering after his first sip.

"Easier to enjoy it if you don't know."

Jolan shrugged. Took another sip.

"So, what's it like working for the witch queen?"

"We're trying to break through Ward's technology, but it's . . . most days I feel overmatched."

"Kes swears you're both consorting with demons now. Fucking them in exchange for power."

"Most days, I spend eighteen hours struggling with mathematical equations to improve our lodestone orientation models."

"Fucking a demon sounds like more fun."

Outside, there was a flash of lightning. Oromir's horse whinnied, nervous.

"It's all right, girl," he called. "Just a storm."

"What's your horse's name?" Jolan asked.

"Doesn't have one."

"Oh."

"You gonna lecture me about that? Spout some dragonshit about how I've changed since I don't name my horses anymore?"

Jolan shrugged. "Naming horses during a war like this doesn't make much sense to me either."

They both drank. Oromir refilled his cup.

"I have nightmares about the day that Cumberland died," Jolan said. "Do you?"

"I used to," Oromir whispered. Then held up the jug. "This stops them."

Jolan understood that. He'd brewed a ginger-root sleeping tonic for himself every night for weeks after Cumberland died. He'd only stopped when he began working with Ashlyn, who refused to abide the foggy head it gave him during their morning experiments.

"The thing is, every once in a while, instead of a nightmare, I dream about the other times we had," said Jolan. "Drinking rain ale in that tavern, where Willem got so drunk. Riding horses along the river. Everyone eating dinner around the fire, pretending that Sten wasn't the worst cook in Almira."

Oromir didn't say anything.

"Sometimes I dream about that night in the skyship cabin, too. Not that often, but it happens. And it . . . what I'm trying to say is that I still feel something for you. Beneath all the pain and regret." Jolan took a breath in. "I know that you blame me for what happened. I blame myself. But do you feel anything else for me? Even if it's buried? Even if it's different."

Oromir stared at him for a long time.

"It doesn't matter what I feel for you, Jolan. Because you're always going to be the idiot boy who got Cumberland killed. I can't forgive you for that. So we can share some cups of this awful drink and we can talk about old times if that'll make you feel better, but all it does is remind me of the biggest mistake I ever made and put me in a dark mood."

Jolan stumbled outside. He was crying so hard that he couldn't find
his own tent. So he just hunkered down beneath a Daintree in the
darkness and the rain, hugging himself and shaking and waiting
until morning.

13

NOLA
City of Deepdale, Cat's Eye Tavern

"How much for the last of the paku?" asked Kellar, eyeing the salted
meat with greedy eyes.

"The answer to that question is what you'd call negotiable," answered Nola as she wiped down the counter to the Cat's Eye tavern.
The previous customer had spent thirty minutes munching on a tiny
handful of cashews while he drank his rain ale, and left a bunch of
crumbs.

Kellar licked his lips. "Two silvers."

Nola scoffed. "Two silvers will buy you a handful of fish scales,
if you want those."

"Three silvers?"

"Don't insult me, Kellar."

A moon's turn ago, three silvers would have bought Kellar the
entire fish, and a free rain ale to boot. But times had changed, and
silver was worth less and less each day. The only thing of real value
was the remnants of the last Dunfarian supply shipment. The lords
had taken most of it, and the rest had been snatched up by the gangs.
Nola needed to earn enough coin today to buy a Dunfarian pig off
the black market tomorrow, and that was going to require some close
trading with what she had left.

"Three's all I got."

"Guess you're not getting my fish, then."

Kellar weighed that. "How about that Papyrian lens I won off one
o' them pirates in the spring? It's made of silver, and you can see all
over the city with it."

"Who'd want a better look at this mess of a city?"

Kellar shifted his eyes from the fish to her face. For a moment,
she thought that he might draw that little thumb-knife he kept in

his belt. If he did that, Nola was in serious trouble. But she returned his gaze with just as much malice—more, even. That was the key to these kinds of deals: Never back down. Never tuck your tail.

"Well, if we're negotiating, and my coin and wares are apparently no good here, make *me* a fucking offer."

"Don't curse around my sister," Nola warned, looking over to Grittle, who was struggling to open a half-empty jar of pickled radishes.

"The words released from your mouth aren't exactly pristine, Nola."

"All the same."

Kellar sighed. "Well? Your offer?"

Nola smiled. She didn't have any use for a Papyrian lens, but the mention of it had given her an idea.

"How's that stash of rice wine you keep in your cellar doing?"

Kellar's face flattened in a way that told Nola his stash was running low, but it wasn't fully depleted.

"Got a few bottles left, I think."

That was good, because while the tavern had a half-full cask of rain ale she could burn through at a high markup, that wasn't going to be quite enough to afford the pig she had her sights on. But there were two old Papyrian sisters who'd come to Deepdale by way of those pirate ships that had brought the Flawless Bershad back home. The two sisters usually visited the Cat's Eye in the evenings to watch the sunset.

Nola had a feeling the Papyrians would pay a heavy markup for the drink of their homeland.

"Bring me two bottles, your silver, and the Papyrian lens. Then you've got a deal."

"Thought you didn't want the lens?"

"I changed my mind."

The thing was useless for trading now—all that anyone wanted was food or drink—but times had to change eventually. That's what she hoped, anyway.

"Fine. Fine. Give me the fish now, and I'll bring the bottles around when I—"

"What, you make a mud totem that would turn me into a moron or something? If so, you did a crap job. You get your fish *after* I get my payment."

Kellar grumbled something, but he slid off his stool and headed for the door all the same.

"And none of the swill!" Nola called. "I got sweet, sweet fish, so you best bring me the good shit!"

After he was gone, Grittle looked up from the jar.

"What word is worse: *fuck* or *shit*?"

"Huh?"

"Kellar said *fuck*. Well, *fucking*. But you said *shit*. Whose was worse?"

Nola weighed that. Couldn't think of a good answer.

"Here. Let me help you with that jar."

————

Nola watched Suko and Kiko—the two Papyrian sisters—drink their rice wine. She smiled. They'd paid a *very* high markup for their bottle. The swine was nearly within her reach. All she needed was a decent night from the regulars, then she'd be kept in bacon for weeks.

Nola's eyes lingered on the two sisters, who laughed as they drank together. She wondered if she and Grittle would live long enough to do that under some other sunset, seventy years from now.

With this war on—and a sky filled with dragons and skyships—that seemed about as likely as her turning a profit on the Papyrian lens she'd coerced from Kellar.

Nola was jostled from that dark thought by the sight of Trotsky and Pern, who were walking down the hill right on time. They were two of her regulars. Retired wardens, both of them. Trotsky made the journey on a pronounced limp he'd earned during the Balarian invasion. Pern didn't carry a limp, but he had the distant look in his eyes that Nola had come to recognize in men who'd spent time fighting Balarians. She saw it in Pern, and she'd seen it in her eldest brother, too. But she also saw it in the younger Jaguars who came back to Deepdale after fighting Wormwrot and the gray-skinned monsters. She hated that look.

"My two favorite customers!" Nola said happily as they came through the door. "I assume you'll be starting with rain ales?"

"Correct!" Trotsky said. "And if you water 'em down again, I will cut your ears off."

"Grittle does the pours," said Nola. "You gonna cut a little girl's ears off?"

"I don't discriminate punishment based on the age of the culprit who's screwing with my beers."

"I take offense to that," Grittle said as she got their drinks. "You know that I'd sooner choke on a seashell than water down the drinks of war heroes."

"You're trying to escape justice with flattery," Trotsky responded, then turned to Nola. "You teach her that?"

"Me? I would never instruct my only sister to resort to such vile means of manipulation as flattering two of the most fearsome and brave wardens the Dainwood has ever known."

In fact, Nola had taught Grittle that exact thing. And while Nola prattled on about some story Trotsky had told her half a hundred times, Grittle watered down both of their beers. Although she didn't dilute them as much as the other customers that day. Grittle had a soft spot for Trotsky and Pern.

So did Nola, if she was being honest with herself.

"Thank you, darling," Trotsky said when Grittle came around with their drinks. "What're our options in terms of grub?"

"Limited. I sold the last of the paku a few hours ago, but Sebita caught some crickets that I've been roasting. Two per person, max. Interested?"

"Hm. Any limes to go with the chirpers?"

"Limes. That's funny. I haven't so much as dreamt of citrus since spring."

"Fine, fine," said Trotsky, pushing his coins across the table. "I'll take two."

"Pern?"

"No, thanks. Chirpers hurt my gums."

"You have to eat something," said Trotsky.

"You aren't my mother," said Pern, taking a sip of his beer. "And rain ale counts as dinner."

Nola had used a mug of rain ale as dinner more than a few times since the war started, but looking at Pern's skinny arms and gaunt face made her heart hurt. "How about I boil yours down so they're a little softer?"

Pern sighed. "Yeah. Sure."

Nola nodded. Headed into the kitchen to work up their orders. As she prepped the bugs, she made the mistake of starting to daydream on the pig she'd buy tomorrow, which got her stomach rumbling and—against her better judgment—she cooked up a third chirper, telling herself that it was because Grittle would be hungry, and knowing that was half a lie. Or half a truth, if she wanted to cut things in a generous direction for herself.

When she came back into the main room, Trotsky and Pern were still the only customers. Damn.

"Come on over, Grittle," Nola said, sitting down with them. "I made one for us to share."

Tiny meals lasted longer if you shared them with good company.

"Grittle, I heard you exchanged words with Lord Bershad when he came through," said Trotsky. "That true?"

She nodded gravely. "He helped me with the paku. It was exactly where he said it would be!"

"That's because the gray dragon told him. They speak a secret, magical language to each other."

"I asked him about that," said Grittle. "He said it wasn't true."

"Well, he obviously can't discuss his magic with a little girl. But how else would he have known?"

"The fact that he grew up in Deepdale might have been a factor," said Pern.

"I grew up here, too!" said Trotsky. "I didn't know where the fish was."

"Maybe the Flawless Bershad is a better fisherman than you," said Nola.

"Bah! Dragonshit. He's using magical powers."

Nola cut the third cricket in half with a dull butter knife and gave Grittle the bigger half. All of them munched on their bugs for a little while.

"Did I ever tell you about the time that I saw him kill a Blackjack?" Trotsky asked after he'd swallowed a bite.

"About three hundred times, yeah."

"It was seven years ago," Trotsky continued, ignoring her. "And I was making a trip through the Gorgon Valley to trade some limes, back before the Balarians incinerated them all like assholes."

Nola listened to Trotsky's story patiently. He usually bought a second and third rain ale on nights when he got to telling stories, and a captive audience was the key to getting him all wound up. Grittle did a good job of asking questions she already knew the answer to, which helped extend his story by half. She knew that telling stories made Trotsky thirsty, too.

By the time he was done, half a score of patrons had wandered in. The shady-side cobbler, Jakell, and his wife Vindy. Dervis, a younger warden who'd lost his arm in the war and just recently healed enough to leave the castle surgery. All the Jaguars got a portion of silver for losing a limb, and Dervis seemed intent on drinking his away. Nola always made sure he got some food in him, too.

There were others that Nola knew well enough to bullshit with, but couldn't place all their names. That was a good thing, though. She couldn't survive off her regulars alone.

Grittle tended to their drink orders and Nola handled the roasted crickets. She also made promises there'd be pork coming tomorrow. She even managed to squeeze a few advance payments off two patrons in exchange for choice cuts.

She cruised by the Papyrian sisters, who'd come inside now that the sun had set and joined Jakell and Vindy at their table.

"I have one more bottle of rice wine if you're interested?" she asked.

"Oh, my," said Kiko in a thick accent. "This one was so good, perhaps we should save the next for tomorrow. What do you think, Suko?"

Shit. You better not save my swine money for tomorrow.

"It was good. Reminded me of home."

Suko smiled. Paused. Before she could answer, Grittle came over.

"Trotsky says it's dangerous to put treats off until tomorrow at his age," she said. "Since there's always a chance he might die in his sleep."

"Grittle!" Nola said. "That's very rude."

But the Papyrians were both laughing.

"No, no, she's right!" said Kiko, still laughing. "These days, it's always a risk. We'll take it. And bring enough cups for our friends."

Nola gave Grittle a little nod of approval. They'd practiced situations like that, where Grittle could get away with saying inappropriate things because she was still little.

Nola went to fetch the last bottle of rice wine, along with an extra set of cups. By the time she came back, Jakell had finished his crickets and was using one of their legs to pick at something stuck between his brown teeth.

"So, Jakell, were you able to finally convince Lord Silas to purchase a pair of shoes from you?" she asked.

"No, he turned me down once again." He eyed Nola. "You enamored with him like all the other women in this town?"

Nola shrugged. "He's not really my type."

Jakell snorted, then smiled, showing off his horrific teeth even more. "Hear that, Vindy? Not really her type."

"I heard," his wife said lightly. She was still munching on the last of her cricket. "And I respectfully disagree."

"My wife here would run away with Lord Bershad in a heartbeat, given the chance."

"His cock is a foot long."

"That's just a story," said Jakell, waving a hand at the notion.

"No, no. Becki Stark used to run a tavern in some Atlas Coast town, and she screwed him *twice*. Once on his way to Vermonth and again on his way back. She confirmed it. A foot long."

"Becki is known for exaggerations."

Grittle frowned. "What's so special about a big cock, anyway?"

All of the women looked at each other. Then broke into laughter. Vindy patted her on the head. "You're a little young for that, my dear."

Nola was old enough to understand what they were talking about in theory, but didn't have any practical experience with the issue. If she was honest, the prospect of letting a cock of any size inside of her wasn't very appealing.

"I never liked the really big ones myself," said Suko. "Turns their owners into lazy lovers."

"The Flawless Bershad does not strike me as a lazy lover," said Vindy, voice wistful.

"Definitely not," said Kiko. "Queen Ashlyn might only be half-Papyrian, but we islanders are famous for molding men into generous lovers. I bet Bershad knows *exactly* how to use his giant cock."

"Can we please stop talking about Silas Bershad's cock?" Jakell asked. "Grittle is too young, and it's upsetting my digestion."

"You're the one who brought him up!"

"No, that was Nola!"

Nola put her hands up in mock surrender. "I asked about shoes. I didn't realize we were going to wind up talking about his cock, either."

"Well, what do you want to talk about instead?" Vindy asked. "This terrible war? The latest man we know to be eaten by a dragon?"

"Lemmy, right?" Nola asked.

"Yeah. Nicked by a Blackjack three days ago."

Everyone went quiet a moment. Lemmy had been a good customer. He never paid with coin—even before the war started—but always had fruit available to trade that he picked from Daintrees. It was a risky way to scrounge food, seeing as you shared those Daintrees with the dragons. And Lemmy's luck had finally run out.

"Well, we can always talk more about making shoes," Jakell said. "I've been trying a new way to cut the soles that works just as well and uses a fraction less material, which is important in these times."

Nola left the women to suffer through another one of Jakell's shoe monologues, which were far less interesting than Bershad's cock.

Three hours later, Dervis—their last customer—stumbled out the door, looking very much like he was going to vomit up his belly of rain ale in some alley on the way home.

Nola locked up, then lit her last dragon-fat candle and started to count the night's proceeds while Grittle cleaned up. Her sister knew the weight of tonight's balance, too. Nola could tell that she was nervous because she wiped the countertop down three times.

When the tally was done, Nola closed her ledger and breathed out a heavy sigh of relief.

"Did we make it?" Grittle asked, her voice so earnest and hopeful it made Nola feel like she might cry.

"Yeah, Grittle. We made it."

Between the rain ale, the crickets, and that little boon with the rice wine, she had enough for the pig. Just barely enough.

Grittle smiled. "I knew we would! Everything's going to be okay now, right?"

"Yes. Everything's going to be okay."

Just like Nola's knowledge of an ideal cock size, that was a theoretical assurance, not a certain one. Because now that she had the coin, she'd need to take it down to the pens and use it to buy the pig from the Ghost Cat Gang. They were the only ones left selling swine to lowborn.

"Can I come with you tomorrow?" Grittle asked.

"Definitely not."

"Why?"

The truth was that the Ghost Cats were just as likely to stab her as sell her one of their swine, but she wasn't going to tell Grittle that.

"Because I need you to watch the tavern while I'm gone, little sister."

Grittle frowned, but eventually nodded, her face determined. "You can count on me."

And again, Nola felt like she was going to cry.

14

BERSHAD
Dainwood Jungle

The Blackjacks' territory smelled like dead monkeys and dragonshit.

He and Ashlyn had climbed a ridge to get a look at the terrain. The Nomad circled overhead, giving Bershad a clear sense of the valleys ahead.

There were thousands of Blackjacks stretched across the treetops, resting lazily amongst the strong Daintree branches. About thirty leagues ahead, Bershad could feel a buzzing noise. When the Nomad got near it, the sound got far worse and she darted away. Bershad checked his ear, half expecting to come back with blood.

"I think the skyship's out there," he said to Ashlyn, pointing to the source of the sound.

"Good," Ashlyn said.

"Speak for yourself, you can't hear the noise it's making," Bershad said, wincing. "But at least it'll be easy to find."

He and Ashlyn made their way down the ridge, where everyone was waiting. Jolan, Kerrigan, Simeon, Felgor, Cabbage, and Oromir's crew. The donkeys were grouped behind them.

"We ready?" Bershad asked.

Everyone nodded. Even Cabbage.

Bershad reached out to the Nomad and called her down. "Let's get on with it, then."

———

The Nomad led the way through the jungle, swooping ahead of them and scaring off the Blackjacks with a series of snarls and screams and cries. Given her size, none of the Blackjacks seemed eager to make a pass at her.

Bershad stayed twenty paces in front of the first donkey, keeping his attention rooted on his connection to the Nomad. They passed steaming, chin-high piles of dragonshit that were full of monkey bones and mango cores.

"That is a powerful odor," Felgor said as they passed an especially watery and putrid pile. He walked by with a hand over his nose, but as soon as he took it away he vomited in the bushes.

"When are you gonna get yourself a stronger stomach?" Bershad asked him.

"Well, I can't grow new ones like you, so I'm stuck with what I got."

Bershad grunted. "Just try not to do it again. It upsets the donkeys."

"Pretty sure the trek through a dragon-infested wilderness is the primary cause of their agitation."

Around midday, they reached a section of the forest that was carpeted by uneaten monkey carcasses.

"This seems a little unnatural, doesn't it?" Cabbage asked. "They didn't even eat these ones. Just killed 'em for no reason."

"It can happen when a group of males join together and take control of a territory," said Ashlyn. "Each predator fuels the aggression of the other, and their behavior becomes erratic and violent."

"In my experience, most erratic and violent situations are caused by a group of swinging dicks getting stuck in close proximity to each other," said Kerrigan as she stepped around a half-rotten monkey.

"Women cause trouble, too," said Simeon.

"Oh? Name a time that a woman's sown swaths of death and destruction across some battlefield over some idiot dispute."

Simeon laughed. Waved at Ashlyn. "You're forgetting who you're walking next to, Kerri."

Kerrigan made a face. "Some Almiran warlord started that fight."

"Wallace started it," Ashlyn said. "I finished it."

Ashlyn turned to Bershad. "Well? What's up ahead?"

He reached out. Sure enough, there was a trio of males up ahead. Their blood was hot and their senses alert. They could feel the Nomad coming.

"Three of them," Bershad confirmed. "They're looking for a fight."

"Think Smokey can take 'em?" Felgor asked.

Bershad shrugged, then sent a questioning twitch to the dragon.

She gave back her version of a middle finger, then leapt from the rafters of the canopy, heading straight for the Blackjacks.

15

VERA
Dainwood Jungle, Sector Thirteen

"Well, I can see why Osyrus Ward didn't want to bother with this," said Decimar. "There are more dragons directly ahead of us than I've seen in my whole damn life."

"Yeah," Vera agreed, looking out at the swarm of Blackjacks that swooped and whirled through the air like a horde of enormous starlings. Others were perched in the Daintrees below, grazing along the canopy.

She turned back to Garwin. He and two of his men were fiddling with Ward's machine, which looked like a bunch of dragon-slaying horns that had been melted together.

"Is that ready?"

"Fuck if I know," Garwin said. "All the engineers did was tell us how to turn it on."

Vera turned back to the dragons. They were less than a league from them.

"Then do it."

One soldier moved to the side of the machine and took hold of a long crank made from dragon bone. Tried to pull it backward with a grunt. Failed. "Uh. Seems stuck."

"Pull harder," said Garwin.

"Don't wanna break the thing, sir."

"Well, seeing as it's made from dragon bone, I don't think that's very fucking likely."

The soldier tried again. When he still failed, Garwin shoved him out of the way, planted his feet, and leaned down on the crank. After a moment of strained muscles and struggle, it shifted backward with a rumble and a click.

Dragon oil poured into the machine through a series of tubes. It began to vibrate on the deck, emitting a low hum.

"That's it?" Vera asked when nothing else happened.

"Supposed to be," said Garwin.

Vera turned to the wall of dragons, which was unchanged.

"Should I turn us around?" Entras asked from the pilot's seat. "'Cause they don't seem to be—"

Entras cut himself off when the impenetrable wall suddenly broke apart, giving them a narrow but clear tunnel leading into the jungle on the far side.

"Put us in a full burn, Entras. I don't want to be in the thick of things any longer than necessary."

"Full burn."

They roared ahead, moving toward the gap. The shadows of the dragons plunged them into wild darkness as they moved through the tunnel. Nobody spoke. Just watched the horde around them.

When they were halfway through, the horns of the machine started billowing black smoke.

"Uh, that can't be good," said the soldier who'd been too weak to work the crank. He peered down at the machine. Screwed up his nose. "Smells like burning hair all of a sudden. I wonder if it's still working?"

Before anyone could answer, a Blackjack swooped alongside the ship and snapped its tail across the gunwale, decapitating ten soldiers in one sweep.

"Everyone down!" Vera shouted, hitting the deck.

Garret was already on his belly. Everyone else followed a heart-beat later.

Dragons started closing in around them. Snapping at the sides of the ship with their jaws and tail. Two latched onto the levitation sack with their claws, then darted away again when the gas started hissing at them.

Vera crawled to Entras. "No matter what happens, you keep this ship moving forward."

Entras nodded, eyes focused on the gap ahead, which was getting smaller with each passing second.

All around them, things descended into a nightmare of gnashing dragon jaws, screaming men, and utter chaos. Vera stayed down, tucked into as small of a ball as she could manage, wondering if this was how she was going to die.

And then, without warning, it all stopped.

Vera waited another moment before she stood up. Looked around. There was nothing but clear sky ahead. The Blackjacks behind them weren't giving chase.

"We made it," she said.

"Most of us, anyway," said Decimar, coming over.

Vera looked around. The men were brushing themselves off and dealing with wounds. There were blood and limbs all over the deck.

"We lose any of ours?" Vera asked Decimar.

He shook his head. "Just minor injuries. Can't say the same for the Ghalamarians, though. Looks like they lost almost a score. Those idiots need to learn how to duck."

Vera nodded. That was a good thing. Their numbers were almost even.

Overhead, the levitation sack was hissing as the gas leaked from a dozen punctures, but they could patch those once they landed.

"Vera, I got something!" Entras called, pointing ahead. She went over and followed his finger to a big swath of jungle where the entire canopy was missing. She pulled out her lens and glassed the area. Saw the wing of a skyship jutting up from the trees.

She smiled. "Make a course, Entras. We've found the *Eternity*."

16

CABBAGE
Dainwood Jungle, Blackjack Territory

Bershad's dragon rose high in the sky, until she appeared to be no bigger than a crow, then dove into the canopy with a feral scream, attacking the Blackjacks. There was a violent series of cries and snarls that made Cabbage's toes clench. The leaves thrashed and writhed. Cabbage could see flashes of gray scales. Then black. A geyser of blood sprayed up and out across the canopy.

And then there was silence.

"We're good," Bershad said, starting to walk forward. "Keep the donkeys calm as we pass through. The blood will spook them."

Bershad led them through the undergrowth. For half a league, there wasn't much to look at aside from more piles of dragonshit.

Then they reached the first dead Blackjack.

It was hanging from the limb of a Daintree—wings spread out across a few trees. Its head was gone. Just a neck stump remained, which was pouring blood onto the forest floor at a rate that a waterfall would struggle to match.

"That is deeply unpleasant," Cabbage muttered.

"I prefer dead dragons to those wretched mushroom people from your island," said Felgor.

Cabbage just shrugged. He didn't have the energy to decide which was worse.

Bershad guided them disconcertingly close to the whole mess, despite there being a nice little path around it to the right.

"Think maybe we should divert that way?" Cabbage asked.

"There are seventeen vipers over there," Bershad said without turning around or slowing his pace.

"Oh."

"Just keep the donkeys calm."

Bershad stepped less than a pace to the left of the pooling dragon blood, but the first donkey froze up and dug his heels in, refusing to budge. Cabbage tried to calm the beast down and coax him forward, but he refused.

Felgor's donkey was frozen, too.

"Uh, Silas?" Felgor said. "Think we're a little beyond muzzle rubs, given the circumstances."

Bershad turned around. The look on his face wasn't impatience or anger. It was sadness. Something he'd never seen on the Flawless Bershad's face.

He swallowed, then walked back to Cabbage's donkey and placed a scarred hand on the beast's forehead.

"It's all right," he whispered. "Everything's going to be all right. You have to trust me. I'll protect you."

The donkey kept his heels frozen in the blood-soaked ground.

"I promise," Bershad continued. "Only way you get hurt is if I'm already dead."

Cabbage didn't know much about donkeys other than they were strong-backed and stubborn as hell. So it was with great surprise that he saw the donkey flip back his straightened ears and relax his tensed hide. When Bershad continued past the waterfall of dragon blood again, the donkey followed.

"He commands donkeys and dragons both?" Cabbage whispered to Felgor.

"Silas would say that he doesn't command either," said Felgor. "But he's a bit of a prick in that regard."

They moved past the bleeding dragon corpse in a single-file line. For a few dozen paces the sound of the blood spattering on the leaves was all that Cabbage could hear. But once they cleared enough distance, a far more disturbing sound arose.

The Nomad was eating a Blackjack.

Back in Burz-al-dun, the clockmaker that Cabbage was apprenticed to kept a dog in the workshop named Iro. He was a black mutt with powerful jaws and a mean look in his eye. Something to dissuade thieves. The clockmaker had given Iro a fresh bone each night as they were sitting by the fire and going over the next day's work. Cabbage had always had trouble focusing on the clock schematics while the sound of cartilage and bone popping in the dog's mouth echoed around the small workshop.

Listening to one dragon eat another was far more distracting.

They came around a Daintree to find the Nomad with her maw buried in the stomach cavity of the second Blackjack. She came up with her muzzle drizzled in gore and looked at Bershad with an expression that was alarmingly similar to one you'd give when silently offering someone a sip of your ale.

Bershad waved it off.

They kept walking.

———————

The good news was that after Smokey killed the three Blackjacks, the dragons ahead of them cleared out real quick, and without a fight. The bad news was that Cabbage started paying attention to their back trail, which was constantly being closed off by the Blackjacks who returned to their roosts as soon as the Nomad moved on.

"Guess we're not camping for the night," Cabbage muttered to himself. "We'd be totally surrounded."

"We're surrounded either way," Simeon said happily. "But if we camp, we'll be eaten."

"Why do you sound so happy when you say that?"

He shrugged. "I like it when things are simple. Ghost Moth Island was simple. Walking through a nest of dragons is simple. This war, though? All the magic and skyships are just a complicated pain in my ass."

"Things can be simple and wretched at the same time."

"Life's generally wretched one way or another, Cabbage. Simple and wretched is better than wretched and complicated."

"I guess."

Simeon slapped Cabbage on the back, which nearly sent him head-first into a pile of Blackjack shit.

"If I can keep you alive long enough, maybe you'll find yourself a stretch of something simple and wonderful."

"Letting me stay behind with the Jaguar Army would have been a good way to preserve my life."

"Doesn't work like that."

"Why not?"

Simeon just smiled at him. Kept moving.

Sometime after nightfall—Cabbage couldn't tell exactly when, just that it was dark enough so that all he could see was the donkey's ass that was directly in front of him—the Nomad stopped her leap-frogging cycle and landed in a tree above Bershad.

Then she retched.

"Is she sick?" Cabbage asked.

"Naw, I'm sure she's puking all over the forest for the fun of it," said Simeon.

When they reached Bershad, the Nomad had dropped into a lit-tle clearing, and was drooping her head like a sick dog. The pile of vomit was full of Blackjack meat and scales.

"What's wrong with her, ate a bad dragon?" Simeon asked.

"The vibration is getting stronger," Bershad said, gritting his teeth. "Feels like a massive dragon horn that won't stop ringing. Feels like . . . like . . ."

Bershad puked, too.

"Ha, who's got the weak stomach now?" Felgor asked.

Bershad spat. Glared at him.

"We're getting closer to the crashed skyship," Ashlyn said.

"Yeah," Bershad agreed, then turned to Smokey. "And this is as far as she can take us."

Bershad went over to the dragon and put a hand on her snout, then rested his forehead against her nose for a moment. Then Smokey lifted herself into the night sky and disappeared.

Once she was gone, Bershad seemed to relax.

"Aren't we pretty exposed without her?" Cabbage asked, already looking around for Blackjacks.

"The Blackjacks are having the same problem she is," said Bershad. "We're safe enough, long as we keep moving forward."

"How're we gonna get back out, though?" Cabbage asked.

"She'll come back when we need her to. Trust me."

That seemed to be good enough for everyone else, so Cabbage had no choice but for it to be good enough for him, even though it seemed thinner than Papyrian silk. They crossed the clearing and headed farther into the jungle that was now devoid of dragons. And it wasn't just the dragons who seemed scared off. The branches were empty of monkeys and birds. The ground clear of rodents and snails and snakes. The only thing that seemed alive was an alarming number of worms, which were fleeing the earth as if it was on fire.

Oromir's men bent down to scoop up mouthfuls of worms as they moved through. Jammed them into their mouths happily, their smiles coated with dirt and half-chewed worms.

Cabbage tried one bite, but quickly spat it out. He decided his next meal would come from the skyship, or in the afterlife. Whichever came first.

Near daybreak, they reached a wide streak of fallen Daintrees that ended at a cliff. Their trunks had all been snapped near the base. Only one thing could have done that.

"The skyship crashed here," Bershad said. "Jolan and Kerrigan, stay with the donkeys. Everyone else, on your bellies and moving up with me."

Cabbage opened his mouth to ask if he could guard the donkeys,

too, but Simeon hauled him to ground before he could get a word
out.

They reached the lip of the ridge, which looked out on a bowl valley.

As expected, the wreckage of the skyship was below. One side of
the hull had been torn off during the crash, making it easy to see the
contents of the cargo holds. Some were packed with sacks of rice.
Others piled with cured meat. Shelves were lined with jars of beans
and pickled vegetables. One entire hold was packed with cheese
wheels the size of a warden's shield. Cabbage's mouth watered at the
sight.

What they hadn't been expecting was a second ship—perfectly
intact—with a steady stream of soldiers and skyship crew coming
in and out of it. They were moving rice sacks into the second ship,
the hull of which was festooned with extra cargo netting. There
were longbowmen perched along elevated positions, looking out
at the forest.

"Well, this is a proper goatfuck, isn't it?" said Felgor.

"Whisper when you speak, Balarian," said Oromir. "The grayskins can hear over great distances."

"Don't see any of those around," said Felgor, although Cabbage
noted he was whispering now.

"Naw," said Simeon. "But there's plenty of clock fuckers." He took
a big breath in. "Some Ghalamarians, too. I can smell 'em."

"Where they're from is less important than the fact they've
got every angle of approach covered with those longbows," said
Oromir.

"Might be we can rush 'em," said one of Oromir's men. "Get in
close before they get a second volley off."

Nobody responded to that right away, but a few moments later
there was a rustling in some ferns about two hundred strides out from
the skyship.

"Movement to the south!" an archer called. Then he loosed an
arrow with smooth, confident efficiency.

The arrow landed in the ferns and a boar came screaming out of
the undergrowth at speed, one arrow jammed in his hide.

A second archer loosed another arrow that plugged the boar just
above the eye, dropping the beast.

"By the fucking forest gods, that was a good shot," the warden
muttered.

"You still want to rush them?" Oromir asked.

"I do not."

"Hey Ashe, what's the range on your death orb things?" Felgor asked, motioning to the satchel where she kept her lodestones.

"Thirty paces, tops. They're too spread out."

They all passed a moment in silence, studying the scene below.

"They do have a few blind spots in their route to and from the ship," Oromir said eventually. "See them? There. And there."

"Aye," said Simeon, then he grinned. Snapped his fingers, which sound like bones being broken in half. "Here's how we'll do it. Oromir sneaks some o' his murderous men down and waylays the porters. Dress up as them and spread out around the whole area nice and quick. Then I'll rush in from the south, making a real big ruckus and attracting their arrows. You and yours take out the bowmen while they're focused on me. Just be quick about it. Even my armor isn't impervious to those arrows."

"Works," said Oromir. "I'll take a score to the first blind spot. Kes, you take the second. Wait for my signal and—"

"Nope," Bershad cut in. "We're not doing that."

"You got a better idea? 'Cause that dragon's not here to help you and I'd rather not get porcupined today."

"I don't want to get porcupined either," said Bershad.

"It's an inconvenience to you. It'll kill me and my men," said Oromir. "So you can politely go fuck yourself, *my lord*."

"Calm down, Oromir," said Bershad. "There's a way to do this without bloodshed."

"Why would we want to do this without bloodshed?" Simeon asked.

"Because we're not all shrouded in dragonscale armor," said Ashlyn. "What are you thinking, Silas?"

Bershad pointed to a slender woman wearing dark armor. She was standing in the shadow of the skyship, scanning the tree line with a lens.

"I'm gonna go have a chat with her."

"That's a Papyrian widow," said Oromir.

"I'm aware," said Bershad. "We know each other."

Ashlyn squinted at the skyship. "Is that who I think it is?"

"Yep."

"I see. Okay. Let's go down and talk to her."

"You all on friendly terms with the rest of those archers, too?" Oromir asked. "'Cause that widow doesn't leave their sight lines, and judging from the fate of that boar, they're gonna shoot on sight."

"There's a way around that." Bershad said. "Felgor, you still have the skyman's uniform in that pack?"

"Oh, there's no way I'm ever parting with this baby. Skymen get all the perks back in Floodhaven. The best part is—"

"Put it on, then follow me."

17

VERA
Crash Site of the Eternity

After scanning the forest for enemies, Vera ran a long, circular patrol around the skyship, keeping an eye on the men who were loading the food.

Garwin had refused to order his men to help, so it was just the regular skymen doing the work. One of them men bumped into her as she made her way around the cargo hold, mumbling an apology and some excuse about jungle heat.

Vera came around to Decimar, who was standing over the boar he'd killed.

"A decent shot," she said.

"Mediocre, I think." He winced. "I was aiming for the eye."

Vera laughed. "You longbowmen are all perfectionist assholes."

"And you widows are all insane. Jumping out of skyships for fun."

Vera shrugged. They both scanned the forest for a few moments.

"Seems pretty quiet," Decimar said. "Apart from the boar."

"Yeah." Vera watched the men load the food. "I wish we could move this along. I want this done so we can go to Pargos."

"You're still planning on going through with it, then?"

"Yes."

"What about Garwin and the Hangman?" Decimar said, lowering his voice and gesturing up to Garret, who was standing in the shadowy nook of the skyship's upper level with his arms crossed, staring at them. He seemed to be waiting for something to happen, although Vera wasn't sure what that could be. "Don't expect they'll be interested in a side jaunt when this is done."

"I'm aware."

"So, what's the plan there?"

"I'll think of something," Vera said, reaching behind her breastplate to dig out her smoking kit. She always came up with better ideas after a smoke.

But her kit wasn't there.

She frowned. Started patting her pockets and pouches. Nothing.

"Black skies," she muttered.

"There a problem?"

"I must have left it on the skyship . . ."

"Left what?"

"My—"

Vera stopped talking when the familiar scent of her pipe tobacco wafted across the open field and filled her nostrils. It was coming from a thicket of ferns that grew beneath the shadow of a massive Daintree.

"Vera? What is it?"

"Nothing," she said to him. "I'm going to scout that undergrowth, though. Tell the men. I do not want to be shot."

"Why's that undergrowth suddenly in need of a one-person patrol?"

"I just want to make sure there aren't any more boars around," she responded. "Can't let you have all the glory."

Vera made her way into the jungle alone. The smell of her pipe got stronger as she moved closer to the Daintree. She knew it might be a trap, but it seemed to her that if someone wanted her dead, they wouldn't have used such an elaborate way to get her attention.

All the same, she approached on the prowl, careful to stay in the shadows of the undergrowth and avoid moving any ferns or branches. She eventually got to a vantage point where she could make out a big man smoking a pipe. She didn't recognize him until he looked up at her and smiled.

"You got some sneak to you, Vera. But if you wanted to ambush me proper, you should really do something about the way you smell. Papyrians have a specific kind of stink to them when they don't bathe for a while."

Vera stood up. Sheathed her blade. "Fuck yourself, Silas."

18

CABBAGE
Crash Site of the Eternity

After Ashlyn, Felgor, and Bershad snuck down through the woods, Oromir ordered his score of wardens to surround the skyship, but stay out of sight. Then he took out a lens and started glassing the crash site.

"This whole situation is a serious misallocation of my skill set," Simeon muttered, crossing his arms and scowling.

"I didn't hear you put up much resistance to *Lord* Bershad's orders." Oromir said Bershad's title like it was an insult.

"Fuck off, Almiran. He slipped away before I could reinforce my case."

"Uh-huh. For such a legendary murderer, you eat an awful lot of dragonshit from Silas and Ashlyn."

On instinct, Cabbage scooted backward from his spot a little bit. He didn't want to get any of Oromir's blood on him after Simeon tore the warden's arms off, but Simeon just threw Oromir that spooky smile he got when he was impressed with someone's grit.

"You wanted a fight, too," Simeon said. "Didn't hear you pushing back."

"I follow orders."

"Sure. When old Flawless will stove your head in for disobeying them, you follow them to the letter."

Oromir put the lens down and gave Simeon a measured look. "I heard he stoved your head in pretty good up on that island of yours. That's what Felgor said, anyway."

"Untrue," Simeon said. "Silas and I were fighting square, and it could have gone either way. Then the witch queen interrupted with her sorcery, which is a cheap way to win."

Cabbage was tempted to point out that all those years of Simeon murdering men in regular armor while he wore the dragonskin wasn't exactly fair, either. But he liked his arms in their present location.

"I don't believe you," said Oromir.

"Cabbage was a witness."

Simeon turned to him.

"Uh. Yeah. I was . . . and the fight was—"

"Don't care," Oromir interrupted, putting the lens up to his eye and continuing to scan the crash site. "Either way, you got cowed, and now you're whipped worse than a farm boy fawning after the warden who took his cherry."

Simeon shook his head. That smile was still on his face. "You got anything to throw out besides idle talk, Almiran? Because if not I'll—"

"Quiet!" Oromir hissed, all his focus on the crash now. "Did you see that?"

"See what?" Cabbage asked.

"I saw a man moving around on that upper tier. Could have sworn he had a rope coiled on his hip."

"Uh, my vision's not so good over long distances," Cabbage admitted. "What's it matter if one of 'em has a rope?"

"I think it was Garret," Oromir muttered.

"Who?"

Oromir ignored him. Closed his lens. "I'm going down there."

"Why?"

"Because if I'm right, there's a man down there I need to kill."

"I like the attitude, kid, but if you go down in a huff the only person you're gonna get killed is yourself," said Simeon.

Oromir's face screwed up into a mess of frustration.

"Don't shit yourself just yet," said Simeon, then pointed. "See that big rut in the ground from when the skyship crashed? We'll use the ferns as cover to reach it."

"We?" Cabbage asked.

"Shut up, Cabbage. We're obviously going with him."

Cabbage didn't feel like that was obvious at all, but knew there was no point in arguing.

"Once we reach the rut, we crawl until we reach that crater formed by an uprooted rock. From there, we'll have an angle on everything."

Oromir nodded. Then gave Simeon a once-over. "That armor stands out. Can you take it off?"

"Don't need to." He turned to Cabbage. "Fetch mud and leaves."

19

VERA
Crash Site of the Eternity

Bershad took a long drag off Vera's pipe, then he offered it to her. "You want the dregs?"

"What are you doing here?" she hissed.

"Same thing as you, I'd imagine. Awful lot of food going to waste in that crashed ship."

"That's our food," Vera said.

"Ah. Well, me and five thousand of my wardens were all set to unleash one of those ambushes we've become famous for, but then I saw a familiar face who appeared to be supervising the operation, and I thought if I could have a little private chat, we might be able to talk this out rather than resort to steel and spilled blood."

"Five thousand wardens, is it?"

"Yup. Got you fully surrounded."

"You're a shitty liar, Silas." A little smile crossed her lips. "Even if the Jaguar Army was five thousand strong—which it isn't—there's no way you marched them all through that dragon-infested jungle." Vera frowned. "How *did* you get all the way out here on foot?" she asked, glancing down and noticing that Silas wasn't wearing any boots.

"Got my ways."

"Uh-huh. And what about stealing my pipe?" she asked. "I don't remember you being so good with your fingers."

"Harsh, but fair. I had some help on that front."

Bershad motioned to a clump of ferns, where a skinny Balarian wearing a skyman's uniform was crouched.

"Hey, Vera."

She squinted at him. "Felgor?"

He stood up and gave her a big grin, putting his minuscule teeth on happy display. "In the flesh."

"Where'd you get that uniform?"

"*Got my ways,*" Felgor said, mimicking Bershad's accent. He frowned. "Hmm, doesn't sound as gruffly heroic when I say it."

"Vera!" Decimar yelled out to her in Balarian. "You okay?"

"I'm fine!" she called back. "Stay where you are."

"Sounds like you've gotten pretty good at the clock fucker's tongue," Bershad said.

"I take offense to the term clock fucker," said Felgor. Then he whispered to her, "Your accent *is* pretty good, though."

Vera snorted. "Look, I'm glad you're both alive and all that, but this isn't a great time for a reunion. If anyone sees you besides me, arrows are going to fly." She jerked her chin to the tree line. "Go back to your jungle. You lost this one."

"No, I didn't."

"Cut the dragonshit about five thousand men. I'm not a moron."

He shrugged. "Might not be quite five thousand, but I do have her."

A woman in a yellow poncho walked out of the woods. It had been a long time, but Ashlyn Malgrave's face was unmistakable.

Vera's jaw hung open. "My Queen. You're supposed to be . . ."

"Dead?" Ashlyn asked. "Not yet."

Vera glared at Silas. "Anyone else you're hiding in those ferns?"

He smiled. "That's all for now. But we do have enough wardens to make things interesting if it comes to a fight. Was hoping you could tell your men to stand down and clear out. You can have whatever food you already loaded, we'll take the rest."

Vera shook her head. "I need that food."

"If you try to tell me that the Balarian army is short on rations, I'll lose my composure."

"It's not for the military. People are starving all over Terra."

Bershad cocked his head, surprised. "And that's a priority for Osyrus Ward?"

"It is a priority for me."

"Huh." Bershad scratched at his dirty hair. "Even split?"

Vera shook her head. "It's not that simple. The longbowmen will follow my lead, but the Ghalamarians who are with me have their own commander, and he's not really the even split sort." She looked at Bershad. "You know him. Garwin."

"Argel's baron?"

"He's a count now."

"What's a Ghalamarian count doing in this war?" Bershad asked.

Vera hesitated. Decided that Bershad didn't need to know the full truth.

"Osyrus Ward compelled him to join the fight."

"If you know him, that's good for us, right?" Ashlyn asked.

"Eh, we didn't leave things on the best of terms."

"What does that mean?"

"Last time we met, I killed a bunch of his men, and his city was destroyed by a Red Skull."

"By the fucking forest gods, Silas, are there any lords in Terra you haven't pissed off or killed?"

He shrugged. "There's you."

Ashlyn just shook her head.

"So, what are we doing here?" Vera asked.

Ashlyn stood up. "I would like the chance to persuade Garwin that a peaceful resolution is best for everyone in this particular instance."

"I can give it a whirl on my own," Bershad offered.

"No. You're a shitty negotiator to begin with, and it sounds like he hates you. We'll do it together."

Vera chewed on that. "I'm willing to try."

"Good," said Ashlyn.

"Felgor, best you wait here," said Bershad.

"Could not agree more," said Felgor.

"Oh, and Vera?" Bershad said. "Best keep the fact that she's the deposed witch queen of Almira between us, yeah?"

Vera nodded. "Decimar!" she called.

"Here," he called back. "Everything okay?"

"I'm coming back out with some visitors. Keep your arrows in their quivers. We're going to have a little chat."

"Acknowledged."

Vera started picking her way back to the crashed skyship.

20

CABBAGE
Crash Site of the Eternity

Cabbage realized far too late that the mud he'd rubbed across Simeon's armor was mostly dragonshit. Now he was stuck trailing the stinking Skojit as they crawled along the rut on their bellies.

When they were about halfway to the skyship, a woman shouted from the jungle.

"Decimar!"

Cabbage was so startled and sure they'd been spotted, he didn't really catch much of what was said after that, but when a few moments passed and he didn't have an arrow through his face, Cabbage calmed down and tried to figure out what was going on.

The widow came out of the jungle, followed by Bershad and Ashlyn. No arrows were loosed at them.

They lost sight of the trio as they got closer to the skyship crash, so Oromir gave a little signal and they kept crawling. Now that the longbowmen's attention was elsewhere, Oromir began to move faster, and they reached the lip of the rut a few minutes later. Oromir and Cabbage crawled up to scout.

"What're they doing?" Simeon asked.

"Talking," said Cabbage.

"Talking?"

"Yeah. They're all clumped together."

"Huh." Simeon spat. "Any Ghalamarians?"

Cabbage now had a clear view into the crash. There were actually twelve men in Ghalamarian armor—two of whom wore officer's plumes. Simeon hated officers the most.

"Uh, I can't quite tell."

Oromir flashed him a look, but didn't contradict the lie. Instead, he raised his lens and began scanning the ship. From here, they had a good angle on the exposed upper levels. There was a man hiding in the shadows. And he did have a rope coiled on his hip.

"That's him," Oromir whispered.

"*Who?*" Cabbage asked.

"Garret the Hangman. And I am going to kill him in the next five minutes."

Oromir hopped down and moved close to Simeon.

"Cabbage is lying to you, there are ten Ghalamarian regulars and two officers in that skyship."

Simeon's face darkened even more than before, which Cabbage hadn't thought was possible.

"What does the sigil on their shoulders look like?" he asked.

"A sun rising over some waves."

"Argel," Simeon whispered. "I fucking hate Argellians."

"One of them is wearing a count's plume."

Simeon smiled. "Oh, I am going to ruin his day."

He moved to charge, but Oromir stopped him with a strong hand.

"Wait. There's a man on the upper levels. You'll draw him to the ground so I can kill him. I kill him. Not you."

"Why's that important?"

"I got my reasons. And they're far better than the ones you got for killing Ghalamarians you've never met." He pulled Simeon close. "Garret is *mine*. Clear?"

Simeon smiled. "We're clear, Almiran. How do you wanna get it done?"

Oromir started drawing a quick map in the mud at their feet. "The officer is here. If you come up from the right, you'll have a decent angle on him. . . ."

Oromir kept talking. Cabbage felt his cock shrivel, way it always did before a fight.

21

ASHLYN
Crash Site of the Eternity

"Who the fuck are you two?" Count Garwin asked Ashlyn as they approached. For now, the Ghalamarians had their weapons sheathed, but their hands were all gripped around the hilts and she saw a lot of white knuckles.

"Emissaries from the Jaguar Army," Ashlyn said. "We're here to negotiate."

"The Jaguar Army sends lots of emissaries deep into dragon-infested jungle looking for negotiating opportunities, do they?"

"They do when there is a crashed skyship full of provisions added to the equation."

"Uh-huh. Well, I'm a little hazy on why that Papyrian cunt allowed two so-called emissaries to tromp into my perimeter," Garwin growled. "But so long as you both fuck off back to your jungle in the next minute, you can keep your lives."

"Can't recommend referring to a widow that way," said Bershad. "They kill for less."

Garwin's eyes moved to Bershad. It took a moment for him to recognize Silas, but when he did, his eyes widened and his face reddened. "You. Fucking. Asshole."

"Guess we're skipping the pleasantries entirely this time?" Bershad asked.

"You destroyed my city."

"No, that Red Skull destroyed your city. And I've got a bit of a grudge myself. You sold me out to the Balarian emperor after we left Argel. Pretty shitty thing to do."

"And yet Mercer is long gone down the river, while you're alive and well and wreaking havoc through this forsaken jungle. How'd that come to pass?"

"Just lucky I guess." Bershad spat. "Anyway, looks like we both showed up here with the goal of getting ourselves fed. How about we split it?"

"Why would I do that instead of just killing you and your bitch?"

"Because we've got five thousand wardens hiding in the trees," Bershad said. "You're totally surrounded."

"And you're so full of dragonshit I can smell it on your breath."

"Signal your men to attack. See what happens."

"I know what would happen. You'd die."

"That's unlikely."

"Can you both put your dicks away for moment?" Ashlyn asked. "We came down here to avoid a fight, not rekindle a stupid one between the two of you."

Garwin shifted his gaze to her. "I don't know how many of your rabble are out there, but if you had enough to launch an attack you would have done it already. I have no reason to compromise with savages."

"Sure you do," said Ashlyn. "Because we savages know where every single dragon warren in the Dainwood is located. I would imagine that Osyrus Ward doesn't really care about this food, nor does he care much about you, if he attached you to the group that flew through a horde of Blackjacks to get it. But what if you came back with ten fresh warren locations? That's a man who would be put in good favor, I think."

Garwin didn't say anything, but she could tell he was interested.

"And a man in Osyrus Ward's good favor is a man who lives a long time," Ashlyn added. "He'd probably be allowed to return to his seat of governance. Enjoy the rest of this war from a comfortable and fortified tower."

Garwin licked his lips. Glanced at one of his men, who was wearing a lieutenant's plume. "The Madman is always looking for more warrens, that's a fact," the lieutenant said, eyes sliding to Ashlyn. "Dunno what this mud-haired woman's word is worth, though."

"Neither do I," said Garwin. He appraised Ashlyn for a few more moments. "All right, *emissary*. Here's what we'll do. Real slow, you're going to draw the locations in the dirt at your feet. Then my men are going to confirm those locations with our charts. Then you can have your split of the food."

Ashlyn pretended to weigh the offer. It wouldn't matter either way—there was no way that the Balarian charts could confirm or deny warren locations, so she planned on giving them a set of difficult-to-reach and useless places to check.

"Half the locations now. Half when all of your men are back in the skyship, and half the food remains on the ground."

"We're just halving shit all over the place, aren't we?" Garwin said. But his face was already changing to the expression Ashlyn wanted to see. "Okay, you have a deal. Start marking locations with that finger of yours so we can all get out of this place before—"

"Ghalamarian swine! Get ready to fuck off down the river!"

Ashlyn turned to see Simeon charging. His armor was coated in a mixture of mud and shit.

She cursed. Crouched. And flexed the muscles of her forearm.

Her bands began to spin.

22

CABBAGE
Crash Site of the Eternity

Cabbage watched the attack unfold through his lens.

Seven archers loosed rounds at Simeon as he crossed the gap between their crater and the parley. All the arrows connected, but only two punched through his armor. Thigh and shoulder, looked like. Not nearly enough to stop Simeon when he had all that heat and hate roiling through his blood. He rushed past Ashlyn and Bershad. Punched the Argellian lord in the face, which sent his teeth spraying out the back of his skull.

"Shit," Cabbage muttered. "I'm gonna get yelled at for letting this happen."

Cabbage assumed the usual murder and mayhem would follow, but before Simeon could cause much more destruction, a hemp rope dropped down from an upper tier of the broken skyship and tightened around his neck. Garret dropped down, and Simeon was yanked out of sight.

Garret strained against Simeon's weight, both hands wrapped tight around the hemp rope. Oromir flashed out of the undergrowth, sword drawn, heading directly for him.

Given everyone else's focus on Simeon's lynching, he'd have had no problem running his sword through the man's back. But at the very last moment, the Papyrian widow's attention shifted, and she threw the scabbard of her sword at Oromir, striking him on the temple and knocking him unconscious.

"Kill them all!" the Ghalamarian lieutenant screamed.

As the archers drew their bows, Bershad sprinted to Oromir and threw his own body over the warden, shielding him from the volley that came a heartbeat later and taking five arrows in his back.

Ashlyn raised her left arm high over her head and made a fist. The bands on her arm spun with furious movement. When the archers loosed their arrows at her, she snapped her fist toward the ground. The arrows seemed to accept the movement as ironclad directions— each of them smacked harmlessly into the mud at her feet.

While the archers nocked a fresh volley, Simeon tore the noose off his neck and dropped to the ground with a loud thump, which sent Garret stumbling backward. The archers fired the entirety of their next volley at Simeon, but he shifted and shimmied like a dancer, causing a bunch of glancing shots.

"Gonna need more than some string and arrows to kill me," he growled, then charged the nearest Ghalamarian.

Ashlyn swept her left arm sideways and Simeon was launched into the air like a coyote who'd just been kicked by a donkey. He landed near Cabbage with a thump and crash.

Ashlyn's bands spun to life again. Five metal orbs the size of apples flew out of the pack she kept on her hip, zipping through the air and stopping directly in front of the faces of the nearest Ghalamarian soldiers.

"Enough!" Ashlyn shouted. "If everyone else stops, everyone else lives. Keep fighting, and I start hollowing skulls."

The Ghalamarian lieutenant didn't have an orb in front of his face, but his mouth twitched as he looked around at the men who did.

"She's bluffing!" he blurted. "It's a trick. Attack them on my—"

A single band on Ashlyn's arm blurred with speed, creating a high-pitched whine. One of the orbs zipped through the air, punched into the side of the lieutenant's skull, and then returned to the exact same place it had been hovering, just with a smear of blood and scrap of bone shard on it. The lieutenant collapsed.

"I am not bluffing, and another volley of arrows won't do anything besides make me angry."

She motioned to the heap of arrows at her feet.

"But I don't want to end any more lives today. Drop your weapons and get out of my sight."

23

VERA
Crash Site of the Eternity

"Do as she says," said Vera.

For a bunch of professional soldiers, the men dropped their weapons awfully fast.

Vera remained outside while everyone else moved back to the *Sparrow.* Garret was the last to leave, and had a strange look on his face, but he eventually followed the others.

Bershad remained still as a corpse while the men withdrew, but as soon as Garret disappeared into the *Blue Sparrow,* he stirred, then stood with a curse on a groan. He looked uncomfortable, but more like a man who'd fallen off a high ladder than someone who'd been shot with five longbow arrows.

A teenage boy had picked his way down from the hills while everyone was getting their bearings. He wasn't wearing any armor, but was carrying a large backpack. He moved to help the unconscious warden, bending down and checking his pulse. He produced a glass vial from his kit, shook it a few times, then held it beneath the warden's nose.

His eyes snapped open, and the warden shot up. Eyes searching.

"Where's Garret?" he hissed.

Vera was surprised he knew the name, but realized she shouldn't have been. Men don't generally charge a group of well-positioned archers to kill a stranger.

"Garret was here?" the boy asked, voice strained and suddenly full of anger, too.

"He's gone now, and you're an asshole," Bershad said, walking over to Oromir. "I told you to wait in the fucking jungle."

"That man was mine to kill."

"No, he wasn't. You screwed this whole thing up."

The two of them glared at each other for a few moments, and Vera wondered if they were going to try and kill each other now. But Bershad softened, then turned around, showing his arrow-ridden back to the warden.

"Pull those out and we'll call it square."

The warden ripped the arrows from Bershad's back with all the gentleness of a gardener pulling stubborn weeds. He dropped the arrows. Spat. Then stalked off into the jungle.

"What's his problem?" Vera asked.

"Oh, he's got a collection of them," said Bershad, rubbing his back as he came over to them. He smiled at Ashlyn. "So, who's a shitty negotiator now?"

"I had Garwin convinced," Ashlyn responded. "Simeon and Oromir are the ones who spoiled it."

"Yeah." Bershad squinted at the remnants of Garwin's skull, then out into the field where the big Skojit had flown. There was a man who appeared to have no ears crouched over him.

"You didn't kill him, did you?" Bershad asked.

"He'll be fine. Jolan, go over and make sure none of those arrow wounds are problematic."

"On it," the boy said, trotting away.

Ashlyn had kept those gray orbs hovering around her head in a loose orbit, but now that they were alone, the bands on her fingers increased their speed, and the orbs flowed back into her satchel like ducks following their mother into the water.

Vera watched them, transfixed.

"It isn't sorcery," Ashlyn said. "It's a combination of—"

"Queen, I've spent the last year surrounded by Osyrus Ward's machines and experiments. I might not understand exactly how you're doing that, but I recognize the general method. There's no need to explain."

"Fair enough," said Ashlyn. She licked her lips, appearing very thirsty. "Is my sister alive? All of the rumors we hear are different."

"Yes. But her spine was completely severed during an assassination attempt last winter. She cannot breathe without the aid of Osyrus Ward's machines. And without his continued help, she'll die."

"That's why you're helping him?" Bershad asked.

"That's right."

Vera looked at Silas a long time, waiting for him to challenge her. But instead, his face softened.

"I understand, Vera." He gave a grim smile. "Looks like we're both still out here in the wilderness, doing work for the Malgraves, yeah?"

She smiled back. "Looks like it."

There was a silence. In the distance, a dragon bellowed out a long screech.

"You two had sex, didn't you?" Ashlyn asked.

Vera's mouth dropped open. "Um. We. I."

"Don't bother denying it, Vera. I've known Silas a long time, and that particular smile of his only gets conjured from one thing. Well, the memory of one thing, anyway."

Ashlyn looked between them again, waiting for an answer.

"Well? Let's have it."

There was simply no way Vera was going to answer that question.

Bershad sighed. "Yeah. Up in the Razorbacks."

Ashlyn kept a stern face for a long moment, then broke into a smile of her own. "Black skies, you always did have a thing for screwing in the woods. I hope you made him bathe first, at least?" she asked Vera.

"I did, actually."

"Good." She paused. "It surprises you, how gentle he is. Yes?"

"Yes," Vera said.

"Okay," said Bershad, "I think we've covered all the necessary ground on this front."

"Now he's embarrassed," Ashlyn said. "I don't have much sympathy for you, though."

Vera did her best to tamp down the embarrassment she felt, too. She didn't have much success.

"Wait," said Ashlyn. "Osyrus's machines might be able to breathe for a person—and I know that he's an advanced healer—but how did Kira survive those injuries in the first place? She should be dead."

"That's the other thing that you need to know." Vera took a breath. Tried to think of the best way to explain. "Kira has carried the Malgrave name all of her life, but it doesn't belong to her. Not completely."

"What are you talking about?" Bershad asked, frowning. Confused. But Ashlyn saw it almost immediately.

"Hertzog isn't her father," Vera said.

"What?" he asked. "Then who is?"

"Leon Bershad," Ashlyn said, almost to herself. "Her father is Leon Bershad."

Vera nodded.

"She's my . . ." Bershad trailed off. "Sister?"

"And she's like you. *That's* how she survived. But she needs to be freed from Ward's machines."

Bershad swallowed. Seemed to recover from his shock. Then he started digging into the pouch on his hip.

"If she's like me, then that's gonna be a real straightforward thing to do."

He pulled out a handful of moss with bright blue flowers growing from it.

"No, I've tried giving her moss already."

"Not this kind," said Bershad. "It's called—"

"Gods Moss," Vera finished. "I know what it is, Silas. And I made Kira eat a nugget the size of a sparrow's egg. It was only a temporary solution. Osyrus says that he was forced to suppress her healing because of some transformation that could occur. I thought he was lying, but didn't want to risk it."

"He's not lying," Ashlyn said, with a pained look in her eyes.

"But that means . . ." She turned to Silas. "You, too?"

Bershad nodded.

"I'm sorry, Silas. Truly."

Bershad shrugged. "I'm used to death sentences. But I appreciate the sympathy."

Vera swallowed. "Osyrus is trying other methods to heal her. He says that Kira will recover in time."

"Maybe she will, but he'll never allow that to happen," said Ashlyn. "People like Silas and Kira are too valuable to him, and she's far easier to manipulate if she cannot move or breathe on her own."

"Yeah, I've figured that much out on my own." Vera swallowed. "I didn't really come here for the food. I needed a way to get that skyship under my complete control. Seeing as you killed the two Ghalamarian officers, I have it."

"Why do you want a skyship?"

"I believe that the alchemists have more information about Seeds than Osyrus Ward lets on. And I believe that information can help me heal Kira. I explored the archives in Pargos once, last spring, but didn't find anything. There must be another location."

"There is," said Ashlyn.

That pricked up Vera's attention. "You're sure?"

Ashlyn nodded. "Okinu once stole records from the alchemists. It was many years ago, but they contained information about Seeds, along with many other secrets that the alchemists are hiding from the world."

"Where was this archive?" Vera asked.

"I'm not sure. Somewhere in Pargos."

"That's not any better than what I already know," said Vera. Although she supposed there was some value in knowing that she was on the right path. "Even with a skyship, if I need to go searching city by city, this will take a long time. And every day that I am away from Kira, her life is in more danger."

"Kira's my sister," Ashlyn said. "I would help you if I could, but I don't know where the archives are. Okinu never told me." Ashlyn went quiet. Seemed to be searching her mind for something. "But I do remember the name of an alchemist who specialized in spinal injuries. She came up in a number of records that I acquired while I was researching the spines of Ghost Moth dragons. Her studies were focused on humans—how our nervous systems bind to bone and tissue—so it didn't help me. But she was clearly a pioneer."

"What's her name?"

Ashlyn paused again, thinking. "Caellan."

"Any idea where she might be?"

Ashlyn shook her head. "I'm sorry, I wish I could help you more."

"A name helps. Thank you." She paused. Looked at the food. "Is this enough for you to keep fighting?"

"Yes," said Bershad.

"Good." Vera looked to the east. "We nearly died coming in here. I have no idea how we're going to get out."

Bershad smiled. "I can help you with that, actually. Us being old friends and all."

———

They followed the Gray-Winged Nomad's path through the horde of Blackjacks. Nobody spoke, as if a single word could break the spell and send all the dragons upon them.

When they were through, the Nomad tilted her wings and rose high into the sky, disappearing.

"Well, that little trick works a whole lot better than Ward's piece-of-shit machine," Entras said.

"How long to Burz-al-dun?" Vera asked him.

"Hard to say, but it's not gonna be quick," Entras warned. "Calling this ship overloaded is a massive understatement. Right now I'm more worried about having enough fuel to cross the Soul Sea at all than I am about arriving in a timely fashion."

"Just give me a range, Entras. I've been awake for three days. I want to know how long I can sleep for."

"Ah, got it." He frowned. "We're riding a decent wind up the coast right now. That'll get us to Glenlock, then we peel off and cross the Soul Sea . . ." He stopped to chew on his lip. "Twenty-three hours, at least."

"Thank you," Vera said.

That was enough time for decent drink *and* a good night's sleep.

Vera went down to the galley—which was now packed with rice and meat—and found a jug of chilled juniper liquor. Poured herself a glass, twisted a lime into it, and took one big gulp followed by small sips. The warmth on her throat and the buzz in her head felt good.

She lit her pipe. Sat for a while, smoking and drinking and trying to relax.

Garret showed up about ten minutes later.

"I came for a drink," he said.

Vera used her pipe to point at the jug of juniper liquor. "Help yourself."

Garret nodded. Came into the galley and poured himself a glass. She noticed that he squeezed a far larger portion of lime juice than she had.

"Don't like juniper liquor?" she asked.

"I prefer rain ale."

"Rain ale?"

"They only make it in Deepdale. Brewed from jungle rain and forest hops, or so I was told. There's a tavern called the Jaguar's Mask that served a good brew."

"How is it that you've been drinking in Deepdale with a war on?"

"This was earlier. For a different job."

"Have anything to do with why that young warden was so intent on running his sword through your back?"

"No." He gave her a look. "That was because of something your empress hired me to do."

"You worked for Okinu?"

"Yes."

Vera was surprised, but realized she shouldn't have been. Okinu had always been a pragmatic person when it came to removing troublesome obstacles. There were plenty of places where a widow would stand out, but Garret wouldn't.

"You work for Osyrus Ward. You've worked for the empress of

Papyria. And it sounds like there's a long list of lords who've used you to do their dirty work. Were you royalty or something?"

"Why do you ask that?"

"I'm wondering how you wound up under the employ of such noteworthy people. The youngest son of a baron with a penchant for danger might have managed to carve this kind of life out for himself."

"My father wasn't a baron."

"How did you wind up in this life, then?"

"How'd you wind up in yours?"

Vera took a long drag from her pipe. Blew it out.

"Before a widow can retire, she must select a replacement. I was chosen by a widow named Sunsu-Ka."

"Don't tell me they give you some test of bravery or something."

Vera shook her head.

"Sunsu came to my village one morning. Didn't say a thing, just visited each household with a young girl. Stared at them. Us. Before she left, she killed my family's goat with a shot from her sling."

Vera paused, remembering.

"I'd raised that goat from birth. She was my responsibility. So, I followed Sunsu through the village with a sharpened rock and threw it at her temple when I thought she was distracted. But widows are never distracted. She caught it. Threw it back at me and knocked me unconscious. When I woke up, I was on a ship heading for Roriku Island, where Papyrian girls are turned into widows."

"How old were you?"

"Ten."

Garret took a drink. Didn't say anything.

"You aren't going to tell me about yourself, are you?" Vera pressed.

"What does it matter?" Garret asked. "I might have been a butcher's son or an orphaned street urchin. A conscripted soldier or the disgraced member of some traveling theatre troupe. Whatever I was before, this is what I've become."

He drained his glass.

"I believe my actions are all connected, though, even if their origin is inconsequential. The first man I killed is tied to that warden who tried to kill me in the jungle. And I am tied to them. Always."

Vera raised an eyebrow. "That juniper liquor works fast on you, huh?"

He gave her a confused look, then a small nod when he understood.

"Another?" he asked.

"Sure."

Garret poured her drink and returned it to her. They both drank a while in silence.

"Something's been bothering me," Vera said eventually.

"Okay."

"Why did you really volunteer to come with us?"

He sipped his drink.

"The Jaguars are running out of food. That skyship crashed in their territory with enough rations to prolong this war for months. I figured there was a chance they'd get wind of it. And if they did, they'd send their best warriors to collect."

"Bershad and the Skojit?"

He nodded.

"Guess you missed out on a lot of gold," she said. "Sorry."

He shrugged. "Those bounties no longer interest me."

"Why not?"

Garret leaned back in his chair. "Last year, there was a job that I left unfinished. I have the opportunity to rectify that."

"Can't abide a loose end?"

"Exactly."

Vera decided not to press him. She took a sip of her drink. Thought of Kira.

"You're happy about something," Garret said. "What is it?"

"I found something that I needed today. A name."

"What name?"

Vera paused. Maybe it was the juniper liquor. Maybe she was starting to trust Garret a little bit. Or maybe it was because when they got to Burz-al-dun, she knew that she might need to kill him. And she wanted him to know why.

"Caellan. She's an alchemist."

"To help your empress?"

"That's right."

Garret nodded. Drained his drink and stood up. "Terra's a large realm to go hunting for one specific person. A skyship would help. Too bad this one's bound back for Floodhaven once we're done in Burz-al-dun."

Vera finished her pipe. Tapped the ashes out against her boot.

"Yeah. Too bad."

24

ASHLYN
Inside the Eternity

As the blue skyship disappeared over the horizon, Bershad took Ashlyn's hand.

"If Vera had offered, I might have gotten in that skyship with you and sailed away from this whole mess," he said.

"Where would we go?" she asked, rubbing his palm with her thumb.

"Beyond Taggarstan. Far as we could fly. When the skyship ran outta fuel, we'd find a hidden, quiet place for you and me to live. Just us."

"What about the Nomad?"

Bershad smiled. "She could come, too. You'd need something to draw. Wouldn't want the witch queen getting bored in her retirement."

Ashlyn smiled. "It sounds perfect, Silas."

They were quiet for a moment. Ashlyn thought of that imaginary, quiet place. Then she thought of the things she'd seen Osyrus do on Ghost Moth Island. The things he was doing still in Floodhaven.

"But we can't run away just yet."

"No," Bershad agreed. "Not yet."

They turned back to the crashed skyship, where the wardens were already loading sacks of rice and dried meat onto the donkeys. Jolan emerged from the wreckage and came sprinting up to them with a flushed face.

"Ashe," he huffed. "I found something you need to see."

As they were following Jolan back into the ship, they ran into Felgor and Cabbage, both of whom had their arms full of Balarian machinery. Felgor was carrying some kind of navigational globe that was wreathed in numbers, complex machinery, and moving parts.

"Where did you get that?" Ashlyn asked.

"This?" Felgor asked, all innocence. "It was just lying around one of the cabins."

"Which cabin?"

"Uh, one of the big ones near the front."

"That would be the main bridge?"

"Could be."

"What are your plans for them, exactly?"

"Sell 'em. That's obvious."

"How is that obvious?" Bershad asked.

"Because if idiot collectors will pay five hundred gold for beat-to-shit breastplates from some forgotten war a hundred years past, they are for sure going to want skyship crap when all this is over. And I've mentioned my concerns that you don't intend to pay me the rather large sum of gold I'm already owed due to my heroic efforts and intelligence gathering. So I've been forced to scrounge."

"Felgor, you don't even know what those do," said Ashlyn. "At least let me—"

"Queen Ashlyn," pressed Jolan, with an uncommon amount of urgency in his voice. "There's a living acolyte in the wreckage."

Ashlyn's pulse quickened. She forgot about Felgor immediately. "Show me."

Jolan led them to the skyship's engine room. The main power source—which Ward called the Kor in his schematics—was still pulsing with the dim light that Ashlyn's dragon thread used to carry. There were four acolytes connected to it by wires and tubes. Three were dead. But the fourth was twitching weakly from its crumpled spot in the corner of the room. One eye was open and staring back at them, the other had melted.

"I've seen a bunch of the Madman's weird shit," said Simeon, who was in the chamber along with Kerrigan. "But this one's near the top of the list. The fuck is it?"

"A ballast acolyte," Ashlyn said. "They were described in the documents Felgor stole. Ward uses them to prevent the skyship Kors from overheating during long flights."

Jolan already had the diagnostic tool connected to the back of the acolyte's neck. He held up the opposite wire to her. "I figured you'd want a look."

Ashlyn plugged the wire into the port on her arm. Nodded at Jolan.

He cranked the diagnostic coils until the gears were fully tightened, then released.

The transfer of information came in a series of pricks against the lodestones in Ashlyn's bands. When they'd first started using the tool back in the Deepdale castle, Jolan needed to run the diagnostic dozens of times before Ashlyn could decipher the orientations they projected, but after so many hours of practice, she had no trouble visualizing the acolyte's system immediately.

"I recognize the general arrangement," she said. "It's similar to what Ward uses in the spines of the war acolytes."

Ashlyn frowned as the diagnostic continued to unwind. There was something else, too. A second loop that was running in tandem with the first, except this one was constantly shifting and morphing. She'd never felt that before in any of the spines she'd tried to breach in Deepdale castle.

"Run it again, please," Ashlyn said when the diagnostic finished. "I want to try something."

Jolan cranked and released. This time, Ashlyn focused on the secondary loop. It was tightly woven against the first, almost like a braid. As gently as possible, Ashlyn spun up a single magnetic tendril from her bands and used it to give the loop a soft pull, like plucking the string of a harp.

The diagnostic tool started to omit a series of taps in a different, but clear pattern. "I'm getting a lot of feedback all of a sudden," Jolan said, listening while the diagnostic completed its cycle. "It's additional information of some kind, but the diagnostic isn't designed to parse it."

"There's a second loop," Ashlyn said. "It's a lot more dynamic than the first one, which will make it harder to follow, but it leads directly into the acolyte's brain."

"But we've run the diagnostic against dozens of spinal loops," Jolan said. "Why is this the first time we're seeing this?"

"We've never run it against a loop that was connected to a living acolyte." Ashlyn paused. "If the second loop shuts off when the acolyte dies, that would block further access and ensure nothing of high value can be salvaged."

"Sounds like something Osyrus Ward would do," said Bershad.

"So we've been wasting our time for months?" Jolan asked.

"Not at all," Ashlyn said. "Those failures led to building the diagnostic and the kill switch. Now that we've found a path forward, we have the tools to walk down it."

"I'm not sure we're ready to do anything without a way to properly visualize the data that's coming through."

Ashlyn chewed her lip, trying to figure something out. "Run it again."

The machine rattled off another long series of clicks that came in four distinct groups.

"Hear the pattern? They sound like Pargossian coordinates, which start in the north, then move east to south to west. That was four points north, seven points east, nine points south, and eleven points west. Then it repeats."

"All I hear are a bunch o' fucking clicks," said Simeon.

"It's a spiral," Ashlyn said, ignoring him. "I think I can use that guidance to breach the loop. That's what I was missing at Fallon's Roost. If I can't adjust with the dynamic shift, the whole system backfires."

"You're making a lot of assumptions," said Jolan. "If he's using Papyrian coordinates, it starts in the south, and moves in the opposite direction."

"Ward hates Papyrians, and he was trained as an alchemist in Pargos. No, he'd have used the Pargossian system."

"Even if you're right about that, the control it will take to wind that precise of a loop is incredibly high," Jolan said.

Ashlyn pulled off her poncho.

"I can do it."

"But even the smallest mistake will—"

"Oh, for fuck's sake, Jolan. That thing is about to die. No time to argue."

Ashlyn filled her bands with current, and guided her five lodestones above the injured acolyte. Then she ramped up the bands on her fingertips, which controlled the fine-tuned movements, and started weaving her magnetic strand between the two loops, using the imagined shape of the spiral as her guide.

It worked perfectly. All the resistance she'd felt trying to barge her way through the dead acolyte spines in the castle was gone. This felt like threading a sharp needle through a piece of silk.

She wove her way up the acolyte's spine and into its brain, completing the loop.

The acolyte jerked upright at the intrusion. Its eyelids started fluttering like moth wings. She felt it attempt to trigger a backfire, but now that she was completely intertwined in the loop, all she had to do was squeeze a little to make the twitching acolyte freeze.

She smiled at Jolan. "See?"

"I can't believe you did that. You could have killed us all."

"But I didn't."

If she wanted to, Ashlyn could rip her strand back out, stripping the lodestones of their orientations so she could add them to her arm bands. But now that she controlled the spine, she could feel another lodestone embedded in the acolyte's brain. It didn't feel like it was part of a loop, exactly, but there was something odd about it. A level of complexity she'd never felt before.

Without thinking, she filled the strange lodestone with current.

The pupil of the acolyte's undamaged eye dilated. Its body stiffened.

"Awaiting command," it said.

"What the fuck?" Simeon growled.

"Invalid command."

"I'll tear your head off, you gray-skinned asshole."

"Invalid command."

Simeon stepped forward. "If you say that one more—"

Ashlyn pulled back on the current. The acolyte's pupil shrank and its body relaxed.

"Everyone except for Jolan needs to leave this room," she said.

Nobody moved. Ashlyn pointed toward the door.

"Right now."

Kerrigan shrugged and left. Simeon did the same, but muttered a few curses under his breath for good measure.

"You too, Silas. I need as little distraction as possible."

Silas smiled. "I'd hate to be a distraction."

He kissed her on the forehead and left.

"So, what's the plan?" Jolan asked.

"It's responding to verbal commands," said Ashlyn. "I'm going to power it up again, and we're going to see what's possible."

Jolan nodded. "Let's do it."

Ashlyn filled the lodestone with power again.

"Awaiting command," the acolyte said.

Ashlyn tried to think of a place to start. Something simple.

"Raise your right arm."

"Invalid command."

She frowned. "Describe your purpose."

"Invalid command."

Jolan raised his hand to show that he wanted to try something. Cleared his throat.

"List available commands."

"Visual diagnostic. Mobility diagnostic. Remote connection. Manual override."

Ashlyn smiled. Gave Jolan a nod of support.

"Execute visual diagnostic," Ashlyn said.

"Accepted."

The acolyte blinked five times in rapid succession.

"Optics operating at fifty percent capacity. Maintenance required."

That made sense.

"Execute mobility diagnostic."

"Accepted."

The acolyte's legs jerked and strained, but there was too much damage for it to stand up.

"Command failed. Multiple fractures detected."

Ashlyn figured she might as well try everything. Get a feel for the system.

"Execute remote connection."

"Accepted."

The acolyte sat motionless for a moment.

"Command failed. No viable port."

Ashlyn wasn't sure what that meant, but she didn't want to waste time on it now.

"Manual override."

"Submit access key."

Ashlyn felt another pathway in the lodestone open. When she probed it, Jolan's diagnostic started a rapid series of taps.

"They're Pargossian coordinates again," Jolan said. "But there are a *lot* more of them. And they're constantly changing. It's not a repeating signal, the shape of each spiral rotation is unique."

Ashlyn nodded. "I want to try and run it. This may be our only chance. Read them out as they change."

"I'll do my best."

Jolan started to read off the coordinates, which shifted so fast that Ashlyn was forced to use all of her available bands to keep up. She started to sweat from the heat her arm was generating. Felt her mouth go dry.

"Fifteen degrees north," Jolan said. "Two hundred and three degrees east, and, um . . . hold on, no that's not right . . . two hundred and *five* degrees east, seventeen south, ninety-four west."

Ashlyn adjusted her bands to follow his guidance, but she was met with a huge and sudden amount of negative energy.

"Incorrect key. System purge commencing."

"Shit."

Ashlyn felt the familiar feeling of a backfire brewing, so she ripped her strand out of the acolyte's spinal loop, stripping the orientation, and activated her kill switch, which severed the connection between her bands and the dragon thread.

As soon as the risk of a backfire was gone, she started shifting her bands through the unlocking sequence.

"We'll try again as soon as I finish this," she said.

"Um. Ashlyn?"

"I'm going as fast as I can, just give me—"

"Ashlyn, I think it's dead."

She looked up. The creature's head was lolled to one side.

She finished the unlocking sequence anyway and tested the loop. Nothing.

She sighed. "We lost it. Damn."

Jolan pulled the diagnostic out of the acolyte.

"I think I was right the first time," he said as he coiled the wire. "Two hundred and three degrees east, not five. Sorry."

"It's not your fault. Like you said, the diagnostic was never meant to parse that much information."

"I wish we'd seen what was behind that last command, though. If Ward put that much security behind the manual override, it might be the vulnerability we've been searching for."

"I agree," said Ashlyn. Although she didn't want to think about how they'd manage to get another living acolyte in such a vulnerable position. Finding this one had been pure luck.

She glanced at Jolan. Saw the miserable look on his face. He was still blaming himself.

"This was a huge breakthrough, Jolan."

"But we don't have anything concrete from it."

"Not true. I cleared the acolyte's spinal loop on my way out." She reached into the acolyte's neck and pulled out the first lodestone, which had a platinum rod drilled through the middle of it. "That means we can finally add more bands to my arm. I'm interested to see what this platinum rod does."

"I'll start on it right away," Jolan said, eager for something to do.

"Let's get out of this dragon-infested jungle, first. We have a lot of hungry wardens waiting for us."

25

ACOLYTE 799
Location Unknown

There was enemy brain matter on Acolyte 799's hands. He did not know how it got there.

"Fuck, but I love having an acolyte on patrol," came a voice. "Seven-Nine-Nine turned those wardens to jelly."

Acolyte 799 turned. Saw a man in black armor and red face paint.

Red faces mean Wormwrot. Wormwrot are tools for victory. Allies.

The thought came to him from nowhere and everywhere at once. A truth that was core and fundamental to his being. There was no way to deny it. That would be like denying the existence of the sun, or the wisdom of his master, Osyrus Ward.

Another Wormwrot came around. Peered at him. Lieutenant Pellin was his name. Acolyte 799 remembered.

"You all right?" Pellin asked him.

A question. Acolyte 799 hated questions. Questions needed answers. Wrong answers meant pain. He decided to ignore it. Make his own question.

"Where is the enemy?"

"None left. You tore 'em to pieces. We got a shitload of masks to turn in for bounties. All that's left now is to march ourselves to the extraction point, get home, then collect our coin."

"Extraction," Acolyte 799 repeated. "Right."

Pellin frowned. "You sure you're all right? You seem a little . . . off."

Weakness in front of Wormwrot is not acceptable.

"Worry about your men, Lieutenant. Not me."

Pellin nodded. "Sure thing." He pointed east. "We've been out here for three days, so the extraction is at Greenbelt Knoll. Eleven leagues that way."

"Maybe we'll run into the Flawless Bershad on the way and get a *real* bounty," said a Wormwrot private.

"Don't even joke about that," Pellin responded.

———

They marched. Acolyte 799 took comfort in the routine of walking. One step. Then another. Then another.

Between each footfall, his thoughts drifted to that name. Bershad. Acolyte 799 had seen him. He was sure of it. But where? When?

No questions! Questions need answers. Wrong answers mean pain.

He shook his head. Pushed the thoughts away.

"Hey, Coller, where'd you get those boots?" asked the Wormwrot private.

"The fuck you care where I got 'em?" Coller responded.

"Because yours ain't soaked through and half-ruined like mine. I want a pair."

"You're screwed on that front, my friend."

"Why?"

"Poor bastard named Rigar made these for me. And he's dead."

Rigar. That name. Rigar. Rigar. Rigar. Why is that so familiar?

"Too bad. I'd have parted with a lot of coin for some decent footwear. How'd he go?"

"Ugly."

"Everyone goes ugly in this war. I mean how, exactly?"

"Way I heard it, his whole unit got torn apart by the fucking Skojit who wears white dragonscale armor."

Acolyte 799 froze.

Skojit. White armor.

"Thought that story was dragonshit?"

"Naw. The Skojit's real. Intelligence confirmed it a while back. Think his name's Sormon or Simon or something like that."

Simeon. His name is Simeon.

Acolyte 799's muscles clenched. Tightened. He couldn't move. Couldn't breathe.

Coller paused. Looked back at him. "Uh, what's up with the acolyte?"

Everyone looked at him. But Acolyte 799 still couldn't move. His mind was flooded with the vision of a red-haired man. A head exploding. Pain. Pain. Pain. He knew Simeon, but who was Rigar?

Acolyte 799 fell over. Started twitching in the mud. Couldn't stop.

Coller laughed. "Appears the Madman gave us a dud, Lieutenant."

Pellin came over. "I knew there was something wrong with it."

"He killed Jaguars without trouble," said Coller. "How's it that he can't handle a march?"

"You're asking the wrong person. But we gotta get him to the extraction."

"These fuckers weigh more than three men in full armor. Why bother? Let's just leave it here and get a new one when we get back to Floodhaven."

"Because any unit that loses an acolyte and lives to tell about it has to give one of their own to the Madman."

"What? Why?"

"Replacement, you idiot."

Coller cursed. Looked around.

"C'mon. We'll cut down some of these vines and drag him along. Watch out for snakes."

PART II

26

VERA
Balaria, Burz-al-dun

Vera stayed aboard the *Blue Sparrow* while Decimar and his men unloaded the rations. She kept an eye out for trouble in the crowd who'd gathered around them, but there were no signs of a fomenting riot or a fight over the food. That surprised Vera, especially given the hungry and gaunt faces that were looking up at her from the ground. Maybe they were simply too weak to fight back.

When the food was fully dispersed, Vera motioned to Decimar and his men. They all took up positions around the deck where they had clear shots on Garret and the remaining Ghalamarians. When everything was set, she stepped forward.

"There are two ways that your time in my service can end," she said. "The first is with an arrow through your heart in the next ten seconds."

That got everyone's attention. She saw a few men's throats bob with rough swallows. Hands moved to swords, but no farther. They'd seen the longbowmen work. At this range, and this outnumbered, drawing steel was an obvious death sentence.

"Think we're all a bit interested in the second version," said a blond-haired man. Vera had never learned his name.

"All of you disarm and get off this ship. Then you head home to Ghalamar. You do not identify yourselves as soldiers ever again, and you do not ever speak of what you saw in the Dainwood."

One man with a thick black beard winced. "How many times am I gonna drop my fucking weapon this week 'cause o' some cunt's command?"

Decimar drew his bow. Aimed it at the bearded man.

"At least once more, if you want to see the end of this week at all," he said.

The blond man took a long breath. Spoke loud enough for everyone to hear.

"Seeing as our officers have both had their skulls hollowed, I believe we're all obliged to decide for ourselves on this." He moved his hand from the grip of his sword to the cross guard, then pulled the weapon out of his belt without unsheathing it. Dropped it on the deck. "Personally, I am going the fuck home. Never wanted a part in this war, anyway."

With that, he threw a leg over the gunwale and hopped onto the ground below. The rest of the men took a varying amount of time to come to the same conclusion, but they all got there.

All except for Garret, who stayed motionless near the middle of the ship.

Decimar shifted his aim. "You choosing the first option, Hangman?"

"I would like to speak with Vera alone for a moment."

"No chance," said Decimar.

Garret ignored him. Kept his gray eyes on her. She saw more emotion in him than she was used to. And she knew from experience that if he meant her harm, she'd have seen nothing there at all.

"It's all right, Decimar. We'll speak." She motioned to the cabin at the stern of the *Sparrow*. "In there."

———

The royal cabin of the *Sparrow* had changed since they'd used it to escape Burz-al-dun last year. All the plush sofas and lounge furniture had been replaced with fletching stations for the archers to make new arrows. Garret moved to a simple bench. Sat down.

"You saved my life back in the jungle," he said. "I would like to know why. Given what you're planning to do, it would have been easier for you if I was dead."

"The truth?" Vera shrugged. "Instinct."

"I see."

"Disappointed?"

"The opposite."

"Are we back to that whole pride-in-my-skills thing?"

"Not exactly. I owe you a debt, Vera. I would like to settle it now. Somehow, I think it's unlikely you and I will meet again. Not as allies, anyway."

"You plan on returning to Almira?"

"As I said, I have unfinished business there."

Vera knew that Garret was a murderer by trade. But so was she. In that moment, Vera found that she had no desire to kill him.

"Well, if you leave the ship without a fight, we'll call that square."

"I need to do that anyway if I don't want Decimar's arrow through my skull."

"True."

"But I do have something that will settle our debt." He paused. "Seven years ago, there was a job floating around Burz-al-dun that was offered through a broker. It didn't take much investigation to learn the actual client was the Royal Engineer of Balaria."

"Osyrus Ward."

"Yes. The task he wanted done was simple. Travel to Pargos and murder a woman named Caellan."

Vera's stomach dropped. "You killed her."

"I didn't take the job. There was something a little more challenging on offer at the time."

"But she might still be dead."

"Maybe. Although I ran into the man who took the contract a few months later. He went looking for her, but never found her."

"Where did he look?"

"The contract directed him to a little village in southern Pargos. He said it was all olive trees and clear lakes."

"Garret. *Where is Caellan?*"

Garret smiled. "In all the work we've done together, that's the first time I've seen you lose your composure. Your feelings for the empress weaken you. Watch out for that."

Vera didn't say anything. Maybe he was right, but if killing all your emotions was what it took to survive, Vera didn't see a point in living at all.

"The village is called Nisena."

"Nisena," Vera repeated. "Thank you."

Garret stood.

"The man who went after her wasn't as good as me, but he was skilled. I never knew him to botch a job, besides that one." He gave her a look. "But you are better than him by a significant margin."

Vera nodded.

"I'll tell Osyrus Ward that I killed you. Good luck, Vera. I hope that you find what you're looking for."

27

NOLA
City of Deepdale, the Swine Pens

The leader of the Ghost Cat Gang was a skinny, terrifying man named Elondron.

The grime and scars and lines on his face made him look to be about forty, but Nola knew for a fact he wasn't a summer past twenty-five. Those twenty-five years had just been filled with rough living and a commonplace sort of violence that came with running a Deepdale gang of criminals.

He was carrying four knives that Nola could see. Butchering tools. All of them within easy reach of his twitchy, grease-blackened fingers.

"So, you want a pig," he said.

"Yes."

"Swine's in high demand, these days. I'm sure you heard that the supply ships are having a little bit of trouble delivering food now that they've been turned to splinters."

"I'm aware."

"And I got eleven other people in the market for a piggy today. Meaning they ain't going cheap."

"Nothing does, these days. But I can pay."

Elondron narrowed his eyes. "How much?"

There was no way to avoid making the opening bid. Not while Elondron and his gang had all the pigs and were holding all the knives and Lord Bershad and his wardens were nowhere to be found in the city streets. But that didn't mean that Nola had to be stupid about it.

She pulled out a pouch of coin—held it for a moment like it was all the money of hers in the world—and then tossed it forward.

"Fifty silvers," she said.

That was half the silver she'd earned from the last few weeks at the tavern, and five times what a pig was worth under normal circumstances. But the circumstances weren't normal. She'd fucked over Kellar for that piece of paku. Fucked over the Papyrian sisters for the rice wine. And now it was her turn to get fucked over.

Wasn't fair. It was just reality.

"Now, where did a young girl like you get her grubby hands on fifty silvers?"

"Since when do the Ghost Cats care about the source of coin that's dropped before them?"

"Hm."

Nola could see him bending. He'd raise her bid up a little—sixty or seventy—for appearance's sake, but not much more. She'd squeeze by without having to barter any of her more valuable supplies, and make triple off that pig inside of a week. Bacon rashers would sell faster than a Red Skull can kill sheep in an open field.

But then one of Elondron's goons stepped up behind him. "That girl owns the Cat's Eye, boss."

A spark of greed lit up behind Elondron's cold eyes. Nola's heart sank.

"A tavern, is it?" he asked, turning to her.

Shit. Shit. Shit.

"That's right," Nola said.

"How is it that a little whelp like you owns a tavern?"

"My three brothers built the place. Ran it for years. But when the wars started up again, they unhooked their masks from the walls and fought for the Dainwood."

Nola took a long turn glaring at each of the men in the room. A few kept their stupid greedy grins up, but most had the decency to be embarrassed. They were all men of a fighting age, but they'd chosen crime over defending their homeland.

"They dead, then?" Elondron asked.

That grinning idiot had pushed her into this fix, but Nola wasn't stupid enough to dig herself deeper.

"Fighting alongside Lord Bershad himself, last I heard."

"Ah, see, there's your mistake. Little too big of a lie, there, all three of them still alive and fighting in this war. One, maybe. Two, possible. But all three? Naw." Elondron spat. "I think your brothers are all ten leagues down the river, which is too bad for you, because you seem like a savvy girl. Savvy enough to still be squeezing silver out of your tavern when there's barely any food left in this shit heap of a city. And I'd imagine that makes you smart enough to know that a tavern without any warden brothers coming back to claim it is very . . . interesting to a businessman like myself."

"You're not a businessman," said Nola. "You're a criminal. Now are you selling me this pig or not?"

"You can have the pig. Free of charge."

"There's nothing free in this world except the seashell that takes you down the river."

"Fair. Let's call it one silver, then." Elondron stood up. Rested his hands on the knives at his hip. "And permission to sell my other wares out of your tavern."

"Wares? You hawking pottery or something?"

"Black sticky," Elondron said, face serious. "Salvaged a whole crateful from a skyship that crashed on the rim of the valley."

Nola stood up, too. Grabbed her coin. There was no chance that she was going to let a slimy criminal like Elondron worm one of his little tentacles into her tavern. It starts with a little sticky in the back and it ends with her owning less than the dirt on the opium den floor they'd turn the Cat's Eye into.

"Forget it."

"Hey, now. No need to start canceling the whole deal. We're negotiating, right? You let us run our sticky through your tavern, you don't just get the one pig. You get one each week. *And* you get our protection."

"I don't need protection. Lord Cuspar owns a stake in my place."

"Cuspar? That bastard's the biggest leech in Deepdale. Not a man known for offering up anything other than an open palm, waiting to get filled with someone else's coin."

"All the same, I'm not interested in new partners or weekly swine."

Nola headed for the door, but two of Elondron's men moved to block it.

"We can do this the easy way," said Elondron. "Which is with a handshake agreement that benefits the both of us, or we can do it the hard way, which involves you leaving this room with a lot fewer teeth than you walked in with."

Nola turned around.

"So, you're the kind of criminals who hoard pigs and beat the shit out of girls so you can sell opium in new places?"

"Please. Nobody told you to show up at our doorstep today trying to make this deal. You could have waited in the scrap line along with everyone else. But *you* wanted to be the tavern with a pig. You wanted the profit."

Nola dug her fingernails into her palm hard enough to draw blood. Tried to think of a way to improve her situation, but failed. Truth was, law and order in Deepdale was hanging on by a very thin thread, and while Elondron and his gang couldn't quite sell their opium in the street, there was definitely nobody stopping them from tuning her up real good and getting away with it.

"A pig a week?" she asked.

"Guaranteed."

"How many pigs did your little gang steal, exactly?"

Elondron smiled. "Oh, don't worry. We got enough to keep your customers in bacon until the Balarians cut through the great lizards and kill us all."

Nola chewed on that a little longer. If it was just her, she might think about taking her silver and disappearing into the Gloom. Leave this rotten city to eat itself from the inside. But she couldn't risk that with Grittle. Couldn't risk watching a Blackjack swoop down and eat her sister because she was too afraid to get her hands dirty.

"Deal."

28

BERSHAD
Dainwood Jungle

After they returned from the skyship crash, the leaders of the Jaguar Army met on a ridge overlooking the Daintree grove where the rest of the army had camped. Below, Bershad could hear wardens laughing, joking, and—most importantly—eating their fill of the rations they'd delivered.

"This is the best food I've ever tasted," Willem said, putting down his spent bowl of rice and beans and pork. He'd been raiding Wormwrot patrols to the north, and had just rotated back through the camp the day before Bershad and the others had returned. "How do you Dunfarians get so much flavor in the swine?" he asked Kerrigan.

Kerrigan smiled. "That's a Dunfarian secret."

"I'd like to know why I was denied my request for a second wedge of cheese," Simeon said, scooping up the remains of his beans and rice with a chunk of flatbread.

"Because you're allergic to it," said Kerrigan. "Your farts damnnear killed us when you ate the first one."

"But a small wedge would be—"

"No!" Willem, Ashlyn, and Jolan all said at once.

"Fine, fine. Assholes." He scratched at the side of his neck.

"You should enjoy the food you *can* digest," said Kerrigan. "We're all going back on strict rations starting tomorrow. Need to make this food last as long as possible."

"How long will that be?" Willem asked.

"All the way through autumn, so long as nobody cheats." She took a bite of rice. "For the time being, our ration problem is solved."

"Which just leaves the whole 'destroying a far larger army in possession of flying ships' problem to contend with," said Oromir.

"I actually might have some ideas there," said Willem. "We had a little discovery while you lot were gone. Turns out those maps Felgor stole are more than just a list of locations."

Willem took out a map and spread it across the ground. Weighed the edges down with tiny rocks.

"It took a while to figure it out, but the Balarians are pairing drop-offs and extractions together based on time. Extractions always come three, six, or nine days after drop-off. The men work their way to whichever location is attached to the day. For example, if Wormwrot gets dropped off here, the extraction is here three days out, here six, and here nine."

"Why bother with something so complex?" Simeon asked.

"I wouldn't call that complex," Oromir said. "And you know how the clock fuckers love time and all that shit."

"Once again, I take offense to that term," Felgor said, using a silver fork to shove a huge bite of smoked pork into his mouth.

"Felgor, where did you get that fork?" Bershad asked.

"Won it."

"Won it how?" Bershad asked.

"Cheating at dice."

"Of course you did, Felgor."

"Anyway," Willem cut in. "To answer Simeon's question, they do it so the Wormwrot patrols always know where to go for the extraction ahead of time without needing to communicate with command. Once you know the pairings, they're pretty easy to follow."

"How many have you figured out so far?" Bershad asked.

"About half. And I have scouts all over the jungle mapping the rest. But here's the real beauty: a skyship comes to each extraction location regardless of whether the patrol is there to be taken out of the jungle. And each time, they're expecting to find a group of Wormwrot in red face paint."

"You wanna do it the same way we got into Blackrock to steal that skyship," Oromir said. "Disguised."

"Yeah. Except this time we don't need to sneak through a whole city and fortress and climb up an anchor wire. We just need a quick way to destroy the skyship and get out again." He turned to Ashlyn. "I was hoping our witch queen could help us out there."

Everyone looked to Ashlyn.

"I could do that," she said. "But it won't be enough."

"Why not?" Willem asked.

"Because Ashlyn can only be in one place at a time," said Kerrigan. "If this is going to work, we need to be hitting skyships all over the Dainwood within a pretty tight timeframe. If we rely on her alone, Ward will rebuild the fleet faster than we can wreck it."

Ashlyn nodded. "Exactly."

"A score of wardens storming those ships have piss-poor odds of success," said Willem. "We might take down one or two in every ten we attack, but the rest'll be shredded by the grayskin that's aboard every ship."

There was a silence.

"I can solve that problem," said Jolan. He removed a copper orb from his pack and placed it on top of the map. There were wires sprouting from the top like the leaves of a beet. "Wardens don't need to go into the ships at all. Just this."

"What is it?" Simeon said, squinting at it.

"For weeks, I've been trying to find another use for the salvage we took from all the dead acolytes," Jolan said. "I finally found a way to trigger a reaction based on the collapsing of gears around the blasting powder we pulled from the artificial heart ventricles, which—"

"What kind of a reaction, kid?" said Bershad.

Jolan licked his lips. "An explosion. Not a huge one, mind you. But in an enclosed space, it should be powerful enough to cripple a skyship."

"How many of these do you have?" Willem asked.

"Right now? Two. But if we send someone back to Deepdale to get the rest of the salvage and bring it to Dampmire, I can make more. A lot more."

"That's not a problem," said Willem. "And while you build more of those orbs, we'll finish the mapping. Then we'll start attacking the extractions. All of them. Every day. We can hamstring the Balarian fleet inside of a week, before they truly understand what's happened. Ward will either have to pull ships away from the other cities in Terra that he's conquered—which will lead to rebellions—or give us a clear road to Floodhaven. Either way, it could turn the whole tide of the war."

Bershad looked at the map. Itched his beard. "It could work," he admitted.

"Definitely," Oromir agreed.

"That won't be enough, either," said Ashlyn.

"Decimating Ward's fleet isn't enough?" Oromir asked. "You drunk, Queen?"

"Think the situation through to the end," Ashlyn said. "What happens when we get to Floodhaven? If we lay a siege, Ward will just send grayskins over the walls and tear us apart. Then he'll rebuild the fleet and we'll be right back where we started, except our army will have been massacred at the gates of Floodhaven."

"Well that's depressing," said Simeon.

"We need to destroy Ward's ships in order to reach Floodhaven, but we also need a way to take the city in a single night."

"All due respect, Queen, but I don't think that's possible," said Kerrigan.

"I do," said Ashlyn. "Jolan and I finally broke through Ward's security measures at that crashed skyship. We found a way to give the acolytes commands. They were pretty basic. Blink the eyes. Stand up."

"You gonna sack Floodhaven by making the acolytes blink themselves to death?" Oromir asked.

"There's another set of commands we couldn't reach. It was called a manual override."

"Doesn't sound that useful," said Simeon.

"We didn't think so either," said Jolan, removing a sheaf of papers from his satchel. "But when I took a closer look through the acolyte schematics that Felgor stole, I found a few mentions of it. One of the commands hidden behind the lock is called the annihilation protocol."

Simeon's face brightened. "I like that much better."

"Of course you do," Kerrigan muttered. "You're a murderous bastard."

"It could mean a number of different things," Ashlyn warned. "But our hope is that if I can access it in one acolyte, I can find a way to apply it wholesale to larger groups. I could kill hundreds of acolytes in seconds."

"And that's how we take Floodhaven?"

Ashlyn nodded. "Exactly."

"I'm sold." Simeon burped. "Let's do it."

"It's not that simple," Ashlyn said. "To test the theory, I need a living acolyte."

"Why?" Willem asked.

"As soon as an acolyte dies, the path to their brain closes. That's why we've never found this before. They've always come back dead."

"Well, yeah," said Bershad. "They tend to cause problems if you don't kill them in a timely fashion."

"I'm aware of that, but we need to capture one that's alive," said Ashlyn.

"You're insane," said Oromir.

"I'm just telling you what I need," Ashlyn said.

"How long would you need to keep it alive once we capture it?" Bershad asked.

"Hard to say. Breaking into the manual override system could take days. Weeks, even."

"There's no way we can keep a war acolyte contained for more than a few seconds," said Oromir. "Forget days or weeks. There's just no way."

"True," said Ashlyn. "But a harvester model would be easier to control."

"What do those do?" Kerrigan asked.

"I'd imagine they fucking harvest," Simeon said.

"Oh, why don't you go bite your own dick off, Simeon, I was just—"

"Enough," Ashlyn interrupted. "Simeon is crude, but correct. The harvesters are the ones they send into the dragon warrens. They have no weapons, no armor. They're far weaker, too. A basic sedative would keep it under control."

"I've read through those protocols that Felgor stole, too," said Willem. "The harvesters always travel with a score of Wormwrot and three war acolytes. So, what's the plan there?"

"We lure them to a place that we control," Ashlyn said, clearly having thought this through already. "Neutralize Wormwrot. Then I'll kill the war acolytes with blunt force, and lock down the harvester's spinal loop before it can backfire."

"As I recall, Jolan had to run a wire from Ashlyn to the acolyte to do that in the skyship," said Bershad. "Doubt you're gonna find another one that's willing to sit still for that."

Ashlyn nodded, but seemed to have a solution for that, too. "Jolan?"

The boy took a breath. "The diagnostic is a problem on two fronts. There's the wire, and the fact that it doesn't parse signals of living acolytes very clearly. But I can build a new tool that solves both issues. I just need a little time." He paused. "I also need to, uh, borrow Felgor's astrolabe."

"My what?"

"That mechanical globe you stole from the crashed skyship. It contains a lot of Ward's existing technology that I need to repurpose. Otherwise, this'll take years."

Felgor considered that. "For a small daily fee, I will rent it to you."

Jolan frowned. "How much?"

"Fifty gold pieces per day."

"I don't have any gold. Nobody does."

"I will of course accept a loan structure with ten percent interest per day, compounding of course."

Jolan's jaw dropped. "But in just a few days that will amount to—"

"We'll take the loan," said Ashlyn. "Just give him the astrolabe and add it to my tab, Felgor."

"Deal."

"I'm more interested in how the queen plans on killing three war acolytes by her lonesome," Oromir said. "Seems awfully ambitious."

"A week ago, it would have been." Ashlyn motioned to the new, thick band set above her elbow, which had three metal pins drilled into it. "But the salvage from the acolyte in the skyship is far more stable than my older bands. I can balance ten lodestones in my system now. Three acolytes. Ten lodestones. I like my chances."

"If you're so confident, how about you just kill everyone while we sit back in camp eating extra rations?" Oromir asked.

"It takes a massive amount of energy to use the lodestones, and their range is limited," said Ashlyn. "I can handle three war acolytes inside a warren. Two scores of Wormwrot out in the open are problematic."

Oromir stood up. "I'll have no part of this."

"You volunteered to walk into a nest of dragons, but won't set a simple ambush?" Bershad asked.

"I did that because we needed the food. This isn't simple. It's another gamble, just like Fallon's Roost. It was my men who got chewed up and killed by the sorcery of our queen then, and it's my men who've been torn apart by grayskins for the last year. Not this time. I said I'll have no fucking part, Bershad."

Oromir stormed off.

Willem cleared his throat. "Being honest, if we're gonna have a hope of mapping these pairings before the end of summer, I'm gonna need every spare warden out in the jungle, anyway. I don't know how many men you need to deal with the Wormwrot escort, but—"

Bershad waved him off. "It's fine. You can take all the Jaguars. I only need Simeon and ten good men from Naga Rock to get this done."

"You sound pretty confident."

"That's because I know the codes Wormwrot uses to rank the size of dragon warrens," Bershad said. "We'll make a map that has a large one marked on it. That'll ensure the harvest acolyte shows up in a timely fashion."

Bershad decided not to mention that marking a large warren would mean that Vallen Vergun would join the escort. No reason to cause a panic.

"Only tricky part is getting a forged map in front of Osyrus Ward." Bershad turned to Felgor. "How about it, you fucking thief? Up for one more trip to Floodhaven?"

Felgor's eyes narrowed. "First you take my collector's items, now you want to send me back behind enemy lines. Is this what I am hearing?"

"We'll add another hundred thousand gold to your tab."

Felgor smiled. "I'll need a haircut. I'll need my officer's uniform cleaned. And by the ass-gears of Aeternita, I will need someone to eliminate this rash from my neck." Felgor scratched at his infected skin. "Meet these requirements, and you can consider the job done."

Bershad laughed. "I'll handle the clothes. Jolan, can you handle the rash?"

The kid peered down at the infected skin. "Yeah. No problem."

"One last thing," Felgor said.

"Clothes, gold, and medical treatment isn't enough?" Bershad asked.

"I need Cabbage. That's the only way my officer bit carries water."

"Fine with me," said Simeon. "The earless bastard isn't any good in a proper fight anyway."

"It's settled, then," said Bershad.

"Not quite," Kerrigan said. "How are you going to kill forty Wormwrot with ten men from Naga Rock?"

"Vash was right. I'm gonna need to carve myself a new mask after all."

29

CABBAGE
Village of Dampmire

Cabbage had agreed to return to Floodhaven on the condition that they were allowed to take a donkey loaded with extra rations with them. Kerrigan had given him the side eye, but agreed.

Once they were on the road, Cabbage convinced Felgor to divert through Dampmire.

"Oh, *I* see why you wanted the extra grub," Felgor said when he saw Cabbage messing with his new ears on the way through the village. "You dipped some fingers into a local honeypot on our last turn here."

"It's not like that."

"Oh, not a fingers man? You just go right in with the tongue, or what?"

Cabbage glared at Felgor. There was no point in attempting to improve the thief's manners. The best you could do was distract him.

"How do my ears look?"

"Fantastic."

Cabbage couldn't tell if he was being sarcastic or not.

Jovita had said that she didn't care about his missing ears. And Cabbage believed her, but that didn't mean *he* didn't care about them.

"Right. I'm going to give her the donkey and food. Wait for me somewhere that you won't be tempted to steal anything. These people don't have much."

"Sure, sure. I'll find a quiet nook and work on my dice throws or something."

Cabbage headed down the narrow wooden causeway. When he reached Jovita's hut, he hesitated, suddenly very nervous. But the donkey crapped twice while Cabbage was stalling, and the smell got him moving again. He took one last a deep breath, and knocked.

"Cabbage?" Jovita asked after she opened the door. "What are you doing here?"

He motioned to the donkey. "Brought you a present."

———

Cabbage brought all the supplies inside and laid them out ono the kitchen table. Rice, beans, and plenty of salted pork.

Jovita was quiet for a long time, looking at it all.

"I don't know what to say, Cabbage. This is . . . too generous." She gave him a sly look. "You trying to earn a spot in my bed with all this?"

"No! I just . . . wanted you to have it is all."

"And you walked all the way back to Dampmire to give it to me?"

"It's on the way to Floodhaven. Me and Felgor are heading back."

"What for?"

"Uh, it's kind of a secret."

"A secret, is it?"

Cabbage nodded gravely. Before he could say anything else, the donkey pushed his head through the window of Jovita's hut. He was munching on something from her garden.

"I was thinking you could have the donkey, too, if you think he and your dog will get along. We can't take him to Floodhaven with us."

Jovita rubbed his muzzle. "What's his name?"

"Well, I'm not sure what his dragonslayer called him, but I've been calling him Rat Stomper, on account of him crushing a rat the first day we set off with him."

"That's a terrible name!" Jovita said, but she smiled while she said it. She rubbed his muzzle a little longer. "Think I'll call you Mustard. It's been ages since I've had some. He'll be my little reminder of better times."

"You like mustard?"

"Love it. But our fields got salted by the skyships last year."

"Sorry," Cabbage said, making a note to look for some fancy Balarian mustard while they were in Floodhaven.

"Please," said Jovita. "Making do without mustard isn't a big deal in the grand scheme."

"I guess not." Cabbage looked down at his boots. "Guess giving one pretty villager some food doesn't do much good in the grand scheme, either."

He kept his eyes fixed on his boots for another moment. When he worked up the courage to look at Jovita, she was smiling.

"Oh, Cabbage. You're kinda sweet."

He laughed. "Don't think anyone's ever accused me of that."

He paused. Hesitated.

"Can I ask you something, Jovita?"

"Sure."

"If we manage to end this war, and I somehow manage to survive it, would you be open to maybe seeing me more often? I like it here, in Dampmire. And . . . I like you."

"You barely know me."

"That's true, I won't argue." He looked down at his feet again. "I guess what I'm saying is that I'd be open to changing that, if you were, too. And you can answer honest. I might be a pirate, but I'm not a man who thinks he's owed anything from a woman she doesn't want to give."

Jovita seemed to think that over really carefully. "What did you do before you were a pirate?"

"I was apprenticed to a watchmaker in Clockwork City," Cabbage said.

"Did you enjoy the work?"

Cabbage thought about that. "The man I trained under was not a kind person. He was harsh with mistakes, and cold to me, even if I did well. But I liked the way so many disparate pieces could be fit together and make something anew. Something with a purpose. In Balaria, telling time is treated with great respect." He hesitated. "Sometimes it reminds me of the Dainwood army. There's the Jaguars, but also us from up on Ghost Moth Island, and Queen Ashlyn with all her sorcery. The Flawless Bershad with . . . whatever goes on beneath his skin. And Simeon, with the dragonscales around his. We're all different gears and pieces, and together we make up a larger whole." He paused to take a breath. He'd been talking so fast that he hadn't been breathing right. "Sorry, that was a long answer."

"I liked it."

"Do you like . . . uh." Cabbage stopped, realizing he didn't know Jovita's trade.

"I'm a weaver," she said, helping him along.

"Ah. Right." He hesitated. "Do you like it?"

"Not really," she admitted. "The work's routine, and useful. But there's not much joy in it."

"Is there something else you would have rather been?"

She thought about that.

"When I was a girl, I wanted to be a traveling merchant. I always loved when they came through Dampmire with stories of far-off places. Seeing something new every day, I would like that, I think."

"Me too," Cabbage said softly.

He didn't know what else to say, or what to do. Suddenly he was afraid that Jovita wanted him to leave, or that he never should have come here to begin with. But then Jovita took his hand and squeezed it.

"See? Now we know each other, Cabbage. A little, anyway. That's a good thing."

She kissed him on the cheek. Held her lips there for what felt like a very long time. The sensation filled Cabbage with a mixture of panic and pleasure that he hadn't felt for a decade or more. Maybe not ever.

Cabbage smiled the whole way to Floodhaven.

30

GARRET
The Soul Sea, Almiran Coast

After Vera spared Garwin's soldiers, they all went to the nearest tavern to drink off the experience. Garret followed them, and poisoned them all. He did not believe in half measures

When that was done, he went to see about a ride back to Almira.

The captain of the *Lucky Second*—which was stationed in the Bay of Broken Clocks—wasn't thrilled by the idea of a stranger melting out of the Burz-al-dun crowds and requesting immediate passage to Floodhaven, but the ship's first mate recognized Garret and after a few hurried whispers back and forth, he was given a private cabin, a hot meal of steamed clams and buttered potatoes, and a jug of crisp, Ghalamarian wine.

The ship crossed the Soul Sea at a full burn.

Garret was met at the skyship port by Engineer Nebbin.

"Hangman," said Nebbin, arms folded behind his back like an asshole. "Master Ward requests your immediate presence."

"Yeah, I expected that he would," said Garret. "Lead the way."

―――――

Osyrus Ward was in a workshop on the forty-third level of the King's Tower. Two acolytes were with him.

Ward was operating on his mechanical spider, whose legs were crumpled together in a surprisingly accurate mimicry of an actual dead spider. Both of Ward's arms were covered to the elbows in green ichor.

Garret had become used to horrific displays like this in the workshops. Last time he'd been up here, Ward had been attaching metal wings to a rat while the rodent was still alive.

Osyrus glanced up at him, then returned to whatever he was adjusting in the spider's chest cavity.

"Garret. As I recall, you departed Floodhaven upon the *Blue Sparrow,* which was fully crewed." He pulled a gray orb from the spider with a grunt. "You have returned to Floodhaven as a stowaway, with no sign of the crew or ship from which you departed."

"The crew's dead."

Osyrus's hands froze. He looked up. "Including Vera?"

"You told me to kill her if she misbehaved."

"In what manner did she misbehave?"

Garret couldn't lie about delivering the food to Burz-al-dun. There were too many ways for Osyrus to learn about it. Beyond that, there was some wiggle room.

"We got the food from the crashed skyship and took it to Burz-al-dun," Garret said. "When we were done, Vera wanted to take the *Blue Sparrow* to Pargos, rather than return to Floodhaven. So I killed her."

"What of the longbowmen?"

"They took offense to Vera's murder, but Garwin and his Ghalamarians had the numbers."

"Where is Garwin?"

"Last I saw them, he and his men were doing a shit job of trying to fly the *Blue Sparrow* over the Razorbacks in bad weather."

"They deserted?"

Garret shrugged. "Give a few soldiers that were press-ganged into war a skyship of their own, they're going to get ideas."

"Why didn't you stop them?"

"If you wanted someone to keep that many soldiers under control, you should have sent an acolyte."

Ward stared at Garret for a while. "I'll send scouting ships along the Razorbacks to look for the *Sparrow,* naturally."

"Naturally."

Thing was, the Razorbacks were a very large mountain range, and they were teeming with Red Skulls. Ward would send a few ships, sure, but not enough to rule out the possibility of undiscovered wreckage. The lie was covered.

"Whether we find the ship or not, this is a disappointing result, Garret."

"No, it isn't."

"Oh? How is a lost skyship and a deserting Ghalamarian count a good thing?"

"You have plenty more skyships. And with Vera dead, you can give up your ridiculous pretense of helping Kira Malgrave and proceed with whatever you actually want her for."

Ward raised his eyebrows. "I'm not sure what you mean."

"Vera was blinded by her affection for the girl," said Garret. "I'm not."

Ward glanced at Nebbin, but said nothing. Garret had the feeling that Ward was on the cusp of having him killed, which was a risk he knowingly took by returning to Floodhaven. But he had an easy way to put himself back in Ward's favor.

"Also, you were wrong about Ashlyn Malgrave," Garret said. "She's alive. And regardless of whether sorcery exists, she is doing something that looks an awful lot like it."

Osyrus's face was unreadable. "How do you know this?"

"She was at the crash site. One of her arms is wreathed in metal, and she can make orbs like the one you're pulling out of that spider fly around her head."

"I want to know *everything* that you saw Ashlyn Malgrave do."

Garret described Ashlyn's body and abilities in detail. When he was done, Ward rattled off a long series of increasingly more specific questions—everything from the thickness of the bands on her arm to the amount of visible sweat on her body and face when she moved the orbs through the air.

"Her system doesn't sound entirely stable," said Nebbin. "But with the proper adjustments, she may be able to deliver the voltage levels we've been unable to reach when purifying the fluid samples."

"Possibly," Ward agreed. "But the system must be intertwined with her biology. We would need to capture her alive. What happened to her?"

"Despite her power, the longbowmen had the range," Garret lied. "She fled into the jungle."

Nebbin cursed. "She could be anywhere by now."

"I can find her," Garret said.

"Are you that eager to make up for your mistake?" Ward asked.

"Not exactly," Garret said. "Ashlyn Malgrave and I have unfinished business. I'll bring her to you alive on the condition that I be allowed to kill her when you're done with her."

Linkon Pommol might be dead, but the contract he'd assigned to Garret was not.

"I see." Osyrus picked up a fresh gray orb, which was engraved with all manner of numbers and symbols, and started implanting it into the spider's guts. "Do you know what happened to Bartholomew, here? He was disemboweled by a tabby cat. Whole swaths of machinery and artificial organs shredded."

Osyrus put another orb into its belly, then began attaching a bunch of different wires to the spider's legs.

"When I discovered the incident, I had a choice. As a specimen, Bartholomew has long since become obsolete. So the only reason to repair him was to test something new. As it turned out, I had an idea for a control mechanism."

Osyrus finished the wires, then cleaned his hands with a rag. When that was finished, he opened a metal case with ten gray rings on it. He slipped a ring onto each finger. Each ring had a small gray ball on it about the size of a pea. The rings that he put on his thumbs had the opposite—a grooved space of about the same size.

Ward locked the ball of his forefinger ring into the groove of his thumb ring, then pulled them apart with a metallic snap, which caused one of the spider's legs to twitch.

"Am I supposed to be impressed by that?" Garret asked.

"I would not expect you to appreciate the myriad applications for this technology."

Ward repeated his snapping with each of his fingers. Each snap caused a different spider leg to twitch.

"But you *do* understand what it means to be obsolete," Ward continued. "Because in a fight against Ashlyn Malgrave, you would be just as overmatched as Bartholomew was against the cat. Would you like me to change that for you?"

"You're not putting anything inside of me."

"No. For you, an external application will be preferable." He glanced at the noose on Garret's hip. "Perhaps a weapon that aligns with your existing skills, but allows you to nullify Ashlyn's power?"

Garret blinked. "I can see the value in that."

"Good. We have a deal, then." He turned to Nebbin. "As Garret pointed out, there is no reason to keep up false pretenses. Begin harvesting samples from Kira's adrenal cortex—as much as her body can withstand. It will take time to engineer her steroid treatments from the hormone scrapings, and I want to have them ready and available."

Nebbin smiled. "Yes, master. Right away."

31

NOLA
City of Deepdale, Cat's Eye Tavern

Lord Cuspar came into the Cat's Eye just as Nola and Grittle were closing. Two wardens in full armor followed him.

"Ladies!" he said with a smile. "How are we this evening?"

Cuspar was an oddly shaped man. Not plump, like most lords from the sunny side of the canal, but not skinny either. More of a strange mixture of both, with an ample belly, but beanpole arms and no ass at all. Generally, his shape reminded Nola of a pear. On the other hand, his two wardens both had thick necks and forearms that were wreathed in muscle. They weren't as tall as Lord Silas, but they were close.

"We're fine, Lord Cuspar. Thank you for asking." Nola gave a bow, as did Grittle. She hated bowing to Cuspar nearly as much as she hated seeing her sister follow her lead. "And you, m'lord?"

"Oh, the answer to that question depends on the status of your finances, Nola." Cuspar moved to the bar, removing a pair of gloves made from a caiman's hide as he walked. One warden stayed by the door, the other moved into the middle of the room and rested his hand on the pommel of his sword.

Cuspar took a spot at the bar and tapped a bare finger against it. "First, a drink."

"Yes, m'lord." She gave her sister a look. "All the way to the top."

Grittle poured his beer, but Nola took it from her by the cask and carried it over. She didn't have a good reason for doing that, but she always did, as if keeping her sister out of arm's reach would also protect her from Cuspar's much larger grip on their fate.

He took a long sip. Licked the foam from his mustache.

"As I recall, you were fifty-two silvers short of our agreed-upon quota last moon's turn. Applying standard interest, that's sixty-two silvers on top of the usual hundred."

Nola didn't say anything.

"Is that your recollection as well?" Cuspar asked pleasantly.

She wanted to argue the ridiculous and very much nonstandard nature of that interest rate, but it was difficult to negotiate when you had no leverage and the man on the other side of the table had two wardens with very large, sharp swords.

"Yes," said Nola, doing her best not to sound pissed, but failing.

"Yes, what?"

"Yes, that is where our debt currently stands." A moment's pause. *"M'lord."*

"Hm." Cuspar took another sip. The beer was half empty. "Of course, if you're unable to cover the debt, we could perhaps adjust the ownership split of the tavern to a different ratio."

Nola reached beneath the counter. As she did so, she noticed that both wardens moved their hands to the grips of their swords and kept them there, even when she came up with a sack of coins and flopped it on the bar with a clink and a rattle.

"Two hundred and ninety silvers," Nola said. "Covers what I owed, plus your thirty percent of this week's profit."

"Profit?" Cuspar repeated. He looked more surprised than if Nola had drawn a blade on him. "How in the name of the forest gods did you turn a profit?"

"As I recall, the terms of our agreement didn't include me detailing my methods of hospitality, m'lord. Just sharing the results." She pushed the sack forward. "I assume you'll want to count it."

"Correct," Cuspar said, voice full of irritation despite the fact that he was coming into more money than he'd expected. That was the sideways thing about lords. They didn't just want to get paid, they wanted to get paid *their* way.

Cuspar tossed the sack to one of his wardens, who moved over to a table and started counting the coins. His lips moved while he worked through the sums. Cuspar drank his beer in simmering silence.

"Well?" he snapped when the warden had gone through everything.

"All here, boss," the man said. "Two hundred and ninety."

"Coin weights all felt right?"

The warden shrugged. "Few might have been shaved a bit, but that's a tavern for you."

"How *many* felt shaved?"

"Fuck's sake," Nola muttered. She reached into her apron and slammed a handful of coppers onto the counter. "Here. *M'lord*."

There was a long silence while Cuspar glared at her. Eventually, the warden behind him cleared his throat.

"That'll probably cover the light ones, boss."

Cuspar turned around. "Did I ask you a question, Ulnar?"

"No."

"Then keep your fucking mouth shut until I do."

There was the smallest moment of hesitation in the warden, along with a tightness in his shoulders and hands. For a heartbeat, Nola wondered if Lord Cuspar might learn to regret speaking so harshly to such an imposing man. But Nola saw the promise of more coin in Ulnar's future sway him away from violence in the present. His face softened.

"Will do, boss." He started putting the coins back into the sack. "Sorry."

Cuspar turned back to Nola. There was a gleam in his eyes that Nola recognized from when she first showed up at his manse, looking for a loan. She'd thought it was lechery at the time, but she was wrong. It was greed. Pure, simple greed.

"You know, if I were to explore your inventory in detail and discover any extra or illicit profits that you've been hiding from me, I would be within my rights to have Ulnar start breaking you and your sister's fingers. Betraying a business agreement with a lord is a *very* serious crime."

"I do know that, m'lord. I can get my ledger if you'd like."

"I'll piss on your ledger. I am talking about every. Little. Detail. Ashlyn Malgrave and her demon dog Bershad aren't here anymore to protect the lowborn. And the way this war is going, they're not likely to return. That means there's nobody to stop me from coming back with ten wardens and pulling up your floorboards. Digging through your attic. Making sure there isn't even one extra silver squirreled away for winter, understand?"

Oh, Nola understood. All too well.

"My floorboards are open to you and your men, m'lord. But the business will likely suffer if my patrons don't have anything to stand on while they drink their morning beers."

Cuspar grunted. Drained the rest of his beer. Burped. Then he spat on her floor for good measure.

"I don't know how you came up with that coin, girl. But unless you can pull it out of your little cunt every month, this tavern's gonna be mine one day. When it is, I'll remember your smart tongue. And I'll throw both of you out on your skinny asses."

He got up. Took the sack of coin on his way to the door.

Grittle took two steps forward and spoke before Nola had a chance to grab her and put a hand over her mouth. "Lord Silas *is* coming back!" she said.

Cuspar turned around. Gave a sly smile. "Is that a fact, girl?"

"Yes. We gave him a beer before he left, so when he does return he's going to protect our tavern from people like you."

"So, a little bit of rain ale is all it takes to bribe the demon of Glenlock Canyon into service?" Cuspar chuckled. "Good to know."

He put his gloves back on, then gave an ostentatious wave. "Until next month, my little chickens. Keep on laying those silver eggs."

When he was gone, Nola locked the door behind him.

"You shouldn't have done that," Nola hissed at her sister.

"Why not?" Grittle asked, frowning. "Lord Silas *will* come back. He'll help us."

"We need to be able to help ourselves. And talking back to Lord Cuspar isn't the way to do that."

"You weren't exactly charming his pants off, Nola."

Nola smiled. Rustled a hand through her sister's hair.

"C'mon. It's time for bed."

———

Nola and Grittle slept in the attic above the tavern.

A year ago, they'd been forced to cram their bedrolls between the crates of extra food and fruit. Nola had gone to sleep each night with the flowery aroma of fresh hops and sharp cheese in her nose.

Now, the attic was so barren that Nola and Grittle were able to spread out as much as they wanted—each with their own space.

"Long enough?" Grittle asked, mumbling around the tooth twig in her mouth.

"No. You need another full minute."

"I already chewed for a minute."

"You chewed for twenty seconds." Nola pointed at the twig. "One *full* minute. Otherwise you'll wind up with a bunch of brown beans for teeth, like Jakell."

Grittle sighed. Then popped the twig into her mouth and started chewing again.

There wasn't a lime tree within fifty leagues of Deepdale that hadn't had its fruit picked clean by Blackjacks or people or both, but at least they could still use the twigs to keep their teeth clean.

While Grittle finished up, Nola played around with the Papyrian lens that Kellar had traded for that scrap of fish. The different tubes were made from brass, and covered with old rope. It wasn't worth much right now—and part of Nola regretted allowing Kellar to tack it onto the trade for his breakfast—but maybe when the war was done, she could take it across the canal and work something out with one of the rich collectors. They always paid too much for crap from foreign countries.

For now, the lens was hers. Might as well use it.

The attic had one big window that looked out over the city. Nola propped it open with a wooden rod and looked out.

It was a quiet night. A bent-backed woman was struggling to move a cart up Canal Street. Two wardens were sitting on one of the bridges; both of them had their pants rolled up and their feet in the water. One of them was missing his right arm, and the other had a set of crutches next to him. Eventually, he pulled his legs out of the water and Nola saw that he was missing a foot.

She moved her lens to the far side of the canal. The highborn side.

Everything about the buildings and shops and manses across the canal was better. The walls were cut from stronger stone. The mortar was fresh and uncracked. The roofs were made from uniform slate and tile instead of old, rain-molded thatch.

Because Nola was in the mood for a little self-inflicted pain, she moved her lens around until she found Lord Cuspar's manse, which was built just outside the castle walls. He had a three-floor manse made from red brick. There was an enclosed yard out back with a big cook fire that was alight with smoldering coals. It looked like Cuspar's servants were cooking a goat tonight. Before he died, their father had run a goat farm to the north. Between the milk and meat, one goat could sustain their whole family for a moon's turn.

Cuspar didn't have a wife. Didn't have any kids. And he was eating an entire goat.

Nola watched a cook come out from the kitchen and spread some herbs over the animal's flesh, then go back inside. The short glimpse inside the kitchen made her stomach churn and her skin crawl. There were jars and jars of rice, grain, spices. Smoked fish hung from ceiling hooks. There was a whole basket of limes.

"Asshole," Nola muttered.

Grittle finished with her twig, and carefully placed it on a cloth. Then she dragged her bedroll over to Nola's and sat down. She always did that, despite the extra space they now had.

"Can I have a story before bed?"

Nola gave her a look. "I should punish you for talking back to Lord Cuspar and cancel stories for a week."

"No, please don't!" Grittle said, looking very concerned.

Nola sighed. Their father wouldn't have liked how lenient Nola was with Grittle. He'd been a strict disciplinarian—stern with manners and chores, always worried about having enough to get by. Nola worried about those things, too. But she didn't have the heart to pass that concern on to Grittle in full doses. So much of life was a difficult burden. Grittle deserved a few more years without feeling the full weight of it.

Nola sighed. "Fine, fine. What kind of story do you want?"

"One about the brothers."

That was the only kind of story that Grittle ever asked to hear.

"A funny one?"

"No . . . a scary one. The one about the Blackjack that got stuck in the field."

"That one's too scary. You got nightmares last time."

"No, I didn't. I just got a little scared."

"Let's do the one about when Janus got his foot stuck in a rain ale bucket."

Grittle seemed to think that over very carefully, weighing the merits of the proposed story. "Okay, but you have to promise to do all the different voices."

"I promise."

Grittle tucked herself tight into her blanket. "Okay. I'm ready."

Nola cleared her throat. "The entire thing started with the unfortunate placement of the rain ale bucket . . ."

Grittle listened carefully, keeping her hands clutched around the blanket.

Nola did her best with the voices.

32

CASTOR
Castle Malgrave, Level 11

Castor was already in the map room when Osyrus Ward burst in, flanked by his little posse of engineers. He'd been sifting through some detailed maps of the Dunfarian coast, looking for a good island to buy after the war. Dunfarian dirt didn't come cheap, but a sailor had told him once that the water near the coast was clear as glass and warm as a freshly drawn bath. That seemed worth the extra cost.

He had his eye on a crescent island with a nice little cove. It'd probably be teeming with crabs and lobster he could catch fresh each morning, then drench in lemon juice and eat for breakfast.

Ward and his men ruined that little daydream with all their bustling and mumbling. Castor folded up his plans for the future and walked over to the massive map of the Dainwood they were all looking at.

"Report," said Ward.

"Six new warren locations have come in," said Engineer Nebbin. "Five are middling in size. But the sixth one, located in Sector Nineteen, appears to be the largest warren that our Wormwrot patrols have found."

"Show me."

He was handed some papers and started reading through them.

"Note the description of the root tendrils," Nebbin said, pointing. "They stretch more than one hundred meters from the mouth of the warren, which is twenty strides in diameter. According to the Seed matrix, we could recover twenty, even thirty pints of fluid. Enough to replenish the recent losses to our war acolyte ranks."

"More than enough," Ward said.

"Shall we dispatch a harvesting team, then?" Nebbin asked.

Ward continued frowning at the paper. "Who wrote this report? I would like to interview them personally."

"Unfortunately, the lieutenant's name is smeared, see here? It happens sometimes. The report itself is actually several weeks old, and was misfiled in the cartographer's manse due to a clerical error. It was pure chance we found it at all."

"Pure chance," Ward repeated. "Hm."

"Is there a problem, Master Ward?"

"No." He set down the report. "We will dispatch a team, but I want an extra ten war acolytes to go with them, rather than the usual three."

Nebbin frowned. "I am afraid with the rebellions in Lysteria heating up again, we only have three spare acolytes who are not currently engaged."

"Then send an extra *three*," Ward snapped. "And double the Wormwrot escort."

"You think it's a trap?" Castor asked.

"I think the discovery of a massive warren located twenty leagues away from any previously patrolled stretch of the Dainwood is suspicious. Don't you?"

Castor nodded. "If Bershad might show up, Commander Vergun will want to go personally."

Ward smiled. "He won't be the only one."

33

GARRET
Dainwood Jungle, Sector Nineteen

"So, why's a legendary killer like the Hangman tagging along for a lowly warren harvest?" asked a Wormwrot sergeant named Yustar.

Garret ignored the question.

"Well?" Yustar pressed, leaning forward. His breath smelled like onions and beer.

"You have your orders, Sergeant," said Garret. "Follow them, and we'll all do just fine."

Yustar didn't like that answer. He spat onto the floor of the skyship to show it.

Unlike the open deck of the *Blue Sparrow*, everything in the newer combat skyships was covered in a shell of armor to protect from dragon attacks. The men were sitting in the main hold, and the pilots were at the end of the hallway in a covered cockpit.

It was hot, made worse by the idiotic face paint he wore to pass for a Wormwrot regular. And it was cramped, made worse by Yustar's terrible breath. But it was preferable to getting snatched by a roaming Blackjack.

"And what the fuck is that thing on your hip?" Yustar asked, motioning to the weapon Osyrus Ward had built for Garret.

"A whip."

"Don't look like no whip I've ever seen."

That was a fair assessment. The whip's braided fibers were made from a strange, translucent material. The grip was molded perfectly to his hand and covered by a dragon-bone guard that was packed with machinery and those little orbs Ward liked so much.

Garret had practiced with the whip before leaving Floodhaven. The barbs that descended from the guard and pierced his skin were unpleasant, but the power they unleashed was worth the pain.

When Yustar realized Garret wasn't going to offer up more details, he spat again.

"You're more of a legendary asshole than anything else, you know that?"

The ship shuddered as it changed course, banking east.

"Two minutes out!" the pilot shouted from the front of the ship.

———

They landed in field of dry grass that was about a hundred paces from the wild and overgrown entrance to the warren. The Wormwrot men rushed out of their skyship and took up defensive positions. Garret exited last. No reason to expose himself.

The second skyship landed to their left. Vergun, Castor, and another score of Wormwrot spearmen trotted out and completed the perimeter. Ten Wormwrot with Balarian longbows followed and set up positions on either side of the skyship.

Behind them, six war acolytes came out of the ship. They ran a patrol around the perimeter Wormwrot had created—all six of them sniffing like bloodhounds, occasionally pausing to squat, pick up a handful of dirt, and taste it. Once they'd performed their check, they nodded to each other in some form of private consensus.

"Harvester," one growled. "Clear to proceed."

A final acolyte came out of the ship. Apart from the gray skin, this one looked nothing like the war models. It was quite thin, and walked with an imperious posture. Gait relaxed, almost graceful. Its arms weren't really arms at all, more a conglomeration of needles and rubber tubes that were bundled together by the same translucent threads that were in Garret's whip.

The harvester moved to the mouth of the dragon warren, which was ringed by orange thornbushes and moss. Extended its arm. A bunch of machinery near the wrist spread apart—needles opening at the tips like flowers, but instead of petals, there were metal parasols that sparked and whirred.

"Viable Seed confirmed."

The war acolytes turned to Vergun.

"The harvester is vulnerable during collection. Keep the cave secure, no matter the cost."

"Not my first time doing this," Vergun growled.

Five war acolytes went into the warren with the harvester. One remained outside, guarding the entrance.

Garret scanned the area, searching for signs of the enemy. There were none, but from a glance at the topography, if an attack was coming, it would arrive from one of two directions: a marshy lowland to the east that was dominated by moss-covered Daintrees, or from the western side of the field, where a set of massive termite mounds formed a complicated maze with good cover.

"Castor, run a patrol along the termite mounds, I will take the marsh," said Vergun, coming to the same conclusion as Garret.

"Aye, boss. On it."

Castor drew his sword and motioned to his men. They headed toward the mounds.

The Madman had been correct. This was a trap. But there was no way to know from where Ashlyn would arrive, so Garret stayed with the archers. As soon as she appeared, he'd make his move.

Not a moment sooner.

34

JOLAN
Dainwood Jungle, Sector Nineteen

Jolan was hiding halfway up a Daintree, doing his best to keep the astrolabe pointed at the harvest acolyte for as long as possible. Ashlyn was on the ground below him, a wire running between her and the astrolabe. She both powered the machine and—if it worked properly—was using it to capture the signal of the harvester's entry lodestone from a distance.

She kept her eyes closed. Stayed completely still.

When the acolytes disappeared into the warren, Ashlyn opened her eyes.

"Did you get it?" Jolan asked.

"Five points north, two points east. Forty-two points south, nineteen points west." She paused. "Repeating. Nice and simple."

Jolan nodded. That was good, but they still had a problem.

"There are six war acolytes with the harvester," said Jolan. "Not three."

Ashlyn didn't say anything.

"Ashe, I'm not sure you can handle six."

"Neither am I," Ashlyn responded. "But I *am* certain the point of no return has passed."

"Oh, it's long gone," said Simeon, who was squatting next to her. He rolled one shoulder in a circle, causing a crisis of clacks from his armor. "Once the shit starts to fly, we'll make our move. Keep an eye out, kid."

Jolan swallowed. Turned back to the skyships. Waited for the violence to begin.

35

CASTOR
Dainwood Jungle, Sector Nineteen

Castor didn't like the look of those termite mounds. Not one fucking bit.

Too many different routes and ways to get separated. Too many little trees sprouting up that might not be trees at all, but armored wardens waiting to draw steel and slit throats. And not nearly enough reliable exits.

If all that wasn't enough, there were also way too many termites on them—each mound swarming with a shimmering film of the wretched bugs.

So Castor called his men to a halt ten strides from the first mound. Waited.

Sergeant Yustar came up next to him. "What're we doing?"

"Shut the fuck up and get back in formation," Castor barked.

He didn't like Yustar. The man had no character.

Vergun halted his men at the borders of the marsh, too. Both groups held fast for a few minutes. The only sound was the rustle of grass in the wind and the heavy breathing of men wearing full armor in the jungle heat. Castor was just starting to think that there wasn't anything around besides the wretched insects.

"Contact right!" a Wormwrot shouted from the edge of the line.

Castor turned. A tall, shirtless man was standing in the middle of the field, wearing a wooden mask that was painted black except for a thick, blue bar running down each cheek.

"A dragonslayer," Yustar whispered. "Think it's Bershad?"

Castor didn't respond. But he didn't have to count the tattoos on that tall bastard's arms for very long before reaching a number that narrowed down the odds in a hurry.

"Why's he just standing there?" Yustar asked.

"Because he wants us to make the first move," said Castor.

"I'm of a mind to oblige him. The bounty on Silas Bershad's head is bigger than a fucking Red Skull."

That was true. Probably enough for Castor to afford his island. But charging the Flawless Bershad without a plan was a real good way to die.

"You'll stand fast until I order otherwise."

Castor didn't take his eyes off the dragonslayer, but he could hear Yustar licking his dry lips. And he could imagine the stupidity that was running through his simple brain.

"Fuck that," Yustar said a moment later. "I'm going for it."

If Castor was still a Horellian—and some regular grunt in the Balarian army did that—he'd have severed the idiot's back tendon and collapsed his throat with a swift kick of his boot. But this was Wormwrot and he wasn't a Horellian, so Castor let the idiot charge across the field on his own, motioning again for the rest of his men to hold fast. Thankfully, they were smart enough to obey.

Yustar trampled across the field, bellowing out a war howl. He was an idiot, but he was also a capable soldier who'd managed to keep himself alive after a whole summer of combat drops into the jungle. So when he came within five strides of the dragonslayer and dropped his shoulder into a strong thrusting position, Castor gave him half odds at becoming a hero on the field today.

It was a good thing Castor didn't gamble.

The dragonslayer remained still until the last available moment, but when that moment came, he darted to the left of the spear thrust and broke the point off with a swipe of his hand. Then he used the spearpoint to disembowel Yustar with a few efficient jerks.

Yustar put up quite a fuss while that happened to him. Enough screaming and shouting that it got Vergun's attention. He ordered the archers who were over by the skyships to loose a volley. They obliged, but while they might have been using Balarian-made long-bows, they were not Balarian longbowmen.

Only one arrow was on target, but the dragonslayer saw it coming and avoided it as calmly as he might dodge a snowball thrown by a small child. Then he turned his back on all of them and walked into the termite mounds.

Vergun still had enough composure to keep half his men watching the marsh, but he ran to Castor's position with a face that was brimming with rage.

"Why didn't you go in after him?" he hissed.

"That's a trap, boss."

"That is Silas Bershad."

"One and the same, in this particular instance." He paused. Scanned the area. "They probably don't have the numbers to fight in the open. We keep our perimeter tight, we'll be in and out with only Yustar down the river."

Vergun responded by drawing his falchion. "Ten men go in with me. Ten go in with you. Take the north side."

With that, Vergun disappeared into the termite stacks.

Castor cursed. He knew Vergun would kill him if he refused, so there was nothing to do but follow his orders.

The place was a proper maze—twisting passages that divided, then divided again so within a few minutes it would be impossible to trace their way back out by anything besides bootprints.

Castor called a halt, not wanting to get lost.

"Was that our fourth right?" he asked the man next to him.

"Fifth."

"You sure?"

A silence.

"No."

Castor cursed.

"Nothing but rights from now on, got it? Then it'll be lefts on the way out so we can—"

"Behind us!" a private shouted, raising his crossbow. Castor turned to find Bershad filling their back trail and holding a white shield. The private fired his crossbow, but the bolt bounced harmlessly off the shield.

Bershad darted out of sight.

"On me," Castor said, moving back through their line until he reached the place where Bershad had been standing.

"Man's not wearing boots," he muttered, looking at the footprints.

"That's because he's a fucking demon," whispered the man next to him. "Demons don't need—"

There was a wet thump from the other side of their line, followed by the clatter of an armored man dropping to the dirt. Someone else fired a crossbow. Cursed when they missed.

"Keep this direction covered," Castor growled, then shoved his way back to the front. There was a dead man with a gaping hole where his face used to be.

"What happened?" he asked the private who was recranking his crossbow.

"Bastard speared Kornut," he said. "Then he ran off that way."

He pointed down a twisting path.

"Did he have a shield?"

"Naw. Just the spear."

"What about boots?"

"What?"

"Was he wearing any *fucking* shoes?"

"I didn't have time to inspect his footwear."

Castor looked around. "Something's not right."

"Not to be rude, boss, but that's pretty obvious."

Shouts rose from the south side of the termite mounds. Then screams.

"How's he moving around so fast?" a man asked.

"Like I said, he's a fucking *demon*. I heard he can transform into a dragon when he wants to."

"He's not a demon, you idiots," Castor growled. "He's just not alone."

"What do we do?"

Castor checked the ground. Took a moment to suss out the footprints that he saw. Found the ones coming from bare feet instead of boots. Those were Bershad's.

"On me."

They moved forward until they reached a wide clearing that was pocked with squat, hip-high trees. Vergun and his men were just coming in from the other side. A masked man was standing in the middle of the clearing. He was carrying that shield again. Breathing hard, skin slick with sweat. His feet were bleeding.

"Silas Bershad," said Vergun, stepping forward. "I am going to cut off your head and put it in a pickle jar."

He motioned for his men to fan out, covering the different paths out of the clearing. The man waited until he was surrounded, then he took off his mask.

Castor had never seen the Flawless Bershad's face, but unless the

legendary lizard killer had been a Lysterian this whole time and nobody had mentioned it in the stories, this was not him.

"Pickle jars, is it?" the man asked in a thick Lysterian accent.
"Seems an odd place to put your head."

Vergun's face twitched with rage. "Who the fuck are you?"

"Name's Goll," the big man said happily. "You're Vergun?"

"Commander. Vallen. Vergun."

"Right, right. Titles, titles. Anyway, Silas Bershad has a message
for you."

"What message?"

Goll cleared his throat, as if he was about to perform the solilo-
quy of some play.

"Not yet, asshole."

The squat trees that filled the clearing came alive and started killing people.

36

JOLAN
Dainwood Jungle, Sector Nineteen

Jolan watched the battle unfold through a Papyrian lens. The sounds
of steel on steel rang out from within the maze of termite mounds.
Wormwrot's perimeter around the marsh broke as men rushed to help
their dying comrades.

"They're starting to thin out," Jolan said.

"Good," said Ashlyn. "How are things looking near the warren?"

Jolan shifted his lens.

"One war acolyte is still guarding the entrance," he called down.

"How many Wormwrot around the skyships?"

Jolan did a quick count. "Seventeen. Most of them have bows."

Ashlyn turned to Simeon. "Go out there and get their attention. I
need the entrance to that warren cleared."

"No fucking problem," Simeon growled, putting on his helmet.

He trotted toward the skyships, picking up speed with each lum-
bering step. When he was out of sight, Jolan raised the lens again
and focused his gaze on the perimeter of the marsh.

Simeon broke free from the undergrowth about a minute later.
Most of the Wormwrot men were focused on the termite mounds,

so only one soldier saw him break out of the mire at a full sprint. Simeon threw a rock at him, which caved in his breastplate and blew a pink smear of organs into the grass behind him. That got everyone screaming, turning around, and forming a shield wall against him.

Simeon met them head-on. Started tearing them apart.

"Any movement from the war acolyte?" Ashlyn asked from below.

Jolan turned his lens to the warren's entrance. "None. I don't think it's going to move."

"Black skies," Ashlyn said. "No choice, then."

"What are you doing to do?"

Ashlyn didn't respond. Just started working her way through the marshy undergrowth.

Jolan turned back to the skyships, where Simeon had massacred about half of the soldiers—reducing them to limbless heaps and smashed torsos. He was currently beating one man to a bloody puddle while four others beat at him with swords that might as well have been big stalks of wheat for all the damage they did.

When Ashlyn appeared at the fringes of the marsh, her armbands were already churning and she had all ten lodestones orbiting around her body. When she was about ten strides away, she zipped them toward the acolyte in a blur. But the acolyte had seen her coming. Its forearms snapped in front of its head, and the orbs were buried harmlessly into his thick muscles. The acolyte lowered its arms. Two massive bone spikes extended from between the fingers of each hand.

"Oh no," Jolan muttered. "No, no, no, no—"

Ashlyn's bands froze. A final lodestone—which Jolan had lost track of—dropped from the sky, slamming through the top of the acolyte's skull.

The creature's spikes retracted back into its arms. It tottered, then fell backward. Dead.

Ashlyn stepped over the corpse and disappeared into the warren, dragging its body with her by using the lodestones that were peppered into its body as anchors.

"Thank the gods," Jolan muttered to himself, relief flooding his veins. "Five more to go."

A strange sound sizzled through the air, and when Jolan turned around, Simeon was no longer pummeling Wormwrot with their own limbs.

He was down on both knees. There was an electrified whip wrapped around his throat.

Jolan studied the man holding the opposite end of the rope. Even with a painted face and Wormwrot garb, he recognized Garret's face.

Jolan climbed down the tree, took one of his explosives out of his satchel, armed it, and ran toward the skyship.

37

GARRET
Dainwood Jungle, Sector Nineteen

Garret had been watching the Skojit tear Wormwrot apart from the shadow of the skyship when Ashlyn Malgrave darted out of the woods and killed the acolyte guarding the warren.

So, the ambush in the termite mounds and the Skojit's assault had been nothing more than diversions. Simple and clean. Garret was impressed.

The only way for him to reach Ashlyn was to go through the Skojit. So Garret had activated the whip and made his move.

Even with a body full of current, the Skojit managed to kill three more men just by thrashing around. Garret squeezed the whip's grip harder, increasing the current flowing through the mechanism. He nearly had the big bastard cowed—which would leave the path to Ashlyn Malgrave wide open—when Jolan came running out of the woods.

He had a wild expression on his face. Full of fury.

"Jolan?" Garret said, frowning. "Get out of here before—"

Jolan threw a copper orb the size of a baby's skull at his feet. There was a little metal tab spinning at the top. Garret had seen enough of Ward's crap to guess what happened once the spinning mechanism stopped. There was no time to untangle the whip from the Skojit, so he disconnected at his wrist and dove behind the skyship's hull.

There was a loud boom and a bright flash. Garret's vision failed him.

When it returned, there was a crater of chewed-up earth where the other Wormwrot used to be. The men had been reduced to chunks of meat that were scattered around the crater. The Skojit had been blown onto his back, but not killed. He was trying to stand up. Moving slow. Disoriented.

Garret's whip was in the crater, about halfway between him and the Skojit.

He darted forward and picked up the whip. Reconnected it with a grunt. The current crackled and simmered, then died.

"Shit."

He tried again. Same thing. Jolan's orb must have damaged it.

"Having trouble with the Madman's toy?" Jolan asked.

Garret turned around to face him. The kid was standing on the far side of the crater. One arm inside a satchel on his hip.

"You got another one of your own toys in there?" he asked.

Jolan took another orb out of the satchel.

"So you work for the Madman now?" he asked. "Just another hired killer fighting for whoever pays?"

"That's all I've ever been, Jolan."

Jolan's jaw tensed. "I wish I'd killed you when I had the chance. More than anything."

"I warned you that would happen."

"You did," Jolan agreed.

There were shouts to their left. Wormwrot men were starting to come out of the termite mounds. They weren't moving like victorious men. The Skojit was still on his knees, but his senses were returning. Without a current in the whip, he didn't have a hope of capturing Ashlyn. Not today.

"If you're going to throw that thing at me, now's the time. Take you revenge, Jolan."

Jolan's face twisted into a snarl. He spun the gear on top of the orb and threw it at Garret.

The whip might have lost its current, but it was still a whip. Garret snapped the tip at the bomb, sending it straight into the air before it exploded.

38

JOLAN
Dainwood Jungle, Sector Nineteen

Jolan's vision turned white when the bomb exploded.

When it returned, Garret was gone.

Jolan cursed. Searched for him in the crowd of retreating men. But there were too many painted Wormwrot faces to find him.

Jolan recognized Vallen Vergun—the albino Wormwrot commander Bershad hated so much. He ordered his remaining men into a defensive line with a few barked orders. Bershad and the others stopped about twenty strides from their line.

"That was a clever trick with the masks, Silas," Vergun called. "Which one are you?"

Bershad stepped forward. Pulled off his mask and dropped it in the mud.

"You and I will settle this alone," he said.

Vergun smiled. "I'm afraid not, Silas. But I'm glad I got to see your face before the acolytes tear you apart."

"Call for 'em. See what happens."

Vallen's face faltered for a moment. Then he shouted.

"Acolytes!"

Everyone looked toward the warren's entrance. Jolan's stomach tensed, knowing that if the acolytes came out of it, everything was over.

But they didn't come out.

Ashlyn did.

The heads of the six acolytes were floating above her, neck stumps dripping black liquid across the dry grass. Her armbands were churning and steam was rising off her sweat-slick skin. Jolan knew that she probably couldn't keep that up for more than a minute or two, but in that moment, she looked downright terrifying. A true witch queen.

"Your acolytes cannot help you, Commander Vergun," she said.

Vergun's eyes narrowed. His face twisted into a mixture of frustration and rage.

"Back to the skyship!" he yelled.

His men didn't hesitate to follow the order. The skyship had its engines fully lit and fired before the last Wormwrot man had clambered into the hull. The skyship was airborne twenty seconds later, burning north.

When it was gone, the bands on Ashlyn's arm froze. The acolyte heads dropped.

Ashlyn collapsed. Put her head between her legs. Vomited.

She spent a few moments taking deep, heavy breaths. When she'd recovered, she wiped her sweat-soaked hair away from her eyes and spun up her bands again. Her lodestones popped out of the acolyte heads and collected in a pile next to her.

Jolan tried to imagine the massive amount of energy and control that had taken—never mind killing them in the first place. He was surprised that she was still alive.

The men of Naga Rock had scattered around the field. Some were clutching injuries. Others were just breathing hard and looking around, glad to be alive. Simeon came over to Jolan and removed his helmet. Even though there was a score of bloody abrasions on his cheek, he was grinning wild and wide.

"You got bigger balls than I gave you credit for, kid." He clapped Jolan on the back hard enough to send him stumbling forward. "Silas! You see what the kid did?"

"Missed it."

"He threw one of his little orbs into a horde of men and turned them to blackened chunks!" Simeon motioned to the crater behind them. "No hesitation. Screaming like a maniac. Fuck, you looked pissed. It was beautiful. How'd you know it wouldn't break through my armor?"

"I didn't."

For some reason, that made Simeon smile even wider.

Silas trotted over to Ashlyn. Jolan followed. Bent down and offered his canteen to her.

Ashlyn took a long drink, throat bobbing with urgency as she swallowed. Jolan noticed there was a single band still rotating near her wrist. She was still connected to something.

"Did you get it?" Jolan asked.

Ashlyn wiped her mouth with the back of her hand, then smiled. Three of her bands spun up to full speed again. A moment later, the harvest acolyte flew out of the warren. It was suspended about a stride off the ground, arms clamped tightly to its torso as if there was an invisible rope wrapped around it.

"Awaiting command," the acolyte said.

39

CASTOR
Castle Malgrave, Level 31

Neither Vergun nor Garret spoke a single word on the flight back to Floodhaven.

After their ship docked, all of them went to see Osyrus Ward.

They found him in one of his workshops in the middle of the

King's Tower, hunkered over a machine that appeared to be built around an enormous dragonslayer's horn. A hatch was open on one side, revealing an inner chamber full of glass tubes and wires.

"Ah. Our intrepid warriors have returned," said Osyrus, putting down his tools. "How did the harvest go?"

Vergun moved to a refreshment table and poured himself a large glass of wine. Downed it in a single gulp. Poured another.

"Your acolytes are dead."

Osyrus frowned. "How many?"

"All of them."

Ward's face darkened. He snapped two of his fingers, which produced a magnetic click due to some rings he had on his fingers. The hatch of the machine closed.

"Explain how that came to pass."

Vergun polished off the second glass, then slammed it down on the table hard enough to crack it.

"It was a trap."

"That was a known possibility, which is why I sent you with *six* war acolytes. That should have been enough to massacre half the Jaguar Army."

"The witch queen was there. She tore your creatures apart with those orbs of hers."

Ward glanced at Nebbin.

"Could she have broken through the countermeasures?" Nebbin asked.

"Anything is possible." Ward turned to Garret. "But that would not be an issue at all if you had done your job."

"The whip was damaged before I could reach her. The only option was to fall back."

"I need more ships," said Vergun. "They're still near that warren. I'll bring a whole company of Wormwrot with me and crush them."

Osyrus walked over to the table and poured himself a glass of wine, but didn't drink it. Just swished it around while he thought.

"You will have your ships, Commander Vergun. But your destination will be different."

"We know where they are."

Osyrus shook his head. "No, you know where they *were*. At this point, we must accept that engaging the troublesome cats in their jungle is not effective. It is time to try something new. If Ashlyn has truly found a way around the countermeasures, then she will likely be planning some kind of offensive. I think it best we put her on the defensive before that comes to fruition. Make her desperate. Panicked. That's the key to capturing her."

Castor cleared his throat. "How're we gonna put her on the defensive, exactly?"

"With this." Osyrus motioned to the machine he had been working on when they came in. "I have been developing an updated version of the beacon Vera used to reach the *Eternity*."

"Didn't that one explode before the job was done?" Castor asked, looking to Garret.

"Yes."

"That prototype was built in an obscene rush," said Ward. "This one is much more stable. With this machine installed on a skyship, that impenetrable blanket of troublesome Blackjacks that protect Deepdale will become decidedly *less* impenetrable."

"You want us to sack Deepdale?"

"I believe that Silas Bershad will react poorly should his ancestral seat be attacked. He'll pull the Jaguar Army back, and whatever Ashlyn Malgrave is planning will be crippled."

Vergun smiled. "Yes. Good."

While Vergun would obviously do anything to get a chance at killing Silas Bershad, Castor wasn't convinced.

"We're gonna be pretty exposed, waiting around for him in a city that's surrounded by dragons," said Castor.

Osyrus waved the problem off. "Ballista units are one of the few resources where we enjoy a surplus. Do not worry yourself, Castor. You will be well supplied and well protected." He paused, then added, "And, as always, exceptionally well *paid*. Any man who goes will receive a bonus of two thousand gold pieces."

Castor thought of his Dunfarian island. The clear water. The taste of fresh lobster.

"I'll go." He turned to Garret. "What about you, Hangman? It'd be good to have you."

Garret shook his head. "One way or another, Ashlyn's path ends in Floodhaven. I'll be waiting for her here."

"As you wish," said Ward. He motioned to the whip. "Give that to me. I'll repair it at my earliest convenience."

Garret turned the weapon over, then walked out of the room. Vergun followed him.

But Castor stayed.

"Something to add?" Osyrus asked.

Castor cleared his throat. "Silas Bershad was using a dragon-bone shield during the ambush. Worked real well for him. Given all the extra bones in this city, I was wondering if we can forge some for Wormwrot."

Osyrus pursed his lips. "That's possible. There is a treatment process required to deal with the weight that is rather costly and time consuming, but I believe this war will be coming to a head in the near future. Shields will prove useful. I'll earmark some surplus bone matter for that purpose and have them ready when you return from Deepdale. How's that?"

Castor nodded. "Works."

40

NOLA
City of Deepdale, Cat's Eye Tavern

The smell of freshly cooked bacon wafted through the common room of the Cat's Eye. Outside, it was raining. The droplets pinged off the rooftops in a gentle and steady cascade. Grittle was eating an extra portion of ribs that Nola had saved for her.

Experiencing those three wonderful things at the same time—the smell of the pork and the sound of the rain and the sight of Grittle eating an extra meal for the first time in a year—was almost enough to counterbalance the vexing presence of Elondron and three of his lieutenants in the Cat's Eye.

Per their agreement, she'd allowed them to set up an opium-peddling operation in the back half of the tavern, where there was easy access to the alley so they could slip away in the event that one of the few remaining wardens of the city wandered through in a mood for enforcement.

But the real advantage to the Cat's Eye was that it gave Elondron access to a fresh set of customers.

More than a few of Nola's regulars had started patronizing the back corner. Dervis, in particular, hadn't bought any food or drink from her in three days, but he'd been making regular visits to Elondron.

Currently, one of the gang members was recounting a story about beating a man half to death in an alley for fun. Elondron was laughing his ass off.

"Nola, I got a question for you," said Trotsky, coming over from his table.

She sighed. "Lay it on me."

"It's not that I'm opposed to sharing the tavern with folks of different strokes," he said, giving a little head jerk in Elondron's direction. "And I'm sure those four have a good reason that they're laughing in their seats instead of fighting in the war. But why is it they've decided to occupy *this* tavern all of a sudden? And how come you're not making them pay for their drinks?"

That had been an addendum to her agreement with Elondron. Along with permission to sell black sticky, his men were all drinking their fill of rain ale and potato liquor, when she had it in stock. That was eating into her profits at first, but Elondron had also come through with a stockpile of fresh hops that allowed her to scale production back up to normal amounts, which counteracted the losses.

"Did you enjoy the bacon you ate for breakfast?" Nola asked him.

"Oh, definitely. And I'm not complaining. Just curious why—"

"And did you like the pork loin you had for dinner two nights ago? Or the ribs from last week?"

Trotsky opened his mouth. Closed it again.

"Do the changes make sense now?"

He lowered his voice. "You threw in with a gang? Really?"

"Not like there's a tree outside my window growing alternative options. This place wasn't gonna survive on crickets and watered-down rain ale."

"Ha! I knew you were adding water."

"But not anymore," she said, moving over to the cask and pouring a fresh mug for Trotsky. "That one's on the house, Trot."

"Aye. On the house." He gave her a sad look. "Sure thing, Nola."

As Trotsky ambled back to his table, Nola returned to tallying up the final numbers from the night before and adding them to the ledger. She wasn't going to have trouble paying Lord Cuspar his next cut. Not at all.

She felt a pang of guilt looking at the health of her ledger, and knowing that so much of the city was still suffering. Still starving. But she shook the feeling off. She was protecting her brothers' memory. And she was protecting her sister. That was all that mattered right now. She could make up for her mistakes later.

"What's the matter?" Elondron asked, coming over and thumping an empty mug onto the counter. "You look like you ate a rotten egg or something."

Nola gave him a look. "Only thing rotten in here is you and yours."

"Uh-huh."

He motioned to the mug. Nola swiped it off the counter and filled it. When she came back, she slammed it onto the bar just hard enough to spill some beer on his sleeve.

"C'mon, there's no need for that. We can be cordial business partners."

"We're not business partners. You're a leech on the inside of my leg."

"Leeches don't do anything but suck blood." He looked around the busy room. "I believe me and my sticky have had a positive impact on this place."

Nola didn't say anything.

"You know, I'm not so different from you, Nola."

She gave him a look. "We're nothing alike."

He shook his head. Took a big gulp of beer. "You're just a little behind me in the journey, is all."

"What journey?"

"You think I want to be the asshole hoarding pigs and selling off black sticky? You think I dreamed of this life when I was a little boy? No." He leaned in close. "But when the lords and wardens of this fucked-up realm took all the other options for themselves, I did what needed doing to stay alive. And now here I am. *That's* the journey, and I see you making good headway."

"This is just temporary," said Nola.

"That's what I told myself, too. Way back. Said I'd change around when things got better. But what you gotta realize is that life never gets better. The desperation . . . the fight to survive . . . it never goes away for people like us, Nola. So you best get used to that dirty skin you're wearing. You can't change out of it, and it ain't easy to clean."

"I don't believe you."

Elondron shrugged again. "It's one of them lessons that takes a while to sink in."

He shoved off from the bar and headed back to his men.

"Hey, El!" shouted one of his men, a man named Lok. "Watch this!"

Lok threw a broken chair leg at Trotsky's head.

He hit the old warden in the temple, dropping him to the stone floor with a smack and a clatter. Elondron and Lok started laughing. The other patrons were looking around, startled and trying to figure out what had happened.

Pern was not laughing. And he'd seen exactly what happened. He was out of his chair in a heartbeat, crossing the room with a surprising amount of speed.

He punched Lok in the throat, which paused his laughter with an urgent purpose.

Lok dropped to his knees, eyes bulging and struggling to breathe. Face turning red. Nola didn't think that he was going to die, but she wouldn't have made a wager against it, either.

A few things happened very quickly.

Elondron drew one of his knives. So did his two remaining men with open airways. Pern held his ground, despite being outnumbered and unarmed. But behind him, without prompting, the regulars of the Cat's Eye tavern snatched up their knives and forks. Nola grabbed Grittle by the back of her apron and yanked her over to her side of the bar.

"Appears we have a bit of a fix brewing here," Elondron said. He looked down at Lok. "A real big one, if he dies."

Everyone was tense and quiet as they watched Lok. Most of Nola's patrons were old or crippled or both. Not fighters. But there were a lot more of them, and nobody seemed eager to back down. Even Jakell and Vindy and the Papyrian sisters had knives in their hands and hard stares in their eyes.

After what seemed like a very long time, Lok finally managed to suck in a proper breath of air. With great effort, he stood up. Pointed at Pern.

"Gonna kill you, old man."

"Give it a try," Pern growled.

"Nobody's killing anyone in my tavern!" Nola shouted, keeping Grittle behind her, but moving forward so she was between the two opposing sides. "We clear on that?"

"Can't let this pass, Nola," said Elondron. "You need to make it right."

"Your man's the one who threw the chair leg," said Nola. "A bump to the throat's about right, I think."

"That was a lot more than a bump," Lok muttered, then pointed at Trotsky, who was getting helped up by Jakell while Vindy held a napkin to the gash in the side of his head. "Look. He's fine."

"So are you," said Nola. "Now how about all of you just fuck off for the day, yeah? Come back when cooler heads prevail."

Lok shook his head. Drew his own knife and pointed it at Pern. "I'm gonna open your wrinkly throat, old man."

A lot of shouting ensued, most of it coming from her patrons, expressing their unhappiness with that statement, and plans to open other throats in return.

"Quiet!" Nola yelled. "Everyone shut up!"

Nola knew that this had spoiled everything. One thrown chair leg, and it was all ruined. But there was no way that she was letting them murder Pern so she could make rent. No way.

"Elondron," she said. "You and your men need to get out of my tavern. *Never* come back."

Elondron absorbed that news with a devious smile. "We'll leave. But we *will* come back."

"Just try it," growled Dervis, coming up next to Pern. "See what happens."

"Please. You only got one arm, and you're gonna be shaking for the sticky in an hour." He smiled again, wider. "And that's when I'll come knocking."

Things stayed tense for another moment. It broke when one of Elondron's men lowered his knife and pointed out the front window of the tavern with a shaking finger.

"Is that one o' the flying ships?"

Most of the people in the tavern assumed it was a foolish trick, but Elondron squinted out the window, and his face changed into an expression that was full of genuine and abject panic.

"Oh," he whispered. "Gods."

That got everyone to turn around except for Nola, who kept her eyes on Elondron just in case he was a better actor than she gave him credit for. But all he did was let his mouth hang open in terror.

"No—Nola?" Grittle asked, tugging at her apron. "Look . . ."

Nola turned.

There was a skyship coming in from the east. It had black sails and iron armaments jutting from its deck. The smell of burning dragon oil filled Nola's nostrils as it got closer.

"How did they get past the dragons?" Vindy asked, ducking down beneath a table, as if that was going to save her.

"It's impossible," said Jakell. "The Blackjacks always protect Deepdale."

"Well, they're not protecting us anymore," said Nola.

The skyship stopped a block away from the tavern. Nola saw black ropes drop to the street. They thrashed and snapped like snakes, then a series of figures slid down them in quick succession.

They all wore black armor with animal fur around the collar. Their faces were painted blood red.

Wormwrot.

The mercenaries drew weapons and fanned out along the street. One of them headed for the tavern with a grim purpose and kicked the door open with muddy boot. He slammed the pommel of his sword into the man nearest the door, spraying teeth across the floor. Six other mercenaries came through the door behind him.

"Come quiet, no kill," said the man who'd kicked in the door. He spoke broken Almiran with a thick accent that Nola didn't recognize. "Make fuss, die with guts jammed down throat."

There was a moment of tense silence as the Wormwrot men realized they'd just barged into a tavern where every single patron was holding at least some kind of weapon. The man with the strange accent frowned, and the smallest look of uncertainty crossed his face.

"Kill these foreign fucks!" Elondron shouted, then rushed forward with his knife.

The whole tavern lit up with a war howl. One Wormwrot swiped at Elondron, but he slid to the side and rammed a knife through his ear. Left it there. Grabbed a bottle and smashed it against another Wormwrot's painted face.

"Nola, knife!" shouted Pern.

She grabbed her heaviest butcher knife and gave it a clumsy throw. Despite her shitty aim and angle, Pern caught it by the handle and then rushed forward, cleaving a mercenary's head apart. Everyone else rushed forward, shoving, stomping, stabbing, and kicking.

"Nola!" cried Grittle.

The man with the strange accent had snuck around the bar and yanked Grittle to the floor. He reared up with his sword, moving to stab her.

Nola didn't think. She threw a jar of pickles at his head, which shattered and got him to stop long enough for her to sprint across the room and start kicking him in the face.

Once.

Twice.

And then a lot more. So many times she lost track and her thigh was aching when it was over and the man's face was bloody, his teeth broken. He finally released Grittle from his grasp, groaning from the boot kicks.

Nola grabbed Grittle and carried her to the far corner of the bar.

Her shoulders were heaving. Her heart was racing. Her mouth felt like she'd been sucking on a copper coin. Gods, she was scared.

But when she looked up, she saw that the other Wormwrot were dead.

In all her life, Nola had never seen a man die. Now, in the space of one minute, she'd seen five of them murdered. Kicked one to the brink of death herself, seemed like.

Outside, the ship was still hovering overhead and casting a shadow on the street. Wormwrot men were yelling and screaming at people in foreign languages, marching them out of their homes and buildings.

"What do we do?" Vindy wailed.

Nola looked to Pern, then to Elondron. Both of them had blood splashed across their faces, but didn't appear to have an immediate answer to that question. Nola pointed to the alley door.

"Out the back. Everyone." She grabbed Grittle's hands and placed them on the belt loop of her pants. "You do not let go of me, no matter what happens. Understand?"

Grittle nodded. There were tears in her eyes.

"It's going to be okay." Nola paused. "I promise."

Everyone made it out of the tavern and down the alley to the first intersection without trouble. But things went to shit in progressive stages from there.

The skyship had dropped men all over the city, so as soon as they left the shelter of the alley, Wormwrot men were on them—shoving people to the ground and binding their hands with lengths of black rope. Lok ran off on his own and got tackled by two soldiers. He resisted, and got his head slammed into the cobblestones until he was either unconscious or dead.

A mercenary grabbed Nola, then Pern grabbed the mercenary and dislocated his shoulder with a hard jerk.

"Keep moving!" he growled through gritted teeth.

"To where?" asked Jakell. He was holding Vindy's hand tight.

"We need to get out of Deepdale," said Elondron. "This way. Quick."

Nola followed Elondron down another alley, but someone grabbed her ankle and pulled her to the ground. Her ear slammed against the road and she lost all hearing on that side. She wormed and kicked and eventually broke free from whoever had grabbed her. Grittle helped her back up to her feet.

They reached the next alley and kept running. Nola's face was blurry with tears and her ankle was screaming in pain. Grittle slipped in a dirty puddle and went down, yelping as she skinned her palms on the rough stones. Nola hauled her back up.

"Keep going," she whispered. "We'll be okay. We'll be okay."

She was saying it for Grittle, but she was saying it for herself, too.

Elondron, Jakell, and Vindy were ahead of her now. She wasn't sure who was behind.

Jakell ducked behind a set of crates and pulled out a set of keys.

"What are you doing?" Nola hissed, when Jakell started to open the door.

"This is my shop," he said, opening the door. "We'll hide inside."

"Wormwrot are everywhere. Your shop won't hide us forever. We need the Gloom."

Pern sidled up next to Nola. Trotsky was behind him. No sign of Suko or Kiko or anyone else. Was that it? There had been twenty people in the tavern.

Jakell got the door open with a click. "Do what you want, we're hiding in here. There's a good spot."

He and Vindy went inside, and Jakell pulled up the carpet of his workshop, revealing a trapdoor underneath. Nola gave Pern and Trotsky a look. "What do you think?"

"I'd reach the Gloom if I could," said Trotsky. "But with my knee, I can't believe I got this far."

Nola turned to Elondron. "Give me a minute. I want to check it out."

Elondron wiped his brow, leaving a dirty smear across his forehead. "No promises."

Nola took Grittle's hand and went inside the workshop. Jakell had a decent-sized crawlspace beneath the floor that was lined with shelves of canned food.

"Jakell," muttered Trotsky. "How did you save all this?"

"Huh?" asked Jakell, who was struggling with the trapdoor. "Oh, well. Everyone needs shoes. Except Silas fucking Bershad. C'mon. Everyone get down here."

Vindy went first, then Jakell. He extended his hand.

Nola grabbed Grittle's hand and pressed it into his. "Go."

Grittle clambered down. Look up at her and extended her hand. "C'mon, Nola!"

Nola squinted at the space. There was only enough room left for one person. Any more, and they wouldn't be able to close the hatch.

"Trotsky, you go," she said.

"What? No, you need to stay with your sister."

"It's like you said, Trotsky. With your knee, you'll never make it out." She looked at him. "And I need a warden to protect my sister. Understand? You keep her *safe*."

Trotsky gave her a slow nod. "I will."

Nola knelt down. "Grittle—"

"No!" her sister cried, batting at her with her hands. "No, no, no. You can't leave me!"

"Grittle. Stop. Stop it." Nola put both hands on her shoulders. Got her to stop struggling. "I need you to be strong now. I need you to be brave."

"I'm so scared."

"I know that you are," said Nola. "I'm scared, too. But you're going to be safe in there until I get back. I'll go get help. I'll get Lord Silas."

Grittle sniffled. "Do you promise?"

Nola's voice caught in her throat. "I promise."

She kissed her sister's forehead. Hugged her tight.

"Now go. Go down with Trotsky. I'll be back as soon as I can."

Once they'd managed to crunch themselves into the crawlspace, Pern helped Nola close the trapdoor and throw the carpet over it again. They locked the workshop behind them.

Elondron was still outside. He opened his mouth to say something cruel, no doubt, but stopped short when he saw Nola's face. He gave a little nod. "I can get us out of the city. Then we can track down the Jaguar Army and bring them back."

"How?"

"Canal gate. There's a route we use to get in and out of the city unseen."

She nodded. "Lead the way."

Wormwrot were everywhere, but they managed to avoid the patrols by sticking to the alleys and side streets, using the shadows and the refuse as cover. By the time they reached the canal gate, Nola was completely covered in mud. Her lungs were burning. The acid feeling of terror was burning through her stomach. Pern was wheezing in a way that made it sound like his lungs were full of dust.

Problem was, there was a score of Wormwrot waiting there. They were rounding up anyone who tried to leave the city and throwing them into a big wagon.

"Why are they bothering to take prisoners?" asked Pern from their hiding spot behind a broken wagon.

Elondron shrugged. "All I know is that I'm not in a rush to become one."

"But we're never getting past them," said Pern.

Nola looked around. Tried to think of something.

"The canal," she said. "We can get out that way."

"Swim the tube?" Elondron asked. "You're crazy."

"We used to do it as kids on dares," said Nola. "It's not that hard,
the current does most of the work."

"The fuck it does."

"It's our only way out of the city."

Elondron chewed on that. "The current does most of the work?"

"Right."

"I'm in."

Pern scanned the canal. Every breath that he took was a dry
wheeze. He looked back at the guards. They weren't shoving anyone in the wagons currently, just watching the different streets.

"I'll distract them."

Nola frowned. "You sure?"

"They're not killing people. Not yet, anyway. Better to take my
chances in the wagon than try to hold my breath in that tunnel."

"All right." She turned to Elondron. "Look, I know we were inch-
ing toward a bit of a problem back there, but—"

"Forget it," he said. "We've got a bigger problem now." He paused.
"It's my city, too. Last thing I'm gonna do is let the fucking Balarians take it. We get out, then we get to the Jaguars."

"Yeah. Okay."

Pern gave her a nod. "I'm ready."

The old warden took a moment to collect himself, then broke from
cover and charged the gate, bellowing out a war cry that turned into
another wheeze. Only two Wormwrot responded to his charge at
first, but when he tripped one of them and slipped past the other,
more rushed him.

That's when Nola broke for the canal.

From the corner of her eye, she saw Pern get stiff-armed and
dropped to the ground. Someone pinned his arm behind his back.

By the time one of the mercenaries noticed Nola running for the
canal, she still had about fifty paces to go.

Shit. Faster. Faster.

Nola heard shouting in a foreign language. Then the clomp of
boots behind her. She cleared the road, then the overgrowth that
bordered the canal.

Leapt into the air.

Someone grabbed her by the hair. Ripped her to the ground.

Elondron had all his momentum going toward the canal, so there was nothing he could do when the man who'd grabbed her hair clotheslined him with a sheathed sword. He slammed into the ground next to her.

Nola gasped for air. Elondron clutched his chest.

The man who had hit them wasn't wearing face paint. That made it easy for Nola to see that both his skin and long hair were as pale as freshly fallen snow.

"It appears we have caught a pair of fish," he said in fluent Almiran.

Nola was still too stunned to do much besides sit on the ground and gasp, but Elondron was apparently faster to recover from being snatched back to the earth with sudden violence. He lunged toward the pale man, who caught him by the throat. Lifted him off his feet.

"Brave fish, as it were," he said.

Elondron didn't respond. Couldn't, really, with the man's hand clamped around his throat.

"Silas Bershad will find out what you've done," Nola hissed. "And when he does, he'll come back for us."

The pale man responded with a smile. "I'm counting on it."

He glanced over the lip of the canal, down at the rushing water. Turned back to Elondron.

"Tell you what," the pale man continued. "I will let you take your chances with the river, under one very simple condition. Should you survive, you will find Silas Bershad and deliver a message to him. Do you agree to these terms?"

He relaxed his grip on Elondron's throat just enough for him to rasp out two strained words.

"What. Message."

"Tell him that Vallen Vergun now rules Deepdale. And so long as I do, none of her people will see the shelter of a roof or a bed. None will taste any food. Meanwhile, I will take each of my daily meals from their flesh. And I will continue doing so until he comes to see me, or I run out of people to eat."

Nola's throat went dry. Vision blurry with panic. That's why they weren't killing anyone. This insane man was going to eat them all.

Nola thought of Grittle. Prayed to all the forest gods she was still hidden.

"Do you understand this message?" Vergun asked.

Elondron nodded.

"Good." Vergun threw Elondron into the water with casual disregard. He landed in the canal's rain-swollen and brown water. Disappeared.

While he was momentarily distracted, Nola got up and ran.

She wasn't heading in any particular direction. Just away from that insane cannibal. But she only made it a few strides before someone grabbed her by the back of the neck and threw her to the ground again.

She looked up to find the battered face of the Wormwrot whose face she'd kicked in at the tavern. He was smiling at her with a set of black, broken teeth.

"Caught you, little fishy."

41

VERA
Pargos, Above the City of Nulsine

Pargos was beautiful.

The landscape was nothing like the brown, lifeless deserts of Balaria, nor was it like the wild and dangerous forests of Almira. Everything was manicured and tame. Vera looked out at long rows of olive trees that extended in all directions around the village of Nisena.

"Seems a little too . . . agricultural to be holding some secret archive, don't it?" Entras asked as he guided the *Sparrow* toward the village.

"Secret archive," Vera replied. "Which makes this the perfect location."

"So, are we going to just go knocking on doors, or—" Decimar stopped midsentence. Squinted. "Shit."

"What?"

He pointed to the middle of the village. "There."

Entras looked, too. "We don't all have your eyes, Soft Star. How about you just tell me what you see?"

"There's a burned-down building," Vera said. She could just make out the blackened beams and scorched rooftop.

"So, it's two Soft Stars we have on board now, is it?" Entras mumbled, mostly to himself. "Fantastic."

"What does it mean?" Decimar asked Vera.

"I don't know, but it's unlikely to be good."

———————

Judging from the ankle-high weeds that were growing amidst the ashes of the building, it had been burned down in early spring.

"Why haven't they rebuilt it?" Decimar asked, picking up a scorched book and leafing through the burnt pages. "Or torn it down, at least?"

"Maybe they wanted to dissuade whoever did this from coming back and burning it down all over again." Vera motioned to the book. "Can you make out the title?"

"*Liam Shates's Sonnets, Volume 23.*"

"Poetry?"

"Yeah." Decimar scanned a few more burned books. "Seems like they had all of Shates's stuff."

"If Caellan was an expert on human spinal cords, why was she posted at an archive full of poetry?" Vera asked.

"We don't know if she was here at all," Decimar said. "Only thing left is ashes."

Vera didn't respond, just kept exploring the burned-out rooms. Toward the back, there was a room where the shelves were arranged in a series of concentric circles. Vera moved through the small gaps in the shelves until she reached the middle.

There was a pit leading underground. The pit was full of ash.

"I think the fire started here," said Vera.

Decimar peered inside. "How deep do you think that goes?"

"I know an easy way to find out," Vera said, then jumped down, dropping waist-deep in ash before her feet hit the floor.

"Vera, why are you always so eager to jump off things?"

"Because it usually saves time."

"Doesn't save time if you'd suffocated on a bunch of incinerated poems just now."

Vera picked up a palmful of ash, sifting around for a scrap of legible remains. There were none. This area must have burned hotter than the upper levels. A lot hotter.

"I don't think this tunnel was full of poems, but whatever was in here is lost." Vera blew out a breath. "C'mon. Help me back up."

Vera went back to the street. Scanned the village. There was a young woman in her twenties helping a much older man with a cane make his way toward the center of town. The woman glanced at Vera, but didn't seem particularly interested.

"Have the men start cleaning this up," Vera said to Decimar.

"Clean it up? Looks like it's been this way for a whole season. You see the weeds growing in there?"

"I do," said Vera. "But I want you to clean it up all the same."

"Why?"

"Just do it, Decimar."

Vera trotted down the marble stairs, heading toward the woman and man.

"Hello. Do either of you speak Balarian?" Vera asked, which comprised the total sum of Pargossian words she had.

The young woman stopped and gave her a big smile full of crooked teeth, then spoke in a thick, but intelligible accent. "Better than you speak Pargossian, anyway."

"My apologies," said Vera, glad to switch to Balarian. "I can understand some, but haven't spoken it in many years."

"That's obvious," said the woman.

"My name is Vera."

"I'm Salle. This is my grandpop, Kyal."

Kyal sucked on his gums and squinted at her, then spoke in a much more thickly accented Pargossian that Vera could barely understand. "Why've we stopped? It's time for my bath."

"You'll have to forgive Kyal. He's a grumpy bastard." She turned to him. "The water garden ain't going nowhere, pops."

"I was wondering if I could ask you a few questions about that building," said Vera.

The woman put a hand over her eyes and appraised the building, as if she'd just noticed it was there. "What do you want to know?"

"How did it burn down?"

"Your lot came through at the start o' spring and did that. Seemed strange, a bunch o' Balarians going so far out of their way to torch a bunch o' love poems, but we all figured it was better than getting our olives took."

"You work the orchards, then?"

"Aye, everyone in Nisena does, just about. My family's been at the groves for seven generations. Got olive juice in our veins, don't we, pop?"

"Olive . . . juice . . ." The man spat. "I hate olives."

"Sure you do, pop. Sure you do."

"Are there any alchemists in the village?" Vera asked.

"Alchemists?"

"People who wear gray robes," Vera prompted. "Healers."

"Oh, sure. That lot. They was always more readers than healers from what I saw."

"Bunch o' soft-palmed pansies," Kyal added.

Decimar snorted behind her.

"Where did they go?" Vera asked.

"They scattered after the fire. Haven't seen any of 'em since. Never had much use for them nohow, 'less someone took a tumble out of a tree and snapped a bone. And being honest, we can take care o' that ourselves. Don't need to read poetry for a decade to set a broken bone."

Vera was tempted to ask about Caellan, but something told her a direct approach wouldn't do her much good in this situation. It wasn't like a Burz-al-dun tavern where she could walk in and intimidate people into revealing their true selves. She didn't have any leverage unless she used force, which she wasn't willing to do. Not yet.

"Any idea where they went?"

Salle shrugged. "Lady, I barely know what's in store for me half a day's walk down that road. They fucked off and that's the last anyone here's seen of 'em." She squinted into the burned-out building. "What're your lot doing in there, now? Came to burn it down a little more?"

"They're cleaning up."

"Seems kinda pointless. The poets ain't coming back, don't think."

"All the same."

Salle shrugged. "Suit yourself."

"Okay. Thank you for your time." She smiled at Kyal. "Enjoy your bath."

Kyal muttered something under his breath that Vera didn't catch. Started limping away. Salle hurried to catch up.

"You might consider having a bath yourself," Salle said over her shoulder. "All are welcome, and meaning no offense, you smell like you could use one."

The duo moved away, each step marked with a strike of the cane on the cobblestone.

"Did that backwater yokel just tell you to your face that you stink?" Decimar asked.

"She did."

Vera started unstrapping her armor.

"What are you doing?"

"She kind of has a point. I'm going for a bath."

"While we clean up all the torched poetry."

"Correct."

Once Vera got her armor off, she pulled the daggers off her hips and passed them to Decimar. "Keep an eye on these while I'm gone."

"Is that a good idea? Those two seemed harmless enough, but if Balarians have come through burning buildings down, might not have curried as much favor amongst the other locals. Wouldn't want you to get an olive corer jammed into the back of your head or anything."

"I'll be fine," Vera said. "Blades aren't going to get me where I want to go."

"Where's that, exactly?"

Vera just smiled. Motioned to her daggers. "Don't fool with those while I'm gone. They're very sharp."

———

The water garden of Nisena was a series of natural springs that pooled amongst a set of terraced rocks. Small, bent trees with wide, parasol leaves kept the entire area in a comfortable shade. Tiny birds the color of Kira's eyes filled the branches. They chirped at each other and ate berries.

Salle and Kyal were already undressed and submerged in the closest pool, which they shared with five middle-aged men—all of them had sun-soaked skin and musclebound arms. They gave her wary looks, but made no move to stop her from entering the garden. Higher up, there was a group of small children splashing each other in one pool, and higher up still, an older couple wedged close together, whispering to each other and smiling.

Vera took a seat near Salle and Kyal. Started working her boots off.

"You came," said Salle, who was rubbing at her pale shoulder with a pumice stone. Kyal was doing the same, but struggling to stretch beyond the easiest spots to reach.

"Surprised?" Vera asked, getting one boot off with a grunt and moving to the next.

"Not as surprised as the fact that you took your armor off. Thought widows weren't allowed to do that."

"Met a lot of Papyrian widows, have you?"

Salle snorted. "You don't need to have met a widow to hear stories about them. Your lot's famous for their fearsomeness."

"Those five don't seem too afraid," said Vera, motioning to the men. She got the second boot off, then started unwinding her shirt.

"As for the armor, it's not that we can't take it off. It's that showing vulnerability is usually a bad idea."

She finished undressing, then slipped into the water, which was clear and cool and felt wonderful on her aching muscles and deep bruises. She closed her eyes for a moment, allowing a few heartbeats of emptiness to calm her worried mind.

"Wow. You, uh, *really* needed a bath."

Vera opened her eyes and looked at the water around her, which had become a murky black cloud that was slowly drifting toward Salle and Kyal.

"Shit, sorry." Vera made a useless attempt at containing the spread of her filthy water.

Salle laughed. "Don't worry about it. We're no strangers to a little dirt, ain't that right, pop?"

"Dirt's one thing," he said in Pargossian, then glared at Vera. "Foreign mud off a foreign body, though. Stinks like Papyrian trash."

Salle rolled her eyes. "If you caught that, you're gonna have to forgive Kyal's manners. He's close enough to death now that he doesn't bother with them."

Vera made a face to show she'd understood, and that it wasn't a problem.

"Here, let me help you with your back," Salle said to Kyal, reaching for the pumice.

"I ain't *that* old."

"Then explain to me why you've got such a large amount of crusted dirt all over your shoulders."

Kyal grumbled, but moved so that Salle could help him. For a little while, none of them said anything. Vera listened to the birds and splashed some water on her face until she couldn't taste the salt from her sweat changing the flavor of the water, which took a while. Then she leaned back on a rock.

"Tell me, do all of the olive farmers of Pargos speak Balarian as well as you?"

Salle smiled. "Dunno. You'd have to conduct one o' them surveys the alchemists liked so much, I suppose." She finished up with Kyal's back and swished the stone around in the water to clean it off. "What did you want with them, anyway?"

"I need a healer."

Salle frowned. "You've clearly taken your share of licks." She motioned to Vera's scarred shoulders, bruised arms, and missing finger. "But I don't see any imminent threats to your health."

"Not for me. For someone who I care about."

"Well, seeing as you got that flying ship and all, doesn't seem like tracking down some other alchemist is gonna be an issue."

"I need someone in particular. Someone who has a very specific kind of knowledge." Vera took a breath. Got ready to take a risk. "A woman named Caellan."

"Caellan," Salle repeated, then glanced at Kyal, who was still frowning at the water. "And tell me, who's this person that needs healing?"

"Her name is Kira."

"The empress of Balaria?"

"I'm not sure that she's empress of anything anymore. Not really. Osyrus Ward controls the ministers and the food and the dragon oil. The soldiers and the skyships."

"You have come here with soldiers and a skyship," Salle said. "Does Osyrus Ward control you?"

"No." Vera shook her head. "Not anymore. And I can never return to his service now that I've broken from it. My only path is forward, to Caellan. And I don't even know if she can actually help me." Vera's voice caught in her throat, against her will. She struggled to pull herself together, and didn't succeed. "But she's my last hope for saving Ki."

"Forgive me, Vera, but I do have one last question." Salle paused. "Why is it that you decided to strip down naked and tell us all of this?"

"Because I wanted to show you that I won't use that skyship and those soldiers to pry information from you with violence. I won't burn down your buildings, like Osyrus Ward did. But I'll risk my own life for an answer. I will *give* my life for a way to get Caellan to help Kira. I'll give it gladly."

There was a silence while Salle studied her.

"What do you think, pop?"

The old man turned to Vera. Face all screwed up and suspicious. Then, without warning, his face softened and his back straightened. He spoke to her in perfect Papyrian.

"I think that Vera has earned a look at Caellan's chamber."

————————

They all dressed, and headed back to the burned-out library.

"Caellan still lives in Nisena?" Vera asked.

"I'm sorry to disappoint you, but Caellan disappeared from this archive more than seven years ago," Kyal said. "Her fate is unknown to any alchemist."

"So, you're both alchemists?" Vera asked.

"Correct," Kyal replied, moving considerably faster than before, but still relying on the cane to stabilize his gate. "I am a master in the order. Salle is my apprentice."

"An apprentice who can practically taste the rank of journeyman on her tongue," Salle said with a little wink. Her Papyrian accent wasn't quite as good as Kyal's, but it was close, and she spoke it with a barely contained energy that made Vera homesick. She hadn't heard someone speak her native tongue that way in a long time. Vera certainly didn't talk that way anymore. Maybe she never did.

Kyal scoffed. "I don't know any journeymen who still cannot complete the equation required to give me the correct diameter of the moon."

"That's the last thing, though!"

"And judging from the mess that was your last attempt, you still have a long way to go."

Salle waved him away. "I'm closer than I seem."

"Mm. Your calculus tells me a different story." Kyal glanced at Vera. "Tell me, do you have close contact with Osyrus Ward?"

"Closer than most," said Vera.

"What is your impression of him?"

Vera chewed on that a moment. "Highly intelligent. His ability to predict a person or group of people's future actions is . . . intimidatingly accurate." She paused. "He's also insane."

Kyal grunted. "A decent summary."

"You know him?"

"Knew him. As a boy, we were both apprentices of a similar age, and our masters were friends, so we saw quite a bit of each other."

"What was he like back then?"

Kyal considered that. "Intelligent, as you said. Also impatient. He couldn't stand the rote learning that apprentices must endure their first year."

"Neither could I," Salle added.

"I found a comfort to the routine, myself. Memorization is a particular skill of mine. How is your memory, Vera?"

"Don't answer that," Salle warned. "Regardless of your answer, he'll have you doing mental drills and techniques in no time."

"My memory is fine," Vera said. "So, Osyrus was trained as an alchemist?"

"Bah, not even half-trained. He was expelled from our order after three years."

"Why?"

"He was torturing animals. Well, as I recall, he described it as experimenting with live specimens. But the order does not offer much leeway when they see that kind of behavior from a pupil. It is often a precursor to more problematic behavior later in life."

"Ward's behavior is certainly problematic now," said Vera.

"Maybe they should have let him stay," said Salle. "Guided him in the right direction, instead of allowing him to forge his own."

"If he'd stayed, he would simply have been imbued with more tools with which to twist the world."

"Not trying to be difficult, master, but he appears to have forged an adequate number of tools without our help."

Kyal grumbled to himself.

"Come, let's pick up our pace. Caellan's chamber was on the second floor, where the fire was less severe."

———

Caellan's room was just a simple cell—eight strides by eight strides. There was some soot around the windows, but it was otherwise untouched by the fire that had raged below.

"It is alchemist procedure to put deceased members' belongings in the deep cellars, but since Caellan is technically missing, not dead, her quarters have been left intact. Some consider this to be a waste of space, but the procedure exists for a reason. Master Epplatus once disappeared for seventeen years on a research mission." Kyal chuckled. "I still remember the day he returned, and complained that someone had been using his forks. The tines were bent or something. Anyway, this is what she left behind."

Kyal motioned to three items. Vera squatted down to examine them: A needle made from some kind of animal's bone. A piece of rolled parchment. And a curved knife that seemed like it was made for cleaving plants.

"Nothing else?" Vera asked.

"Nothing."

She unrolled the paper to find that it was a map of the realm of Terra, but drawn with thousands of circular swirls that gave the illusion of elevation.

"What's this?"

"Oh, I wouldn't give that as much attention as it might seem to warrant. Every alchemist must draw one in their fifth year of study, before they're allowed to embark upon surveys in the wilderness. The lines are topographic delineations, and help display accurate elevation levels, which impact the warrens and wildlife of the world greatly."

Vera scanned the map, eyes lingering over the myriad lines that comprised the Razorback Mountains. It made her think of her journey across that nightmare.

"Do all alchemists keep the maps they make?" Vera asked.

"Not all of them," Kyal admitted. "But it's a common practice. Many of us consider our maps to be a mark of pride. Mine is still in my quarters."

Vera glanced at Salle. "You?"

"I got mine somewhere folded up, yeah. Bastard took so long to draw, it seemed like a sin to get rid of it."

"After Caellan left, several of the masters dedicated significant time to studying her map, thinking she may have marked her location for some reason. They did not find anything."

"Hm."

Vera picked up the bone needle. There were a few markings along the side that seemed more about measurements than any kind of code or clue as to where Caellan had gone. The knife had some dried bits of long-dead grass crammed into one of the notches. The handle was worn smooth from use.

"What was Caellan like, generally?"

"Well, your information is correct in that Caellan knew more about spinal cords than anyone else in the order. It is a very complicated aspect of our bodies—bones and nerves and tissue all woven into an intricate and delicate braid. She was incredibly adept at tracing damage back to its original—"

"No, not her work," Vera interrupted. "Tell me about her. As a person."

Kyal hesitated. "To be frank, she was not so unlike Osyrus Ward. Her experiments and studies often stretched beyond the bounds of what our order was comfortable with, and so did her behavior. She was brusque. She hoarded materials. Drank liquor often, and in great volume." He hesitated. "Generally, she was not well liked."

"Why wasn't she expelled?" Salle asked. Apparently, all of this was new information to her as well. "I haven't had more than half a glass of wine in five years because of your intolerance of a little fun."

Kyal rubbed his hands together with clear discomfort. "At the time, the king of Pargos had two sons. One was healthy and strong, his heir." He cleared his throat. "The second was born with a degenerative condition that impacted his spinal column. Caellan was . . . quite helpful with his treatments."

Salle scoffed. "I see. Generating favor from a king does tend to earn some leniencies."

"Yes." Kyal opened his hands. "Her work was truly brilliant. She was just . . . eccentric."

"She seems like someone in whom Osyrus Ward might have an interest."

Kyal shrugged. "To my knowledge, the two of them never met."

Vera believed that Kyal was telling the truth, but she also believed that his knowledge was both incomplete and deliberately limited. She walked around the room. Ran a finger along the windowsill, then flicked away the small layer of ash that accrued on her glove.

"Tell me more about when she disappeared."

"When, or why?"

"Both."

"The when is simple. Seven years and three months ago. The why . . . nobody knows. She came back from a contract in northern Balaria and spent three days getting drunk in this very room. Then, on the fourth morning, we found several obscure documents missing from the archives, and she was gone. The masters were furious. Stealing documents is strictly forbidden, and while it seems a bit moot now, it was agreed that she would face strict punishment upon her return."

"But not expulsion," Salle added, her voice bitter. "Because of the *prince*."

Kyal gave a helpless groan. "As I said, the point is moot."

"What was the contract that she took in Balaria?" Vera asked.

"The contract? Oh, something to do with a governor's old war injury."

"She didn't say anything about it?"

"Just that it was a success. Although I remember that she did not seem particularly happy about that."

Vera paused. "This is all useful information, but . . ."

"It does not bring you any closer to Caellan," Kyal finished.

Vera nodded.

"I don't want to dissuade you from your search, but as I said before, many people have searched for Caellan. Members of our order, and others. None found her."

Vera left the chamber. Looked down the hallway, where there were nine more identical doors.

"Where are the others?" Vera asked.

Vera searched Kyal's face, then Salle's. Both of them were filled with a deep sadness.

"They didn't survive, did they?"

"They had their job," Salle said. "And we have ours."

"What job?"

"Should the library be discovered, they were to preserve and protect the records if possible, but destroy them should they be at risk of falling into the wrong hands."

Vera finally understood. "Osyrus Ward didn't burn this building down." She turned to them. "Alchemists did."

Kyal nodded. "He arrived with his gray-skinned creatures and stormed the building. I do not know what transpired exactly, only that no alchemist nor records survived."

"How did you two survive?"

"Protocol," Salle whispered. There were tears in her eyes, which she blinked away.

Vera looked to Kyal for an explanation.

"Many years ago, Empress Okinu's operatives infiltrated our archive and stole . . . information of great value." Vera noted Kyal's word choice sidestepped the fact that Okinu's operatives had almost certainly been widows. "After that loss, new protocols were created to prevent the incident from being repeated. It was decided that it was better to destroy the physical records than allow them to be misused. In that event, one master and their apprentice would break off from the order and hide among the populace. I held the responsibility as an apprentice for many years, and now as the master."

"What responsibility?"

"He remembers," said Salle. Then smiled bitterly. "And I write."

"I don't understand."

"Perhaps it is easier to show you, than to explain," said Kyal. "And I, for one, relish the chance to leave this place for a time. Come to our home, please. I believe we could all use some refreshment."

———

Kyal and Salle lived in a small cottage on the outskirts of town. It had four rooms. Two of them were small bedchambers. One was a small kitchen. The other was a common room that was crammed from floor to ceiling with sheaves of paper. Kyal entered the common room while Salle moved to the kitchen to brew a pot of tea.

"We're nearly finished with Lionel Cha's survey of Lysterian dragon warrens," he said, picking up a sheaf of paper and giving it a quick scan. "Always liked that one."

"I've found the dictation quite dull," Salle called from the kitchen. "He didn't even find anything useful. All the Gods Moss in that warren had been picked clean by an invasive beetle. Can we *please* do one that's more interesting next?"

"They're all interesting," said Kyal, then tapped the side of his temple. "But I will see what the darkened room has for you."

Vera finally understood. "You *memorized* the entire archive?"

"Yes."

"How long did that take?" Vera asked.

"The burden is a heavy one," Kyal said. "But the knowledge must be passed on."

"It wouldn't be so easy to lose if the alchemists did not keep so much of it a secret," said Vera.

"Perhaps that is true," Kyal admitted. "We are an order so steeped in rules, they have become wrapped around us like chains. I am too old to change, but Salle . . . she may carry on as she sees fit."

Vera looked around at the freshly written books. "Is there anything here that can help Kira?"

"I am afraid that while Caellan was a most brilliant individual, she did not contribute her work to the archives before disappearing."

Vera sat down on an olive crate. Sank her shoulders. Despite everything she'd learned about Caellan, this was a dead end.

The teakettle started to whistle. Salle came in with a mug and put it in Vera's hands. "Something to remind you of home."

Vera took a sip, savoring the old but familiar flavor. She hadn't had a good cup of *Oricha* in years.

"Thank you," she murmured, then took another sip.

"Will you stay for dinner?" Salle asked.

"No. I need to be moving on."

"Where will you go?" Salle asked.

"I'm not sure. Maybe to the city in Balaria where Caellan took her last job. Do you remember what it was called?"

Salle snorted. "Vera, by now you should know that you don't need to ask Kyal if he remembers something."

"Right. Well, let's have it, then?"

The old man smiled. "Craz-al-dig."

Vera nodded. It was a shitty lead, but it was something.

She blew on the tea, mostly so she could cool it down enough to drink it faster. It was good, but it reminded her of a place where she no longer belonged, and she could never return.

That reality was enough to turn any drink bitter.

———

When Vera was halfway back to the *Sparrow,* she heard the footsteps of someone following her.

Normally, she'd have taken cover in a shadowy corner, but she already knew who it was. She'd gotten a good sense of Salle's footfalls during their time together.

Vera turned and waited in the street. When Salle came around, she was carrying a familiar roll of parchment.

Caellan's map.

"When did you take that?" Vera asked.

Salle shrugged. "Kyal would have grumbled. Procedure and all. But I figured you should have it."

"Why?"

"Seems you're willing to scrape this realm down to the bone to find Caellan. You'll need a map."

"There are maps on the skyship."

"I know." Salle smiled. "And like Kyal said, there's nothing special about this one."

Vera narrowed her eyes. "So you came running all this way to give me a map that isn't special?"

"I did." She paused. "And to tell you something about the ways these get made."

"All right."

"The process for drawing the topography is very particular—each swirl is drawn in a clockwise motion, so as to keep the look uniform and consistent across different maps drawn by different alchemists. But alchemists don't learn that until their fourth year of study."

Vera chewed on that. "Osyrus was expelled after his third year."

"He was," Salle agreed. Then held out the map. "Always thought that was kind of interesting."

Vera took it. "Kyal doesn't know?"

"Funny, isn't it? Man has a perfect memory, but never did put the pieces together. Or if he did, he wasn't willing to tell you."

"Why are *you* willing to tell me?"

Salle took a breath.

"I love Kyal like a father. But he's an old man. And old men have been running this realm for a long, long time. They've been running the alchemist order, at least. And look where that's gotten us.

All we do is hoard knowledge and abide protocols. Maybe it's time for us young ones to break things up a bit. That's what I think."

"I agree."

"There's something else you should know about Caellan. She was an expert on spinal columns, but that wasn't the only aspect of study she mastered."

"What was the other?"

"Poison."

Vera frowned. "The two don't seem related."

"There is a logical alignment, actually. There are a large number of animal venoms that cause paralysis, so in theory if you understand how those work, you can reverse them. But given that Caellan has gone through so much trouble to keep herself hidden, I thought . . . well . . . I thought that the person who goes looking for her should know the full extent of her abilities."

"Thank you, Salle."

Salle gave her a sad smile. "Good luck, Vera."

Vera spent the entire night poring over the map in her cabin on the *Blue Sparrow*. But she soon found that even with the clue from Salle, there were thousands and thousands of swirls, and as far as she could tell, they'd all been drawn with a counterclockwise hand.

"Black skies," she muttered, pinching the bridge of her nose between thumb and forefinger.

"Trouble picking a destination?" Decimar asked from behind her.

She turned around. "Something like that."

"You know that's not actually the right kind of map for aeronautic courses. You need a nautical sky map to track the wind currents, which we have in the navigation cabin."

"I'm not concerned with the wind," said Vera, returning her gaze to the map. "Caellan left a hint to her location on this map. I just can't see it."

Decimar crossed his arms. "You need a way to narrow the field."

"Huh?"

"It's an archery term. You find yourself with a field full of targets, you have to narrow the options down to the one you've got the best chance of hitting. Now, range and speed of motion's the biggest thing with an arrow shot. Wind, too, because once you arc an arrow it's the wind that it belongs to and—"

"Decimar, stop talking about wind."

He was babbling like an idiot, but he had a point. She needed another piece of information about where Caellan might have gone. She tried to think. A bone needle and a knife didn't mean anything. And there was nothing special around the area of Craz-al-dig—the last place Caellan had taken a contract—either.

But there was that story. That rumor of a witch in Lysteria who healed the paralyzed kid.

"What was the name of that Lysterian village we went to after the governor thing?"

"Huh? Oh. Kunda-kin, or something."

"No." She paused. "Kunda-*lan*."

"Well if you knew, why'd you ask me?"

Vera ignored him. Found Kunda-lan with a finger, then started searching the area around it. When one circle revealed nothing, she went wider. Then wider still, until she was searching a series of mountains and hinterlands almost fifty leagues from the village.

And that's where she found it.

A single valley within the range, where the swirls were made with quill strokes moving in the opposite direction of all the others.

Vera smiled. Got up.

"Where are you going?" Decimar asked.

"To give Entras a new course."

42

BERSHAD
Dainwood Jungle

While Ashlyn and Jolan were tinkering with their captured acolyte and the army was mapping the skyship pickup locations, Bershad found that he had an unexpected amount of free time on his hands.

He spent it in the wilds outside Dampmire, hunting with the Nomad.

There were still plenty of rations from the cargo skyship, but nothing lasted forever. Plus, more and more, Bershad preferred the taste of raw, fresh meat over rice or cheese or bread. He knew that change was because of his bond with the dragon growing stronger. He knew that his inevitable transformation was getting closer.

And he didn't care. It had been weeks since Jolan had needed to give him an injection, and his connection to the Nomad had never been stronger. It felt natural. It felt right.

He'd left Dampmire an hour before dawn and headed west, working his way along the spine of a ridge that was covered with moss and blooming, purple flowers. For the first few hours of the day, the Nomad had sluggishly hopped from Daintree to Daintree, following him slowly and lazily while her blood warmed up. But the sun was almost halfway to its highest point in the sky now. She shook her wings and sprang into the sky, flying west with a purpose.

"Glad you've summoned the energy to find us a late breakfast," he said.

That was another reason he liked hunting with the Nomad on his own. Nobody was around to look at him funny while he talked to a dragon that was a league up in the sky.

He let the Nomad's senses wash over him. The heartbeats of a hundred animals shimmered across his skin like sweat. A few minutes later, the Nomad picked up the thick, gamey scent of a boar.

"We had boar two days ago," Bershad muttered. "And it makes you constipated."

The Nomad tugged harder.

"I said no. Variety's important."

She tugged one last time—apparently she was in a stubborn mood—then banked south and started flying in a tight loop. She ignored a troop of monkeys and a wandering deer, both of which Bershad would have enjoyed, but since he'd put a stop to the boar, he wasn't in a position to be picky.

Next, she fixated on a jaguar napping in the low rafters of the canopy.

"Very funny," Bershad said. "Move on."

The Nomad headed a little farther south. Gravitated to the reptilian pulse of a fully grown male river snake that was twisting its way up a tributary of the Green River. Judging from the strength of his pulse, Bershad guessed he was about ten strides long.

"You sure?" he asked. "The last one you tried got wrapped around your throat and I had to hack the bastard off with a machete, remember?"

The Nomad tightened her loop.

"Fine, fine. But you're doing the heavy work on this one."

Twenty minutes later, Bershad was sitting by the riverbank, munching on the tail end of the snake. The Nomad was working her way down from the head. The meat up there was sweeter, but she'd been true to her word and dealt with the massive snake on her own, so he figured she deserved the better portion.

Bershad had eaten his fill long before the Nomad was finished. So he leaned back against a river willow and waited for her. There was a white king vulture circling high overhead, waiting for his turn at the carcass. Above her, the smaller black vultures were making their own gyre. They'd wait for the king vulture to finish, and the crows and foxes would wait on them. Eventually, it would just be ants and maggots picking away at the last shreds of meat.

Bershad was a part of that system, too. He hadn't spent much time contemplating the gravity of eventually turning into a dragon warren. Didn't seem worthwhile to get all twisted up about something that you couldn't change. But out here on his own, he couldn't help but linger on it for a moment.

"Guess there are worse fates than turning into a tree," he muttered. Then looked at the Nomad. "Just don't let your hatchlings shit all over me, yeah?"

The Nomad looked up from the snake. Licked her snout. Then went back to eating.

"Good. Glad we agree."

Bershad stood up and stretched his legs. Brushed a few fire ants off his foot. He was about to start heading back to Dampmire when a scent passed over his nostrils that didn't belong in this forest.

A human.

"You smell that?" he asked the Nomad.

By way of response, she took one last bite, then leapt into the sky and flew south, toward the source of the smell. When she was directly overhead, she started circling. The scent sharpened in Bershad's nostrils.

It was a man. Badly wounded, judging from the smell of pus and infection. Not Wormwrot, though. The smell of their face paint was easy to recognize. This was an Almiran.

And he smelled like the canal waters of Deepdale.

Bershad ran into the jungle.

———

He found the man crumpled between two big boulders. A mess of sticks and logs had been trapped between the rocks, forming an overhang and a semblance of shelter. The poor bastard had collapsed there and been too weak to move again. There were ants all over his legs and mosquito bites all over his face.

"Hey," Bershad said, clambering down to squat in front of the man. "Hey, you awake?"

He swallowed. "Barely," he said in a Deepdale accent.

"Take this," said Bershad, handing over his canteen.

The man emptied the canteen in a few desperate gulps.

"Better?"

"A little."

Bershad took the canteen back. "What's your name?"

"Elondron."

"What are you doing all the way out here on your own?"

"Came . . . looking for the Flawless Bershad."

"Well, your methods could use some refinement, but you found him."

That got Elondron's attention. He wiped some black crap out of his eye and gave Bershad a closer look, lingering on his arm, counting the tattoos.

"Lord . . . Bershad," he said, voice trembling. "Vallen Vergun has a message for you."

43

JOLAN
Village of Dampmire

After Ashlyn had been attempting to break into the acolyte's manual override controls for three straight hours, her hair caught on fire.

"Bucket!" Ashlyn shouted, gritting her teeth and continuing to spin the bands at a high speed.

Jolan put down the astrolabe and picked up their last bucket of fresh rainwater.

"Ramp down, first."

"But I'm almost through."

"No, you're on fire. Ramp *down*, Ashlyn."

She cursed, then froze her bands.

Jolan poured the bucket on her head. The water turned to steam against Ashlyn's flesh, which made the Dampmire hut they were using feel like a bath house.

Ashlyn picked up a needle filled with sedative and jammed it into the acolyte's neck, putting it to sleep. Then she grabbed the singed ends of her hair and sliced them off with a knife. Dropped them in a pile with the rest. That was the third time she'd caught on fire this week.

"How far did I get?" Ashlyn asked.

Jolan glanced at the astrolabe, which was still lit up with readings. They'd learned the sheer volume of coordinate shifts was too overwhelming for Ashlyn to digest through her direct connection to the astrolabe, so Jolan monitored them visually, keeping an eye on the broader picture while Ashlyn focused on the immediate spiral.

"You made it through one hundred and seventy-seven spirals."

She sighed. "Last time I made it to one hundred and eighty."

Now that the astrolabe delivered more accurate coordinates, the risk of Ashlyn making a mistake was essentially gone. The problem now was the length of the lock. There weren't ten or even twenty layers to weave through, as they'd expected.

There were hundreds. Possibly thousands. Ashlyn kept overheating before she could break into the manual override commands.

Ashlyn took a long, deep breath. She looked terrible.

"You need to rest for a while. At this point, all we're doing is scraping against diminishing returns."

"I want to try one more time."

"You'll never succeed if you give yourself a stroke."

Ashlyn chewed on her lip and stared at the acolyte. "We spent months in that pantry banging on dead acolytes, and now that we have the living one, I'm not strong enough to get what we need."

"Osyrus knows this is a vulnerability. It makes sense that he's making it as difficult as possible to reach it."

"He's succeeding. We're getting nowhere."

"Our progress just doesn't have concrete results yet," Jolan said. "But Master Morgan always said that experiments take patience and time and careful—"

"Jolan, we don't have the luxury of a years-long project like some alchemist contract. We need results, and we need them now. Willem and his Jaguars are going to be finished mapping the skyship pairings soon. I can't walk up to Floodhaven with ten lodestones circling around my head. I need to have his *entire* system under my control, and as of right now, I can't even get my foot through the door."

"Get some rest. We'll try again tomorrow."

She took a drink of water. "I'm still bothered by that other command."

"Remote connection?"

"Yeah. You don't see anything in the astrolabe when I give the order?"

"I'll show you."

Jolan manually cranked the machine backward to the readings he'd gotten when Ashlyn had tried that command. Once he got there, all the lights on the machine went out.

"Nothing, see?"

"Ward doesn't build things that have no purpose. It must do *something*." She pressed her thumb and forefinger against the bridge of her nose. Closed her bloodshot eyes.

"Ashlyn, I just think—"

"You're right, I need to rest." She unplugged herself from the astrolabe. "I can clean all of this up. Go check on Cabbage. Make sure he hasn't blown himself up."

Jolan could tell that she wanted to be alone. "Sure, Ashlyn. I'll check on you later."

He made his way along the treetop pathways of Dampmire village, heading to the empty hut where he and Cabbage were building the bombs.

Jolan ducked inside to find Cabbage hunched over a set of timers, frowning and sticking his tongue out of one corner of his mouth. There were piles of machinery behind him—all the salvage they'd taken from the dead acolytes that had been brought from Deepdale.

"Hey, kid," said Cabbage, looking up. "How's it going?"

Jolan took a seat at his workbench. Placed the astrolabe on a pedestal and stared at it. "Not good."

"Still can't unlock the grayskin's secrets?"

He shook his head. "How are things here?"

"Got another fifteen timing mechanisms done, with four more on the way."

"Gods, you work fast."

When Cabbage returned from Floodhaven, he'd volunteered to help Jolan, so that they could produce as many bombs as possible. Jolan had been wary of giving a pirate access to such a large amount of explosives, but Cabbage had proved him wrong. He had a gift for working with the tiny gears they used for the timing systems.

"My old master would have disagreed with you there," Cabbage said. "And if he was here to help us, we'd have enough bombs to fill every house in this village. Guy was an asshole, but he was good at his job."

"Do you miss it?" Jolan asked. "Being an apprentice, I mean."

"It was a long time ago, and I'm no good for that kind of life."

"What makes you say that?"

"If I was, I wouldn't have ruined the whole thing." Cabbage put down his tools. "What about you?"

"I think about going back to Otter Rock and rebuilding the apothecary sometimes. Thinking about it feels good, but hurts at same time. You know?"

Cabbage nodded. "I do."

"Skyship coming!" someone shouted from outside the hut. "Cover! Cover!"

Seeing as they were already in a camouflaged hut, there was nothing for Jolan and Cabbage to do besides go quiet and wait. Jolan used to run panicked prayers to the forest gods each time a skyship passed, but now it barely got his pulse elevated.

The skyship's approach made the hut's support beams groan.

"Sounds like a combat model," Cabbage muttered.

"Yeah."

They sat still as the ship got closer. Jolan was about to close his eyes, but was extremely glad he didn't because right at the point where the ship's engine was at its loudest, the astrolabe lit up with a matrix of dots. Jolan studied them as best he could, but before he could make sense of them, they disappeared, along with the sound of the skyship.

"Did you see that?" Jolan asked.

"See what?"

"The astrolabe. Did you see those lights?"

He shook his head. "Sorry, kid. Must have missed it."

"There was probably still some latent energy from Ashlyn running through the astrolabe. It could have caused a misfire, but that doesn't make sense. We never got anything from this position before."

"Jolan!" came Ashlyn's voice from outside the hut. "I need you in the surgery. Right away."

———

When Ashlyn and Jolan got to the surgery hut, Silas was sitting in front of a cot where a skinny, dirty man was laid up. A quick look at the bites and scrapes and dirt across the man's skin told Jolan that he'd seen weeks of hard exposure to the jungle.

Silas looked up at them, eyes filled with fury.

"We have a problem."

44

ASHLYN
Village of Dampmire

Silas appeared intent on bringing every available knife back to Deepdale with him.

He picked through the makeshift armory in cold silence. Jaw set and eyes focused. Grabbing up a knife, testing the edge, strapping it to his body, then grabbing another. After you passed the threshold of five or six blades on your person, Ashlyn was unclear on how a seventh or eighth could possibly be useful, but she knew better than to question Silas on that front. There were larger problems with his plan that needed addressing.

"Vergun is baiting you," she said. "Same as we did to him back at that warren."

"It worked." Bershad tested the edge of a meat cleaver. Grunted. Dumped it back in the pile. "I am going to skin that pale fucker and wear his hide as a cape."

"Our objective lies ahead, not behind."

"My *objective* is to prevent Vallen Vergun from eating the people of Deepdale."

"Deepdale doesn't have any strategic value to us anymore."

"It has value to the people who live there."

"We can't get bogged down in that. It's a war. And if we turn the army around and converge on an obvious trap, we'll lose it. Do you understand, Silas?"

Bershad glared at her. "You're right."

She relaxed her shoulders slightly, glad that Silas saw reason, no matter how painful.

"I'll go back alone," he added.

"What? You can't."

"You and Jolan don't need me to finish what you've started with that grayskin."

"Maybe not, but the Jaguars are going to start ambushing the skyships soon. They *will* need you."

He waved at the shield and spear, which were both propped up in a corner. "I'll leave those."

"One spear and a shield isn't enough."

"It has to be."

"Why?"

He stopped collecting knives. Turned to her

"Because I am the last lord of Deepdale. The last of the Bershads. And I have broken every oath and promise that I've ever made, but I won't abandon the people of that city." He swallowed. "I'm going back. Give me the rest of the Gods Moss."

Ashlyn pressed her lips together. Realized that she wasn't going to talk him out of this.

She moved to the dirty, worn pouch where they kept the moss. She pulled out a big pinch and held it out to him.

"No," Bershad said. "All of it."

"If you use all of it, you'll trigger the transformation."

He shrugged. "Doing it in Deepdale is a better place than most."

"Silas . . ."

"I don't have time to argue with you, Ashe. Give me the fucking pouch."

Ashlyn shook her head. Gave it to him.

Silas tied it around his belt. Then he went back to packing gear and weapons. When he was done, he moved to leave.

"Both of us could die," Ashlyn said, stopping him. "Is this how you want to leave things between us?"

He looked back at her. Softened a little. "If I wind up down the river ahead of you, I'll try to find a decent spot for us in the afterlife. And if you go first . . ." He trailed off. Swallowed. "Well, I don't see much point in staying around in this mess without you. So I'll be following right behind. I promise."

Bershad left. Jolan had been waiting just outside, and Ashlyn could hear his footsteps chase after him.

"Don't go!" the boy called.

Bershad stopped. "If Ashe couldn't talk sense into me, neither can you."

"But—"

"You need to protect her now. She's far crazier than I'll ever be. You keep her *safe*. If you don't, I will come back from Deepdale—or the dead—and murder you. Understand?"

"Yes," Jolan said in a brittle voice.

Ashlyn took a deep breath. Gathered her emotions together before Jolan came back into the tent. The poor boy looked like he was about to burst into tears.

"I couldn't stop him," he said, sniffing.

"Like Silas said, if I couldn't convince him, then you didn't stand a chance."

"But what are we going to do?"

"We move forward," she said. "There's no other direction to go."

Jolan nodded. Paused. "How much of the Gods Moss did you give him?"

"All of it."

"But if he takes all of it, then—"

"I know," said Ashlyn, putting a hand on his shoulder. "That's why I need you to brew a full dosage of the suppression tonic, and I need it to be stronger than any of the ones before it. I'll be back before you're done."

"Where are you going?"

"To find the only person Silas won't murder if he tries to follow him."

45

BERSHAD
Dainwood Jungle

Bershad picked up Felgor's scent two hours after leaving camp. He'd stolen some of Simeon's cheese, and was munching on it while he hiked through the wilderness.

Bershad could have lost him in the woods, but Felgor had crawled through the bowels of Osyrus Ward's Balarian dungeon to rescue him from torture. He'd stowed himself aboard a ship bound for an island in the Big Empty and followed Bershad into that horrific experience. Bershad knew in his bones that Felgor would keep after him, even if he lost the trail. And the jungle was full of hungry dragons.

So Bershad stopped at a cool spring and waited for his friend.

Felgor made surprisingly quick progress along Bershad's trail. He got tripped up twice, but worked his way backward within a few minutes both times and found Bershad's footprints again. By the time he reached the pond, he was drenched in sweat and scraps of foliage.

"Silas," he said, then turned to the Nomad, who was roosting in a tree overlooking the spring. "Smokey."

"She hates that name."

Felgor shrugged. "So, what's the plan?"

"I'm going back to Deepdale to kill Vallen Vergun, and every Wormwrot soldier in the city."

"Sounds good," Felgor said, as if Bershad had just delivered plans to buy a beer at a local tavern. He bent down and filled his canteen in the spring.

"Felgor . . ."

"Don't even bother with that shit, Silas." He screwed his canteen closed. "You wanted to put up a genuine fight regarding me going with you, you wouldn't have left such an easy trail to follow, so let's skip the part where you tell me to turn around."

"Wasn't going to, idiot."

"Oh. Good."

He pointed to the alchemist's pack on Felgor's shoulder.

"But I do want to know what Ashlyn gave you before you left."

Felgor unslung the pack and produced one of Jolan's massive needles. Bershad could see the canister inside was filled with the black sludge. "The kid showed me how to use it. I practiced on a banana."

"I don't want that shit in my veins."

"Emergencies only," Felgor said. "But the queen was very specific about me making sure you didn't get yourself turned into a tree due to idiot heroics. And being honest, she is scarier than you. So I'm coming, and I'm bringing the needle with me."

Bershad shook his head. "Fine," he muttered. "Just don't slow me down."

"Wouldn't dream of it."

Bershad started walking again. Felgor trotted after him.

"You know what nickname I would have given you, if you didn't already have so many when we met?" he asked.

"Don't care."

Felgor pinched an ant off his neck and flicked it away. "*Sunshine.* On account of your pleasant disposition."

Bershad grunted. "I hate it."

"That's the point."

Bershad quickened his pace as they reached a hill, moving into more of a run than a jog. He crested the hill and looked back. Felgor was barely halfway up the hill and gasping for air.

"I told you not to slow me down," said Bershad when Felgor finally caught up.

Felgor put his head between his legs. Spat. "Didn't realize you were gonna run to Deepdale."

"If we walk, it'll take three days. That's too long."

"You can't run for three days straight."

Under normal circumstances, that was true.

Bershad pulled a hunk of moss from the pouch and ate it. The burning in his lungs and ache in his muscles disappeared. Bershad took a knee.

"We're only going to do this one time, and you're never going to tell anyone about it. Clear?"

Felgor smiled. "Clear."

"Good. Now get on my back."

46

NOLA
City of Deepdale, the Swine Pens

After getting captured, Nola and Pern were taken to the covered pens in the livestock district and locked inside, along with the other captured citizens of Deepdale. Wormwrot men wrapped each pen three times with a strange and thick black wire to prevent them from breaking free.

That had been seven days ago.

Suko, Kiko, and Dervis—the one-armed warden—ended up in the same pen as Nola. Every day, stragglers were dragged in by Wormwrot and thrown inside. Every day, Nola prayed that Grittle wasn't among them.

So far, there'd been no sign of her.

Nola didn't know if they were dead, captured and taken somewhere else, or still hiding underneath Jakell's floor. She had no way of finding out. All she could do was sit in the cold mud and stew in a private mixture of rage and sadness and fear. The only small bright spot in the whole experience was when Lord Cuspar was brought in on the second day, covered in mud and crying. There was no sign of his two wardens. Nola assumed they'd been killed.

Nola had mostly avoided Cuspar. So far, he'd done the same. But she knew that he recognized her. She caught him staring at her every once in a while with a guilty look in his eyes.

The gates to the livestock district opened up and a Wormwrot man came in. He headed directly for her.

"You miss Grungar?" he asked, pulling a steel bucket over to No-la's spot and sitting down.

Grungar was the man whose teeth she'd kicked in on the first day of the attack. Today, he'd brought a plate of Dainwood snails with him, which she knew that he was going to eat in front of her using a silver fork with a pearl-inlaid handle. She knew this because that was the same thing he'd done the day before, except that day he'd eaten a rack of pork ribs drizzled in a honey sauce that was still stuck to his beard. The day before that, it had been a perfectly cooked paku fillet, which burned Nola up because it reminded her of the one Grittle fished out of the canal before the whole world went to shit.

Nola had learned the first day that ignoring him—or moving deeper in the pen—just made him angry and caused problems, so she met his eyes.

"Sure, Grungar. I missed you like a warden misses cock rot."

Grungar paused—a forked snail halfway between the plate and his mouth—as he tried to decipher the meaning of what she'd just said. He didn't do so well with similes that were spoken in Almi-ran. Eventually, he gave up his study of her words, and popped the snail into his mouth. Chewed it with all the grace and manners of a Blackjack munching on a goat.

Grungar insisted on tormenting Nola each day by making her watch him eat, which hadn't been so bad the first few days, but was now abject torture. She hadn't had a bite of food since her portion of bacon the morning the skyships arrived. She'd debated having sec-onds, but decided it would do more good to sell it.

That decision haunted her now, when the only thing that had filled her belly in seven days was the dirty water the Wormwrot poured into the pig troughs each morning.

Nola was running out of ways to quantify her hunger. Last night, she'd spent three hours talking with Pern, describing how good it would be to eat a baked potato full of butter and chives and shreds of smoked pork. Today, though, she couldn't even summon specific desires. The hunger felt like a gaping mouth that had swallowed her soul.

"Where friends?" he asked, grabbing another snail.

"I don't have any friends in this cage," Nola lied.

"Don't believe girl," Grungar said. "Seen you talking."

He peered around the pen. "That one," he said, pointing a greasy finger at Pern.

Nola just shrugged. For such a brute, Grungar was pretty observant.

"Them, too," Grungar continued.

This time, his finger went to Kiko and Suko, who were huddled on the far side of the pen.

Nola winced. Very observant. But she still didn't say anything.

Grungar bit into another snail, which had been cooked in butter and sprinkled with cracked pepper. Fucking. Pepper. It had occurred to Nola that Grungar's elaborate and seemingly limitless food supply hadn't come from the skyships, but from the sunny side of the city across the canal. While Nola had been bartering her tavern away to criminals for one pig a week, the lords had been munching through stores of spiced meats without a care in the world.

Who knows, maybe those snails had come from Lord Cuspar's personal pantry. That notion gave her a scrap of satisfaction, seeing as Cuspar was sharing a pigpen with her now. Coated in the same shit as her. Suffering through the same empty belly. But sharing a shitty situation with an asshole lord didn't really improve the situation from her end.

Grungar speared a new snail, then held it out to Nola, close enough for her to grab it if she tried.

"You want?"

Nola knew that Grungar was baiting her. Taunting her in the hopes that she'd lunge for the food, so he could snatch it away with a snarl and a smile. But she also knew that what he *really* wanted was for her to say yes. To beg for it. And that was something that she refused to do.

"Naw," she said, starting to pinch a mud totem. "I'm not hungry."

She worked the figure together, fingers quickly making the shape of a man. Then she flattened the head with her thumb and spat on it.

"But I'm more than happy to curse those snails with the forest gods' blight, so you fucking choke on them."

Grungar's smile faded. "Take it back."

Nola smiled. "No."

Like a lot of the Wormwrot men, Grungar was petrified by the threat of forest god magic. Nola figured all the totems that the Jaguars had been making during the war had made an impression. Or maybe Grungar was just from a particularly superstitious country, wherever that was. Pern said he was from beyond Taggarstan, which was the same as saying he didn't know, since that land was just a big mystery.

Grungar stood. Towering over her like a giant.

"You squash the mud-demon's magic, girl. Or you pay."

"You can't hurt me. I know about the rules. Vallen Vergun said it himself. The people of Deepdale aren't to be harmed, just starved."

Well, one person was harmed each day. But Vergun made that choice. Not Grungar.

"Rules can't be broken," said Grungar. "But bent? Like fingers of girl's friends? This, not problem."

Nola swallowed. She'd have kept screwing with Grungar if it was only her fingers that were at hazard, but she wouldn't put her friends in danger. She pushed the totem into the earth with her palm. Spat again to squash the imaginary spell.

"Satisfied?"

Grungar sat back down. Eyed the flattened mud with suspicion for a moment before returning to his snails.

Nola stayed put. Did her best to think of something besides how good those snails would taste, or what kind of things she would do just to eat one. She'd kill people for certain. She'd kill Grungar. Lord Cuspar. She'd kill one of the strangers sharing her pen, probably.

And in a few more days, she'd probably kill Pern and Suko and Kiko, too.

Nola had always been realistic about this world. She'd done what needed doing to survive. But it wasn't until now—stuck in this pen—that she realized the hidden truth of humanity: they were all just animals who stayed civil and kind because there was food in their bellies and a roof over their heads at night. Take those things away, and the goodness of people got taken away with it.

While she was marinating in this grim reality, there was a commotion by the entrance to the livestock area, which always portended the same dismal and daily event.

Vergun had come to choose his next meal.

He strode across the muddy yard. Surveyed the crowd with discerning, red eyes. Nola didn't move, and neither did anyone else. Hiding seemed to attract his attention more. They'd learned that on the second day, when he'd chosen a woman who'd cowered behind her husband. Best thing you could do was freeze like a rabbit caught in the middle of a field by a hawk, and hope you were passed over.

"Commander," said Grungar, standing up and moving over to him. "Might be you to take girl today?"

Vergun studied her. Nola's pulse hammered in her chest. Her throat went dry.

"No," he said after what felt like an hour. "There's a bravery behind those eyes that creates a bitter taste in the flesh." He turned to
Grungar. "What's your problem with the girl, soldier?"

"Bitch broke Grungar's teeth."

"That does not seem to be stopping you from enjoying the fruits
of the city," said Vergun.

"Still. Want girl to suffer."

"Mmm. I know the feeling." He licked his lips. "But today is not
her time. Perhaps when some of that bravery has been watered down.
Nothing is more delicious than the taste of complete surrender."

"Grungar can make girl surrender."

"I look forward to surveying your progress," said Vergun. Then
he returned his attention to the pens, spending a few moments with
each muddy, starving face. Nola kept her eyes on him, even though
she'd apparently been passed up for the foreseeable future. After
the first few days, people started thinking that if you looked back
at him, he wouldn't choose you. That theory went out the window
yesterday when he picked a beet farmer who'd glared at him the
whole time with icy eyes.

Nola didn't know what Vergun had seen behind those eyes that
he wanted to eat, but apparently it wasn't bitter bravery.

Eventually, Vergun's gaze halted on Lord Cuspar.

"What is your name?" he asked.

Lord Cuspar looked like he'd just swallowed a hot coal. He opened
his mouth, but nothing came out.

"Your *name*," Vergun hissed.

"El-Elias Cuspar."

"You are highborn?"

Cuspar nodded.

"What type of lands does your family hold?"

"Some coffee farms to the south. And . . . businesses in the city."

"What kind?"

"Different kinds. Taverns, mostly."

"Show me your palms."

"Wh-What?"

"Your hands. Put them through the bars."

Lord Cuspar did as he was asked.

"Hm. Not a callus in sight," said Vergun. "Makes for tender
meat . . ."

"Oh, gods . . . gods . . . gods." Cuspar's gasps made it sound like he had been running for a long time rather than sitting in a muddy pen. He started crying.

Vergun left him in tears. Shifted his attention to a young woman nearby. Nola recognized her—she came into the tavern once a moon's turn and always shared a single pint of rain ale with someone who looked like her sister.

Vergun stared at her for a long time. Her shoulders were trembling.

"Your name?" he asked.

"Sh-Shelley."

"No family name?"

"No."

"What is your trade?"

"I used to keep chickens."

"Not anymore?"

Shelley looked up at Vergun. "Your skyships killed them all."

"They aren't my skyships, but I take your point." He gestured to her. "Hands."

She obeyed. A tear streamed down her cheek as Vergun examined them.

"What were you doing to form this callus here?" he asked, pointing to a ridge along the heel of her palm.

"Breaking through the wing joints on chickens."

"Did your mother have them, too?"

"Yes."

"Interesting. Very interesting."

While they'd been talking, Lord Cuspar had slowly begun to relax, thinking that his time had passed. Nola noticed that he had almost managed to get a grip on his breathing. But Vergun turned back to him without warning.

"Lord Cuspar, I have a proposition for you."

That got his breathing all shallow and weak again.

"Prop-prop . . . what proposition?"

"I would like you to choose my dinner for me."

"What? I don't understand."

"I am either going to eat you tonight, or I am going to eat Shelley. You get to choose."

Cuspar glanced at Shelley, whose eyes had become wide as saucers.

"Is this a trick?" Lord Cuspar asked.

"No trick. Just a simple choice that you need to make."

"But, why me?"

"Well, I'm certainly not going to put such a weighty decision on the chicken girl's shoulders. You're a noble. This is what you're meant to do, isn't it? Make difficult decisions that cost people their lives and keep other people fed?"

"You're sick!" someone shouted from farther back in the pen.

Vergun ignored him.

"I am waiting, Lord Cuspar. If you do not decide soon, I will eat both of you."

Cuspar was breathing so quickly now that Nola thought he might pass out.

Eventually, he hung his head like a condemned man waiting for an axe. "Take her."

"Are you quite certain?"

"Yes," he whispered.

Vergun motioned to a blond-haired Wormwrot. He approached the pen, and placed a gray disc into a strange lock, which slackened the rope around the pen, allowing two Wormwrot to open the gate and drag Shelley out. People cursed and cried and some even shouted to go in her stead. For Shelley's part, she seemed too shocked by the events to fully register them. She just stared at Lord Cuspar as she was dragged away, her worn-down shoes leaving two lines in the mud.

Vergun lingered. Surveyed everyone with those creepy red eyes.

"My initial intention was to deprive you all of food until Silas Bershad returned. But I believe that a small exception is in order. Lord Cuspar has chosen my dinner for me. Should the rest of you desire a meal tomorrow evening, you can have it." He pointed at Cuspar. "But it must come from his flesh."

Cuspar retched. Tried to, anyway. Nothing came out except a small amount of green bile.

"One more thing," Vergun added. He pointed at Nola. "She's the one who decides. And she alone." He smiled. "We'll see how much further that bitter bravery will carry you."

Vergun left.

Grungar laughed. Then he scooped up the remnants of butter and pepper from his plate with a dirty finger and licked it.

"Girl might be brave today," he said. "But soon, girl loses bravery. Grungar knows it. Then girl pays for breaking Grungar's teeth."

Once he was gone, people started to whisper.

"Dunno about you all, but I'm not eating a person."

"He let Shelley get eaten instead of him."

"That's different."

"I wasn't saying that it's the same. I'm saying the highborn fucker deserves to die, is all."

"Cuspar is a bastard," said Dervis. "And I haven't eaten in days and days."

"Everyone, please!" hissed a younger man with gold rings in his hair. "Can't you see that he's a sadistic monster? He's trying to divide us."

"You're saying that 'cause you live on the sunny side o' the canal, too!" shouted Dervis.

"I know a silk merchant who was trapped in a mountain pass over Lysteria for three months after an avalanche. Some in his crew died . . . and . . . well . . . he said that it tasted like pork, kind of."

"Wormwrot can throw us into pens like animals, but we don't need to become animals!"

"Nola. Please. I'm *starving*."

"We're all starving."

Lord Cuspar was still staring at the ground in shock. Pern was looking at Nola. He shook his head slowly. She wasn't sure what that meant.

So she closed her eyes. Clamped her hands over both ears and pressed down as hard as she could to dampen the whispers.

She couldn't take this, on top of every other horrible thing that had happened in the last week. She missed Grittle. She tried to think back to a time when it was just them running the tavern and there were no skyships or wars or people debating whether eating someone was acceptable. But she couldn't conjure a clear memory of that time. She knew that it had happened—knew that she'd spent entire, slow afternoons sipping a rain ale and playing hide-and-seek with Grittle and Trotsky—but those memories were foggy and far away.

The only thought that gave her comfort was that Grittle was safe. And she wasn't here.

That meant she wouldn't ever have to know what Nola decided.

47

ASHLYN
Dampmire Village

When Willem and Cabbage walked into Ashlyn's hut, she had just failed to penetrate Ward's system for the seven hundred and seventeenth time.

"Queen Ashlyn," said Willem. "I have bad news."

That was obvious from the look on his face and the fact that he'd returned half a moon's turn early.

"Tell me."

He took a breath. "We started the ambushes as planned. Six of the first seven attacks went perfectly. Wardens approached in disguise, waited for the hatches to open, and threw the bombs in. The skyships were destroyed."

"And the seventh?"

"Sounds like it was a mixture of screwups. A few men missed their throws. A few bombs didn't go off, or blew up in a place that didn't cause enough damage. Result was that the skyship managed to take off and fly for about two leagues before crashing again. The men tracked the ship and blew up the remnants."

Ashlyn relaxed. "We were never going to be successful one hundred percent of the time."

"No, Queen. And we didn't lose any men." He paused. "But the skyships aren't coming anymore."

"No more drops?" Jolan asked.

"Oh, there are still plenty of those. But the extraction points changed."

Ashlyn frowned. "You're sure you mapped them correctly?"

"The first seven all checked out. We've set fifteen ambushes since then and they all came up empty. That's when I headed back to you."

"They switched up the pattern."

"Yeah. That was my thinking, too."

"Black skies," Ashlyn hissed.

Everyone went quiet.

"We could start mapping the locations again," Willem said eventually. "I doubt they changed the general approach, just the pattern."

"That will take another full moon's turn," Ashlyn said. "And

Wormwrot will just change them again when we start the ambushes. Plus, they'll be ready for attacks now. No, that pathway is closed to us."

Another silence.

"I just don't see how they adapted so quickly," Willem said. "It should have taken days, even weeks, for them to realize what we were doing. Lost ships. Salvaged wrecks. Trips back and forth to Floodhaven where captains could speak to each other . . ."

Ashlyn tried to think. "Unless the skyships have a way to communicate with each other," she said. "The skyship that was able to take off might have sent a message before it was destroyed."

"We kept archers in the trees looking for pigeons. Didn't see any."

"Not pigeons," Ashlyn said. "It would be invisible. Two machines linked by a lodestone system."

Jolan perked up. "Ward was able to bring the entire fleet to Floodhaven last winter with some kind of long-distance communication. Maybe he's adapted that?"

"What does it matter how it happened?" Oromir asked. "It's done."

"Oromir's right," said Ashlyn. "All that's left is to decide how to react."

"Well, how's progress going on your end?" Willem asked. "If you figure out that annihilation protocol, maybe we don't need the armada gone anyway?"

Ashlyn shook her head. "I'm blocked, too."

Everyone went quiet again. Lost in their own dismal thoughts.

Jolan cleared his throat.

"I do have one idea," he said. "Well, more of a guess. But the mention of long-distance communication between the skyships made me think of it."

"Go on."

"This whole time, we've been able to execute the remote connection command. The problem is that it always fails. But when I accidentally left the astrolabe on that setting, the whole thing lit up when a skyship flew over Dampmire. It was just for a moment—I barely got a look at the matrix—but it happened. And I guess I'm just wondering if . . . I don't know . . . they're all related."

"Related how?"

"We know that Osyrus Ward built a back door into the armada so that he could draw them to a single point. I'm wondering if that door is still open, and the acolyte is our key to walking through it." He motioned to Ashlyn's arm. "You might not be strong enough to break through the acolyte system, but Ward designed that specifically to stop you. The back door to the armada was built long before that. It might not have the same level of security."

Ashlyn thought about that. "You could be right."

"I could also be very wrong," Jolan added. "And if Osyrus closed his own loophole, this won't work, either. I just . . . I can't think of anything else to do."

"Neither can I," Ashlyn said.

"We'd need to increase the range of the astrolabe as far as possible."

"Definitely," Ashlyn agreed.

Willem cleared his throat. "Hey, uh, you guys realize you're not really communicating the complete picture of the issue, right?"

"Huh?"

"What the fuck are you two talking about?"

Ashlyn swallowed. "We need to get me and that acolyte as close as possible to a skyship, for as long as possible."

Willem frowned. "Why in the name of all the forest gods would you want to do that?"

"Because if Jolan's right about this, I'll be able to take control of the entire armada—just like Ward did. I'll bring the ships to me, then I'll destroy them."

"But even with the armada destroyed, there's still the issue of storming Floodhaven, remember?"

"Yes," Ashlyn said. "But without the skyships, Floodhaven will be isolated. Ward won't be able to bring more acolytes to the city. We can use our surplus of explosives to break through the walls of Floodhaven and sack the city." She looked at Oromir. "No sorcery. Just a simple attack."

Oromir gave her a long look. "That's something I understand, at least."

"We still have one real big problem," said Willem. "I can't think of a single place in the Dainwood where you can get close to a skyship and stay there without getting porcupined."

A silence.

"I can," said Cabbage. "The Gorgon Bridge."

"Oh, the bridge with a fortress on either side that's been crawling with Wormwrot and grayskins nonstop for the last year. That bridge?"

Cabbage shrugged. "That's the one."

48

BERSHAD
City of Deepdale

Bershad ran through the Dainwood jungle at a full sprint with Felgor on his back, only stopping to take bites of Gods Moss and hiss at Felgor to stop whooping and hollering as if he was riding a horse.

They reached Deepdale less than a day later.

When they got there, Bershad and Felgor climbed a Daintree outside the city to look at the fortifications and enemy positions. A black skyship was anchored above the castle. It was flying Wormwrot's flag—a red face on a black field. The main gate to Deepdale was sealed and bolstered with caltrops and razor wire. Twenty sentries stood watch above it.

"Well, this doesn't seem at all good," said Felgor.

"Agreed."

"Can't you just sic ol' Smokey on 'em?" Felgor asked.

"No."

"Why not?"

"They've got ballista teams set up all over city. Too high a risk of her getting shot. I've gotta go in first and soften the ground. Need to free the people of Deepdale, too, so Vergun doesn't have the chance to start killing them once the chaos starts."

"Do you know where they are?"

Bershad could feel a cluster of human pulses in the livestock district. Their scent was roiling with a mixture of panic and fear. That had to be them.

"They're pretty deep in the city. And there are about two hundred and fifty Wormwrot between us and them."

Felgor scratched at the rash on his neck, which had cropped up as soon as he returned to the Dainwood. "This is a nightmare."

"Could be worse," said Bershad, eyeing the city ramparts.

"How could it possibly be worse?"

"They're expecting an attack. Got every section of wall covered. But if I can get over the wall unseen, the city itself is lightly guarded."

"How are you gonna get over the wall? Wait. Could you ride Smokey in?"

"She isn't a fucking horse."

"Then how?"

Bershad gave him a look. "Do you know how to work a catapult?"

Felgor smiled. "Oh Silas. I don't know what you're planning, but I think I'm going to like it."

They climbed down from the Daintree and hiked away from the city for about half a league, until they reached a shallow ravine.

Inside the ravine, there were three catapults gone to rot in the jungle.

"Still here," Bershad muttered, picking his way down and examining the rigging and ropes. "And between the three of them, I'm thinking we can scrounge enough rope for one final shot."

"What're they doing here at all?" Felgor asked.

"Before the Balarian Invasion, my father and Cedar Wallace got into a years-long piss fight over who controlled the different bridges of the Gorgon."

"Why spend years fighting over bridges?"

"Control the bridges, collect the tolls."

"Ah."

"They'd been skirmishing. Trading off control of the different crossways for years. Before the war, my father and King Hertzog didn't really know or like each other, so Hertzog let the thing drag out. Weak high lords are the best high lords, from a king's perspective."

Bershad started untying the hemp ropes that seemed the strongest and bundling them in a pile.

"Wallace got tired of the endless exchange, so eventually he took a bridge, but instead of waiting for my father to come take it back from him, he rolled a score of catapults across and spent the whole spring sneaking them down to Deepdale, through jungle and over hills. My father hated Wallace to the bone, but he was always impressed with that feat. He said that nobody was as good as Wallace at moving men unseen through unfamiliar country."

Bershad tested the strength of some hemp by giving it a hard tug.

"Anyway, Wallace started a siege that summer. I was very small, but I remember the sound of the catapults firing in the night."

"How'd the siege end?" Felgor asked.

"My father put Deepdale on starvation rations. Waited until the Blackjacks had picked the surrounding trees clean. Then, just before they were about to migrate again, he launched massive stores of meat and fruit back over the walls, targeting the places that Wallace had positioned his siege engines." Bershad wiped some sweat off his brow. "Didn't take much for the Blackjacks to swarm. Most of Wallace's men were killed. The few catapults that weren't destroyed got dumped into this ravine."

Felgor nodded. "History's interesting and all . . . but if it took all those men months to lug the catapults down here, how are you and I going to drag this decrepit thing back into range in the next few hours?"

Bershad glanced up at the Nomad, who was watching them from a nearby Daintree.

"I'm going to ask her real nicely for a little help."

49

NOLA
City of Deepdale, the Swine Pens

People continued debating the merits of eating Lord Cuspar all day.

Nobody had anything particularly original or compelling to say. Some felt that eating people—especially highborn—was wrong no matter what. Others were so hungry they didn't really care about right and wrong anymore.

Others still thought Cuspar was an asshole for what he'd done to Shelley, and deserved to be eaten.

Nola said nothing. Eventually, people gave up and hunkered down into their respective groups and corners. That's when Cuspar had come over to her.

"I'll give you back your tavern," he said. "Full stake."

"Gee. Thanks."

"I own four more taverns on the sunny side," he added quickly. "They're far larger. More profitable. They're yours, too."

"Do you honestly think I care about taverns right now?" she asked him. "I left my sister locked in a cellar. She might be dead, or dying. Our city is under siege. We're *all* more likely to get eaten than released. You're just at the front of the line is all."

Cuspar blinked, rapid and panicked. "I could . . . I could help you find her! My household wardens are—"

"Dead."

"But there must be something," he whispered. "Please. I don't want to die. I don't want to be eaten."

"Neither did Shelley," said Nola. There was no venom in her voice. She didn't have the energy for that anymore. But what happened had happened. And seeing as there was no way out of this cage, there was no way to avoid what was coming next.

Around sunset, the gates opened with a rusty rattle. Nola's heart sank as a shadowy figure approached. But it wasn't Vergun, returned to hear her decision.

It was Grungar. Again.

He'd brought a massive shank of venison that was coated with a thick layer of mustard and pepper. He ate it using a hunting knife and that same fancy silver fork with pearl inlay. And he offered each bite to her with a smile, sometimes waiting ten or fifteen heartbeats before popping it into his own mouth.

"Girl hungry," he said while chewing. "Girl starving. Grungar see it."

Then he looked around the pen.

"Others hungry, too. Want meat?"

He motioned to Cuspar, who'd retreated to his lonesome corner. "Eat lord?"

"Maybe I'll eat you," said Pern. "You ass—"

Fast as lightning, Grungar pulled a stone from his pocket and threw it at Pern. Hit him square in the temple. The old warden dropped to the mud with a curse. Put a hand over the impact spot. Blood poured from between his fingers.

"Talk more," Grungar said. "Plenty rocks."

He cut another slice of venison, slow and clean and against the grain so Nola could see the marbling of the meat. Took another bite.

Behind him, the gate opened again. Vergun walked through it.

He marched forward with his hands clasped behind his back. Two Wormwrot trailed behind him. The blond one, and a stocky bald man.

Vergun strolled over to Nola like a man selecting flowers in a shop.

"Good evening," he said pleasantly. "How did you sleep last night?"

"Wonderfully," said Nola. "I dreamt of a warm bath and a Blackjack eating you alive."

Vergun smiled. "See?" he asked Grungar. "Bitter bravery."

Grungar just grunted and stuffed another slab of venison into his mouth.

"Time for a decision about the good Lord Cuspar," Vergun said. "Let's have it."

Nola swallowed. Each time she'd tried to think about her choice directly, her fingers had started shaking and her thoughts had locked down. "What happens if I refuse?"

He shrugged. "Nothing particularly sinister. You and your people continue to go hungry. But I think I'll give Lord Cuspar as much food as he can fit into his stomach." He waved a hand outside the pen. "This would be a good place to set up the dining table."

Nola tensed. Glanced at Pern, Suko, and Kiko, who all stayed quiet.

Dervis stirred. Whispered to her. "If you don't pick Cuspar to die, I will kill that coward myself anyway. Might as well get him cooked for those of us willing to eat him."

"I'll kill *you* if I have to watch that bastard eat a meal in front of me," said someone else.

"Everyone shut up!" Pern shouted, standing. "Can't you see that this is what he wants? He revels in the suffering and the anguish. He wants us to turn against each other. He wants us to *eat* each other like demons. And you're giving it to him. I'm ashamed to call you my countrymen. I'm ashamed to call you *Almirans*."

There was a silence.

"Old man, if you think a little patriotic pep talk is going to fill our bellies, you're dumber than I thought," said Dervis. "And it'll be you who goes next."

Pern straightened. "Is that fact?"

"Enough," Nola hissed. Stopping them. "Enough."

She turned back to Vergun, who'd watched all of this unfold with an expression of barely contained glee.

"Take Lord Cuspar. Do whatever you want with him."

"Oh, I am afraid I will need you to be a little more specific if you want—"

"Fucking cook him!"

Vergun's smile widened. "By your orders. I will even do the members of your pen the courtesy of preparing him elsewhere. A nice spice rub, I think, with plenty of turmeric." He turned to his men. "Take him."

The blond Wormwrot opened the cage and dragged the screaming Cuspar out of it.

"Commander." Grungar stood. "What of girl?"

Vergun weighed that.

"An interesting question. Was it bravery that forced the girl's decision, or the opposite? Are you stronger for choosing one life over

the comfort of many, or weaker for giving into a coward's compul-
sion?"

"Grungar doesn't know."

Vergun sighed. "This is the problem with an army of brutes. They
lack introspection."

He stared at Nola for a while, no doubt giving her fate serious
introspection.

"She broke your teeth. So, you may break hers. Nothing more."
He turned to the two men who'd come in with him. "Stay here.
Make sure Grungar does not get carried away."

Vergun left.

Grungar sat back down and stabbed at the hunk of venison.

"First Grungar finish dinner. Then, Grungar take teeth."

50

BERSHAD
Outskirts of Deepdale

The hemp ropes strained as the Nomad hauled the catapult up the
last hill before they reached the city. The sun was about to set.

"I've changed my mind," Felgor said, wincing as one of the ropes
snapped off into the woods. "I don't like this at all."

"Trust me, the Nomad hates it a lot more," Bershad said. "But
we're almost done. Just need to reach this little clearing."

The Nomad snorted. Kept going.

When the catapult had reached the middle of the clearing, Bershad put a hand on the dragon's shoulder. "That's perfect. Right
there."

The Nomad stopped. Waited patiently while Bershad unstrapped
the hemp ropes from her hind legs.

"Seems like you and her are developing a pretty good rapport,"
Felgor said, watching from a distance. "Kinda reminds me of how
you were with Alfonso."

Bershad stopped working the ropes. A shot of sadness moved
through him.

"Yeah," he said softly.

Felgor seemed to realize what he'd done. "Sorry," he said. "Didn't
mean to dredge up bad memories."

"You didn't dredge them up," said Bershad. "What happened in

Taggarstan is always on my mind. Always fresh. But tonight, Vallen Vergun will pay for what he did." Bershad threw Felgor a bundle of rope. "Now help me get this rigged up."

Half an hour later, they had the catapult aimed at a small gap in the canopy.

"What about the trajectory and all?" Felgor said, looking at the hole. "You sure of things on that front?"

"No."

"I thought they trained all the young lords of Almira to run siege engines and do the, uh, calculations or whatever."

"I had a career change before I got deep into the mathematics of catapults."

"That's too bad, because it seems to me the aiming of the thing is a critical part of this plan." He eyed the gap. "Little screwup in any direction, and you'll wind up impaled by a tree branch."

"I'll be fine," Bershad said, climbing up into the seat of the catapult and getting situated. He arranged the belt of knives that he'd brought so there was a relatively small chance that a major organ would get impaled on landing. He didn't want to waste the moss's strength on injuries he could avoid. This was going to be a long night.

He gave the Nomad a little nod, and she leapt into the sky, climbing high above the cloud cover within a few seconds. With all the Blackjacks around, Bershad wasn't worried about her drawing any special attention.

"I just feel like a slightly larger hole in the canopy is in order here," Felgor pressed.

"No time." Bershad opened the pouch of Gods Moss and ate a large pinch. Felt the strength of it expand in his belly, then radiate through his limbs. He pulled the pouch closed again. Tied it against his right hip.

"Lever's over there," he said, gesturing. "Wait for my signal."

Felgor shook his head. Went over to the release.

Bershad used the Nomad's senses to locate the patrol on the nearest wall. Waited until they had their backs turned.

"Now," he said to Felgor.

"You're *sure* you don't want to prune that opening a little?"

"Pull the fucking lever, Felgor."

"In a second. This might be the last time we see each other. Got to say some words."

Bershad sighed. Felgor pursed his lips. After a good measure of quiet contemplation, he slapped Bershad on the leg and smiled.

"Try not to die."

He pulled the lever. The counterweight plummeted to the ground, and Bershad careened into the air.

Almost immediately, it became clear that the catapult's trajectory was screwed up.

51

NOLA
City of Deepdale, the Swine Pens

Grungar finished his meat. Then he set the plate down in the mud, took the fork, and motioned for the blond-haired man to open the gate again. As the Wormwrot men came inside, everyone moved to the edges of the pen, except for Pern.

"Nola, behind me," he hissed.

"Old man," said Grungar. "Move."

"No."

Grungar shrugged. Strode forward.

Pern coiled his body and threw a quick punch, but Grungar blocked the punch with his bracer. There was a loud, bone-crunching snap. Pern howled in pain. Grungar grabbed him by the head—his meaty hand fitting around the warden's bald pate like it was a river stone—and threw him down into the mud. The stocky Worm-wrot man slammed his shield onto Pern's back to make sure that he stayed there.

Grungar turned his attention back to Nola. Held up his fork.

"Girl pay now."

Nola tried to struggle against him as he grabbed her by the throat, but she might as well have been struggling against a Blackjack.

"Open mouth," he snarled.

Nola clamped her jaw shut.

"Fine. Grungar open it for you."

He tapped the fork against her lips. When she pressed her lips tighter, she could taste the remnant of mustard that was still on the prong.

He wedged the prongs past her lips, and Nola prepared for what-ever terrible pain was going to come next.

52

BERSHAD
Above the City of Deepdale

Bershad's head slammed into a branch as he flew through the canopy, slicing his forehead down to the bone and sending him dramatically off course as he tumbled erratically through the air.

He tried to tuck into a ball but the violence of his spinning was forcing his arms and legs apart. His knives went flying from their sheaths. The city below was hard to focus on as he flipped over, details coming and going in rolling fits and starts.

Bershad had hoped to get lucky and land in a muddy yard or on a thatch roof. Something relatively soft to avoid a slew of broken bones and ruined organs. Instead, he slammed belly-first into the edge of shale roof. Sliced his stomach open on the gutter. He groaned. Struggled to get a grip on the wet shale. Just barely managed to dig two fingers underneath a broken tile and prevent himself from falling.

"Perfect," he muttered, gritting his teeth.

While his wounds healed, he tried to get his bearings. He'd cleared the outer walls and armaments by a good distance and landed on the roof of dragon lookout tower about three blocks away from Canal Street. Judging from the lack of an alarm bell, the patrol on the wall hadn't noticed a man flying into the city, so at least one thing had gone properly.

He could also sense two heartbeats below him.

"Did you hear that?" a man asked in Ghalamarian. Bershad smelled roasted beets and garlic on his breath. "Sounded like a catapult."

"Naw," responded another. "That was just a dragon farting."

"Very funny." He coughed. "I think it was a catapult."

"Good for you. You gonna throw those dice or what?"

"Sounded like something hit the roof, too."

"Maybe it was a shit, not a fart. And our roof was impacted."

"Stop talking about dragonshit, Wump. It's unpleasant."

"Stop hearing made-up noises and toss those dice, Trent."

The man muttered something that Bershad didn't catch. He heard the jostling of bone dice in a palm, followed by the sound of them scattering across a wooden floor.

"By Aeternita, I've got no fucking luck today," Trent complained.

Bershad's fingernails started to strain, but when he tightened his grip on the tile, it snapped free. He slid off the roof and fell about a dozen strides before landing on a little watchmen's platform and breaking his ass bone.

"You definitely heard *that,* right?"

"Yeah. That, I heard."

Someone drew a sword.

"Let's check it."

Footsteps climbed up the interior of the tower.

Bershad reached out to the Nomad while they moved toward him. There was still a lot of city between him and those pigpens, and—unfortunately—a lot more Wormwrot men than he'd realized, cutting competent and tight patrols through the alleys and streets that surrounded the pens.

Sneaking his way over to the people of Deepdale without being seen would take all night, and he needed to get them out of there with at least a few hours of darkness left so that they could disappear into the Gloom.

That meant he needed to draw those patrols away.

The two Wormwrot men had almost reached Bershad. His stomach and ass bone were healed, but his blood was everywhere, so he just stayed where he was, playing dead.

"Seems we've found the source of your sound," said Wump when he saw Bershad.

"Yeah," Trent agreed. "Question is, we got a dead source or a live one?"

"Awful lot of blood around for him to be alive." Wump took a step forward. "How'd he get onto the platform?"

"I told you that I heard a catapult."

"Fuck off with that."

"You explain it some other way."

A pause.

"I think my idea actually had some merit."

"What idea?"

"Might be a dragon crapped him out."

"That's the dumbest thing I've ever heard."

"Dumber than catapulting yourself into the middle of an occupied city?"

"If he had been crapped out, there'd be shit all over him. I do not see any shit. Do you?"

"Just check and make sure the flying man is dead, yeah?"

"Fine."

Trent moved forward, creaking the rickety, waterlogged boards of the tower platform. He jabbed Bershad in the shoulder with his sword, cutting deep into the meat of his flesh. Bershad didn't move.

"Seems pretty dead," Trent called. "Guess one of us should go report it to—"

Trent stopped talking when he saw Bershad's wound knit itself back together.

"What the fuck is—"

Bershad shot up and grabbed Trent's sword by the blade and ripped it out of his hands.

"That hurt," Bershad rasped.

He batted Trent in the face. Sent him cartwheeling off the platform in a spray of teeth and blood. Trent screamed the entire way down. Landed with a thump and a splash.

Bershad had lost his grip on the sword when he hit Trent, throwing it somewhere into the city by accident. So he rushed Wump with a purpose, grabbed his face, and slammed him into the far wall of the watchtower hard enough to stun him, but not hard enough to kill him.

Wump tried to stab at Bershad's belly, but he was too close for that. Bershad squeezed down on Wump's fingers until they all broke and he dropped the blade. Then he grabbed his jaw and pressed his fingers into the joint by his ears.

"Tell me where Vergun is," he hissed. "Lie to me, and it's your jawbone that I'll use to kill him."

Wump swallowed. "Castle," he whispered.

"It's an awfully big castle," Bershad said. "Be specific."

"L-Lord's quarters. That's where he's been waiting . . . for . . . for . . ."

Wump trailed off. Bershad tightened his grip.

"*Say* it."

"Waiting . . . for the Flawless Bershad."

Bershad smiled. "Well, I'm here. And I'm coming for him."

He gave Wump a hard shove, sending the mercenary sprawling across the floor. Then he jumped off the tower, free-falling for a few heartbeats before hitting the cobblestones below at a roll. Both his feet broke, and his shirt got soaked in Trent's blood. His feet healed in seconds, and he was up again, sprinting toward the castle.

"Attack!" Wump shouted. "The Flawless Bershad is heading toward the castle!"

53

NOLA
City of Deepdale, the Swine Pens

Before Grungar had time to pry Nola's mouth open with the fork, a strange noise snapped in the distance. Nola had never heard a noise like that in her life. But it came from the south and it perked up the ears of Grungar, the Wormwrot men, and all the wardens who shared her pen.

"Catapult?" whispered Dervis.

"Yeah," said another. "Sounded sort of rotted out, though."

"Shut mouths," said Grungar. He dropped Nola and ducked out of the pen, motioning for the other two Wormwrot to follow and shut the gate. When that was done, all of them went still, listening for another occurrence of the sound.

For a long time, there was nothing. Long enough for Nola to catch her breath and realize that if the sound didn't happen again, she'd be right back in Grungar's grasp and that fork would be right back in her mouth.

Far off, a man yelled. Went silent.

Then another man shouted, much louder.

"Attack! The Flawless Bershad is here, and he's heading toward the castle!"

"We should go check it out," said the blond-haired man.

"Grungar not interested in lizard killer." He looked back at Nola. "Interested in girl."

"Yeah?" asked the blond-haired man. "Well, there's a ten-thousand-gold-piece bounty on that motherfucker. Still not interested?"

Grungar seemed to weigh these options very carefully in his head. After some thought, he dropped the fork, which made a plinking sound when it hit the plate in the mud. Drew his sword.

"Lock pen," he said. "We go."

"Excellent," said the blond-haired man, taking out a key.

"What about them?" asked the short man. "Should one of us stay and guard 'em?"

"You can stay if you want, but this anchor wire can keep a dreadnought in place during a cyclone," the blond-haired man said, tightening the black wire. "They're not going anywhere."

"Screw 'em, then. Let's go."

The three Wormwrot left the livestock yard. People stayed quiet. Kiko came over and put her hands on Nola's shoulders. Rubbed them until she stopped shaking.

"It's okay," she whispered. "It's going to be okay."

Nola didn't see how that was true, but she was too terrified to say anything. She ran her tongue over her teeth, thinking about how much it would hurt to have them pried out.

"Do you think Lord Silas really came back?" asked Suko.

"No," said Dervis. "What'd he do, catapult himself into the city?"

"Yup."

Everyone looked up. The Flawless Bershad melted out of the shadows and walked toward them. He was covered in blood.

"And now I'm gonna get all of you out of there."

54

BERSHAD
City of Deepdale, the Swine Pens

"Any chance you brought the entire Jaguar Army with you?" asked a warden with one arm.

"I came alone."

"Don't mean to be ungrateful, but how's this going to work? The city's full of Wormwrot."

"First step is getting you out of these pens," Bershad said, moving closer.

He frowned when he saw a plate of venison and an expensive fork on the ground.

"The hell?" he muttered.

"That's Grungar's dinner," said a girl who was squatting close to the front of the pen and reeked of fear more than the others. Bershad took a closer look at her. Remembered her from that tavern.

"Nola, right?"

"Yeah."

"Where's your sister?"

The girl paused. "I'm not sure. We had to separate during the attack."

Bershad nodded. Put his hands on the cages. "Step back from there."

With a belly full of moss, it shouldn't be a problem to rip them open, even if they had been built to contain Dunfarian swine. But when Bershad planted his feet and gave the gate a powerful yank, the lock and chains around the pen held fast. He gave them a closer look. Saw that they'd been wreathed in black fiber.

"It's a skyship anchor," Nola explained. "Vergun had it done the first day so we couldn't break out by pushing together."

The mention of Vergun turned Bershad's blood cold. "Vergun's been down here?"

"Every day," Nola whispered. "And he's done awful things to us while he waited for you to return."

"Well, I'm back," Bershad growled. "And I am going to kill him. But first I'm setting all of you free." He pointed at the Balarian lock. "Who has the seal for this?"

"Seal?"

"It's a little gray disc that can open these types of locks."

"Oh. One of the Wormwrot men. He left with Grungar to go look for you by the castle."

"Know his name?" Bershad asked. With the Nomad so close, he'd be able to focus in and pick up scraps of conversations without a problem.

"No. Sorry."

"What's he smell like?" Bershad asked.

"Smell?"

"I need a way to isolate him out from all the other Wormwrot."

"Well . . . I don't know about his smell . . . but he has blond hair."

"Lysterian?" Bershad asked.

"Maybe. I'm not sure. They all wear that face paint."

"Hm." Bershad had learned that unlike Goll—who always reeked of rum—most Lysterians carried a sweet, vaguely hay-like smell to them.

Problem was, all Bershad could smell was Trent's blood, which had soaked through all his clothes. The power of it was overwhelming him and the Nomad. Screwing up her tracking. He unbuttoned his shirt. Pulled it off.

Better, but not enough. Pants, next.

"What the fuck are you doing?" asked the one-armed warden.

"He's not even wearing a breechcloth," said a Papyrian woman.

Bershad ignored them both. Knelt down and pressed his palms into the cool mud. His senses sparked even more, and on the far side of the canal he picked up that distinct Lysterian smell. It belonged to a man who was a little drunk and a little out of breath, jogging toward the castle.

Bershad snatched up the fork that was laid out on the venison plate. Looked at Nola.

"I'll be back with the seal."

He left the livestock area at a full sprint.

55

NOLA
City of Deepdale, the Swine Pens

"Silas Bershad is fucking crazy," said Dervis.

"And his dick isn't nearly a foot long," Suko added.

"What's he gonna do with that fork?" Pern asked.

"No idea," said Nola. "I just hope he does it fast."

Twenty minutes later, nothing had happened.

No sounds from inside the city. Nobody coming back their way. And no sign of Lord Bershad.

When someone did finally return to the pens, it was the familiar and large outline of Grungar, ambling back to the cages. The short man was still with him, but there was no sign of the blond man with the key to their cage.

"Frundy's an idiot to keep looking for him," the short man said. "The Flawless Bershad's not here. Trent and Wump play dice in that tower all night, and one of them is always bitching about the other one cheating. Wump probably threw the poor bastard off the platform his own fucking self, and now he's trying to cover it up with a big story."

Grungar didn't respond. He was standing over the plate of venison he'd left behind, frowning. "Where's fork?"

"What?" asked the short man.

"Fork gone."

The short man blinked. "Grungar. We've looted this shithole city down to the bone. Who cares about one missing fork?"

"Was Grungar's favorite. Had plans for girl's mouth." He turned. Glared at the prisoners. "Who took?"

"You see any of us hiding ten-foot arms beneath our clothes?" Pern asked.

Grungar squinted at him, as if he was considering the possibility that someone was indeed hiding massive arms from him. Eventually, his gaze landed on Nola.

"You. Where fork?"

"Dunno."

"Fork did not disappear." Grungar drew his sword. "Give back, or Grungar starts cutting throats."

"You know how possessive Vergun gets about his chattel," the short man warned. "We can't get in there until Frundy comes back with the key anyway. Now how about we head back to the fancy side of town and find you a new f—"

Silas Bershad darted out of the shadows, jumped on Grungar's back, and stabbed him in the eye.

"Here's your fork back, asshole."

Grungar howled in pain. Bershad dropped to the ground and punched Grungar in the spine so hard the massive Wormwrot crumpled down in the mud and started twitching like a spider who'd been stepped on.

Somewhere during Grungar's journey to the ground, Bershad had taken his sword, which he flashed across the short man's throat. He collapsed, holding his bleeding throat and trying to scream out an alarm but only managing to spray blood all over his chest.

Grungar was still twitching on the ground. Bershad stalked over to him. Bent down.

He pulled the fork out of Grungar's eye, then rammed it into his neck—tearing his vocal cords apart with a series of rough stabs and rips.

When it was done, Grungar's throat was a complete mess. Nola couldn't make herself look away. She felt a strange mixture of joy and horror at the sight of his corpse.

When she finally did manage to pull her eyes away, Bershad was inserting the gray disc into the lock. The black ropes around the cages sagged. Bershad jerked the cage open.

Dervis shoved his way out of the pen first and grabbed the remnants of Grungar's venison. Tore into it with ravenous hunger. He only managed a few bites before someone else snatched it away. The feral process continued for a minute before the meat was gone.

Dervis looked at the crowd with a guilty eye. Then he threw up.

"Gods," he muttered. "I've been dreaming about doing that for three hours. Didn't pan out like I'd hoped."

"Everyone stay calm and quiet," Bershad whispered. "You make a ruckus, you'll be back in those pens in an hour."

"Ruckus or not, that seems like the most likely outcome," said Pern. "You might be able to strip naked and sneak through the city, but we can't and there are Wormwrot everywhere."

"I'm aware. But I'm gonna get a strong fix on their attention," said Bershad, taking his blood-soaked pants from where he'd left them and pulling them back on. "Once I have it, escape through the western gate. They might leave a few sentries there, but you'll have the numbers. Run them down and get into the Gloom."

"How will we know when you have their attention?" Dervis asked.

"It's not going to be ambiguous," Bershad said, already heading back out of the yard.

Nola had no idea what he meant until she saw the Gray-Winged Nomad swoop down from the clouds and follow him into the city.

Alarm bells started ringing.

All of them.

56

CASTOR
Deepdale Castle, Inner Walls

When Wump raised the alarm, Castor had led the search for Silas Bershad. When their patrols near the castle didn't turn anything up, he went to meet Vergun on the castle walls.

"Anything?" Vergun asked.

"Nothing." Castor paused. "Starting to think that Wump threw Trent off the tower himself, and is trying to cover it up with a story about Bershad."

Then the dragon showed up.

It careened over the rooftops—swooping so low that shingles sprayed across the streets from the power of its wingbeats.

"What the fuck kind of lizard is that?" asked Sergeant Rummy, commander of the ballista defense teams, who was also on the walls.

"Gray-Winged Nomad," muttered Castor.

"Never seen a dragon that big."

"Me neither," said Castor.

The dragon snatched a big wagon in her claws and dropped it through the roof of a manse. Released a high-pitched scream.

"It's wrecking the city just for the fun of it," Rummy said.

"Doesn't matter," said Vergun. "As soon as she stops, she's dead."

They'd placed fifteen ballista teams throughout the city to pro-tect against the Blackjack hordes surrounding the city. That was more than enough to deal with a single dragon. Didn't matter how big it was.

The Nomad swooped through the city and perched atop a big manse.

"There," said Vergun. "That's it."

The three of them waited for the sound of ballista bolts firing. But they didn't arrive.

"She's right in the middle of team four's zone," Rummy said. "Why haven't they released?"

Castor glassed the ballista position with his lens. It didn't take long to identify the problem.

"Team four is dead."

"What?" Rummy asked. "How?"

Vergun snatched the lens and surveyed the team himself. Saw the same thing that Castor had—five men with their throats cut. All of them looked like they'd died surprised.

"Silas," he growled.

The other ballista teams took shots at the Nomad, despite only two being remotely close to the proper range. The bolts that didn't fall short missed. The Nomad darted into the sky, disappearing into the low-hanging clouds.

Castor could hear the grunts and shouts of men, followed by the mechanical cranks of the teams reloading.

Before any of them could finish, the Nomad came down on one of the teams from directly above—tore the ballista apart with her jaws, then swiped a claw across the armaments, destroying the ma-chinery and killing ten men as easily as a kid smearing ants to paste with a finger.

The Nomad was up in the clouds again before any other teams had a chance to shoot.

"Look, there." Rummy pointed below them. Another ballista team had been killed.

"He's close," Vergun said, then drew his falchion. "Castor, on me."

57

NOLA
City of Deepdale

With all the chaos from Bershad and the dragon, the few Wormwrot they saw didn't appear to have an interest in stopping the people of Deepdale from fleeing the city, so that's what most people did.

But Nola went in the opposite direction.

"Nola?" Suko asked, stopping her. "Where are you going?"

"Jakell's shop. For Grittle."

"But there are soldiers everywhere!"

"I don't care. She's my sister."

"But—"

"Would you leave Kiko?" Nola asked.

Suko shook her head.

"Then you understand. Now get out of here."

Suko gave her one more sad look, then she headed toward the western gate with the others.

But Pern stayed. Put a hand on her shoulder.

"I'll go with you," he said. "I need to find Trotsky, too."

Nola nodded. "Thank you, Pern."

They moved through the city as quickly as they could. The only Wormwrot they encountered were dead.

"Did Lord Silas do all of this?" Nola asked as they passed two men, one with his throat torn out, the other with his head wrenched into a violent, broken position.

"I don't think it could have been anyone else," said Pern.

The front door to Jakell's shop had been torn off the hinges. It was a mess inside—scraps of leather and tools and tanning supplies were strewn everywhere. There was a fallen shelf blocking the trap-door.

"Help me!" Nola said, moving to one end of the shelf. She was already pushing as hard as she could when Pern reached the other side and shoved. They moved the shelf up in a series of grunts and fits and starts. After so long without food, the effort made Nola feel like she was going to pass out. Gods, she was weak.

"Grittle?" she asked when they got the shelf moved. "Grittle, it's me! It's Nola!"

Something broke underneath the floor. A jar, maybe.

"Grittle! Just hold on!"

Nola grabbed the latch of the trapdoor. Felt a splinter sink deep into her hand. Didn't care. Just hauled it open.

There was nobody inside. Just a rat that scurried away, knocking more jars off the little shelf.

"No," she whispered. "I thought . . . with the shelf over top . . ."

"They must have found them at some point," said Pern. "Thrown the shelf on after."

He jumped down into the little room. Looked around. He picked up a few of the jars.

"Most of these are eaten," he said.

"I don't care about getting food," said Nola. "I care about getting Grittle."

"I mean that if they had time to eat these, they weren't taken right away," said Pern. "They might still be alive somewhere."

That sparked a flicker of hope in Nola. "But where would they have gone? I never saw her in the pens."

Pern shrugged.

Nola went back outside. Looked around. Everything was chaos and destruction. Soldiers were yelling in the distance. The dragon swooping down from the sky in irregular intervals, screaming wild and mean as it tore Wormwrot apart.

Pern came out behind her, moving slow and wheezing hard from getting the shelf open.

"I need to get higher," Nola said. "Get to where I can see."

Pern didn't say anything, just kept on with the ragged wheezes.

Nola squinted. There was a lot of movement farther up in the city, but all of it was too vague to make out. Then she remembered something. That last trade that she'd made with Kellar for the rice wine. That stupid trade.

"C'mon, Pern. We need to get back to the Cat's Eye."

She headed farther up the street. Behind her, Pern collapsed.

When she turned around, he was clutching the wall of the shop, trying to get himself back on his feet and failing. She went back to him. Slipped an arm underneath his armpit and tried to get him up. But she just wound up toppling over with him.

"Forget it," he said. "I'm no good to you like this. No good to anyone . . ."

Nola didn't say anything, but that was obviously true.

"Rest here," she said. "Get some food from that cellar. I'll find

Grittle and the others, and then we'll come back for you and leave the city together."

Pern wiped some sweat off his brow. "Yeah. All right, Nola."

"Do you need help getting back inside?"

"I'll be fine. Go." He took a breath. "And Nola?"

"Yeah."

"If you find Trotsky and he's . . ." His voice quivered. He pulled something from his pocket and gave it to her. "Give him my seashell. He never carried his own around . . . stubborn bastard."

Nola took it. "I will."

———

Nola made her way to the tavern as quickly as she could, following the line of corpses that Bershad had cut down the middle of the city. She burst through the front door, ignoring the destruction, and dug up Kellar's Papyrian lens from a chest in the basement. Then she headed to her attic and opened the window. She wiped the stingy sweat out of her eyes. Raised the lens and looked out over the city.

She started with the castle, where she could make out men running along the ramparts. None of them had weapons in their hands. They were running away from something.

A moment later, the shirtless and blood-covered Bershad came into view. He was carrying a spear in one hand and the fork in the other. One of the fleeing Wormwrot stumbled. Fell. Bershad put a hole through his skull without breaking stride.

Nola continued glassing the manses around the castle.

Her lens stopped on Lord Cuspar's compound. The once pristine yard had been replaced with a gruesome scene. Armless men were impaled on long spears. Intestines were strewn across the shrubs and flowers.

The door to the kitchen was ajar. Nola looked inside and saw something that made her heart stop.

Vindy was chained to the floor. Alive. Her face was streaked with soot and tears.

If she was there, Grittle might be with her.

58

CASTOR
Deepdale Castle, Outer Walls

By the time Vergun and Castor reached the outer wall of Deepdale's castle, the Wormwrot who hadn't been killed by Bershad had begun to run away from him.

"He's a demon!" one of them huffed as he shoved past Castor. "Run away! Get to the skyship so we can—"

Vergun thumped his blade into the back of the man's skull as he passed.

"Coward," he muttered.

Castor wasn't sure if killing their own men added much value at this juncture. But there certainly wasn't any harm in murdering a deserter, either.

Soon, there were too many fleeing Wormwrot for Vergun to bother killing them. Castor noticed that while some of them had clean blades—or had dropped their weapons entirely—others had wet steel and blood-splashed faces.

"If Bershad came alone, how is it they haven't killed him yet?"

"Just be ready," said Vergun. "He's close."

They reached a muddy yard with a bunch of old, unused surgery beds on one side and a well on the other.

In the distance, the Nomad wrecked the last of the ballista nests. Then she made a long loop over the city, wings lilted at an angle. She came to roost on top of an old tower that overlooked the main castle gate. Vergun and Castor both stopped short. Waited under the cover of an archway to see what the beast would do. For the moment, she seemed content to simply look out and survey the destruction she'd caused.

The castle gate had been closed and barred in a hurry, but with nobody left to defend it, there was also nobody to do anything when a shadowy figure climbed over the crenellation. Jumped off the rampart and landed in the muddy yard.

Silas Bershad.

He strode across the yard with confidence, carrying a spear in one hand and what looked very much like a fork in the other. He was covered in blood, but there were no wounds that Castor could see.

"Welcome home, Silas," said Vergun, who'd somehow managed to keep the confidence in his voice.

"Afraid to fight me alone?" Bershad asked, glancing at Castor.

Vergun motioned to the Nomad. "Seeing as you've brought a friend with you to help, I thought it was only fair."

Bershad shrugged. "I needed her help to get the people of Deepdale out of the city. But I'm gonna kill you myself."

The dragon spread her wings and careened into the sky, disappearing into the clouds.

Castor couldn't believe it. The bastard really could command dragons.

"On me," Vergun whispered, stepping out from beneath the arch, moving left. Castor went right.

Bershad turned to Castor. "Got no fight with you. Leave now, and you'll keep your hide. Stay, and I'll skin you along with your commander."

"I'll stick," Castor said, drawing his sword and angling up.

Castor was a lot of things, but a coward wasn't one of them.

"Your choice."

Bershad darted toward Vergun with a speed that seemed inhuman. He was halfway across the yard before Vergun had managed to plant his back foot and get into a defensive posture. Bershad snapped a spear thrust at Vergun's thigh, snatched it back when Vergun moved to parry, then thrust again at his face, which forced Vergun off balance when he dodged.

That might have been it. Two lightning fast strikes and one dead cannibal. But Castor had caught up by then. He ran his sword through Bershad's back at heart-level.

Generally speaking, when you stab a man in the back, it creates a jerk followed by a sag. The man doesn't know he's been skewered yet, but this muscles and nerves do, so they give out.

Bershad jerked. But he did not sag.

Instead, he rammed the butt of his spear into Castor's jaw. Sent him stumbling backward. Castor took his sword with him, which was a good thing seeing as Bershad came after him with the spear next, jabbing and thrusting with far more strength than a man with a hole through his heart should have.

Castor kept pace with the vicious blows as best he could, but it was a losing game. Bastard was too quick. Castor missed a parry and got the spearpoint slashed over his sword-hand for the trouble. Dropped the weapon into the mud.

Castor would have died then if Vergun hadn't hacked his falchion into Bershad—the heavy blade cleaving through his collarbone and deep into his chest. That put Bershad on his knees, but he immediately tripped Vergun with a sweeping kick, bringing him down with him.

Bershad tried to stab Vergun in the throat with the fork, but Vergun got his arm up so the utensil went into the meat of his forearm instead of his food pipe. He was too close for the spear to be much good anymore, so Bershad just got on top of Vergun and started punching him again and again with powerful, bone-crunching blows.

Castor picked up his sword.

It was in this moment—when Castor saw that while the falchion was still in Silas Bershad's chest, all the sundered meat and bone the blade had cleaved apart was now healed to scar tissue—that he realized they truly were fighting a demon.

And while Castor didn't have much experience with demons, he knew what you were supposed to do with them.

He grabbed Bershad in a tight hold, pinning both his arms behind his back—using every ounce of strength he had to keep the thrashing bastard restrained—and threw him down the well.

The Flawless Bershad went down with a wild clatter of flesh and steel slamming against stone. Landed with a splash that wasn't nearly as far away as Castor would have hoped.

Vergun got to his feet. Spat a mouthful of blood and several teeth onto the ground. Ripped the fork out of his forearm.

"Thank you, Castor. That was good thinking."

"Didn't kill him. And it isn't going to hold him."

"No, I don't believe it will." Vergun held out his hand. "Give me your sword, and go back to the skyship."

"What're you going to do?"

"Keep him occupied while you run through takeoff preparations."

There were already sounds of grunting from the well. Bershad was climbing out.

"Boss. Being honest, I don't think you can handle him alone."

"Nor can we handle him together," said Vergun. "But there is a very large ballista on that skyship. And you are a very good shot."

Castor nodded.

"Understood, boss. I'm on it."

59

BERSHAD
Down the Castle Well

The well was full of rats and mud and it smelled awful. It was too narrow for Bershad to do anything about the sword through his chest, so he just popped another nugget of Gods Moss into his mouth, then shimmied up with a series of grunts and curses.

Vergun tried to cut Bershad's head off as soon as he cleared the lip of the well, but Bershad had been expecting that. He dropped down again—letting the sword pass harmlessly above his head—then vaulted off the lip and took a few quick strides. Now that he had some space, he ripped the falchion out of his chest and turned around.

Vergun had retreated to a set of stairs that led to a rampart above. He backed up the stairs as Bershad moved toward him.

"What did you do, let some mud demon fuck your asshole as a kid?" Vergun called. "Always heard you Almirans were into weird shit like that."

Bershad didn't respond. Just kept moving forward. When he reached the rampart, he lunged forward with a brutal hack.

Vergun skipped backward, executed a graceful riposte, then whipped his sword around to decapitate Bershad. He batted the blade away with his forearm, the steel sinking deep into the bone and sending a shock of pain up his arm.

"Not so keen on having your head removed from your body?" Vergun asked.

Bershad growled. Rushed forward and attacked again and again. Vergun parried and dodged and gave ground, effortlessly rebuffing the attacks. Vergun had always been the better swordsman.

"I must give you my compliments," Vergun said, swatting away another attack. "Despite all of the farms we've destroyed and citizens of the Dainwood we've slain, you managed to keep your people somewhat well fed. I recently ate a delicious series of fried highborn fingers. They're so tender and juicy when they've never done a day's work in their lives."

"You won't rile me up by talking about eating the lords of this city."

"Right, right. You never were on the best of terms with the nobility of this world. Always the rebel. Always apart."

Vergun reached the end of the rampart.

"Of course, I didn't restrict myself to the greedy lords," Vergun continued. "You took so long to return, I had plenty of time to sample a full range of cuts. Women. Children. The little slumrats don't have much flavor—too many bugs and rats in their diet. But there is something so savory about their screams when I—"

Bershad screamed. Charged.

Vergun smiled, then leapt off the castle wall, grabbing hold of a thick vine on his way over the edge and swinging into the yard of a manse, which was decorated with impaled men. Vergun darted inside a back door.

Bershad jumped off the wall. His kneecaps popped out of place on landing. He shoved them back into position and limped toward the manse, blood filled with acid rage.

60

NOLA
City of Deepdale, Lord Cuspar's Manse

Nola had to move through the front chambers of Lord Cuspar's manse before she could reach the back kitchens. The place had been ransacked by Wormwrot men. All the tapestries were torn off the walls. The furniture had been smashed. Someone had taken a shit in a corner. Nola pushed through the wreckage and into the back corridors.

Lord Cuspar's kitchen was the most horrific place that Nola had ever seen.

Severed fingers had been left in cast-iron pans, the digits burned black in pools of butter and pepper. Limbs were hanging from meat hooks, caked in spice rubs. But worst of all were the seven heads that had been put into glass pickle jars and arranged on a shelf. She recognized their faces, because they belonged to the people Vergun had taken away to eat.

Shelley's head was among them. Cuspar's wasn't.

Nola made a private promise to herself in that moment that if she managed to live through this night, she would never cook, serve, or eat another piece of meat in her life. Never again.

The interior door to the pantry was locked. Nola didn't even bother looking for a key, she just grabbed that big cast iron pan, closing her eyes as she shook the fingers out of it, then she smacked the pan against the lock again and again until the whole thing snapped off and she could push through.

The captives were on the other side. All of them arranged along a set of shelves, sitting on the floor with their hands chained behind them. Cuspar. Trotsky. Vindy. Jakell.

And her sister.

"Grittle!"

Nola rushed to her. Felt her warm cheeks and breathed out a sigh of relief. Kissed her head. She was dazed, and seemed to have trouble focusing her eyes at first, but she gave a little confused smile.

"Nola?" she asked. "Is that you?"

"It's me, Grittle. It's me. I'm here to get you out."

The others were all stirring now. Vindy seemed even more dazed than Grittle, but she was alive. They were all alive. For now.

"What's happened?" Jakell asked from his spot. "We heard dragons."

"The city's under attack."

"Blackjacks?" Trotsky asked. His hair was still matted with blood from the chair leg that had been thrown at him a week ago.

"No. Lord Silas came back with his gray dragon."

Trotsky's eyes widened. "I was right?"

"There's no time, Trot." Nola examined the lock around Grittle's wrists, which was attached to a steel bar that had been hammered into the cabinets. "How do I get this open?"

"They keep the key over there." Trotsky jerked his head toward a ceramic jar meant for bread flour.

Nola wasted no time smashing the jar onto the kitchen floor, digging up the key, and unlocking them. When that was done, she ripped the iron rod out of the hinge, setting them all free.

"Are you hurt?" she asked Grittle, touching her arms and face and hands in rapid succession.

"I'm fine." She sniffled. "They only found us yesterday. The soldiers brought us here as a gift to the commander. Said we'd be a nice . . . nice . . . snack." She paused, then whispered. "We could hear what he did to Shelley."

Nola's stomach dropped. Her throat went dry. All this time, she'd held out hope that Grittle had been safe in the cellar—shielded from the horrors of Vallen Vergun. She didn't care about the terrible things she'd been put through—the things that she had done herself—but seeing those same things in Grittle's eyes broke her heart.

She glared at Cuspar. A living reminder of the dark decision she'd made.

"What about you? Are you hurt?"

The lord held up one hand. There weren't any fingers left on it.

"Good."

"Nola!" Jakell gasped. "Please. We're all in this together."

"Tell that to Shelley's head, which is brining in a glass jar in the next room."

"What does that have to do with him?" Vindy asked.

Nola glared at Cuspar.

"It's not important right now. We need to get out of here." She helped Grittle stand up. "We'll go out the same way I came in, through the front—"

Someone burst through the back door of the kitchen and slammed into the shelves, sending porcelain plates clattering to the floor. Vergun. He rushed back to the door and closed it. Flipped the wooden bar down to block it. He was breathing hard and his face was battered and swollen and bleeding. He seemed just as surprised to find them there as she was to see him.

"Little rats," he snarled.

Trotsky charged him, picking up a meat cleaver as he crossed the kitchen. He hacked at Vergun, who parried the attack easily and sent Trotsky stumbling into a cabinet. Vergun reared back to run his sword through Trotsky, but before he could, Lord Cuspar picked up a shard of broken porcelain plate with his good hand and stabbed Vergun in the meat of his back, causing him to drop his sword.

"Run!" Cuspar shouted.

Jakell and Vindy did exactly that, disappearing through the manse. But Nola reached down and grabbed her own shard of broken plate—not thinking, really, just reacting.

The fight was over so fast that Nola couldn't tell exactly what had happened. One moment, Trotsky and Cuspar were piling on Vergun from both directions, punching and beating and screaming and grunting. The next, Vergun had slashed Cuspar's throat wide open with the cleaver and Trotsky was on the ground, groaning and holding his stomach.

Vergun turned to Nola and Grittle. Smiled.

Before Vergun could do anything, the barred door shuddered from impact. Once. Twice. On the third hard pound, the bar started to splinter.

"Stubborn bastard," Vergun muttered.

A heartbeat later, he had a handful of Grittle's hair and the cleaver pressed against Nola's throat.

"Struggle even a little, and you die soaked in each other's blood. Understand?"

Nola gagged. Nodded.

There was another shocking impact on the door. The bar shattered, and Lord Silas came through. He was coated in black mud from navel to toes. The rest of him was covered in blood.

Vergun threw the meat cleaver at his head.

The blade hit him in the temple and he crumpled to the floor in a heap.

Nola's heart sank.

"No!" Grittle screamed.

Vergun drew a strange knife made from bone and pressed that against Nola's neck.

"Is that enough to kill him?" Vergun muttered. There was a hint of fear in his voice, which didn't make sense given that there was a cleaver blade embedded in Lord Silas's skull.

But a moment later, Silas pulled the cleaver out of his head and stood up. Nola watched with horrified fascination as the wound closed, leaving a long scar and a streak of blood. Nothing else

"He *does* have dragon magic," Grittle whispered. "I knew it."

"Take one step forward, and I'll gut them both," Vergun warned.

Lord Silas glared at him. There was a wild look in his eyes that made Nola's stomach churn.

"Do it," he rasped. "Fuck if I care."

"Please. You didn't run all the way back to Deepdale just to put two more children's souls on your conscience. You can save their lives if you walk back out that door."

"Their souls have nothing to do with it. I came back to kill you, Vallen. And that's what I'm about to do."

Bershad took a step forward. In that moment, he didn't look at all like the man who'd enjoyed a beer in her tavern or told her sister where to catch a fish. He looked like a true demon, full of fury and rage.

Vergun pressed the bone knife harder against Nola's throat, making her gag.

"I'm warning you."

"You already warned me." Lord Silas took another step. "Now finish it. Soon as that girl's throat opens, I'm gonna tear your fucking head off."

"Have it your way, Silas."

Nola felt the bone knife skim forward a little, and she'd seen enough Dunfarian pigs killed over the last few weeks to know what came next: raking it back across her throat and killing her.

She brought her hand up to Vergun's wrist, pressed the shard of plate against his skin, and yanked down. Felt his flesh catch, then his muscle tear. He grunted as the bone knife fell away from her throat for the smallest of moments. An instant later, the point came careening back toward her, aimed directly at her eye.

Before it could connect, Lord Silas threw the cleaver.

There was a wet smack. The bone dagger flashed across her cheek instead of going through her eye. Vergun thudded against the wall behind her. She turned to see the cleaver lodged in his right shoulder. He struggled to his feet and ran toward the front of the manse.

"You all right?" Lord Silas said, crouching down next to her. Putting a hand on her face.

"It's not deep, I don't think," she said, even though it felt very deep. The pain was searing and strong. Her legs were weak.

Lord Silas grabbed a rag from the counter and pressed it against her cheek, hard.

"Take this. Push hard. Hard as I'm pushing now." He looked down the hallway, eyes still wild and full of rage. "Get out of the city as soon as you're able."

He moved toward the kitchen.

"Lord Silas?" Grittle asked.

He stopped. Turned around.

"Did you mean what you said?" she asked. "That our souls don't matter to you?"

He gave Grittle a long look. There was a flicker of some softer emotion on his face. But it didn't last very long.

"I never said your souls don't matter. I said they had nothing to do with it."

Lord Silas ran after Vergun. The sound of his bloody feet moving down the hallway made a sticky, wet noise, then faded away.

Grittle started crying.

"It's okay," Nola said, hugging her sister. "Lord Silas saw the broken plate in my hand and he knew that I'd help." Nola looked at her sister. "Understand? He cares about me and he cares about you."

But Grittle wasn't looking back at her. She was looking beyond her, tears streaming down her cheeks.

It wasn't until Nola turned around that she saw Trotsky had died.

61

BERSHAD
City of Deepdale, Lord Cuspar's Manse

Bershad followed Vergun's muddy footprints through the manse until he reached his boots, which had been kicked off in the main foyer to eliminate his trail. The front door to the manse was wide open, leading down into the city.

"Not gonna be that easy, asshole," Bershad muttered.

Everything smelled like charred human meat, making it hard to pick up Vergun's scent, but it was there—acid adrenaline and the earthy smell of turmeric on his breath. And it led upstairs, not outside.

The rooms upstairs were numerous and connected by a maze of doors. Vergun had woven through them in an erratic pattern, but it didn't matter. Bershad followed his scent to the back of the house, bursting into a bedroom just in time to see Vergun's pale feet hanging outside a window, then rising out of sight.

Bershad followed him.

By the time he had crawled out the window and climbed up to the roof, Vergun was already halfway across, running full tilt toward the next manse. He'd hit Vergun in the shoulder socket with the cleaver, and that arm lolled broken at his side, but the bastard still managed to leap across the gap and land with a surprising amount of grace.

Bershad hopped the gap. Caught up with Vergun just as he was realizing that the next manse was too far away to jump again.

He was trapped.

"They should call you Vergun the Fucking Squirrel," Bershad said, coming up to him.

Vergun turned around. Pale hair slick with sweat. "So, this is what you had to become to kill me? A demon."

"This is what I've always been."

Bershad darted forward. He coiled his arms and unleashed every ounce of moss-fueled strength that he had left in his body.

But Vergun parried with the dragontooth dagger.

Bershad had put so much momentum into the attack that the falchion was broken in half by the dagger. The point skittered off the roof and into the darkness. Vergun rammed the dagger straight through Bershad's liver. His legs gave out, but he took Vergun down with him. They fell together in a heap. Bershad shoved the broken edge of the falchion through Vergun's rib cage. Twisted it. Felt his bones spread. Bend. Snap.

Vergun hissed out a rough curse, then head-butted Bershad so hard that his entire nose shattered. But Bershad didn't let go of the sword. He kept twisting with one hand. Put the other on Vergun's throat and started to squeeze. Vergun's eyes bulged. Pale skin started turning red, then purple.

Bershad was so overcome with rage that there wasn't a clear thought in his head. Just the maniacal desire to watch Vallen Vergun die. But before he could snuff out the last scrap of life from Vergun's lungs, the roar of a skyship filled Bershad's ears. Vergun's bulging eyes shifted to a point over his shoulder, and he smiled.

There was a metallic click. Suddenly, Bershad was flying through the air.

62

CASTOR
Above the City of Deepdale

The ballista bolt took Bershad off the rampart like a spider flicked from a table, but Castor couldn't see what happened to him after that. Too much smoke and darkness.

"That must have killed him, right?" Rummy asked.

Castor didn't respond. He was focused on Vergun, who was still on the ground, a broken sword jammed very deep into the side of his chest. He was writhing in pain, which meant he was still alive. For now.

Castor didn't feel a particularly strong inclination to save the life of a sadistic cannibal. But Vergun had stopped Bershad from killing him back at the castle.

He had to square things, at least.

"Just keep the ship steady while I get the commander."

————

Castor hauled Vergun back onto the deck a minute later, lifting him over the gunwale real careful so as not to jostle the hilt sticking out of his chest. Castor didn't know how to fix an injury like that—wasn't like he was a damn alchemist—but he knew enough to know that he should leave the blade where it was until they could get him to somebody more qualified.

"Where did he go?" Vergun rasped.

"Off the wall. Didn't see where."

"Fucking look, then!" he hissed.

"It's too dark, and you're dying." He paused. "Commander. We have to get you back to Floodhaven."

Osyrus Ward was the only one who could fix the damage that the Flawless Bershad had done.

Vergun didn't give the order. Just a tiny nod of tacit approval.

"Raise elevation!" Castor shouted to the crew. "Turn on that dragon beacon, then make a heading north-northeast. We're getting out of here."

63

NOLA
City of Deepdale

"We have to go back and help him!" Grittle screamed as Nola hauled her toward Jakell's shop.

As they were leaving the manse, they'd seen Lord Silas get shot by the massive bolt the skyships use to kill dragons. Nola hadn't seen him land, but she'd heard a terrible noise near the castle wall.

"No, I have to get you out of Deepdale."

"Grittle, thank the gods!" Pern said, coming over to meet them. There were four mud totems on the rim of Jakell's broken window. Pern gave Grittle a big hug, then looked to Nola.

"Trot?" he asked.

She shook her head. "I'm sorry, Pern. Trotsky . . . he didn't . . . I gave him your shell."

Pern nodded. Swallowed. "What happened to Bershad?"

"He got shot with one of the big arrow things."

Pern bowed his head. "Then he's dead."

"No, he isn't!" Grittle yelled. "He has magic, just like Trotsky said."

"I don't think anyone has magic that's strong enough to survive a ballista bolt," said Pern.

"You're wrong," Grittle insisted.

An hour ago, Nola would have agreed with Pern. But he hadn't seen Lord Silas's skull knit itself back together in that kitchen.

"He might be alive," said Nola. "I'm not sure."

Grittle looked at Nola, pleading with her eyes. "Please, Nola. We can't leave him. He came back for us, and now he needs *our* help."

Nola hesitated. She wasn't sure what to do.

"Hey! Hey, is anyone up there?" someone shouted from farther down the street. It was a man with a Balarian accent.

"Wormwrot!" Pern hissed, grabbing Grittle and ducking back into Jakell's shop. Nola followed.

A few moments later, hurried footsteps crunched up the road. But they belonged to a man who didn't look like a soldier.

He was definitely Balarian, judging from his short hair and long nose, but he wasn't wearing any armor and didn't have a weapon. He stopped a little bit beyond the shop, panting.

He muttered something to himself in Balarian that Nola didn't understand. Then cupped his hands.

"Silas!" A pause. "Silas, you out here?"

"I know him," Grittle whispered in Nola's ear. "He came into the Cat earlier in the summer and beat everyone at dice. His name's Falcup, I think. Trotsky said that he cheated."

"Silas? Where are you, you reckless bastard."

"He's going to bring whatever Wormwrot are still alive down on our heads if he doesn't shut up," Pern whispered.

"Agreed."

"Silas!" Falcup shouted again.

"Hey, Falcup, stop shouting, you moron!" Nola hissed to him.

He whirled around, surprised. When he saw Nola he relaxed. "Oh. Hey. My name's actually Felgor."

"Whatever. Just be quiet, okay?"

"Have you seen Silas Bershad?"

"He got hurt up by the castle. We didn't see where he went." Nola paused. "He might be dead."

Felgor swallowed. That news put him on the brink of tears.

But a moment later, the big gray dragon landed with a loud crash behind him.

"Smokey!" he yelped, more happy than terrified.

The dragon cocked its head, studying him. Nola was pretty sure that Felgor was about to get himself eaten.

"Where is he?" Felgor pressed.

To Nola's surprise, instead of devouring Felgor, the dragon pointed back toward the castle with her snout, then flew off in that direction.

"Right," said Felgor. "We follow the dragon."

"Are you insane?" Pern hissed.

"I'm just trying to save my friend," said Felgor, already running toward the castle. "You all can do what you want!"

Nola gave Pern an uncertain look. Despite what she'd told Grittle, she had no idea whether Lord Silas had seen that shard of plate in her hand. No idea if he'd been willing to let her die to get to Vergun.

"I'm going to help Lord Silas," Grittle said with all the confidence that Nola lacked. "He saved us. Now we save him."

"Grittle, I'm not risking your life again to—"

"It's my soul to risk," Grittle interrupted. "And I'm going to help Lord Silas."

Grittle ran after Felgor.

"Gods," Nola muttered.

If her ten-year-old sister had the courage to run back into that mess, Nola figured that she did, too.

64

BERSHAD
Deepdale Castle, Outer Wall

Bershad had blacked out when he hit the castle wall. The crash of the Nomad landing on a nearby manse woke him up. She looked at him with curious concern for a moment. Leaned forward and licked Bershad's bloody foot. Then sniffed the bolt that was jammed through his chest.

"Yeah. Got a bit of a problem there."

Bershad's vision was all hazy and twisted. It felt like his veins were pumping river sludge instead of blood. How long had he been pinned to this wall? Ten seconds? Ten minutes? Was he dead and just hadn't realized it? Seemed possible. But his chest hurt an awfully large amount for a dead man. He could feel the moss fighting against the ruination of his body, and he could feel the moss losing.

The point of the ballista bolt had burrowed into the stone wall behind him. No way to pull it out himself. He turned to the Nomad.

"Hey, girl. Could use some help here." He tapped on the shaft of the ballista bolt. The fletching was made from braided metal wire. "Think you can yank this out?"

The Nomad leaned forward again, sniffing the bolt curiously. She gave the nock an exploratory lick, which shifted the bolt, and Bershad's lungs. He groaned from the pain and the Nomad backed off.

"No, no. It's fine. You just gotta . . . you just gotta pull it out."

The Nomad blinked. Let out a skeptical snort.

"If you can tear this city apart, you can pull one fucking bolt out of a castle wall!"

The Nomad spread her wings and leapt into the sky, disappearing into the night.

"Great," Bershad muttered. "Really great."

With the last scrap of strength he had left, Bershad reached for the pouch of Gods Moss on his hip, grunting at the pain it caused in his lungs and chest. He tore it off his belt, pried it open with his teeth, and then dumped the contents into his mouth.

He knew that was a bad idea, but getting pinned to a wall by a bolt that was made for killing dragons had a way of forcing you to adjust your plans. Bershad swallowed the rest of the moss in three big gulps. Then he sucked the remnants off his teeth and gums to make sure he got everything. He'd need every scrap of strength for what he was about to do.

"Well. This is gonna be unpleasant."

He grabbed the bolt with both hands, wiped away some of his own slippery entrails so he could get a better grip, then hauled himself forward. Screaming the entire way. He felt his lung tear. His heart pumped furiously, trying to produce enough blood to make up for the buckets' worth he was splashing all over the cobblestones below.

Bershad hauled himself forward a finger's length at a time. Grunting and cursing. Howling. Legs twitching from the pain. His body spasmed, and he coughed up a black streak of blood onto the ballista bolt. He stopped pulling. Looked back at his progress.

"Shit."

He'd made it half a stride. Maybe. The bolt was ten strides long.

This wasn't going to work. And it was a pretty shitty way to die, pinned to the wall like a rat. But maybe it was better than turning into a tree. He wasn't sure, and he was in a little too much catastrophic pain to really weigh the two options carefully. Bershad closed his eyes. Wished that he hadn't eaten so much Gods Moss. It was going to take him a long time to die.

He drifted off. Wasn't sure for how long. When he did come out of the fog, it was because of a familiar voice.

"Silas, you big idiot!" called Felgor. "I told you *not* to die!"

65

NOLA
City of Deepdale

"Fuck yourself, Felgor," Lord Silas groaned.

Then he vomited more blood and went limp. Nola would have assumed he was dead if she couldn't see his blue, exposed lung slowly filling with air, then deflating.

Gods.

Nola didn't understand how Lord Silas was still alive. There was so much of his blood dripping down the wall that it was forming an ankle-deep puddle on the street.

"Okay," said Felgor. "We need to get him down from there."

"That's pretty obvious, Balarian," said Pern. "The method we're gonna use is less clear."

Nola looked around. The street was littered with debris and wreckage from the dragon attack. The gray dragon had torn one of the ballista stations off the castle wall and dropped it on the street. There were corpses and twisted metal and gears.

And rope. A lot of rope.

"We'll use this," Nola said, running over to the closest length, which was clumped and knotted around a man who'd been torn in half by the dragon. "Who knows how to tie a noose?"

There was a silence.

"I do," said Grittle.

"What? Why?"

"Trotsky taught me."

Nola choked up a little at that for reasons she could barely think about. "Okay, then get to it. We need four good ones."

Twenty minutes later, Grittle had tied the nooses, and they'd managed get two of them around Bershad's wrists. The ankles were proving to be more difficult.

"Silas, you gotta lift it up so we have a target!" Felgor called.

"Trying to," he mumbled.

Lord Silas had been moving in and out of consciousness during the rope-throwing process. Nola wanted to get this done before he passed out again.

"Please, Lord Silas!" Nola called. "Just try one more time. I can get it. I know I can."

He gave her a look. Then, with what seemed like a very large amount of effort, he lifted his right leg up as high as he could, which wasn't much, but it was enough to give her a target.

She threw it.

Hooked him. Tugged to tighten.

"Yes!" Felgor said. "Thank fucking Aeternita."

"Keep your time god out of this," Pern hissed.

"Well, we can thank your mud gods, too. I wasn't gonna be exclusive about it." He squinted up at Lord Silas. "You think three's enough?"

"I think that I'm real tired of throwing ropes at him," said Pern.

"Agreed. Let's do this."

Felgor, Pern, and Nola all took a rope.

"Grittle," said Nola. "I want you to close your eyes and cover your ears."

But her sister shook her head. "I was in that kitchen. I've seen a lot worse."

That hurt Nola's heart to hear. "Okay. At least step back so you don't get any blood on you."

They pulled Lord Silas to the fletching of the bolt without much trouble aside from his agonized screams. But things became more difficult from there.

The wire fletching was too thick and long to pull him through. He screamed and howled as they pulled. Eventually, they got him over the first bundle of wire with sheer force, but there were still three more to go and it just didn't seem possible that Lord Silas would survive that. The fletching behind him was slick with blue lung tissue.

But that wasn't what stopped them. It was the fact that while they were trying to get Lord Silas over the next braid, his shoulders started sprouting vines and roots.

"Oh, shit," said Felgor, dropping his rope. "Stop! Stop pulling!"

"What's the problem?" Pern asked.

"Hard to explain, but it's a pretty big one." Felgor chewed on his bottom lip, suddenly looking very worried. "All of you need to get out of here."

"Why? What's happening?"

"He's, uh, gonna turn into a tree type thing. And you all need to be elsewhere when that happens."

"Tree? What are you talking about?"

The gray dragon crashed down onto the rooftop of the manse across from the castle wall, drowning out whatever explanation Felgor was going to give with a deep roar that made Nola's stomach turn. They all backed off, using the corner of the manse as cover. Nola peeked around it. Whatever was going to happen next, she wanted to see it.

The dragon nuzzled her snout into the crook of Lord Silas's arm. She seemed to want to give him comfort, but not help. Lord Silas was dropping in and out of consciousness, but his eyes turned clear for a moment and he patted the side of the dragon's face.

"I can't go yet," he whispered to the dragon. "Not until it's finished. Please . . ."

The dragon reared up. Studied him with an intelligence that Nola had never seen in a great lizard. Never seen in any kind of animal.

She leaned down, took the ballista bolt in her mouth, and tore it free from the wall. With the gentleness of a cat moving one of her kittens, she laid Lord Silas down on the street. More roots were pouring from his back. Spreading across the street.

"Help me!" Felgor shouted, already running to him.

"There's a fucking *dragon* in the road," Pern hissed.

"Me and Smokey have a relationship. C'mon!"

Pern cursed, but he followed. So did Nola and Grittle.

The dragon watched while they got Bershad off the ballista bolt. The point had broken off in the wall, which made it easier to slide him off the rod. Nola could see directly into his chest, where Lord Silas's heart and lungs and bones were weaving together in fits and starts, almost like he was choking himself back together in pieces.

But the roots coming out of his back and shoulders were also spreading along the cobblestones. Digging into the earth between the bricks.

Felgor pulled the strange bone dagger out of Bershad's chest, then started rummaging around in his pack. He produced a massive needle that was filled with a black liquid. "Need to wait until he's healed," he muttered to himself. "But not much after."

Lord Silas was shaking. Covered in sweat. "Don't mess this up, Felgor," he hissed.

"Trust me. I've got this."

Silas just gave him a little nod. The hole in his chest was almost sealed. The vines coming out of him were starting to sprout yellow flowers.

"He really does have demon's blood," Pern muttered.

He bent down and starting pinching a mud totem from the wet mixture of rubble and Lord Silas's blood. Nola wasn't sure if making a totem with demon blood was a good idea, but she didn't say anything.

Felgor raised the needle over his head, poised to jam it into Lord Silas's chest.

"Wait," he gurgled, putting a hand up.

"Silas, we got a real bad situation brewing all around."

"And I still only have half a fucking lung . . . just . . . a little . . . more . . ."

The wound in his chest morphed into a dark scab. Lord Silas turned to the dragon, who was watching the entire thing unfold with that same intelligent interest.

"Sorry about this, girl," said Lord Silas. "Hope you'll come back to me down the line." Then he turned to Felgor. "Do it."

Felgor plunged the needle directly into Lord Silas's heart. As soon as the dark liquid entered his body, the scab on his chest sloughed backward in the healing process, turning runny and red again. But the regression stopped there. All the flowers that had bloomed along the vines shriveled and died within a few heartbeats. The roots turned twisted and brown, as if they'd spent a week under the hot summer sun with no water.

The dragon let out a wild, pained shriek. Grittle put her hands over her ears and started to cry. Nola felt a click in her left eardrum, then nothing at all from that side. The dragon arched her wings and leapt into the sky—flying south and disappearing over the big hills.

"Grittle?" Nola asked, shaking her sister. Her voice sounded far away in her own head. "Are you okay?"

She nodded. Pointed at Lord Silas. "Is he . . . ?"

Lord Silas vomited what seemed like a whole bucketful of black liquid onto the street. Spat a few times. Then stood up. Looked around at the sky, which was filling with Blackjacks.

"We need to get out of the city right now."

"You sure you don't want to take a minute?" Felgor asked.

"Can't. The Blackjacks are riled. They're going to swarm Deepdale."

66

BERSHAD
City of Deepdale

The first score of Blackjacks started swooping into the streets and snatching up corpses just as Bershad and the others were moving through the main gate of Deepdale. Bershad led everyone to a high hill, and they watched as the dragons took over the city. He thumbed the familiar, worn grip of his dragontooth dagger, which Felgor had given to him once he was healed.

He was glad to have the weapon back, but he'd lost something far more important.

His connection to the Nomad had been completely severed by the injection. He couldn't feel anything beyond his own senses, which made him feel like he was carved from a block of stone. The world around him seemed quiet to the point of being lifeless.

"You gave me too much of Jolan's crap," he said to Felgor.

"Oh yeah?" Felgor asked. "Well you can politely go fuck yourself, Silas. You were halfway done turning into a tree person. I saved your life."

"It wasn't that close."

"Wasn't that *close*?" Felgor turned to Nola. "What do you think, kid? Did that situation appear to contain a casual amount of urgency?"

"That's not the word I'd use."

"Would a complete goatfuck be more appropriate?"

The girl hesitated. "I'm not sure what word to use, if I'm being honest."

"You lied to me!" Grittle pressed.

"What?"

"You said you couldn't talk to the dragon, but you obviously can. And she *does* give you magic powers. You lied."

"Sorry."

Bershad looked out over the forest.

"Any Wormwrot out there?" Felgor asked.

"I don't know, Felgor."

"Huh? What do you—" He paused. "Oh. Right."

They all looked around for a few moments, each person regrouping in their own way.

"Did a man named Elondron find you?" Nola asked him.

"That's right."

"Is he alive?"

"I'm not sure. He was in rough shape."

Nola nodded. "I wanted him dead so badly. But he saved us all."

Bershad didn't know what to say to that, so he didn't say anything. Nola went quiet.

Eventually the older warden cleared his throat.

"So, what happens now?"

"Felgor and I need to go back to Dampmire. Meet up with Ashlyn." He scanned the sky. "Sun's almost up. We can cover a lot of ground between now and nightfall if the weather holds."

"Can we come with you?" Grittle asked him.

Bershad shook his head. "There'll be more fighting. A lot more. It's too dangerous."

"But what are we supposed to do, then?" Nola asked.

"Head into the Gloom with the others."

"Into the Gloom?" Nola repeated. "And what? Just . . . try to survive?"

Bershad sighed. "These days, surviving's difficult enough to be your sole focus. Find a spot with good water where the fruit hasn't been picked clean by Blackjacks, and hunker down until summer's over. They'll clear out of the city by then, and you can come back. Rebuild your tavern, maybe."

Bershad turned around. Started walking down the hill.

"You were wrong," Nola said.

That stopped him. "About what?"

"Back in that manse. You said that our souls have nothing to do with this. But we *do*," Nola said, voice quivering with emotion. "All of this happened to us, too. We don't just disappear when you walk out of a room or march back into the jungle. And now you're telling me to just hunker down? I tried that already."

She stepped toward him.

"While you and the wardens fought your war, I scraped and scrapped and made a demon's bargains to keep the Cat's Eye open.

And what came of it? Men with painted red faces dropped out of the sky and took a hot shit over the whole thing. They killed Trotsky. Shelley. Cuspar. So many others." She choked back tears. "They turned us against each other. Turned us into *animals*. I don't want to rebuild the tavern. Are you fucking insane? I want to fight them. I want to kill them. All of them."

Bershad looked at her for a long time. It burned him up inside, to see so much fresh hate in such a young girl.

"You're right. I was being an asshole. Sorry." He knelt down so they were at eye level. "I know what it's like to feel nothing but rage. You want a place to pour all that anger. But running blind and furious into a new fight doesn't work."

"You seem to do it all the time."

"And look at what's happened to me because of it. Most of my friends are dead. Most of my enemies are still alive. I have nothing to show for my life except a head full of nightmares, a body covered in scars, and a trail of corpses left in my wake." He paused. "You and your sister need to survive this war. Keep the parts inside that are good and soft. *That's* your revenge. You don't need to turn yourself into someone like me."

"Why not?"

"Because I'm still alive. And I'm going to kill everyone responsible for what happened to you."

"Is that a promise?" Nola whispered.

"Yes. So long as you promise me that you'll rebuild the Cat's Eye." Nola nodded. "Okay."

He turned to Grittle. "And you promise me you'll serve up that rain ale that isn't watered down."

Grittle sniffed. "Are you gonna come back to drink it?"

"I'll try."

67

VERA
Lysteria, Above the Frutal-Kush Valley

"Some view," Decimar said, looking east.

The valley was deep and vast, with high peaks on all sides. The green bowl was dominated by birch and pines, mostly.

"Yeah," Vera said.

"Any idea where the witch is?" Entras asked.

"Caellan's an alchemist, not a witch."

"Once, maybe. But if she really is that Lysterian woman we heard stories about, then she's clearly adopted some witchlike tendencies. Remember what the village people said? All the business with dead frogs in her belt and bubbling tonics that stop your cock from working."

Vera shrugged. "Might be she has one to get a cock working again, too." She glanced at him. "Something you could use."

Entras smiled and shook his head. "More than you know, Vera. More than you know."

"Where do you want to start looking for her?" Decimar asked, changing the subject. Unlike Entras, he had a low tolerance for conversations about cocks.

Vera consulted the alchemist map, then compared it to the valley. The reversed topographic lines aligned with what she saw, so this was the place. She took a long time studying the ground below. Eventually, she smiled.

"That copse of goat willows," Vera said, pointing to a group of trees that were blooming with purple leaves.

"You're pretty confident."

"Goat willows bloom naturally in early spring, then lose all their petals a month before the solstice. Seeing as we're two weeks past that, the fact they're still purple might belie a witch's presence, don't you think?"

"Ha! You think she's a witch, too." Entras frowned. "But I have to say, making a tree bloom out of season seems a little light in terms of sorcery."

She gave Entras a look. "I'm sure she has plenty of cock-shriveling potions bubbling as we speak. We just can't see them from the sky."

Again, Decimar stopped the conversation by pointing to the south. "We could put the *Sparrow* down in that meadow. Approach along the gully that runs north."

Vera followed Decimar's finger. That would mean covering almost two leagues of forest on foot before reaching the willows.

"This is Caellan's territory, and we are showing up uninvited. I would rather not cross through so much of it before speaking with her."

"Why not?"

"Because there's no reason for her to think of us as anything but enemies, and Salle said that Caellan was also well versed with poisons. She may have rigged the area with traps."

"See?" Entras said. "Witch."

Vera ignored him. "I want to get as close as possible, as quietly as possible."

"Oh, no. Not again."

"What?"

"You want to do a sling drop."

"You don't like sling drops?"

"Nobody likes the sling drops except for you. You know that more than half the people who have tried your little trick never walked again? I've ordered the men to stop telling stories about it."

"It's not that hard. The key is timing the roll so you disperse the load on your joints."

"Tell that to Ulric Bant."

"Who's that?"

"One of my idiot bowmen who tried a drop back in the jungle and separated himself from his kneecaps by about a league."

"Look, I'm not asking you to do it with me. I'm only asking you to swoop the ship down into the valley."

Decimar squinted. "Still not in love with the idea."

Vera looked at him. "When was the last time you were in love with anything we had to do, Decimar?"

Decimar cracked his knuckles and looked away, out over the valley. "Don't remember."

Vera nodded. Then pointed. "We'll come in from the east, riding that ridge."

"Now?" Entras asked.

"No. We'll wait until nightfall. For now, take us to the next valley over so we're out of sight."

"You're gonna do it in the dark this time?" Entras asked. "By Aeternita, you truly are crazy."

"I'll be fine. Just make sure you get a good look at that ridge. I do not want my landing fouled up because of a bad approach."

———

Entras fouled up the approach.

That, or Vera screwed up her landing, but either way she hit the ground at an off-kilter angle and careened ass-first into a willow trunk hard enough to drape the ground in purple petals.

"Black skies," Vera muttered in Papyrian. She limped to the nearest shadow. Tried to regain her bearings. The *Blue Sparrow* continued over the next ridge, carried on the wind in near silence, and was only visible if you were already looking for her.

Vera didn't move for ten minutes. Just waited. The forest was quiet, but it was an eerie and unnatural silence. No birds. No squirrels in the pine trees or rabbits rustling the ferns.

Vera stalked forward.

She moved slow—dropping down on her belly to cross areas with poor cover. Rising to a crouch only when she was certain she could stay hidden from view.

The first trap was obvious. Just a simple trip wire. Vera spotted the steel fiber reflecting in the moonlight like a fishing line drawn by a midnight sailor. She stepped over it, and traced it back to a metal case full of poisoned needles. Moved on.

The wilderness changed as she moved closer to the center of the willow grove. It didn't become clearer, exactly. But there was an order to it. Vera found herself moving without hesitation to her next spot because the best line of stealth approach was so obvious.

She stopped. Glared at the next patch of shadows she was going to slink into: a fallen tree that created an overhang against a boulder. It was too perfect. Nature didn't offer such obvious paths to protection. You had to hunt for them. Sacrifice something to reach them.

Instead of crawling into the shadow, she wormed her way to the left of it, even though the maneuver left her more exposed. When she came up on the far side, she found a metal claw half-covered in leaves. The fangs of the claw were made from Balarian steel—screwed in place with the same style bolt that Osyrus Ward used for his automatons. There was a tension lever keeping the device in place, which was connected to a pressure plate located in the middle of that tempting shadow.

Clever.

Instead of forging ahead into the dangerous blackness, Vera decided to readjust her strategy. She might have avoided two traps, but she had no idea how many more were out there, and she only had to screw up once.

She drew *Owaru* and carefully used the tip to unscrew one of the fangs. Then she dug around in the undergrowth until she found a decent-sized rock. Threw it into the shadow. The metal claw snapped forward. There was a loud impact, followed by a spray of mud and leaves.

Vera wailed in pain. Then released a lower, gurgling murmur.

Then she scaled a nearby pine tree with good cover and waited.

For several minutes, nothing happened. Vera was concerned her gambit hadn't worked, but she couldn't try another howl and risk giving away her position. Then a soft, chemical-blue light illuminated farther ahead in the forest. It had the dim glow of light being refracted through a window.

Caellan's hut.

The light died a moment later, and a door opened. Closed again. After that, the alchemist moved without a sound as she traveled toward the trap, but Vera could make out little flickers of her in the moonlight. She was shrouded in some kind of cloak with a ragged outline. Too dark to see clearly.

When Caellan was about ten strides from the trap, she froze. Clucked her tongue.

"I see we have a clever intruder in our midst," she said in Papyrian. Her voice was sultry and smooth. "A welcome change. Grakus was getting tired of eating morons."

Vera didn't say anything. She did not believe the woman knew where she was.

"Trying to keep your position secret? Also smart. But a fool's errand. Grakus can find anyone."

Caellan opened her hand. A green puff of smoke rose from her palm.

"He just needs a little incentive."

Again, Vera kept still. But a few moments later, the ferns to her right started thrashing. A beast was charging through the undergrowth, heading directly at her. What was it? Seemed to be about boar-sized. She tightened her grip on the poisoned fang, got ready. But it wasn't a boar that came careening out of the forest.

It was a Yellow-Spined Greezel.

The dragon had a dozen yellow spikes jutting out from his back. Glowing yellow eyes and a scarred maw. The lizard bolted forward and rammed his head into Vera's tree at speed. The shock vibrated up the trunk and into Vera's palms, forcing her to shift her weight and grip. At the exact moment that her fingers were grasping for a better hold, the Greezel slammed both his front claws against the trunk, sending Vera falling toward his waiting jaws.

She grabbed a lower branch just as the dragon was jumping up to snatch her, tucked her legs to avoid his razor-sharp teeth, and swung herself through the air. Landed behind Caellan. Pressed the poisoned fang against her throat.

The dragon spun around, glaring at Vera but not advancing. He dug his claws into the ground, instead, tearing long marks in the earth. Nostrils dilated. Eyes angry.

"Call that thing off," she whispered.

"Why?" Caellan asked. Her breath smelled of strong liquor, but there was no sloppiness to her words or movement. "Right now, Grakus is the only thing keeping that poison outside my veins."

"No," Vera said, pushing the fang closer. "My arm is the only thing keeping that poison out of your veins. Call. Him. Off."

Now that she was pressed against her, Vera realized that Caellan's cloak was made from raven feathers. They shimmered purple and black in the moonlight.

"Kill me, and that dragon kills you a heartbeat later," Caellan said, voice calm.

"I'd rather avoid bloodshed entirely."

"Then you should not have snuck into my valley."

"I found this valley because of the map *you* left behind, Caellan. You must have wanted to be tracked down by someone."

"Not by a Papyrian widow. As I recall, there is only one reason for a widow to travel without her charge."

"My charge is Kira Malgrave, one of the last members of Okinu's line. She suffered a catastrophic spinal cord injury. Complete severance of the fifth vertebrae. I came to you for help getting her to walk again."

"Walk? If what you say is true, then she is already dead."

"She's a Seed."

That gave Caellan pause. When she spoke again, there was a hint of fear in her voice. "How do you know that word?"

Vera swallowed. "Osyrus Ward has been helping me keep Kira al—"

Vera's words froze in her mouth. She tried to take a breath. Couldn't. Looked down.

Each raven feather in Caellan's garb had a copper needle running down the middle of it. And three of them had suddenly pricked up and stabbed through her armor—filling her veins with ice.

Vera fell over—her limbs frozen like a woman who'd been dead for a day. She couldn't move her arms. Couldn't shout. Couldn't even blink.

"I do not bargain with Osyrus Ward's dogs," Caellan said in that smooth, silky voice.

Vera's vision blurred as her tear ducts stopped working. Everything went dark.

68

CASTOR
Castle Malgrave, Level 77

Osyrus Ward removed the sword hilt from Vergun's chest with a grunt. Dumped it into a metal basin. Examined the damage that the Flawless Bershad had done.

"Ruptured stomach and spleen," he said. "Collapsed lung. And a rib cage that is essentially splinters." Osyrus pressed on part of Vergun's stomach and a large stream of blood sprayed from his wound. "This is a substantial injury."

"Can you fix him?" Castor asked, not really sure which answer he wanted to hear.

"Yes, yes," Osyrus said with the confidence of a parent who'd just been asked by their child whether the sun would rise the next day. "But I fail to see the concrete value in doing so. You have failed every task to which you have been assigned, Commander Vergun."

Vergun gasped for air. Didn't seem to be finding enough of it.

Osyrus mumbled something about lungs, then produced a needle and injected it downward through Vergun's collarbone, into his chest. He flipped a valve on the needle, which released a hiss of air and left a putrid smell in the laboratory.

"Try again, Commander."

"Silas . . . Bershad."

"Blaming your failure on an external source is not acceptable."

"This was a pretty powerful external source," Castor said.

He told Osyrus Ward about the things they had seen Bershad do. The wounds he'd taken, and healed almost immediately. Ward did not seem surprised by any of the information.

"It sounds as if Silas Bershad has learned to make the most of his abilities. Good for him."

"What is he?" Castor asked.

"He has a rare blood disorder that makes him vital to the reproduction cycle of dragons, as well as resilient to tissue and bone damage."

"I shot him with a ballista before we left," Castor said.

"That is unlikely to have killed him," Ward said.

"Fix me," Vergun rasped.

"That would be a waste of resources that could be better allocated elsewhere. Silas Bershad has proven himself to be far more powerful than you are. If I repair these injuries, you will simply go out and get more of them."

Castor felt a swell of relief and excitement at the possibility of Vergun dying on this table. He could take the gold he'd been paid so far and get out of this city. Out of this fucking war. He didn't have enough to buy a whole island, but renting a small fishing shack in the middle of nowhere was sounding more appealing to him with each passing day.

"The more productive action would be to improve you, rather than simply repair you," Ward continued.

"Won't . . . become . . . gray . . . slave."

"That's fine. The acolyte project has largely run its course anyway. But I have finally gathered enough materials to move to the next phase of trials, which require an alpha test subject."

"What will it do to him?" Castor asked.

"Answering that question is the point of the test. But if successful, the process will make you far stronger and more . . . *durable*. It will give you the edge against Silas Bershad that you need."

Vergun's eyes were hungry. He nodded slowly. "Do it."

Ward smiled. Castor's heart sank.

"Let us alight to the upper reaches of my tower."

———

Osyrus Ward led them to the highest chamber of the King's Tower. For months, Ward had been funneling the bulk of his precious resources to this room. Castor had to admit he was curious what it was all being used for.

When Castor saw what Osyrus had built, his pulse completely escaped his control.

One side of the room had seventeen impaled men against it. Well, *impaled* wasn't exactly right—they were strung up to the wall by steel beams and clear wires. And neither was the word *men*. They had human forms, but seemed to have been carved from trees rather than built from meat and bone. Branches with black leaves sprouted from their backs. Their legs had been shorn off and plopped into vats of green liquid. Their mouths were bolted shut with strips of metal, but they were definitely alive. Their eyes were open and full of fear.

The other side of the room had two tables. One had a Red Skull's severed head on it. The other, two claws.

Despite these horrors, the machine in the middle was the most disturbing thing in the room.

It was about the size of a merchant wagon, and comprised of hundreds of sacks that looked kind of like half-filled wine bags. Each sack was stitched together from a horrific amalgamation of flesh and bone, and they were connected to each other by those rubber gaskets and tubes that Ward was always bitching about. Fluids burbled back and forth between different parts of the machine, causing the bags to shake and shudder, and causing Castor to feel very much like he was going to puke on the floor.

"I call it the loom," Osyrus said.

"Why the fuck would you call it that?"

"I'll show you."

Ward stepped toward the middle of the machine, where there was a particularly large sack that was a few shades darker than the rest, and festooned with bones. He grabbed one of the bones and gave it a pull, which brought a whole framework of bones extending outward with a sticky shudder.

Castor hadn't seen a loom in a long time, so it took him a moment, but the framework was a pretty close representation of the sewer's tool.

"Don't see any thread," said Castor.

Ward snapped his fingers at the acolyte who had carried Vergun's stretcher up the tower. "Place him in front of the loom, and mulch the Red Skull."

The acolyte deposited Vergun, who was having trouble breathing again and seemed like he was quite close to death. Then he picked up the Red Skull's head with two meaty hands and fed it into the right side of the machine, where there was a much larger gasket that looked a lot like a massive cow's asshole.

The Red Skull was sucked into the machine. The sound of crunching, digesting bones that followed was a noise that Castor knew would haunt him for the rest of his life.

"Should I mulch the claws as well, master?" the acolyte rasped.

"No," Osyrus said, moving over to the wall of tree people. "Until we obtain a more powerful energy source, we must rely on the dragon oil reserves for fuel. There is no reason to process more than necessary."

The vats beneath the tree people were all connected by copper pipes that ran into the side of the loom. Osyrus bent down near one of them, cranked a lever back and forth a bunch of times, then pressed a button on the side of the pipe.

Castor couldn't tell exactly what the button did, but it appeared to cause the tree people an enormous amount of pain. They shook and shuddered, dropping leaves all over the floor and attempting to wail, but the steel bands over their mouths muffled their cries.

A black fluid spread through the different sacks, and several moments later, a series of wet, black threads were pushed from the sacks and guided into the bony frame of the loom.

Osyrus ran a finger along one thread, then wiped it against a machine in the corner of the room. A bunch of dials sputtered and turned.

"Purity levels at sixty-two-point-three percent," he muttered.

"Is that good?" Castor asked.

"Good enough."

"So, they're some kind of special stitches?" Castor asked.

"That is an adequate comparison. Stitches bind disparate elements together. And we are going to bind Commander Vergun to an entirely new set of elements." He glanced at Castor. "You may leave, if you'd like. The process is . . . messy."

Castor swallowed. He had seen and done his share of horrible things in his life. Only thing worse than doing them was being too soft to look at the results head-on.

"I'll stay."

Osyrus went to work.

Castor knew this would be unpleasant, but figured it couldn't be much worse than a field amputation on a dying man after a battle, and he'd seen dozens of those.

He was wrong. The things that Osyrus Ward did to Vergun were a thousand times worse.

PART III

69

ACOLYTE 799
Location Unknown

Acolyte 799 woke up in the dark again. It was cold.

"The bindings along his nervous system are frayed," came a familiar voice. His master's voice.

"Damaged in his last combat sortie?" asked the man with the nasally voice.

"No. There is no evidence of exterior damage. Hm."

Acolyte 799 felt an extreme amount of pressure around his right temple. For a moment, it felt like his entire brain was going to pop. Then it released.

"I see. An old pathway was retriggered."

"That's possible? How?"

"Coincidence, most likely. I can patch the error, but it will always be weaker now, and prone to further error. Too risky to redeploy the unit into combat situations."

"Do we scrap it?"

"No. After Vergun's trial, we're far too short on resources to waste him. Reassign him to a pacification ship stationed in a remote location, where the odds of a confrontation are low. All he needs to do is intimidate the crew enough so they don't mutiny. One job he can still perform."

"I'll see to the details."

70

VERA
Frutal-Kush Valley, Caellan's Cabin

Vera woke up with a desperate gasp.

She wasn't restrained, and she went for her weapons before she fully got her bearings.

"I took those," came Caellan's voice. She was sitting at a table across the room. A mug in front of her. "Wouldn't want my mercy to bite me in the ass so soon after doling it out. I am sure that you know a thousand ways to kill me without your blades, of course, but trust me when I say those attempts would not end well for you. Not in my home."

Vera looked around the hut. The walls and ceiling were made from a smooth and uniform lattice material. There were dozens of glass orbs hanging from the low ceiling. Each orb seemed to contain a miniature world of its own. One held a sandy landscape with a lone, black scorpion sunning itself under a heated orb the size of a marble. A field of headless grasshoppers were littered around its hairy claws. Another orb contained a lush rainforest full of moss and tiny ferns. Two brightly colored frogs hid amongst the leaves. And another still was nothing but dark green water and churning black snakes.

"I should note that my mercy is decidedly temporary. Back in the woods, I filled your bloodstream with a paralyzing agent. I gave you an antidote once I hauled you back here, but only the first in a sequence. If I do not administer another dose in twenty minutes, the paralyzing agent will take effect again, and you will die."

"Why show me mercy at all?" Vera asked. "Temporary or otherwise."

"Curiosity. I would like to know how a Papyrian widow wound up serving Osyrus Ward."

"I was in the process of explaining that when you poisoned me."

"I felt our conversation would be more fruitful without that claw at my throat. The results of contact with that specific toxin are extremely unpleasant. Turns your entire bowel to jelly."

"You're the one who made it."

"Yes, I am. Along with so many other monstrosities. Now tell me, how did you become Osyrus Ward's dog?"

"That's not who I am."

"Then who are you?"

"I am the last Papyrian widow. And I came here to get help for Kira."

"That person is just a name to me. For all I know she could be worse than Osyrus."

"No. She was trying to bring peace to Terra. Fill starving bellies. End useless wars. But the world is black and cruel and full of sharp teeth that chewed her apart. She was betrayed by her husband. Betrayed by her aunt, Empress Okinu. Betrayed by everyone."

"She seems to have attracted a rather diverse amount of ire. That does not typically happen to magnanimous rulers full of kindness. Perhaps Kira simply overextended herself before she had the chance to grow black teeth of her own. Perhaps your teeth were not sharp enough to protect her. The rulers of this world will always disappoint you."

Vera narrowed her eyes. She recognized those words. "Osyrus Ward said that to me once, back in Balaria."

"The man is insane. That does not make him wrong. At least not about everything."

Vera knew she wasn't going to get anywhere by starting a philosophical argument with this woman, so she tried a different approach.

"Maybe Kira will turn rotten," she whispered. "Maybe I already have, trying to protect her. But I am not going to let her remain in a *fucking coma* because I'm afraid of who she might become. I love her. I have for a long time, I think. But when the time came to tell her, I was afraid . . ."

Caellan took a sip from her cup. "Spare me the emotional plea, yeah? That might have convinced the softhearted alchemists back in Nisena to help you—it's always effective to see the sensitive side of a fearsome warrior—but a decade of isolation and heavy drinking has hardened my heart a bit. I don't give a shit who you love, and I don't give a shit who Kira might help or not help if she's healed. Do you think I came out here to the middle of nowhere because I was interested in drumming up new business from intrepid strangers? I want to be left alone."

"Why did you leave that map behind, then?"

"Ah, right. That fucking map." Caellan drank more. Refilled her cup from an earthenware jug. "I told myself that it was to allow a properly trained alchemist to find me, if they truly desired, so I might pass on my knowledge to someone worthy. I figured it

would be a young disciple who'd figure out the map's secret. Someone who hadn't been tainted by the order and their precious protocols." She let out a breath. "But I suppose the truth is that I always
wanted someone to show up at my doorstep and make me pay for
helping Osyrus Ward. I didn't care who it was—one of his agents,
or someone who'd found out what I had done. I just wanted them
to earn it."

Vera motioned to the Caellan's cloak. "I've been around Osyrus
Ward long enough to recognize his work. He made that for you,
didn't he?"

She nodded. "He called it his most elegant prototype, but like all
of Ward's creations, whatever exterior beauty they possess is belied
by a skeleton of poison and pain."

"What did you do to earn such a gift?"

Caellan stared into the corner for a long time, then shifted her
gaze back to Vera and spoke in a cold monotone. "I broke the alchemist protocols that prohibit experimentation on Seeds. I discovered
a way to suppress a Seed's natural response to trauma, which allows
them to endure in their human state for an unnaturally long period
of time. Seeds appear resilient, but they are actually quite delicate,
in their own way. I taught the method to Osyrus Ward. He gave me
the cloak as a reward."

She went to drink from her cup but found it empty. Instead of
refilling it, she set it down on the table again, and continued to talk.

"I soon learned what he was planning to do with the knowledge
I had given him. He doesn't want to give Seeds normal lives. He
wants to be able to torture them in perpetuity. When I discovered
this, I tried to kill him. Failed. Then I ran. First, back to Pargos,
where I asked the alchemist order for help. They told me that I had
brought the guilt that I felt upon myself by breaking protocol, but
offered no other insight or aid. So I left. Came to this valley."

There was so much information within those words from
Caellan—and so much of it impacted Kira—that Vera had a difficult time keeping her emotions under control. All this time, Kira
had been tortured by Osyrus Ward, and she'd allowed it to happen
under her very nose. But there was nothing she could do about that
now except move forward.

"I know what it's like to be abandoned by an order you've given
your life to in service," Vera said. "And I know what it's like to be
weighed down with guilt. But I *will* help you, Caellan."

"How is that?"

"Once Kira is safe, there will be nothing stopping me from killing Osyrus Ward. And I want him dead just as much as you do."

Caellan studied Vera for a long time. Eventually, she went to a different earthenware jug and poured a mug of liquid that smelled like a mixture of piss and vinegar. Brought it to her.

"Drink that."

Vera sipped the drink. Coughed at the bitter taste. Then gagged. She put the mug down.

"Oh, I'd finish the balance if I were you," Caellan said. "As in so many other aspects of life, half measures aren't effective when it comes to antivenom."

Vera did as she was told. Choking down the entire contents. She didn't feel any different, other than wishing her tongue didn't register the rotten taste, but that was probably a good thing.

"Does this mean that you'll help me?"

"It means that you aren't going to become paralyzed and die in the next ten minutes."

Caellan poured herself a fresh mug of liquor. Vera could smell the potency of it from across the room.

"Now, I need you to tell me every single detail that you can about Kira's condition, starting from the moment of her injury until the last time you saw her."

Vera did as Caellan asked. She described the machines that surrounded Kira, down to the color of every last vat. She described the lung apparatus that Kira was attached to. All their efforts to get her off the machine. And the temporary effect of the Gods Moss.

"You're rather resourceful for a bodyguard," Caellan said when she was done. "The Gods Moss is one of the alchemist order's most closely guarded secrets. How did you acquire it?"

"I got wind of a merchant who was transporting a small amount by caravan."

"If the merchant knew the value, it must have been very expensive to acquire."

"It was."

Vera blinked. The merchant had had four bodyguards traveling with him. Vera had killed them all.

"And for all it cost me, the effects were only temporary. We only had a few minutes to speak. From what I had been told, it should have been enough to heal her completely."

"Under normal circumstances, it would have," said Caellan. "But Ward has most likely been feeding her the suppression tonic intravenously since the initial injury. After so much time, it will not be simple or easy to reverse his work, but it is possible. I have the materials."

"How long will that take?"

Caellan sucked on her teeth. "Thirteen days."

"When can you start?"

"Right away." Caellan glanced at the door. Sighed. "Unfortunately, the first step is the most unpleasant. The Yellow Greezel's venom is the only substance powerful enough to stimulate the reaction that we need from Kira's body, and we need a rather large amount of it." She stood. "Follow me."

———

While Vera had been paralyzed, Caellan had secured the dragon to a massive tree about a hundred paces from her hut. The creature stirred as they approached. Glared at them with suspicious eyes.

"There is no way to tame a dragon," Caellan said. "No domestication flows through their cold blood. But Grakus and I have an understanding with each other. An uneasy truce, I guess you'd could call it. I always expected it'd be the lizard that broke our terms and made me his lunch one day." She paused. "But we humans' capacity for wretchedness will always surpass the great lizards'."

Caellan squatted down near a shrub, and fiddled with something unseen in the bushes. There was a click, and then movement in the tree above the dragon. A metal orb dropped down from a rope, then popped open, releasing a large shank of wet meat near the Greezel. The dragon started tearing the meat off the bone. Caellan watched patiently.

"The meat is poisoned?" Vera asked.

Caellan shook her head. "No. But after protecting me for so long, the beast deserves a final meal."

When the dragon had stripped away all the meat, it started licking the bone. That was when Caellan extended one arm and jerked her wrist back. A needle flew from her cloak and struck the dragon's tongue. The needle was so thin, the dragon didn't notice. Just kept on licking.

A minute later, it slumped over. Dead.

"I also needed a good view of his tongue," Caellan said, already walking toward the carcass.

She drew a butcher's knife from inside her cloak. Arranged herself so she had clear access to the joint where the Greezel's spine met a scale. Then she made a very precise hack, which left a small rend. She examined the result, nodded to herself, and then made another, just slightly deeper.

"Describe these acolytes in more detail," Caellan said, rearing up for another hack. "Numbers. Behavior."

"When we were in Burz-al-dun, there were only a few of them. Ward treated them more like servants and mechanics for the skyships—said that he couldn't keep the *Blue Sparrow* in the air without their help. He meant that literally. He uses them as stabilizing devices for the skyship engines."

"How does he make them?"

"They start as humans, I think. Injured, usually. He fills their bodies with metal and dragon bone and fibrous strands cut from Ghost Moth dragons. With the war on, there have been plenty of subjects. There are hundreds of acolytes spread across Terra now—each of them ten times stronger than any man has a right to be. Ward used the skyships to take power, but his acolytes are the ones holding it for him. Ghalamar. Lysteria. Dunfar. Pargos. The only place left outside of his control is the Dainwood."

"I see." Caellan stopped hacking and tested the spine. She was breathing a little hard from the work. When the spine didn't come loose, she resumed her work. "So, he finally found the key to reigniting the Ghost Moth hunter-killer nerve to full strength. That's too bad. When I met him, his progress had been blocked for decades because of that little mystery. But that's what makes Osyrus Ward so dangerous. He soaks up information and techniques and materials from every source imaginable, then twists them around for his own purposes."

"What is he really doing? He's amassing all these materials but it's unclear what he'll do with them. He told me he was building a better world."

"Yeah, he fed me that dragonshit line, too."

Caellan made another hack. Stood back and wiped her forehead.

"A better world," she continued. "A cleaner world. One where the animal struggle for resources was no longer necessary. Blah. Blah. Blah. I'm sure that in some ways, that's what he still thinks he's doing. But he lies, even to himself. The truth is far more terrifying."

"What truth?"

"He doesn't have a plan at all. To Osyrus Ward, this entire plane of existence is just one big specimen for him to poke and prod and transform. The output of his experiments—whether for good or ill—is irrelevant to him. He just wants to keep *going*."

Caellan reared up and slammed the blade down again. This time, a splash of dragon blood sprayed across the raven feathers that ran along her wrists. She pulled the poisoned spike from the dragon's hide with a yank and a grunt. A long tendril of tissue and meat and nerves trailed from the bloody stump.

"He'll push the limits of our world, and he will never stop pushing. Stopping would not even occur to him. The problem is that ten years ago, he was torturing Seeds and rebuilding rat spines. Now he's rebuilding people. If he keeps going at this pace, he'll cross over from the mortal realm, and into the stuff of gods."

"I don't believe in gods," said Vera.

"Neither do I," said Caellan. "But that doesn't mean Osyrus can't create them."

71

JOLAN
Dainwood Jungle, Southern Bank of the Gorgon

Jolan moved down the muddy trail carrying two mugs of steaming coffee. All around him, wardens were either chopping at Daintrees, or lashing logs together to build rafts that could cross the Gorgon River.

He found Ashlyn sitting with Willem, Simeon, and Kerrigan.

"I brought coffee," Jolan said, handing Ashlyn a mug.

"What, none for the rest of us, boy?" Simeon asked.

Jolan shrugged. "None of you stayed up all night working on the astrolabe with me."

"Balls the size of apples," Simeon said, grinning and reaching into a little goatskin pouch. "I got you a present."

"Really?" Jolan asked, surprised.

Simeon produced two silver rings from the pouch. Held them out.

"What are they?"

"You're Almiran, ain't you? And you proved yourself to be a true warrior at that warren." He motioned to Willem's ring-laden hair. "You need the decorations to reflect that."

"But I'm not a warden."

"Think we're all a long way past giving a shit about that. Lean over and I'll tie 'em in."

Despite Simeon's armored gauntlets, he got the first ring tied into a strand of Jolan's hair without trouble.

"What're they made out of?" Jolan asked.

"Some scraps I stole from all that shit you had brought to Damp-mire."

"What?"

"Yeah. Figured it should come outta your scrap pile, since that's what you used to turn those Wormwrot to chunks. Label said it was modified lead or something."

"I need those!" Jolan said. "They're specifically designed to block electrical charges."

"Too late, I'm done tying." He slapped Jolan on the back. "Wel-come to the bloody life of a true warrior, kid."

Jolan touched the heavy rings. Looked around and saw that every-one was smiling at him.

"Uh, thanks, I guess."

Ashlyn took a sip of her coffee. "I was just telling them that you and I finished extending the range of the astrolabe, which means we're ready to head to the Gorgon Bridge." She turned to Willem. "How much longer before you have enough rafts?"

"A day to finish the ones for the men. Another for the barges we'll take the bombs on."

Ashlyn nodded. "The donkey cart moves slow. Jolan and I will need three days to reach the bridge, so you'll have a little time be-fore you cross."

"Whole riverbank is gonna be pocked with mud totems in that case. Between the skyship patrols and the River Lurkers, the men aren't exactly thrilled at the prospect of crossing the Gorgon."

"If we're right, the skyships won't be a problem for you," Ashlyn said. "But there isn't much I can do about the Lurkers."

"You're sure you can control the skyships from that bridge?" Ker-rigan asked.

"No," Ashlyn said. "But I am sure you'll be able to tell whether I'm successful or not. Don't start crossing until you're sure."

"And the signal we're looking for is, what?"

"A skyship that's under my control," Ashlyn said.

"How are we gonna know that?"

"Because I am going to start crashing them."

Kerrigan shrugged. "If you say so."

"Once you're across, make your way to the fifth bend of the Fox-paw River."

"What's there?"

"A massive cave. I'll meet you there, and we'll make a frontal as-sault on Floodhaven together."

Willem dug some dirt out of his ear with one finger. Flicked it away. "Never thought I'd do something so risky and be the one on the safer side of things. If you and Jolan don't make it, we can always head back to the Gloom. Not that there'll be much point in that, other than dying on familiar ground."

There was a long silence.

"I wish Silas was here," said Jolan.

"Kerrigan will go back to Dampmire in case he returns," said Ash-lyn. "But we can't afford to wait for him."

She left the last part unsaid, which was that he might not be com-ing back at all. There'd been no word from Deepdale.

"What's the matter, Kerri?" asked Simeon. "Scared of a little fight?"

"I never was much of a warrior," she replied. "And someone needs to take all those donkeys back to Vash and Wendell eventually."

"Kerrigan the donkey herder. Quite the fall from grace you've had since being in charge of Naga Rock."

Kerrigan just shrugged.

Simeon's face softened a little. "Well, no point in talking the thing to death," he said. "Let's just get on with it."

Everyone went their separate ways, leaving Ashlyn and Jolan alone.

"You don't need to come with me to the bridge," Ashlyn said. "I can read the astrolabe on my own."

"If you split your attention, you'll be more likely to make a mis-take."

"That's true, but if something goes wrong, there's no reason for both of us to die."

"This was my idea. There's no way that I'm letting you go there alone. I couldn't live with myself."

Ashlyn nodded. "I understand."

Jolan took a sip of his coffee. Pointed at Ashlyn's arm. "That's the most powerful source of energy in the realm of Terra. There should be something better that we can do with it than destroy things."

"One day, there will be. But right now, we need to do this."

Ashlyn finished her coffee. Dumped the dregs into the grass.

"We'll leave within the hour," she said. "You need to go see Oro-mir before that."

"What? Why?"

"Jolan." She put a hand on his shoulder. "Are there things that you want to say to him?"

He hesitated. "Yes."

"Do you want to go down the river holding onto them?"

"No."

"Then go. I'll get the donkeys ready to travel."

Oromir and his men were helping to build the barge that was meant for the explosives, which were packed into a bunch of crates next to the half-built barge. Jolan spent a full minute going crate-to-crate, rechecking random bombs before working up the courage to ap-proach him.

"Hey, Oro."

Oromir turned around, saw who it was, then went back to tying a lashing around two logs.

"I'm busy, Jolan."

Jolan walked around the barge's skeleton so that he was in front of Oro. "Look at me."

Oromir raised his pale blue eyes. Held his gaze.

"I used to think about you all the time," Jolan said. "After the skyship crash. After Cumberland died. You were always in the back of my mind. I kept the memory of you so close. It was my one scrap of comfort in this whole mess. But after that night that I came to your tent, I let you go. The same way you let me go. Truth is, until Ashlyn said your name to me just now, I hadn't thought of you for weeks."

He paused.

"I've killed people since then. I'm not sure how many. Ten. Twenty. I turned them into chunks of smoking meat. And I didn't feel a fucking thing when I did it."

Again, Oromir said nothing. Jolan stepped closer.

"But I don't want to be like this. I don't want to go numb. Or twist into something wretched and evil, like Osyrus Ward. I remem-ber the person that you were. And I miss the person that I was. I hope you survive this, Oro. I really do."

Oromir still didn't say anything. So Jolan walked away.

72

VERA
Frutal-Kush Valley, Caellan's Cabin

While Caellan brewed the tonic, there was nothing for Vera and her men to do besides wait and work on their weapons. Vera had gotten both her daggers keen enough to cut silk during the first few days. Decimar and his men had fletched a month's worth of arrows.

Entras paused his work fletching an arrow, lifted one ass cheek, and broke a long, putrid stretch of wind.

Entras—and most of the men—refused to eat or drink anything in Caellan's hut. Instead, they relied on the *Blue Sparrow*'s backup rations, which consisted of canned beans and salted meat. The diet did not have a pleasant impact on the longbowmen's digestive system.

"Will you please eat something besides that canned crap," Vera said as she polished away the rough edge of a shot for her sling.

"Up until that bath of yours in Pargos, you smelled far worse than my broken wind."

"But I took a bath, didn't I? Caellan has plenty of food, which makes this a solvable problem."

Entras glanced at the glass orbs on the eastern side of the cabin, where Caellan kept her foodstuffs. Nuts and berries and mushrooms, mostly. As far as Vera could tell, the alchemist didn't eat meat or rice or bread.

"She keeps her food in the same glass worlds that she grows her poisons," Entras said. "Only a fool would eat from those."

"You calling me a fool, Entras?" Vera asked. "The mushrooms are delicious."

"They could be poisonous."

"At this point, I would rather die an unnatural and violent death than continue living under the yoke of your rancid gas."

"I didn't realize widows had such delicate sensibilities."

"And I didn't realize that longbowmen have rotting bowels."

Entras shrugged.

Caellan burst through the door of her cottage in a flurry of movement and muttered curses. She flitted between the different globes—snatching at red tubers and glowing green mushrooms. She threw the ingredients into a sack, then grabbed a needle and began extracting goo from the ass of a massive black spider covered in crimson hairs. She cursed to herself the entire time.

"Trouble?" Vera asked, getting nervous.

"You dick-swinging bowmen are farting too much," she said without looking away from the spider.

"Don't *you* start with me, too, witch," Entras said. "Your work is out back in the shed. We're stuck in here waiting on you."

Caellan stopped. Stared at him. "That is not a shed, it's a laboratory. And you are filling the atmosphere around it with methane, which is screwing with my work!"

Entras frowned. "That can't possibly matter."

"Oh, you're an expert in nerve-stimulating agents now, are you?"

"We haven't set foot in your . . . laboratory."

"When you invent a way to keep the exterior air from getting into an enclosed space without suffocating the person inside, you let me know. Until then, pass out some fucking wine corks and tell your men to stick them up their fat asses!"

Caellan left.

Entras looked at Vera. "Do we have fat assess?"

Vera smiled. "Not the word I'd use."

They were quiet a moment.

"But, all things being equal, maybe have your men wait on the ship until she's done? I'd hate to endure the ruckus caused by Caellan passing around corks."

"Aye." He looked around. "Place gives me the creeps, anyway."

———

Vera didn't mind the solitude during the days that followed. That was the one aspect of a widow's duty that had always felt unnatural to her: you were almost never alone. More often, you were surrounded by scores of lords, preening like roosters.

She basked in the quiet of Caellan's hut. Meditated. Stretched. Exercised. Did her best to prevent her mind from getting bogged down on thoughts of Kira, alone and unconscious in that tower. Surrounded by metal and machines. Most of the time, she failed.

Ten days later, Caellan emerged from her laboratory with three vials. Green. Black. Red. She laid them on the table and poured herself a full mug of liquor. Her first, since she'd begun working on Kira's tonic.

"Inject them in a series, starting with black at the top of her spine, then red, then green. The first two will reverse the effects of Ward's suppression tonic. The green will activate Kira's healing capabilities and allow you to take her off the machine."

"Is there a risk of her transforming?"

"There is *always* a risk of her transforming. But, I did the best I could to mitigate it."

"How long will it take to work?"

"Best guess? A few minutes. But to be perfectly candid, this is uncharted territory. I designed the suppression tonic, but I have never tried to reverse it before. She will be extremely weak at first, but should improve quickly."

Vera nodded. Went quiet.

For the last thirteen days, when her mind wasn't bogged down with thoughts of Kira's eyes and voice and smile, she'd been trying to think of a way to break into that chamber and get her out. So far, she hadn't come up with any ideas.

"Is something wrong?" Caellan asked.

"This gets me past one obstacle, but there are others in my way. Some of them are very large."

She told Caellan about the place Kira was kept, and the massive acolyte who guarded her.

Caellan chewed on this information. Then she moved through her hut and opened one of the chests in the back. Came out with the cloak she'd been wearing the night they'd met. In the low light, Vera could see the copper wire and bone barbs beneath the black sheen of bird feathers.

"Take it," Caellan said, holding it out.

Vera hesitated. "Are you sure?"

"There was no point in me toiling away for all those hours if you get stomped to mush by Osyrus Ward's creature. *Take* it."

Vera ran her hand down one of the feathers. Felt the barbs.

"You and I are of a similar size, which is lucky," said Caellan. "Try it on."

The cloak seemed to automatically attach to the places where it met Vera's bare skin—at wrists and along her neckline—tightening to her body with a strange tug that felt both natural and wildly foreign at the same time.

Caellan gave her a long once-over. "It suits you, I think."

"How does it work?"

"The barbs will open if you clench your muscles twice in quick succession."

Vera backed up. Tried it with her left forearm. The feathers prick-led. Barbs extending like a cat's claw.

"I removed the paralysis venom from the barbs," Caellan said. "Replaced it with the most destructive mixture that I have ever brewed. Funny, how easy it is to take a lifetime's knowledge of heal-ing, then twist it backward upon itself. Long ago, I designed it spe-cifically for Osyrus Ward's veins, should he have ever found me. I suppose I should have been more proactive. Maybe none of this would have happened."

"I have my share of regrets, too." Vera put a hand on Caellan's shoulder. "But once I get Kira to safety, I *will* kill Osyrus Ward. I promise."

Caellan nodded. She ran a hand down one of the cloak's feath-ers. "There is one more aspect of this garment that you should know about. I've been too old to take advantage of it for quite some time, but the way those gassy Balarians talked about your propensity to jump off skyships, I think that you might find it particularly useful."

"What is it?"

"When Osyrus gave me this cloak, he didn't make it from scratch. He retrofitted an existing prototype in which he was pursuing a dif-ferent goal."

"What goal?"

Caellan smiled. "Flight."

73

BERSHAD
Dainwood Jungle, Southern Bank of the Gorgon

After leaving Deepdale, Bershad and Felgor went to Dampmire, where they found Kerrigan. She told them where Ashlyn had gone, and what she was planning to do when she got there.

Bershad and Felgor headed for the Gorgon.

Bershad's feet started getting torn up during the journey. He tried smearing dabs of moss into the wounds, but it was no good. The injection back at Deepdale had taken away his ability to heal. There was nothing to be done but wrap his feet in strips of cloth and keep moving.

He also didn't have the Nomad to help him locate the Jaguar Army, but he didn't need her. Once they were within a few hundred paces of the river, there were bootprints and sign everywhere. Bershad slowed down. Motioned for Felgor to stay behind him and stay quiet. Then he started creeping through the ferns. He was stopped when he heard two wardens talking.

"Why are you always putting coffee beans in your totems, Sem? Use steel like a normal person."

"Steel's never brought anything but trouble into my life," Sem responded. "Coffee is delicious and never hurt anyone."

"I dunno, didn't Elden Grealor go to war with Cedar Wallace over coffee plantations a few years back?" said a third man.

"Look, assholes. All I'm saying is that if there were forest gods protecting the Dainwood—which there ain't, 'cause one look at the state of our fucking forest proves that, but if there were—their divine wings and haunches would be dusted with rich dark coffee grounds because coffee is the only good and pure thing left in this mess of a world, and I think they'd appreciate me making totems in their likeness."

There was a silence.

"Did you just make that up?"

"Yeah. Why?"

"It was beautiful."

"Fuck off."

"Seriously. We manage to avoid getting torn apart by dragons or grayskins you should become a poet. Specialize in coffee limericks or something."

Bershad stood up and walked out of the undergrowth. "Evening."

There were five wardens gathered in a circle, each man with a handful of mud and chain mail links for their mud totems. Except Sem, who had a handful of coffee beans.

Those chain mail links and coffee got dropped in a big hurry. Weapons were grabbed and raised. Then lowered again when they saw who it was.

"Lord Bershad," said Sem. "You're back. How was—"

"Where's Ashlyn?" Bershad pressed.

The wardens all looked at each other. "Best you hear it from Willem. C'mon. I'll take you to him."

———

"You let her and Jolan take a fucking donkey cart to the Gorgon Bridge?" Bershad hissed.

"She's the queen of Almira," said Willem. "I don't have purview over her decisions."

"You could have talked her out of it."

"Not true. And even if I could have, it's not like we're swimming in other options here, Silas. If she can pull this off, it's our best chance. Shit. It's our *only* chance."

Bershad just shook his head, trying to think. He wished that he was still connected to the Nomad. She could fly ahead and find her.

"Look, this whole thing is supposed to get started tomorrow morning," Willem said. "Wait here and cross with us. If this works out, you'll meet her at the Foxpaw river with the rest of us."

"No. I'm going after her now."

"She's got a two-day head start. You'll never catch her on foot."

"Not going on foot." He started walking toward the river. "Need one of your rafts."

"Wait," Willem said, following him. "You take a raft down the Gorgon now, you'll get spotted by a patrol and blown to pieces. Maybe you can survive that, but I don't like the odds."

"Silas actually kinda lost the whole healing from moss thing at Deepdale," Felgor said.

"Really?"

"Doesn't matter. I'm going." He looked west. "Sun's almost down. I'll go at dark when the skyships can't see me."

"You try to ride the Gorgon in the dark, you're gonna get eaten by a River Lurker."

"Don't care."

Willem cursed. "At least let me spend the time between now and nightfall trying to talk some sense into you."

———

Willem tried. Didn't do any good. As soon as the last wisps of sunset were gone, Bershad hauled the raft out of the canopy and headed to the water. Felgor picked up an oar and followed him.

"Felgor, you're not—"

"Close your mouth, Silas. You want a chance at making it down this river at night, you need another oar. So it's you and me on this. One last time."

Bershad looked into Felgor's eyes. Saw that he wasn't going to change his mind, either.

"All right, Felgor. One last time."

They were just about to shove off when the rattle and clank of Simeon's armor came down from the canopy.

"You gonna try and come, too?" Bershad asked.

"Fuck no. I'd sink that little thing. They're still building one big enough for me."

"What do you want, then?"

Simeon held out the shield and the spear.

"Thinking you might need these more than me, where you're headed."

Bershad took them. "Appreciated."

Then he shoved the raft into the dark water and started rowing.

74

VERA
Almira, Atlas Coast

Vera watched from the edge of the pine forest as Decimar and Entras made their way to her on horseback. The *Blue Sparrow* was hidden in the trees behind her, invisible from the sky or surrounding valley.

Decimar and Entras dismounted as soon as they were past the tree line.

"Get the mounts water," he said to one of his men. "Damn near killed 'em riding back from Floodhaven."

"You have news?" Vera asked.

Her face was too recognizable in the capital for her to return. But Decimar and Entras were just two Balarian officers in an occupied city.

"Seems we've missed quite the commotion. Vallen Vergun and Wormwrot got themselves ambushed by the Jaguars, but the story going around is that Silas Bershad, the Skojit, *and* Ashlyn Malgrave herself were all there. They tore Wormwrot a new one, but also managed to kidnap a living acolyte."

"That's bad?"

"Seems to be. Osyrus Ward's pulled most skyships back from the outer territories and has them patrolling every inch of the Dainwood's border. Apparently, they're expecting some kind of attack."

"Interesting," said Vera.

"There's something else," Decimar said. "Involves your old friend, Silas Bershad."

"What?"

"After the goatfuck by the warren, Vallen Vergun took the loss a little personally, because he flew into Deepdale with a crew of Worm-wrot men and sacked the city."

"Deepdale? He got past the Blackjacks?"

"Used the same kind of beacon we did, although his wasn't a total piece of shit. But that isn't the craziest part. Bershad actually came back. Alone. And he unsacked the city in a hurry. Rumor is Ver-gun's either dead or turned into a grayskin himself."

Vera chewed on that. Hard to say whether it impacted their plans one way or another. "Between that vicious bastard being dead or turned grayskin, you have to hope he's dead."

"Agreed." Decimar looked back over the valley. "Not sure where this leaves us in terms of getting Kira out of the city. Only reason we got this far without trouble is because Ward has all his eyes on the Dainwood. But if we try to drop you into Floodhaven like last time, we're gonna get spotted on the first pass, and destroyed when we come back through to retrieve you."

"There's only going to be one pass," said Vera. "On the pickup."

"How's that going to work?"

"You're going to drop me off from above. Very high above."

"You're really gonna trust your life on some feathered cloak?"

"I've been testing it while I waited for you." Vera motioned to the tall pines behind her. "It works."

"Swooping off a pine tree and jumping off a skyship that's half a league up in the air are two different things."

"Don't forget the narrow window that I need to slip through on my way down."

Decimar just shook his head. "Crazy fucking Papyrians."

He squinted at the sky.

"Clouds are coming in. If you really wanna do this, tonight is the night."

Vera nodded. "Agreed."

———

The air above Floodhaven was cool. The wind almost nonexistent. That was good, because despite Vera's outward confidence to Deci-mar, she was nowhere near sure this was going to work. The fewer variables the better, since any one of them could kill her.

"Well, we're just about here," Entras called, working the pedals and lulling the *Sparrow* into a fixed position. He kept his hands on the controls, making small adjustments to their levitation mixture levels to keep them still. "Doesn't seem like anyone's spotted us."

Vera examined the old acolyte's mask in her hands. Decimar had found it in one of the lower holds of the ship and cut it to fit her. He'd also reinforced the skullcap with an extra layer of steel, per Vera's instructions. She pulled it over her head and tightened the straps. The mask smelled of leather and chemicals and made it difficult to breathe, but something with the tinted glass actually made it easier to see at night. Any scrap of light was amplified, and any structure or building was alight with a golden glow around the edges.

As much as she hated Osyrus Ward, there was no denying that some of his inventions were useful.

Vera hopped onto the gunwale and looked down, scanning the clouds below. Between the little breaks she could make out the winking, white-blue lanterns that illuminated the four towers of Castle Malgrave. They were almost directly underneath her.

"By Aeternita, even looking at you on that ledge makes my stomach turn," said Decimar.

"C'mon, Decimar. What kind of a skyship captain gets queasy from heights?" Vera asked as she fastened the cloak to specific points on her wrists and ankles.

"Last I checked, I was still a lieutenant. We're afforded sensitive stomachs."

She looked at him. "Consider yourself promoted, then. Captain Decimar."

Decimar sucked on his teeth, then consulted the watch on his bracer. "How long do you need?"

"Come through at four o'clock. We'll still have the advantage of darkness."

"By your orders."

She gave him one last look. "If I'm not there . . . don't let Osyrus Ward have this skyship back. Become a pirate or something. The first skyship pirate of Terra. Suits you."

Before Decimar could respond, Vera jumped off the gunwale.

For the first three seconds, she kept her arms flat against her thighs. Legs together. Body gaining momentum and speed as it plummeted toward the earth.

She pierced the clouds. Castle Malgrave came into view. Vera spread her arms and legs apart.

Since the cloak was latched to her wrists and ankles, that created two big pockets that trapped the wind and slowed her descent so that she was able to tilt her body and start spiraling downward rather than falling, moving the way a hawk rides a thermal into the sky, but reversed.

Vera focused on the King's Tower. Located the tall, narrow window that marked the entrance to Kira's chamber. Focused on it as she spiraled around the tower. Once she was closer, she got a short glimpse of the giant acolyte standing in front of Kira's dome.

Right where I left you.

Vera wrapped around the tower one final time. When the window came back into view, Vera snapped her arms and legs together, which turned her into a human arrow.

She crashed through the window headfirst, using the acolyte mask as a battering ram. There was a shock of impact and a wrench in her neck, then she was through the gap. Vera spread her arms and legs again, slowing her descent enough so she landed on the hulking acolyte's back instead of splattering herself across the ground.

The acolyte grunted. Reached up to pluck her off his back as if she was an annoying mosquito. But Vera tightened every muscle in her body twice, causing the poisoned barbs in every feather of her cloak to straighten and sink deep into his gray flesh.

The acolyte's skin swelled around each barb—boils rising like bubbles from a thick soup. His arms tensed, fingers splayed out wide.

"Intruder," it rasped. "Intrud . . . intr . . . in."

His entire body began to convulse. Fingers doubled back on themselves like peeled plantains. His face started to swell and bloat.

He screamed. His spine arched and his belly and chest burst open. A wet bundle of metal parts dumped onto the floor. Some of the gears and levers were still working—rotating the broken pieces in jerky, incomplete circles.

Vera climbed off his corpse. Pulled off her acolyte mask and took a deep breath in, only to find the air reeked of rot and bile and acid stink. She managed not to vomit, but just barely.

Vera took out her seal. Said a silent prayer that Osyrus hadn't changed the codes. She slipped it into its corresponding slot, which prompted the now familiar series of clicks and snaps and unlocking metal pins. The thick metal door released from its lock and opened. A cloud of humid, jungle-thick air poured from the opening.

Vera went inside.

In the time that she'd been gone, Osyrus Ward had added significantly more machinery to the room. Everything was out in the open, siphoning Kira's blood from her body and running it through a series of vats and spinning centrifuges that led into the ceiling.

Vera removed a glove. Put a hand on Kira's cheek.

Her skin was still clammy and cold. A dirty yellow film crusted the edge of her eyes, since nobody had been around to clean her up. That gave Vera a swelling storm of anger in her chest and stomach. Made her want to run the halls, turning the rest of Osyrus Ward's creatures to rotting heaps.

Instead, she removed the three vials of liquid from behind her breastplate and rolled Kira on her side. There were fresh scars over both of her kidneys. Some kind of surgery had been done.

"Black skies," Vera muttered.

She shook her anger away. Took a breath. Then she injected each vial of tonic into the place Caellan had specified along her spine.

Nothing happened for a minute. Then two. Then three.

"Come on, Ki," she whispered. "You can do this."

Four minutes. Nothing.

"Please, Kira. You have to wake up. Please."

She kept counting the seconds on her wrist bracer. Lost track of them somewhere around six hundred.

Then Kira's turquoise eyes shot open, wide with panic. Her back arched. Toes curled.

"Stay calm!" Vera said, relief washing over her. "I'm going to take you off the machine."

Vera unhooked the hoses from Kira's chest, then she pulled out the metal ports. Watched as the wounds healed seconds later, leaving nothing but a small scar against her skin.

Vera helped her sit up. Kira took a slow, long breath.

"Vera," she said. "You took a bath."

Vera couldn't help but smile. "How do your legs feel?"

Kira wiggled her toes. "Weak. But they work." She shivered. "I'm cold."

Vera had expected that, seeing as the bandages Ward gave her barely covered her nakedness. She pulled a cotton shift from inside her cloak and helped Kira put it on.

"I'm getting us out of here. Decimar is going to pick us up in the *Blue Sparrow,* but nobody can see us leave. Understand?"

Kira nodded. "Yes."

Despite the healing power flowing through Kira's veins, she could barely walk. All of the muscles in her legs had gone soft and weak while she'd been asleep. Vera had to hook a strong arm around her waist and practically carry her out of the dome.

"What happened to him?" Kira asked, looking at the puddle of gore that the acolyte had become.

"Don't worry about it," Vera said.

They descended three levels without being seen. From there, Vera guided them to a little storeroom that was located a level above the bridge leading to the Queen's Tower. The room had no windows, but Vera pulled a shelf aside to reveal a little wooden hatch. She yanked on the rope handle to open the hatch, which looked out on the top of the bridge.

"Why is this here?" Kira asked.

"Servants use it to go out on the bridge and clean off the bird shit."

"Really?"

Vera nodded. "I never liked it. Too much of a security risk. But it's coming in handy now."

Vera scanned the bridge. There was a clear path to the center, where Decimar would pick them up. Satisfied, she leaned back on her haunches and checked the time on her bracer.

"We have a few minutes," said Vera.

Kira nodded. "I'm starting to feel better. Stronger."

"That's good."

Vera hesitated. Went quiet. She had so much that she wanted to say to Kira, but no idea where to begin.

"How did you heal me without Osyrus Ward?" Kira asked.

Vera told her about the last few weeks. The food they'd taken to Burz-al-dun. Pargos. Caellan. The raven cloak she'd used to fly into the tower.

"You've had quite the adventure," Kira said.

"Not what I'd call it, exactly." Vera paused. "I'll be glad when it's over."

"I'm not so sure," said Kira, smiling. "Decimar is right about you."

"Right about me. How?"

"You pretend to have ice water in your veins. Always scowling. Always gauging risks for others. And then you jump from skyships wearing an untested cloak made by a witch."

"Alchemist."

"Whatever. You love the thrill."

Vera shrugged. "All the same. When this is done I am going to soak in a bath for a month. Replace thrills with cold rice wine and warm water."

Kira smiled. "I like the sound of that."

Vera checked her watch. "It's almost time. Let's get out there."

Vera helped her across the bridge, but Kira was telling the truth;

her movements were already feeling much steadier and stronger. They reached the center of the bridge.

"Hold onto me here," she said, moving one of Kira's hands to a thick strap at the base of her left hip. "And here." She moved her other hand to the middle of her back. "Tightly."

"I will."

Vera looked past Kira's swirling hair, into the sky. Squinted. There was movement in the distance, barely perceptible unless you were looking for it. Then a quick, double flash of a blue torch. *The Sparrow.* That signaled them as one league out.

"Twenty seconds," said Vera. Opening and closing her right fist to get it ready. "Don't be scared."

Kira squeezed herself closer. Looked up at her.

"I'm not scared, Vera."

Without thinking, Vera kissed her. Allowed herself to be overwhelmed by the feeling of Kira's lips and the taste of her mouth while the bracer pulsed out ten perfect seconds and her heart went wild in her chest.

They broke apart.

"Vera," she whispered. "That was . . ."

Kira's next words were lost to the wind as Vera caught the rope from the *Sparrow,* and they were both snatched into the sky.

75

JOLAN
Southern Side of the Gorgon Bridge

"It's bigger than I pictured," said Jolan, looking down on the Gorgon Bridge. They'd left the wagon with the comatose acolyte hidden in a grove a few hundred paces back, and crawled up to a ridge on their bellies so they were hidden from view.

Most bridges in the Dainwood were made from wood. The few stone bridges that existed in the jungle were narrow and ancient. Overrun with moss and lichen so they seemed a part of unconquered wilderness, too. The Gorgon Bridge was the opposite of that. A massive intruder on the landscape that was wide enough for eight carriages to ride side by side.

"Elden began construction as soon as he took control of the

Dainwood," said Ashlyn. "He knew he'd never get rich off the lumber if he relied on river barges."

Jolan swallowed. Remembered seeing Elden's corpse hanging over the street of Deepdale with piss dripping off his boot. He pushed the memory away. This was no time to get lost in the past.

He shifted his gaze to the skyship that was hovering over the halfway point of the bridge.

Unlike the heavily armored combat ships that flew over the Dainwood or the agile cutters that patrolled the Gorgon, this was a cargo ship with a bloated hull. It was anchored about two hundred strides off the ground.

"How close do you want to get?" Jolan asked her.

"Directly underneath," said Ashlyn. "Which means we need to get through there."

Ashlyn pointed to the large, covered gatehouse on the near side of the bridge. A wagon was approaching the checkpoint. The guards outside took seals from the driver, checked the descriptions, ran them through the checker machine, then waved them inside for inspection.

"You're sure you can manipulate the machine?" Jolan asked.

"No," said Ashlyn. "But if I can't, we were never going to get the rest of this done."

Jolan nodded. "I'll get the donkeys ready."

––––––––––

They waited until the road was clear before making their approach. The donkeys got skittish as they reached the shadow of the gatehouse, slowing their pace and braying unhappily.

"It's all right," Jolan whispered. "Everything'll be fine."

"You don't seem scared," Ashlyn said.

"This isn't the first time that I've approached a fortified Balarian checkpoint with bad intentions on my mind. I was piss-scared last time, but I didn't have a sorceress with me."

Ashlyn scoffed. Shook her head.

There were nine sentries guarding the exterior of the checkpoint. One man in front of the gate, who was motioning Jolan forward, and four men on either side holding crossbows.

"That'll do," said the man in front when Jolan had rolled the back wheels over a slight bump.

As soon as Jolan got the donkeys stopped, two men in the rear bent down and lifted a metal grate from the ground, blocking their exit.

"What's the matter, your oxen get sick or something?" asked the man in front.

"No," said Ashlyn. "They were killed by one of your skyships."

The man shrugged. "Hand over your seals."

With her right hand only, Ashlyn produced two discs from a pocket inside her poncho and tossed them to the sentry. He gave them a quick read, then looked back at them. "What happened to the descriptions?"

"Siphoning rubber for you clock fuckers is rough work," Ashlyn said in a thick Almiran accent. "Things break."

In truth, Jolan had filed them off during their journey to the bridge.

"Maybe they do. Or maybe you're a bunch of fools who are about to get porcupined when the codes don't match. Don't matter to me none."

The sentry moved over to his machine and deposited the seals.

Ashlyn's poncho covered her left arm, and the hum emanating from her rotating bands was so quiet that it could have been a cat's purr. Both of their seals were accepted with a satisfying click that clearly disappointed the sentry. He handed them back as the checkpoint gate was opening.

"Inside for inspection." He smiled. "Say hello to Acolyte Two-Oh-Two for me."

The mention of an acolyte caused a pit of fear to form in Jolan's stomach. They'd anticipated one being stationed in the gatehouse, but knowing it was there for certain was different.

Jolan roused the donkeys and moved them forward.

The soldiers closed the gate behind them as soon as they were through, trapping them inside the windowless gatehouse, which was illuminated by dragon-oil lanterns that ringed the walls.

Acolyte 202 was a stride taller than Bershad. Veins the color of rubies bulged along his neck and massive arms. Dragon bones shaped like ram horns protruded from the sides of his head. His eyes were cold and dead.

In addition to the acolyte, there were two men on the ground level. Ten more stood in the gallery above, each armed with a repeating crossbow.

"Stay where you are," said one of the men on the ground in a bored tone. He had his crossbow cradled lazy in one arm. "If you move, Two-Oh-Two will cut you in half."

Acolyte 202 corroborated this threat by extending a long, dragon-bone claw from the middle of each meaty fist. A smear of blackened blood glistened along the side of each claw.

The other guard trotted around to the back of their wagon and undid the latch. Dropped the tailgate.

"The fuck is all this?" he muttered in Balarian.

"What're they hauling?" called the man in front.

"Dunno. But it sure as shit ain't rubber. Bunch of machinery." He took a closer look inside. "By Aeternita. There's a fucking acolyte back here."

The sentry's eyes widened. His mouth opened to shout an order.

Whatever he said, it was drowned out by the roar of Ashlyn's bands screaming to life beneath her poncho. Two lodestones darted from her satchel like startled sparrows and blasted through Acolyte 202's eyes and out the back of his skull.

As the acolyte fell to the ground, the two lodestones zipped to either side of the sentry's head. They hung there for a moment—shaking like angry bees—before smashing through either ear and meeting in the middle of his brain with a wet click.

"It's the witch queen!" someone shouted from above.

"Porcupine her!"

More lodestones streamed from Ashlyn's satchel.

Jolan closed his eyes. He didn't want to get blood in them.

He heard the metal zip and pop of lodestones careening through the air, followed by the wet thumps of human flesh being pierced and battered and broken.

When he opened his eyes again, everyone was dead. There was blood dripping from the upper gallery and one of the donkeys had crapped all over the floor.

Ashlyn hopped off the cart and moved to the gate mechanism behind them. She put her hand on the gearbox and jerked her bands in a quick rotation, which shattered the contents of the box.

"Unhitch the donkeys and let them cross the bridge," she said. "Their part is done."

Ashlyn destroyed the second gate's gearbox once they were through it.

"That won't hold them forever," Jolan warned.

"We don't need it to," Ashlyn said.

The far side of the bridge was empty except for a single rubber farmer's wagon in the distance that soon disappeared into the morning fog.

Ashlyn pulled their wagon across the bridge using two lodestones on the tongue as an anchor. Other than two bands rotating near her elbow, pulling the cart didn't seem to require much of her energy.

Jolan eyed the skyship. They were about a hundred paces away.

"Think anyone up there will notice there aren't any animals pulling our wagon?" he asked.

"Not likely," said Ashlyn. "And when we stop, it'll make more sense."

They closed the remaining distance at a slow, methodical pace. As they entered the shadow of the skyship, Jolan felt a shiver run up his spine.

When they were directly beneath the skyship, Ashlyn moved to one of the wagon wheels and activated her finger bands. The iron bolts of the wheel shot off into the water, and the wheel fell off the wagon, causing it to crash in a heap.

"I get it," Jolan said. "They'll think our donkeys ran off."

"That's the hope," said Ashlyn. "Let's get started."

They both got into the wagon. Jolan connected the astrolabe to Ashlyn's arm.

"Just give me a moment to weave down to its brain," she said, her fingerbands already whirring.

While Ashlyn's bands shifted and spun, Jolan peeked out of their wagon and looked down the bridge. He didn't see anyone, but he wasn't sure how long that would last. Then he dug around in his satchel until he found the jar of smelling salts.

Ashlyn's bands stopped. "I'm ready. Wake it up."

He shook the vial of smelling salts, then uncorked it and held it under the acolyte's nose. The muscles beneath its gray skin twitched and roiled and then its eyes snapped open. Ashlyn clamped down on it immediately, freezing its body.

A moment later, its pupils dilated.

"Awaiting command," it said.

Ashlyn took a deep breath. "It was your idea. You want the honors?"

Jolan nodded. Licked his lips. "Remote connection."

"Accepted."

What followed were the longest five seconds of Jolan's life.

"Success," it droned. "Now connected to the *Steady Cog* cutter model skyship."

Relief flooded Jolan's body. He'd been right. Thank the gods, he'd been right.

"Protocol dictates a status transmission," the acolyte said. "Transmit now?"

"No!" Ashlyn and Jolan both said at the same time.

"Accepted. Awaiting command."

Jolan moved closer to Ashlyn. "Are you getting anything useful?" he whispered.

"There's an open loop that leads into the skyship above us. From there, it expands outward in dozens of different directions." She frowned in concentration. "There aren't any coordinates or spirals to slow me down, though. Just smooth pathways."

"That means it won't take nearly as much energy to travel through them, right?"

"Exactly." Ashlyn took a breath. "I'm going to push through them all at the same time. After this, there's no going back. Ready?"

Jolan stuffed a wad of cloth in each ear. "Ready."

Ashlyn's bands started to spin faster. Then faster still. Eventually it sounded like they were sharing the cart with a forest demon who was getting his teeth pulled out.

Just when Jolan thought his eardrums were about to explode, the sound stopped. Ashlyn's bands froze again.

She was smiling.

"What is it? What did you get?"

The astrolabe lit up with pinpricks of golden light—the same matrix that Jolan had seen back in Dampmire.

"Are those what I think they are?" he asked.

"Every skyship in the armada," Ashlyn confirmed. "This is Osyrus Ward's back door."

"Can you control them?"

She frowned. Probed with her bands a little. "All I can do to the ones that are far away is pull them toward our location, but I have a lot more access to the skyship above us. I can feel the doors. Locks. Flight controls. Everything. Ward left it all completely unsecured so he could pilot the ships remotely." She paused. "Hold on, I'm going to try something."

Her armbands started whirring again.

Overhead, Jolan heard the sounds of metallic crunching and snapping and breaking as doors and hatches slammed shut all over the skyship deck. Jolan peeked out of the cart and looked up. Men were banging on exterior doors. Shouting at each other in confusion.

"Good," Ashlyn said. "They can't interfere, but I can still use them to reach the other skyships. We need to start pulling them toward us, but now that I'm connected to all of them, I can't parse out exact locations—there's too much information."

Jolan scanned the skyship locations on the astrolabe. Some were in fixed positions over the different cities of Terra, but a lot of them were patrolling the coastlines and riverways of Almira.

"I'll read the locations out to you. Where do we start?" he asked.

"We need to let Willem know that it worked. Find a skyship that's out west, over the Gorgon."

Jolan nodded. Studied the astrolabe for a moment. "Okay, I have one. It's on grid forty-three. Negative four west. Positive fifteen east."

Ashlyn's bands shifted in a slow, probing rhythm for a few moments, then froze.

"Got it."

Her bands increased speed, sustained and loud.

The glowing pin that represented the skyship started to move east.

"That's it," Jolan whispered, barely believing what he saw. "You've . . . you've got it."

"It feels like dragging a wolf around with a leash made of silk thread," Ashlyn said. "Let me know if I move off course."

Jolan watched the dot. "You're drifting a little too far south."

One of Ashlyn's bands froze while another reversed direction. "Better?"

"Better."

They carried on like that for a few minutes, with Jolan giving occasional course corrections to keep the ship moving down the Gorgon, and Ashlyn adjusting as needed. Jolan became so absorbed in the work that he didn't notice the roar of the skyship's engine until it was pounding in his ears.

Jolan inched toward the back of the wagon and lifted the flap. His jaw dropped.

The cutter was facing away from them. It was lilting far to the aft side and its engines were fully lit, but it was being dragged backward by Ashlyn.

"Almost there," Ashlyn whispered. "Just a little further, and I can overload the engine."

Jolan watched the ship. There were men scrambling into position along the gunwale. They had bows drawn, and were nearly in range.

"Ashlyn, whatever you're going to do, you need to do it—"

The skyship exploded in a flash of white light. Jolan closed his eyes on instinct. When he opened them again, the skyship was gone and the bridge was peppered with shards of metal and bone. There were charred bodies everywhere.

"Gods," Jolan said, transfixed by the destruction. "There must have been a hundred men on that ship. We . . . killed them all."

"Jolan, look at me."

He turned away from the wreckage to see Ashlyn staring back at him, hair damp with sweat. Eyes bloodshot and glassy.

"We don't have time to hesitate," she said. "I need you to give me more targets. A lot more."

Jolan nodded. Looked down at the astrolabe and found another skyship.

Started reading off its location.

76

CASTOR
Castle Malgrave, Western Tower

Castor was awoken from a deep sleep with the news that Kira Malgrave had escaped. He dressed. Armed himself. Splashed some water on his face, and made the long trek to her chamber in the King's Tower.

The giant acolyte that stood permanent guard in front of her dome had been reduced to a pile of putrid mush. There were ten engineers bustling around the area, muttering to themselves in small groups. Ward was bent over some kind of modified astrolabe, which had scores of wires spilling out of it. Knowing Ward, he'd altered the thing to blow a man's head off from ten leagues away.

"I can't fathom what substance could have caused such catastrophic destruction," said Nebbin, who was standing over the pile of mush, frowning. "Or who brewed it."

"Oh, I know exactly who brewed it," said Ward as he dropped a pea-sized lodestone into a hole in the astrolabe. "Her name is Caellan. And I wish I'd killed her years ago."

"Who?"

"It doesn't matter," Ward replied. "The priority is finding Kira and getting her back inside this dome."

"My men searched the castle pretty good," Castor offered. "Didn't find a trace of the empress."

"But where could she have gone?" Nebbin asked.

"That is what we are about to find out," said Osyrus, closing the panel of the astrolabe. "At least, we will as soon as someone gives me two pints of dragon oil!"

A junior engineer came running over with a tube of oil, which Osyrus pressed into a separate port.

"I am not sure that I'm familiar with that mechanism," said Nebbin as he watched Ward configure a few things.

"Why would you be familiar with something that I never fucking told you about?" Ward snapped.

Castor worked to hide a smile. He found the old man's frustration a little amusing.

"As a security precaution, I always install one half of a unique lodestone pair into each of the Seeds we harvest," Ward continued. "Should a specimen ever go missing, all I need to do is run a charge through the other half while it's attached to this tracking device, and it will give me the Seed's location."

Ward wound a lever on the side of the astrolabe a few times, then pushed a button that caused a loud pop. A few dials turned and a set of coordinates rolled across the number slates.

"Hm. She is nearly ten leagues east, over the Soul Sea. The only way that could be true is if she's on a—"

"Master Ward!" cried an engineer, running up the steps and panting hard. "Master Ward, there is an urgent problem with the skyship armada."

"What's the problem?"

The engineer swallowed. "We no longer have control over it."

To Castor's surprise, Ward smiled at that news. "Ashlyn Malgrave is making her move."

"That's a good thing?" Castor asked.

"It means that she's exposed." Ward stood up. Headed for the door. "Follow me, Castor. If Ashlyn is making her move, we must make ours."

77

VERA
Above the Soul Sea

"We have a problem, Vera!" Decimar called from beside Entras.

Once they'd been picked up by the *Sparrow,* Vera had ordered a full burn to the east, with plans to adjust course once they were beyond the sight of land.

"Give me a moment," said Vera, tightening a blanket around Kira's shivering shoulders. "Stay right here. Take deep breaths. Your body will calm down soon."

"I'm all right," said Kira. "Go see what he needs."

Vera nodded, then crossed the deck to the pilot's cockpit.

"What are you doing, Entras?" Decimar asked. "Throttle up."

"We're fully lit."

"Then why are we slowing down? We'll be going backward in a minute."

Entras rechecked his controls and dials. "I have no idea. It's like we're tethered to something that's pulling us—"

He stopped talking midsentence. Pointed east.

The entire horizon was filled with skyships. All of them seemed to be having the exact same problem that they were. As Decimar warned, the *Sparrow* slowed to a stop, then started getting pulled backward.

"Is Osyrus Ward doing this?" Vera asked. "Trying to bring us back to Floodhaven?"

"We're not being pulled back to Floodhaven," said Entras.

"Then where are we going?"

Entras studied his instruments. Glanced at a map of Almira he kept inside the cockpit.

"The Gorgon Bridge, looks like." He scanned the sky, which was now filled with skyships—most of them lilted at odd angles. A few were completely upside down. "And the entire armada appears to be coming with us."

78

BERSHAD
Southern Side of the Gorgon Bridge

Bershad and Felgor watched the skyships exploding as their raft surged closer to the Gorgon Bridge.

"Think that's Ashlyn's work?" Felgor asked.

"Don't see who else it could be," Bershad said, taking a deep dig with his oar.

"You sure she needs our help?" Felgor asked. "Seems to me the situation's pretty well under control."

"I'm not gonna sit on my ass hoping that it's gonna stay that way. C'mon. Row."

Bershad guided them to the Dainwood shore of the Gorgon, hauled the raft into the reeds, then he and Felgor worked their way up to the bridge.

The portcullis leading into the gatehouse was closed. Eight sentries were trying to force it open with a long string of grunts and curses. A ninth man was standing with his back to Bershad, shouting at the workers.

"Haul this gate up!" he shouted. "Men are dying!"

"I told you, Sergeant, it's bloody *jammed*!" one of the men hissed. "That Almiran bitch must have cast a spell on it or something."

"Just fucking haul!"

The Balarians continued their labor. Bershad and Felgor dipped back under cover.

"Nine men's kind of a bigger deal without the moss, huh?" Felgor asked.

Bershad nodded.

"Okay, no problem. Here's what we'll do. I still have my Balarian officer's uniform—I knew that garment would come in handy again. We'll run what I like to call the Pargossian Prisoner Con, with a little bit of a Lysterian Milk Maid thrown in at the end. It's pretty simple, but there are a few specific aspects that need to go *just* right or else—"

"Forget all that," said Bershad, hefting his shield and spear. "There's an easier way."

Bershad walked down the middle of the muddy road that led to the bridge. Stopped when he was two strides from the sergeant.

"Hey, asshole."

The sergeant spun around. He was an ugly bastard with mutton-chops and a frying pan face.

"Who the hell are you?"

Bershad stepped forward and slammed the shield into his face, splintering the sergeant's top row of teeth and sending him stumbling backward on his ass. Bershad let him crab walk toward the gate as his eight men armed up to face him.

"I am the Flawless Fucking Bershad," he growled. "And if you don't get out of my sight in the next ten seconds, I'll kill each of you where you stand."

———

After the Balarians had fled into the woods, Bershad gave the gate a long once-over. He even tried the chain, but the reality was that if eight soldiers couldn't get the thing open, he wasn't going to, either.

"This is totally jammed," he told Felgor. "Ashlyn must have shattered the gear boxes."

"What do we do?"

Bershad peered around at the edges of the gatehouse. "Might be we can climb around it."

"Don't they design these types of structures to make that particularly difficult?"

"Yeah."

"And I doubt this rain'll help."

"It won't."

Felgor sighed. Started digging into his pack. "All right. Guess I can part ways with yet another collector's item."

He produced one of Jolan's bombs, looking at it like a child staring at their last morsel of chocolate.

"Felgor, where did you—"

"The same place I always get shit, Silas. By Aeternita, are we going to do this every time?"

"Do you know how to set it off?"

"Kinda."

"How many do you have?"

"One."

Bershad shook his head. "Best pick a real good spot for it, then."

79

ASHLYN
The Gorgon Bridge

Ashlyn destroyed a massive cargo skyship that she'd pulled in from the southern coast of the Dainwood. Then a cutter from the Gorgon Valley. Her ears were ringing and her lips were chapped. She felt like her bones were on fire.

"There are fourteen more coming in from across the Soul Sea," Jolan said. "They'll be in range in four minutes."

Ashlyn looked to the east. She could see them on the horizon.

Before they were in range, Ashlyn felt a strange signal spear through the system, burrow into the acolyte's brain, and begin to spread. Unlike Ashlyn's signal, which had to be carefully woven and twisted into the acolyte, this one flowed rapid and uninterrupted, like water through a pipe.

The acolyte bolted upright. Jolan was so startled he nearly fell out of the wagon.

"Ashlyn Malgrave," the creature said in an imperious tone. "What exactly do you think you're doing?"

Ashlyn released the skyships she'd been reeling in and tried to tighten her grip on the acolyte's spine and stun it again, but the new signal blocked her.

"You will find it is not so easy to throw me out of the system that I created, Queen of Almira."

"Osyrus Ward."

The acolyte smiled. It looked like someone was pulling on his cheeks with hooks.

"At last, we meet. I am a great admirer of your work with the Ghost Moth tissue. You have no idea how many barriers that has allowed me to break."

Ashlyn swallowed. "Oh, I have some idea, Ward."

He studied the bands on her arms.

"So, this is the apparatus you've used to cause so much trouble. Interesting. But I'm afraid we'll need to put a stop to your antics."

The acolyte's eyes followed the wire in Ashlyn's arm to the astrolabe in Jolan's hands. Then it chopped out in a clumsy but powerful motion, hitting Jolan in the neck and throwing him from the cart.

The astrolabe went with him. Ashlyn's connection to the skyship above was severed.

Before she could do anything, the acolyte grabbed her by the throat. Its long fingers snaked up her neck and around her head.

"I could crush your skull like an eggshell," it hissed. "But that arm of yours may still prove useful."

Ashlyn tried to summon her lodestones, but her bands were still wrapped up in the harvester's system, and Ward refused to let her out. She was stuck.

Overhead, there was a metal groan, then the rattle of cargo hatches opening.

Ward pulled the acolyte's face into that creepy smile again.

"You were smart to lock down the *Steady Cog*," he said. "Her holds were recently stocked with a new type of acolyte that I've been tinkering with. The feral model. They are a somewhat rough precursor to my final project. I'm interested to see what you think of them."

Acolytes started dropping from the sky in groups of three and four. These weren't the hulking war acolytes she was used to. Their bodies were deformed and swollen. Teeth sprouted from shoulders. They each had dozens of eyes placed in random locations along their misshapen skulls.

"Black fucking skies," Ashlyn hissed.

"Yes, they're quite horrifying. But we wouldn't want the Jaguar Army mounting an ill-advised rescue attempt before someone can come collect you, would we?"

The Jaguars weren't coming to help her, which meant she needed to help herself. She focused on the harvester's system. Osyrus was preventing her from extricating herself, but she had a little room to wiggle deeper inside.

She carefully shifted her hand behind her back, then started rotating her bands—slowly guiding her magnetic strand to the manual override pathway.

The lock was wide open now. But Ashlyn would still need to travel through it.

She would only have one chance at this. She blinked tears into her eyes. Forced her lip to quiver.

"Please, Osyrus. I'm begging you to let me go."

"That is not going to happen."

"I'll turn on the Jaguar Army. I'll kill them all for you."

The acolyte craned its head. "Pity. I expected you to have a stronger character."

"Can I just . . . can I just say one more thing in my defense?"

"If you must."

Ashlyn filled her bands with current, rushing down the manual override pathway. She reached the end in less than a heartbeat, and a massive array of commands opened up to her.

But she only needed one of them.

"Execute annihilation protocol."

"Confirmed," the harvester said in its normal, rigid voice.

Then its head imploded.

The acolyte's entire system shut down. Its fingers went slack, releasing her.

Ashlyn jumped out of the wagon and ran to Jolan. He was unconscious, but alive.

All around her, the feral acolytes turned their twisted faces and wild claws toward her. Their warped hackles rose. Their wretched bodies coiled.

Ashlyn summoned the lodestones to her. Then she flooded her bands with power, causing the lodestones to rotate around her and Jolan in a wild blur.

The ferals howled before they charged.

Ashlyn howled back.

80

GARRET
Castle Malgrave, Level 79

Garret had been on a balcony of the Queen's Tower—practicing with his repaired whip by snapping it at empty wine bottles—when a skyship careened overhead, lilting almost completely sideways as it was pulled south by some unknown force. Garret started coiling up the whip. He had a feeling practice was over for the day.

Less than a minute later, a pale-faced and panicked engineer came for him. Said he was needed in the upper workshops.

———

When he arrived, Castor was already there. Osyrus Ward was sitting in a big metal chair. There was a pair of needles in each of his wrists. Those needles had wires running to the spine of a comatose acolyte that was submerged in a tub of translucent goo. The tub was connected to a bunch of pipes running deeper into the castle walls.

Ward's eyes were closed and he was muttering to himself.

"That isn't the most fucked-up thing I've ever seen," said Castor, eyes fixed on Ward. "But it's high on the list."

"You know what's going on?" Garret asked him.

"Not really. Ashlyn Malgrave's up to some shit, and Ward's trying to stop her with, uh, that."

Garret frowned. "How's it work?"

"No idea."

Before Garret could ask more questions, the acolyte's head collapsed on itself, turning to red mush and releasing a foul odor in the room.

Ward's eyes snapped open.

"Clever bitch," he muttered.

He yanked the needles out of his wrists and sprang up from the chair.

"Ashlyn is on the Gorgon Bridge," he said. "She was using the *Steady Cog* as a conduit to control the armada. I've dropped a payload of ferals onto the bridge to keep her busy, but that is a temporary measure. Where is Kira Malgrave, currently?"

Nebbin consulted some kind of orb, which he was clutching like a baby. "Seven leagues east of the Gorgon Bridge. They're dead in the sky. Engine was probably damaged during Ashlyn's attack."

"Good. Mark her location. Since Kira isn't going anywhere, Ashlyn is the priority. Fly to the Gorgon Bridge and subdue her, then collect Kira on your way back. I'll pay each of you one hundred thousand gold once they're both safely returned to the castle."

"Fly to the bridge in what?" Castor asked. "Every skyship in Floodhaven just got dragged over the Gorgon and blown up."

"There is one that remains. The first skyship that I built. Its design is rudimentary, but she has more than enough room for a few passengers." He turned to Garret. "I want Ashlyn Malgrave brought back *alive*. When I am done with her, you may kill her. Not a moment sooner. Understood?"

"Yes."

Castor cleared his throat. "I'll fly your ship over to that bridge, but if you don't trust a horde of acolytes to handle the witch queen, how's the Hangman gonna capture her alive on his own?"

Ward smiled. "He won't be alone."

81

BERSHAD
The Gorgon Bridge

Felgor's bomb blew the first gate off its hinges, but only left a long diagonal tear in the second one. Bershad used the dragontooth dagger to widen the opening a little, then climbed through the narrow gap, cutting his stomach as he pulled himself through.

"Shield and spear," he called to Felgor, who passed the weapons through, then started to follow.

"Hurry the fuck up, Felgor," Bershad hissed when a few moments had passed and all the Balarian had managed to do was squeeze one foot through the crack.

"I'm trying," he grunted. "It's pretty narrow, and I can't heal my stomach with moss if I slice it open. Neither can you anymore, I might point—"

"Forget it. Catch up when you can."

Bershad ran down the bridge. There were broken bits of steaming dragon bone everywhere, along with the splattered corpses of men who'd been thrown from their exploding skyships. In the distance, there was a noise like a hurricane and a flurry of movement in the foggy distance. He ran faster.

When he was close enough to see through the fog, he saw something that he didn't understand.

There was a horde of deformed creatures throwing themselves at a patch of churning red mist in the middle of the bridge. The creatures were torn apart on impact, but they just kept coming.

Through the haze of gore, Bershad saw flickers of Ashlyn's yellow poncho. The mist broke for a moment, and he saw that her arm was extended, her hair was on fire, and she was screaming.

"She can't keep that up much longer," Bershad muttered.

He charged forward and started spearing the creatures in the backs of their skulls. He got through six or seven before any of them turned around and attacked him instead of Ashlyn. He bashed them backward with his shield, throwing them into Ashlyn's curtain of lodestones and reducing them to bloody scraps.

There were still two of the creatures alive when Ashlyn's lodestones started spinning out of control—flying into the air with a wild hiss, or skittering across the cobblestones. Within a few heartbeats the shroud was gone and Ashlyn was on her knees, chest heaving.

Bershad speared one of the creatures through the face and shoved the other one off the bridge and into the muddy water below. Then he ran back to Ashlyn and smothered her burning hair with both hands. Her poncho was soaked with blood and covered with bone chips.

"Ashe," he said. "Ashe, it's me."

She blinked at him. "Silas?"

He nodded. Squeezed her into a tight embrace. "I never should have left you. I'm sorry, Ashe. I'm so sorry."

"Did you save Deepdale?"

"I saved the people. The city belongs to the dragons now."

"Then you did the right thing, because my plan was destined to go to shit no matter what." She turned to Jolan's limp body. "Is he alive?"

Bershad moved to the boy. Checked his neck. "Yes."

Ashlyn nodded. Got to her feet. "We need to get off this bridge. I can walk if you can carry Jol—"

She was interrupted by the roar of a skyship engine passing through the sky above them.

A moment later, Vallen Vergun landed between Bershad and Ashlyn with a bone-crunching snap. He was wearing black leathers. Carrying no weapons.

His knees popped back into place almost instantly. Healing faster than Bershad ever could, even with a belly full of Gods Moss.

He turned to Bershad and smiled. "Hello, Silas."

Bershad cocked his spear and charged.

Vergun sidestepped his spear thrust, then lashed out with one arm. Bershad raised the shield to block the impact, but it was far stronger than he'd expected. The shield kicked back into his temple, flashing his vision white. When it returned, Bershad was twenty strides away and crammed against the side of the bridge.

Ashlyn's bands whirred to life. A lodestone zipped out of the wreckage and careened toward Vergun's bare chest. But his skin shifted to a patch of black scales a moment before impact. The lodestone shattered.

"You'll need to do better than that, Queen."

"As you wish," she said, bands spinning even faster. This time, nine lodestones rose from the wreckage. Two of them tottered and fell back to the ground again, but the other seven flew forward at speed, surrounding him and smashing into different points on his torso. His scales shattered about half of them, but the others blasted through his bare, pale skin, sent him reeling backward.

Ashlyn screamed. The lodestones swarmed back around her, gaining momentum.

Before she could attack Vergun again, a whip snapped around her arm and shocked her.

Her back arched, violent and strained. Her bands froze. Then she crumpled to the ground, lodestones falling around her.

"Ashlyn!" Bershad screamed, body surging with panic.

That gray-eyed Balarian emerged from behind a broken piece of skyship, face blank and calm as he walked toward Ashlyn.

Vallen was back on his feet. The wounds from Ashlyn's lodestones had healed.

"Ward wants her alive," said Vergun. "But he did not express the same desire toward you, Silas. Are you ready to die?"

Bershad gathered the shield and spear. Stood up.

Before he could charge, Felgor appeared out of the smoke and tackled him, taking them both over the edge of the bridge and into the swirling, brown waters of the Gorgon.

82

GARRET
The Gorgon Bridge

For a moment, it looked like Vergun was going to follow Bershad off the bridge and into the river. Garret wouldn't have stopped him. The man had always been insane. Now he appeared to also be invincible.

But Vergun came to his senses after glaring out at the water for a few angry moments. He stormed back to Ashlyn Malgrave.

"She is alive, right?" he growled.

"Yes," said Garret. "As ordered."

Garret had given some thought to increasing the current and killing her. But cleaning up an old mess at the cost of creating another one bothered him. He'd give Ward a chance to keep his promise and let him kill Ashlyn when he was through with her.

If Ward broke that promise, he'd simply kill them both.

Vergun licked his lips. "I'm hungry."

Garret thought that was a pretty odd thing to say, given the current situation, but he didn't respond because it was at that point that he noticed Jolan was also lying unconscious on the bridge. His pulse quickened.

Before he could do anything about Jolan, Castor swung Ward's little skyship around and landed it on the bridge. Nebbin rushed out of it, flanked by three war acolytes.

The engineer checked Ashlyn's pulse. Nodded approval.

"Pick her up," he snapped at one of the acolytes.

Then he looked around. Saw Jolan. Motioned to the other acolyte. "You get the boy."

"Why bother with the kid?" Garret asked.

"He was assisting Ashlyn Malgrave. He might have information."

"No. The boy stays here."

Nebbin smiled. "You don't give the orders, Hangman. I do. Now drop your weapon and surrender."

"What are you talking about?"

"You told us that the *Blue Sparrow* was commandeered by Count Garwin. And yet we have received three separate reports that the *Blue Sparrow* is the very ship—currently dead in the air—that kidnapped Kira Malgrave. You *lied,* Hangman."

Garret's happiness for Vera was stunted by the immediate problems it caused for him. He didn't know how Ward planned to punish him, and he didn't want to find out. He squeezed down on the whip, drawing more blood and fueling the current. But before he could turn Nebbin into a pile of ash, the engineer produced a rectangular piece of machinery from his pocket and pushed a white button made from dragon bone.

The current from Garret's whip reversed flow, shocking his body and sending him to his knees. His jaw clenched. Muscles spasmed and went tight, freezing him in place.

"Should I kill him?" Castor asked.

"No need," Nebbin said lightly. "He's incapacitated."

"The man's dangerous. Leaving him alive is a risk."

"That weapon is bound specifically to his blood, and Master Ward would like to attempt an unbinding experiment on him at his leisure." He waved his hand around at Garret, Ashlyn, and Jolan. "The acolytes can guard these three until another skyship arrives to collect them. We're done here. On to the runaway princess!"

Castor shrugged. "Works."

Nebbin glanced at Garret and smiled. "I will see you later, Hangman."

He pushed the button on his device again.

Everything went black.

83

VERA
Above the Soul Sea

"Decimar, if this this skyship doesn't start moving again soon, we're all going to die."

"I'm aware of the stakes," Decimar said, grunting as he tightened a metal nut. Then he moved to a hulking rubber belt and hauled it back into place. "But we blew half our pistons fighting against whatever force was pulling us back to that bridge."

"How long to fix it?"

"I can give you a detailed estimate or I can just fix it as fast as I can," Decimar said.

"Fine. Do it."

Decimar worked for a few more minutes on various parts of broken machinery. When he had things in some semblance of order, he moved to a big lever. Grabbed hold.

"Please work," he whispered. "Please, please, please."

He pulled the lever. The engine roared to life.

"Thank fucking Aeternita!" Decimar said, stepping back.

Relief flooded Vera's body, but it didn't last long.

"Vera!" Entras shouted from above. "We got a real big problem coming our way. You both need to get up here."

Vera and Decimar climbed onto the deck. Entras pointed west, where a flying object was approaching fast.

"Dunno if it's a skyship or the most fucked-up dragon in existence," Entras said. "But it's coming right at us."

"It's a skyship," Vera said, although not one she'd ever seen before. It was made from the skull of a dragon and cobbled together with iron sheets. It was smaller than anything else in the fleet and there was a trail of black smoke in its wake. "Throttle up the engine and head east."

"I've only got one piston working. That won't be enough to out-run that thing."

"I know. I want arrow volleys on it as soon as it's in range."

Decimar nodded. Turned to his men. "Prep weapons."

While the longbowmen were getting ready, Vera went to see Kira in the royal cabin. She'd been asleep last Vera checked, but was sit-ting up now and seemed more alert.

"How do you feel?" she asked.

"Doesn't matter. What's happening outside?"

Vera swallowed. "There's going to be a fight. You need to stay in here, no matter what. Understand?"

Kira nodded.

Decimar was right, they couldn't outrun the ship. It only took twenty minutes for the bone ship to close the gap between them. Once it was in range, Decimar and his men peppered the ship with arrows, but they bounced harmlessly off the hull.

"I think they're going to ram us," Decimar said.

Vera backed up toward the door of the royal cabin and loaded her sling.

The skyship slammed into the port side of the *Sparrow* and got stuck there. For a few moments, nothing happened.

Behind her, the door opened.

"Vera?"

"It's not safe, Ki. Close the door and—"

A man vaulted out of the dragon skull and landed in the middle of the deck.

Vallen Vergun.

Vera whipped her sling in three tight arcs and released. Hit him in the right temple. But instead of tearing a canyon through his skull, there was a flash of black against Vergun's alabaster skin. Her shot shattered as if it was made of mud, not steel.

Next, the longbowmen turned and loosed their arrows at him, but his skin shifted again and the arrows glanced off him, skimming uselessly into the sky.

Then the killing began.

Vergun darted forward and punched straight through a man's chest. Tore out another's throat. The longbowmen drew their swords and attacked, but their blades bent and broke against his skin. Vergun tore all of them apart in seconds.

Decimar had moved to protect Entras, and had a fresh arrow nocked. Vergun stalked toward them. Decimar waited until he was five strides away, then loosed the arrow. At that range, it punched straight through Vergun's heart.

Vergun looked down at the arrow, smiled, then ripped it out and rammed it through Decimar's eye. He came over to Entras and tore his head off, threw it overboard, then reached into the cockpit and killed their engines.

Vera's body filled with blind rage.

She didn't think of Kira. She didn't think of herself. She just screamed, then charged Vergun, extending the poisoned barbs along her arm as she ran. She had no idea whether Caellan's barbs could pierce Vergun's skin. She had no idea if the poison inside of the barbs would kill him.

And she never found out.

When she was ten paces away from Vergun, a strong hand grabbed her by the back of the skull and threw her overboard.

84

CASTOR
Above the Soul Sea

Castor watched Vera fall. That strange cloak made her tumble and rip through the air in an odd way—kind of like a wounded bird catching random wind currents on a broken wing—but it didn't seem to slow her down much.

He didn't see her land in the violent, choppy water. Too much rain.

Castor took a quiet moment to lament the fact he'd never hear Vera speak in that silky accent of hers again, but the private vigil was cut short when the empress of Balaria came out of nowhere, jumped on his back, bit his ear off, and spat it back in his face.

"I'll kill you, you fat cheeked turtle-fucker!"

She dropped to the deck and started harrying him with a series of surprisingly well-placed attacks, aiming for his throat, eyes, and balls. For royalty, the girl cursed and fought like a demon. Castor was tempted to simply punch the girl in the face, but one hundred thousand gold coins will stir a remarkable amount of patience into your body, even when you're missing an ear.

Castor grabbed the girl's wrists and clamped them down against her body. "Stop. Struggling."

Kira froze, eyes wide, and Castor thought his orders got the wild bitch to behave until he followed her gaze to Commander Vergun, who was eating the entrails of one of the men he'd killed.

"Commander?" Castor asked. "What are you doing?"

Vergun didn't respond. Just shoved another handful of intestines into his mouth, barely chewing before he swallowed.

"Gods . . ." Kira whispered.

The girl started thrashing around again, but while she was doing that, Engineer Nebbin crawled out of the bone ship. His forehead was bleeding from the impact when Castor had rammed the *Blue Sparrow*. He hurried across the deck and injected a needle into Kira's neck. She went limp in Castor's arms.

"That will keep her sedated until we can return her to the machine," said Nebbin.

He looked back at the bone skyship.

"You've destroyed Master Ward's prototype with that ramming maneuver. We'll have to return to Floodhaven on this vessel, and who knows how long—"

The moron went quiet when he saw what Vergun was doing.

"Why is Commander Vergun ingesting that corpse?"

"You're the engineer. You tell me."

Nebbin's mouth opened. Closed. Opened again.

"I believe his loom fabric has become corrupted. We need to get Commander Vergun back to Osyrus Ward for treatment." He moved closer to Castor and lowered his voice. "Bring the Malgrave specimen into this skyship's cabin and keep her away from Vergun. I will get the ship on a course to Floodhaven as quickly as possible."

———

Castor sat with Kira in the cabin, listening to the rain and trying to weigh the balance of all the gold he'd been paid to fight this war against what Vallen Vergun was doing on the deck outside. Truth was, eating raw corpses wasn't any worse than the things he'd done at Deepdale. No reason to go soft now.

Not like he was about to switch sides on this war now, anyway.

Without their witch queen, the Jaguars were fucked.

PART IV

◆

85

BERSHAD
Coast of the Soul Sea

Bershad hadn't given himself stitches in ten years. He was out of practice. But the cut along his stomach was wide and deep, so he did the best he could.

"You sure you don't want me to do that for you?" Felgor asked, wincing.

"I'm almost done," Bershad said.

They'd managed to grab hold of some skyship flotsam and ride it down the Gorgon River until the current let up in the harbor. Then they'd paddled to shore under the cover of darkness.

The towers of Castle Malgrave were just barely visible through the heavy fog. Each tower pulsed with a blue, artificial light.

"You think Vergun took Ashlyn back to the castle?" Felgor asked, poking at a tiny puncture wound on his left palm.

"That's what Vergun said."

"What are we going to do?"

"I have no fucking idea, Felgor. I'm trying to work that out."

Bershad didn't say anything while he finished his stitches. Just tried to think through their options, none of which were good.

"You shouldn't have pushed me off that bridge," Bershad said, wincing as he made another stitch.

"I saved your life."

"I could have figured out a way to deal with Vergun. Could have saved Ashlyn."

"No, Silas, you really couldn't have. He'd have killed you, and Ashlyn would be totally screwed. At least we have a chance to rescue her now."

"What chance?" Bershad snarled. "There's no shitpipe we can crawl through to get to wherever Osyrus Ward took her. And without the moss, any one of Ward's acolytes can tear me apart like a lamb."

Bershad pulled too hard with the needle and tore a stitch out of his skin. He cursed. Threw the needle into the water. Decided to just pack the rest of the wound with a wad of mud. Looked off at the castle, too angry to think.

"We could go meet the Jaguar Army," Felgor said after a while.

"They might not have even crossed. Or they might have died trying."

"But if they made it, they'll have those bombs."

"The bombs aren't much good if the skyships aren't destroyed."

"Well, it's better than knocking on the city gates! Fuck, Silas. I'm trying to be helpful here."

Bershad sighed. Ran his hands through his hair. "I never should have left her. If I'd stayed . . . I might have been able to stop this whole mess."

"But you went to Deepdale and you saved all those people," Felgor said, voice softening. "Look, there's a lot of walking between here and the fifth bend of the Foxpaw river. Plenty of time to figure something out."

Felgor started heading down the beach.

"Come on," he called over his shoulder. "Less moping, more walking."

Bershad stewed for another moment, then he gathered the spear, shield, and dragontooth dagger, and followed.

————

They marched through the night. The cut on Bershad's stomach stung with each step. His feet were torn to tatters. The world felt dead and cold and quiet to him. He missed the Nomad. He couldn't stop thinking about Ashlyn. And he was so wrapped up in his own misery that he didn't notice the woman walking toward them until she was almost on top of them.

"Vera?" Felgor asked. "Is that you?"

She was wearing a strange cloak made from what looked like raven feathers. There was seaweed in her hair and she was cradling one arm with the careful tenderness of someone with a bad injury. She gave them both a long look.

"Do either one of you have some water?"

Felgor reached into his pack. Held out the half-filled waterskin.

"I need some help," she said, motioning to one shoulder with her chin. "This one's dislocated."

Bershad held the waterskin above her head and squeezed the balance into her mouth.

"So what happened to you?" Felgor asked.

"I got thrown off a skyship."

"Why?"

"Long story."

"How'd you survive?"

"An even longer story. And neither one matters right now. I need a way into Floodhaven."

"So do we," said Bershad.

"Guess that makes us allies again."

Bershad nodded. Scanned the coast. "The sun'll be up soon. We need to find some cover and deal with that shoulder of yours."

Vera used her good arm to wave at the forest. "Lead the way."

86

ASHLYN
Castle Malgrave, Level 60

Ashlyn woke up to the sound of something eating. Sloppy, loud, and greedy.

"How long is the hunger slaked after a meal?" someone asked.

Ashlyn's head was pounding. She was on her knees. Both her ankles had iron manacles around them, which were bolted to the floor. The room was cold, but well lit. An acolyte guarded the door.

There were two men on the far side of the room. The first was sitting at a desk with his back to her. He had greasy gray hair. The second was Vallen Vergun. He was crouched beside the desk, tearing meat off a long bone with his bare fingers and then wadding the meat into his mouth. He barely chewed before swallowing.

"Doesn't get slaked at all," Vergun said between mouthfuls. "I'm hungry all the fucking time."

"Interesting," said the other man, scratching a few notes on a piece of paper.

That must be Osyrus Ward.

"Interesting?" Vergun asked. "You turned me into a monster."

"That is a matter of perspective. Think of your predecessors, the feral models. They contained far more undesirable outcomes."

"Fuck your perspective and your outcomes!" Vergun shouted. "What did you do to me?"

"Your condition is an unexpected side effect of the procedure," Osyrus said. "Possibly caused by impurities from the Seed specimens we ran through the loom. It could have also been a splicing error of some kind. . . ."

Osyrus kept on talking. Ashlyn tried to get her bearings.

The room was round. The floor and ceiling were made from hundreds of carefully cut sections of dragon bones. It reminded her of Kasamir's bone wall from Ghost Moth Island, but the arrangement of the slats was more functional than ornate. One entire wall was dominated by machinery—hundreds of different levers, dials, cranks, and gears ran from the floor to the ceiling.

Someone had cleaned the blood from her skin and hair. Her poncho and traveling clothes had been replaced with simple, white linens that covered her except for the left sleeve, which had been neatly cut away.

Her left arm was splayed out from her body, held and in position by scores of translucent wires that ran between her arm and the ceiling. It took Ashlyn a moment to realize they were dragon threads. There was a thread attached to each of her bands—even the thin ones at her fingertips. Mechanical spiders the size of coins were climbing up and down the threads. She could feel them probing her with tiny magnetic pulses. Probably trying to activate her system.

She took a small comfort in the knowledge that when that electrified whip had knocked her unconscious, her kill-switch had been triggered. Those spiders would never get her bands turning again.

Only she or Jolan could do that.

"Stop spouting nonsense!" Vergun snarled at Osyrus, who'd continued an esoteric rant while Ashlyn was looking around. There was blood dripping from Vergun's chin. And Ashlyn could now see that he'd been eating a human arm.

"You asked for an explanation," said Ward.

"And now I'm telling you to fix it."

Osyrus stopped writing. "Once I am able to produce a pure form of thread for the loom, that will not be difficult to do." He glanced at the half-eaten arm. "But I can see the value of an interim solution. As it happens, I have recently finished processing the Malgrave specimen's steroids, and we have a small surplus. I'll arrange to have a series of injections set aside for you. The steroid will temporarily cleanse your impurities and quash your undesirable . . . urges."

"I want a permanent solution," said Vergun. "How do you purify the thread?"

"The material has an extremely high decomposition voltage, which has been an irritating barrier. But our queen will help us hop over it."

Osyrus waved a hand at Ashlyn. Vergun's red eye shifted to her.

"She's awake."

Osyrus twisted in his chair. "Ah. Good. You may leave us, Commander Vergun. I will have Engineer Nebbin bring your injections to you as soon as they are ready. Until then, please stay in your quarters. I'll ensure there is plenty of food there."

Vergun left through a large door on the wall to Ashlyn's right, taking the half-eaten arm with him.

Osyrus picked up his notebook and approached Ashlyn.

"Ashlyn Malgrave, at last we have a proper introduction. Our discussion through Acolyte Three-Nine-Eight was interesting, but far from an ideal platform for conversation."

"This situation isn't exactly ideal for me, either."

Osyrus shrugged. "Perhaps not. But you destroyed a significant amount of my resources with your apparatus. Scores of ships. Thousands of crewmen. I've been forced to empty Floodhaven to fill the gaps, which has been an unpleasant distraction from my real work. You are lucky that I haven't simply killed you."

"You won't do that," Ashlyn said. "You need me to break that irritating voltage barrier."

Ashlyn was familiar with the basics of purifying metal through electrolysis: run a strong enough current through a substance, and the impurities were pulled away from the raw material. Whatever Osyrus planned to purify, it seemed to work under the same principle.

"I need the apparatus attached to your arm," Ward corrected. "The rest of you is useless to me."

Ashlyn didn't say anything.

"I don't suppose you would be willing to save me some time and unlock your security mechanism so that I may continue?"

"That isn't going to happen."

"Suit yourself."

He started scratching more notes.

"Where is my sister?" Ashlyn asked.

Ward ignored the question.

"What about Jolan?"

Again, nothing.

"I am curious how you were able to worm your way so deep into my systems with such limited resources," said Ward.

"You left a lot of your precious notes lying around Ghost Moth Island."

"Who told you about the island?" Ward asked, distracted.

"You know who."

He stopped writing. Looked at her. "Okinu was always a cunt. I could have made her a goddess. But all she wanted was a pile of dragon bones to bolt onto her silly water-bound ships. She had no vision."

"Now you'll make yourself a god instead? Is that what the loom does?"

"The concept of divinity is a weak abstraction for my work. But I *will* create a better world."

"By destroying the people and creatures living in this one."

"And what would you have done instead, oh righteous protector of the great lizards? If you were to follow your plans to their logical end, you would arrive at a world that is devoid of humans and ruled by dragons."

"There is a balance to strike between the two. A harmony."

"Harmony?" He said the word like a curse. "That is a child's dream. This world is perpetually hamstrung by the chaotic, animal struggle for resources. One must make dramatic changes to fix that."

"The same way you've fixed Vallen Vergun?"

"True progress has a cost. Few are willing to pay it."

"You're insane."

He shrugged.

"I must commend the resourcefulness of this apparatus, crude as it is. Your use of salvaged ballast pins was messy, but admittedly inspired. I expanded your work while you were unconscious. The extra stability will be necessary once we begin. The purification process is extremely taxing."

Ashlyn looked at her arm. Ward had drilled a trio of holes in each of her bands and added a platinum stabilizing pin into each one. That would increase her stability by several orders of magnitude. Ashlyn couldn't fathom what he would need that level of power for.

"What are you purifying?" she asked.

"Your method for treating the dragon threads to restore their potency was rather simple to replicate," Ward said instead of answering her question. "However, I found your method of activation undesirable. Relying on a single specimen's blood is not scalable. And anything that is not scalable is not useful. I have implemented a more elegant solution."

Ward opened a metal box that was full of gray rings. He spent nearly a full minute putting them on—three to each finger. When that was done, he pressed each thumb and forefinger together, which caused the rings to click into a magnetic lock.

He snapped them apart in the same motion you'd use to spin a top.

The spiders twitched into action, moving up the dragon threads with a synchronized alacrity. The movement generated a controlled current within each strand.

Ward admired his spiders for a moment.

"They are the perfect servants. Decentralized. Tireless. Expendable."

"If they were perfect, you wouldn't need me."

He turned to her. "I will admit that the decentralization comes at the cost of raw power. The potency you've achieved by fusing the thread to your muscle and bone is as remarkable as it is difficult to replicate. I've destroyed seventeen specimens thus far. I am curious how you survived the process."

"You haven't heard? I fuck forest demons and bathe in infant blood."

Ward frowned. "This conversation has been civil so far, and it can stay that way if you will deactivate the locks on your arm and allow me to continue with my work."

"No."

Ward seemed to have expected that response. "If you will not open the locks willingly, I will break through them."

Ashlyn smiled. "Give it a try."

"As you wish."

Another snap of fingers. The current that was stored in the threads cascaded into her bands. It hurt, but not nearly as much as the things that Ashlyn had done to herself.

"That it?" Ashlyn said.

"Hardly. I just don't want to accidentally kill you with too strong a charge. We'll do this in very short, increasingly painful chapters."

Osyrus snapped at the spiders to reset their positions and refill the threads with current.

The second shock did hurt a little more, but Ashlyn kept smiling anyway.

87

VERA
Atlas Coast

"So, the cloak makes you fly?" Felgor asked Vera, shifting positions in the oak tree, which shook the branches and would give their position away to anyone in the area with decent eyes.

"Stop fidgeting," Bershad said.

"I wasn't fidgeting, I was asking a question. Vera, can you fly?"

"If I could fly, Silas wouldn't have popped my shoulder back into its socket two hours ago."

"But if you couldn't fly a little, you wouldn't have survived jumping off a skyship at all."

"I didn't jump. I was thrown."

"Whatever. Far as I'm concerned, you can fly."

There was a silence.

"Did Osyrus Ward make that for you?" Bershad asked.

"Not for me. Someone else."

"How'd you get it?"

"She gave it to me so that I'd have a way to kill him. Which I very much intend to do when we reach Floodhaven."

"Good," Bershad said.

After dealing with her shoulder, Bershad had told Vera about the Jaguar Army and the bombs they were supposed to have brought across the river. Vera wasn't sure how much good that would do, but she knew she couldn't get back to Kira alone. So, for the time being, she'd go with them.

Felgor shifted in the tree again.

"Stop moving," Bershad hissed.

"I wasn't."

"Then who's shaking the fucking leaves?"

"Squirrels?"

"Will you both stay still until dark?" Vera hissed.

It started raining. Skyships continued to come and go from the city in large numbers. Acolytes and Wormwrot moved through the forest below them in sporadic patrols.

"Awful lot of activity in Floodhaven," Felgor said. "What're all those skyships doing?"

"Ashlyn Malgrave destroyed half the armada," Vera replied. "Those ships were the only thing keeping Osyrus's grip on Terra. Now he's scrambling to fill the gaps. The city'll probably be half empty by tomorrow morning."

"Interesting," Bershad said, but didn't elaborate as to why.

Darkness fell. When an hour had gone by without a patrol passing beneath them, Bershad started climbing down the tree.

"We need to reach the Foxpaw before daybreak," he said. "Stay close to me."

––––––––––

Bershad kept up a grueling pace, tracking along the bank of a shallow river and selecting the different branches they'd follow with the confidence of a veteran fruit merchant selecting good apples from the market.

"Are you sure this is the right way?" Felgor asked when Bershad had them ford a knee-deep stretch that branched off the main current. He then started to scramble up a short, wooded hill. "They said fifth bend in the Foxpaw. That was the third bend, and now we're following something else."

"Shortcut," Bershad grunted.

"But should we really be taking shortcuts we're not positive about? Because you don't have Smokey to help you out this time and—"

"Felgor, if I started telling you the proper way to pick a lock, you'd tell me to go fuck myself, right?"

"Well, you're a lot bigger than me, so I'd be a little more polite about it."

"All the same. Ease up on the questions. I've been through here before with Ashlyn. If we take the long way around, it'll be midday tomorrow before we arrive. This'll get us there before dawn. Just watch out for Lake Screechers. They like the ponds at the top of the hill."

Bershad led them across another few leagues of steep forest until they reached a flat area that was all sharp rocks and scattered ponds. Vera could see the glowing red eyes of dragons lurking in the shadows.

Bershad wove between their little territories, keeping just far enough away to avoid being attacked.

After spending the deep hours of the night cutting through the rough country, they reconnected with the Foxpaw river at a hard bend, just as Bershad had said they would.

"We're here," said Bershad.

"I don't see anyone," said Felgor.

Vera frowned. Scanned the riverbank. At first, she didn't see anything out of the ordinary—just weeds and sagging cottonwoods. But then her eyes caught a lumping arch that was a little too pronounced and uniform to be part of the natural landscape. She looked closer. The arch was caused by a deep tunnel dug into the shoreline that was about as wide as Vera was tall. Too big to be a fox or badger burrow.

"There. What is that?"

"River Lurker den," Bershad said, heading toward it. "And it's also where our friends are hiding."

"If everyone's in there, how come there are no tracks?" Felgor said, looking around the entrance.

"Because the Jaguars aren't morons," Bershad said before ducking into the gloom of the tunnel.

Felgor scratched his head.

"They entered during the rain, when the water was high," Vera said from behind him.

"Oh. Right."

The tunnel smelled like mushrooms and earth. The darkness was impenetrable, but Bershad didn't seem to have a problem navigating, so Vera just kept a hand on his right shoulder to guide her. The tunnel sloped slightly upward for about ten strides—probably to prevent things like afternoon rains from flooding the main chamber—then dipped sharply for about a hundred winding strides. Vera got the sense they'd doubled back toward the river, then away again, but she couldn't be sure in the winding darkness.

Eventually, they turned a corner and the soft, orange glow of a distant torch returned her vision.

There were bootprints in the mud. A lot of them.

They approached another corner. Bershad stopped. Sniffed. Then called out.

"Smells like someone's been letting Simeon get into the cheese again."

There was a silence. Then an almost impossibly loud and long fart from around the corner that would put Entras's gas to shame.

"Fuck yourself, Silas. Life's short and I eat what I want."

"Life's gonna be a whole lot shorter for all of us if you don't stop breaking your evil wind-of-poison!" came another voice with a Lysterian accent.

"Goll?" Felgor asked, voice raising to a half shout. "Goll, is that you?"

"Aye, Balarian. It's me. Come out, will you? We ain't gonna shoot."

They entered a chamber that made no sense to Vera. It had been

carved from the earth by dragon claws, but it was adorned with human trappings. There were lengths of teakwood boards laid out to
form a kind of floor, and half-rotten carpets thrown across them.
There were bookshelves bursting with sheaves of paper and two
rusted alchemy stations must have been at least ten years old.

There was also a pile of new crates in the middle of the room, and
there were hundreds of Jaguar wardens perched in various places,
looking back at her.

A tall warden with a narrow face and bulbous chin stepped forward. Smiled.

"Gods, it's good to see you, Silas." His smile faded when he turned
to Vera. "You fight for the Balarians."

"Now she's fighting with us, Willem."

"If you say so. And what about Ash—"

Willem was interrupted by a bone-clacking rattle as the big Skojit
shoved forward from somewhere deeper in the cave. He was eating
from a rusty tin can with a silver spoon.

"Silas, you survived. Good. You hungry?" He held up the tin.
"We got lots o' this stuff."

"Simeon, those tins are almost twenty years old. Ashlyn and I
brought them down here when we were teenagers."

"Yeah, that's what the others said. Which is why I got 'em all to
myself." He took a bite. "This one is some kind of meat situation with
a decent cheese that—"

"Simeon, will you shut the fuck up? Ashlyn and Jolan aren't here."
The dark-haired warden who'd tried to kill Garret came forward.
Oromir. He stalked over to Bershad. "Are they dead?"

"Ashlyn's alive. I'm not sure about Jolan, but I think they were
both captured."

"What happened?"

Bershad told them about the bridge. Vera could tell from the rough
edges around his words that he was barely holding back his emotions.

Everyone was quiet for a while.

"What are we gonna do?" asked a miserable-looking man with
no ears and a Balarian accent.

"That's easy," said one warden. "We're gonna wait till nightfall
comes around again, then we're gonna swim back across the Gorgon
and get lost in the Gloom."

"That's an option for anyone who wants to take it," said Bershad.
He motioned to the crates. "But I have a mind to take those to the
walls of Floodhaven and break through them."

"Might be we can get through the walls," said Willem. "But there's gonna be an awful lot of grayskins waiting for us on the other side."

"There'll be some," Bershad agreed. "But we saw skyships coming and going all day from the tree we hid in. We're thinking that Ward is rushing to fill in the gaps that Ashlyn created, and he's using the reserves of men and grayskins from Floodhaven to do it. It'll be skeleton crews guarding those streets. That's my bet."

"But once we attack, Ward will call the skyships back," said Willem.

"Yeah."

"And then we're screwed," Willem finished.

"Nonsense," said a red-haired warden with a blue mask on his hip. "That's when Lord Bershad'll call the dragon down to help us, right?"

Bershad gave him a look. "Who told you I could do that?"

"Felgor."

Bershad turned to Felgor, who just shrugged. "Didn't think it was a secret."

Bershad shook his head. "The Nomad's gone. She's not coming back."

"Then there's no chance," said Willem. "It's suicide."

"Maybe," said Bershad. "But if I'm gonna die, it's gonna be trying to reach Ashlyn. Not running away."

There was a silence. Oromir stepped even closer to Bershad.

"I've hated you since the moment I met you," he said. "You're impulsive, violent, reckless, and you've squandered every gift and advantage you've ever been given." He lowered his voice to a whisper. "Just like me."

Bershad didn't say anything.

"But Jolan is better than both of us. He always has been." Oromir swallowed. "If there's a chance that he's alive, and a chance you can help me get to him, I'll follow you. Doesn't matter if we die, so long as there's a chance."

"There is," Bershad said. "I promise."

Simeon belched loudly.

"There'll be Ghalamarians in the city," he growled. "So I'm in."

Willem sucked on his teeth. "Me too, I guess. Gods know that Jolan's dealt with my cock rot enough times to warrant a rescue attempt."

Goll stood. Hefted his axe. "I've failed to repay my blood debt to you, Flawless. So I have no choice but to die by your side."

Felgor cleared his throat. "This display of bravery and devotion is really touching and all, but there's a way to do this that isn't completely guaranteed to end with all of us swallowing shells."

"If there's another option besides attacking the most fortified city in Terra with a thousand men and some apple-sized bombs, I'm all ears," said Willem.

"Well, actually you lot are still going to have to do that. But me and Vera can sneak into the castle while you have everyone's attention. We'll free Ashlyn, and she'll save our asses. You all should have seen the damage she did on that bridge. It was incredible."

"How are you going to get into the castle?" Willem asked.

"Please. I've snuck in and out of Floodhaven four times this year." He patted Vera on the shoulder. "Plus, I'll have this little murderous assassin with me, who will be my prisoner." He pointed to Oromir. "You'll be my muscle."

"That's idiotic," said Oromir.

"You'd be surprised how many stupid decisions get made when there are large explosions outside the window. Trust me, I can get you into the castle. From there?" He shrugged. "Guess we'll just see."

Bershad looked at Vera. "What do you think?"

The truth was, she thought the entire thing was suicide on all fronts, but the alternative was leaving Kira to die.

"I'll do it."

Bershad turned to the wardens.

"Any man who doesn't want a part of this should leave now. I won't stop you. And you'll leave with your honor intact. Get back to the Dainwood. Protect the people for as long as you can. That's all I ask of you."

A few men blinked. Spat. Adjusted their armor and their weapons. But nobody moved to leave.

Willem cleared his throat. "We're all with you. *Lord* Bershad."

Bershad nodded. "Rest up today. We'll move out after nightfall. Attack at midnight."

88

JOLAN
Castle Malgrave, Level 37

Jolan woke up to the sound of coffee being poured. He was laid out on a simple cot in a room illuminated by the pale light of ignited dragon threads that were bunched inside glass vases.

His neck was so stiff it felt like his vertebrae had been fused together. He went to rub his muscles and found a perfectly wrapped, cold seaweed poultice swathed around his trapezius muscles.

"I apologize for the injuries you sustained," came a man's voice. "That poultice will minimize the pain and swelling."

Jolan sat up. His head hurt almost as much as his neck.

An old man was sitting behind a desk, staring at him with sharp eyes. There was a steaming mug of coffee next to him.

"Would you care for a cup? Freshly brewed."

"You're Osyrus Ward."

"Yes."

Jolan desperately wanted to ask about Ashlyn, but forced himself not to. The less Osyrus knew about Jolan and his relationship to Ashlyn, the better.

"And you are Jolan Fent, of Otter Rock," Osyrus continued when Jolan stayed silent.

Jolan's stomach twisted. He hadn't heard anyone speak his last name in a very long time.

"How did you know that?"

"The same way that I knew you appreciated a fresh pot of coffee in the morning."

Osyrus tapped a stack of loose-leaf papers that was tied together with a strip of red leather.

Jolan frowned. There were only a handful of people who knew Jolan's last name, and only one of them knew how to read and write. "Morgan Mollevan."

"A quick and accurate deduction. You probably weren't aware, but every master alchemist is required to submit annual progress reports of their apprentices to the main archives in Pargos. Those glorified librarians never did anything with the information, but the alchemists do love collecting facts for no reason."

"I don't believe you," said Jolan.

"No?" Osyrus pulled a page from the pile and read aloud. "'Jolan displays great creativity with his poultice concoctions, as well as natural instincts as a forager. But his lack of detail orientation holds him back from greatness. And his forgetfulness when it comes to daily chores is extremely annoying. The morning coffee, in particular.'"

Jolan swallowed. That was Morgan. Hearing his words made Jolan's heart long for the quiet life he'd once led. And longing for it made him feel ashamed.

"Is that supposed to mean something to me?" he asked. "Morgan Mollevan is dead. I never became an alchemist."

"No," Osyrus agreed. "You became something far greater. I know that you have been aiding Ashlyn Malgrave. Half the mechanisms installed in her body were crafted by your hand. Sprung from your mind."

"I'm just her assistant."

"False modesty? No. Caution, I think." Osyrus scratched at his greasy beard. "Would you like to know how your mother died?"

Jolan knew that Osyrus was probing for a weak point in his mind. Something that he could manipulate. He wasn't going to let that happen. "My mother is a stranger. I barely remember her."

"I see." Osyrus smiled. Stood. Walked to the door of the chamber. "Please. Follow me. I would like to show you one of my workshops. I think you'll find my current experiment relates to something that you do remember."

Ward took him to a large room that was filled with rows and rows of glass tanks.

"If you'll lead the way, we're looking for specimen tank #9907."

Jolan headed down the first aisle. He wasn't sure what else to do.

Ashlyn had told Jolan of the things that they'd found on Ghost Moth Island. Gruesome experiments and torture performed in the darkness. But that wasn't what Jolan saw in the tanks that he passed.

Each tank was filled with a different, and carefully manicured ecosystem. Some had flora from the jungles of the Dainwood. Others the deserts of east Pargos. Others still were somehow kept cold enough to contain Lysterian snows.

Then there were the creatures.

The first ten tanks contained buzzing, mechanical re-creations of normal insects and animals. Beetles. Hummingbirds. Scorpions. But then he began to pass animals that seemed perfectly normal except for their size. Pargossian elephants the size of rabbits. Thundertail dragons no larger than sparrows, roosting on twigs.

"Size and scale are interesting variables to manipulate," Ward said as they moved down the aisle. "But these changes were mere precursors to my actual aims. Here we are. Just on the left."

The things they'd passed were so strange that Jolan was taken aback to find that tank #9907—marked with an embossed, steel placard across the top—contained something very familiar.

Four toxic, red-shelled snails, and one squirrel, which was chewing on an acorn that was laced in the snails' poisonous mucus. Given the squirrel's size, a few nibbles of the tainted acorn should have killed it. But the rodent looked perfectly healthy.

"I had the specimens plucked from the stream half a league south of a burnt-out apothecary in Otter Rock," Osyrus said from behind him. "I wanted to ensure my experiments matched your own previous efforts."

Jolan wasn't sure what to feel. He could cast off memories of a mother he barely knew, but he'd dedicated most of his life to finding an antivenom for the red-shelled snails with Morgan Mollevan, and they had failed.

"What did you use to purify the antibodies?" he asked. That was the problem they could never solve.

"Oh, I can certainly show you the method at a later time. I am not stingy with my knowledge, like the alchemists. But right now, I believe the details of my success will be less compelling than the time it took for me to implement them."

Jolan turned away from the tank. "Are you going to make me guess?"

"No. The samples arrived by skyship four hours ago. I created the antibodies while I was waiting for you to wake up."

Despite Jolan's best efforts, that bothered him. He and Morgan Mollevan had toiled for years. *Years.* And when Morgan died, they'd been nowhere close to a solution.

"I must acknowledge, of course, that I was able to adapt an existing purification process for this purpose. But the point I am trying to illustrate is that my work has reached a stage where applications such as this are, to be blunt, very easy."

"Why are you telling me this?"

"Because I was once like you, Jolan. Brilliant. Creative. And afraid of my own strength. Afraid to take the next steps."

"I'm nothing like you," said Jolan. "And I'm not afraid."

"Yes, you are. I can see the hesitation and fear in your eyes. You see the faces of the men you've killed for the sake of progress. The weapons you've built to oppose me are haunting you. Do you know why you feel that way, and Ashlyn Malgrave does not?"

Jolan didn't respond. He felt sick to his stomach.

"Because she's *royalty.* Everything she has was given to her because of the blood running through her veins. You and I had to fight for it. Struggle. We had to earn it."

"She's earned it, too."

"Not in the same way."

"I've seen your other work, Osyrus. I've seen the burnt-out villages and charred corpses that *your* skyships leave in their wake. I've seen the gray-skinned abominations you've unleashed on Terra."

"That is a small fraction of my work. In Balaria, there is clean, potable water flowing into every home because of me. With a few more advances, I will pull tumors from children's brains without harming them. I can create a new genus of Ghalamarian wheat that doesn't go to rot in its field when Green Horns are eradicated from the area. I can end famines. End the *suffering*. Nothing is out of reach anymore, Jolan."

"A few more advances," Jolan repeated.

"Yes. All that I need is access to a stronger power source."

Jolan understood immediately. Ashlyn must have triggered her kill switch when she was captured. He gave Osyrus a nasty smile. "Having trouble breaking through the lock on Ashlyn's bands? Must be annoying."

"Pettiness does not suit you," Osyrus said.

"Maybe not, but Ashlyn and I spent three months struggling to break through your system. It's only fitting that you struggle a bit with ours, too."

"Ours?" Ward repeated. "So, you *did* help her build it?"

Jolan went quiet. He needed to be more careful with his words.

"This is about progress, Jolan. You can help me change the world."

Jolan turned to the rows of lush, incredible experiments in front of him. He knew that despite the wonders in front of him, there were rooms full of horrors above and below. He looked back to Osyrus.

"I don't know the sequences. Even if I did, there is no way that I will betray Ashlyn Malgrave in exchange for a coffee and the vaporous promise of some imaginary future where suffering doesn't exist."

Osyrus gave a sympathetic nod. "I've also been seduced by the trappings of royalty. I was not much older than you when Ashlyn's own aunt, Empress Okinu, took me into her service. At first, she was kind. Supportive. Made me think that she deserved my undying loyalty. But I was always just a servant in their eyes. When I pushed against her royal goals, she betrayed me. Ashlyn will do the same thing to you."

Jolan shook his head. "Ashlyn treats me as an equal. She always has. Maybe the reason Okinu betrayed you is because you're completely insane. I will *never* help you."

"Certainty is such a brittle thing," Osyrus said. "Just like Ashlyn, you would have been a more productive asset if we had formed a mutualistic relationship, but alternative methods of obtaining your cooperation are available."

"You can tear every limb from my body, I still wouldn't help you."

"Speaking from a rather large data set, you most definitely would. Everyone breaks eventually. But I've always had a soft spot for wayward alchemists. And because of that, I would prefer to avoid causing you physical harm until necessary."

"What does that mean?"

"You have the run of my workshops on this level for the time being. Explore them. Enjoy them. And give my offer deeper consideration." Osyrus smiled. "Just know that while you wait here in comfort, I am causing Ashlyn Malgrave a considerable and growing amount of pain with each passing moment."

89

BERSHAD
Outside Floodhaven

There were dead wardens hanging in the trees outside of Floodhaven. They'd rotted down to nothing but bones and rusted bundles of armor. Bershad, Vera, Cabbage, and Simeon sat beneath them, looking out at the walls of Floodhaven, which were bathed in artificial light.

"Who're these poor bastards?" Simeon asked, motioning to the nearest skeleton.

"Malgrave wardens," said Bershad. "They were strung up by a lord named Cedar Wallace during a siege."

"What happened to Wallace?"

"Ashlyn killed him."

Simeon laughed. "Of course she did."

"They remind me of the Line of Lornar," said Vera.

"You've seen the Line?" Simeon asked.

Vera nodded. "Crossed it, too."

"How'd your time in Skojit country pan out?"

"I've got one less finger than when I went in."

"Yeah. That'll happen." Simeon adjusted a dangling scale on his armor, which fell out of place again a moment later. "If we survive this deal, I'll take you all back to the Razors myself and show you around. You'd like it up there, Cabbage."

"I would?" Cabbage asked.

"Definitely. There are these villages in the high hills where the air is so clear you can see straight to Pargos. It's beautiful."

They were all quiet for a moment.

"Vallen Vergun is going to be waiting for the two of you on the other side of those walls," said Vera. "If you want to survive this mess, the first thing you'll need to do is kill him. And I am not sure that's possible anymore. Osyrus Ward did something to him. He has this . . . shifting skin. Almost like dragon scales."

"Yeah," said Bershad. "I'm familiar."

"What's your plan?" Vera asked.

"I'll figure something out."

"So, no plan?"

He shrugged. "The thing you learn real quick when you're killing dragons is that plans tend to go to shit in a hurry. Sometimes it's better not to have one at all. That way you're not disappointed when it gets ruined."

"You're crazy, you know that, Silas?"

"You're the one who jumps off skyships, Vera."

She smiled and shook her head. Oromir and Felgor came up to their position and dropped into the trench. Felgor was dressed in his officer's uniform and Oromir had a stolen set of Wormwrot armor on, plus the red face paint. Felgor threw a pair of irons to Vera.

"To apply at your leisure," he said, then produced a comb from a pocket and started running it through his hair.

"Is orderly hair a big priority right now?" Vera asked.

"It's the little things that matter for these kinds of deceptions. Speaking of which, Vera, I'm going to need you to punch me in the face."

She screwed up her face. "Why?"

"You'll see, but it's important." He leaned forward, pointing to his right cheek. "Right here, if you please. Hard enough so it swells, but not so hard it swells shut."

Vera shrugged. Then punched Felgor the face.

He took the blow with a surprising amount of composure. Pressed against it with two fingers, winced, then nodded approval.

"Perfect. The little things, Vera! That's what'll get us inside the castle."

"Thought you said it's a matter of people making bad decisions when bombs start exploding around them," said Cabbage.

Felgor paused. Thought about that. "The big things matter, too."

He started combing his hair again, which had been mussed up when Vera punched him.

"Speaking of bombs, when's the show starting?"

Everyone turned to Bershad. He figured it was just about midnight.

"Right now."

Simeon smiled. "Finally."

He turned to the bomb that Cabbage had spent the day building specifically for him. It was the size of a beer cask, and sprouting with dozens of tubes and wires. "Get me going, Cabbage."

Cabbage started adjusting a bunch of different cranks on the bomb. Bershad signaled Willem, who was in the trench next to them. He then passed the order down to his men. The wardens started prepping weapons and bombs and shields.

When Cabbage finished, he stepped back. "It's ready. Any pressure greater than twenty pounds, and it'll explode."

"Well, that's terrifying," said Felgor. "Please get it out of this trench."

"Yeah, yeah." Simeon put on his helmet, then squatted, shoved the bomb onto one shoulder, and stood. The effort caused his armor to shudder and whine. "See you ugly bastards on the other side of the wall."

Simeon climbed out of the trench and started across the field at a trot.

Bershad turned to Vera. "Let us push into the city a bit before you follow. When you get to Ashlyn, tell her . . ." He trailed off, struggling with the right words. "Tell her that I'm not going down the river without her. So she best come find me, so we can do it together."

She nodded. "I will."

Felgor smiled. "You know what I'm gonna say. At this point, seems redundant to waste the breath."

"Agreed." Bershad pulled him into an embrace. "Good luck, you fucking thief."

Bershad hopped out of the trench and ran toward the walls of Floodhaven.

The wardens of the Dainwood followed him.

90

CASTOR
City of Floodhaven

When Osyrus Ward called Castor into one of his castle workshops, he'd assumed some new atrocity had revealed itself. He couldn't remember the last time he'd gotten good news, why expect some now?

But he'd been wrong. Turned out the Madman had kept his word. There were two hundred freshly crafted tower shields made from dragon bone waiting in one of the lower workshops. Since they were operating on a skeleton crew, that was enough for every man on duty to have one.

Castor personally managed the distribution. Since Vergun was busy eating corpses in his private chambers, Castor didn't trust anyone else with the task. When that was done, he headed to Foggy Side, where he planned to find a tavern that was still open and get hammered drunk while lamenting the loss of his ear.

Those plans were put on hold when a spiral of blue flames hurtled into the air above the main gate. A massive explosion followed. Every nearby shop window shattered. Soldiers ducked for cover in the confusion.

Alarm bells started ringing. They didn't stop.

"Did a skyship crash?" some private asked, brushing broken glass from his hair.

"We're under attack, you fool," Castor hissed.

"Attack? From who?"

Castor grabbed him by the top lip of his breastplate. "You better at running than you are at thinking?"

The idiot nodded.

"Good. Run back to the castle and grab the first engineer you can find. Tell them to call the armada back to Floodhaven. And tell them I need the commander released from his quarters and sent to station one as fast as possible."

The idiot nodded again. "You can count on me, sir."

"Good." Castor drew his sword. "The rest of you, come with me."

Station one was a crow's nest built atop the roof of a warehouse that had a clear view of the main gate. By the time Castor got there, it was pure mayhem.

The gate itself was just a smear of smoking rubble. Masked Jaguars were pouring through the opening with impunity.

"Where are the acolytes?" Castor asked.

His question was answered when two war acolytes came around a corner—sprinting headlong at the Jaguars, spikes extending from their arms as they ran.

With a level of composure that made no sense given the situation, a warden stepped forward to meet them. He threw what appeared to be a brick at the charging acolytes. It bounced once near their feet, then exploded. Turned their legs to ruin.

That didn't kill them, but five Jaguars pounced on the wounded acolytes a moment later. Hacking their skulls apart.

"Shit."

More Jaguars were pouring through the hole in the wall with each passing second. There were hundreds of them, and if even half of them carried one of those bombs, this was quickly becoming a fight they couldn't win. Not with a few scores of Wormwrot spread across the city and caught by surprise.

The tiny skyship they'd used to intercept Ashlyn at the Gorgon Bridge boomed overhead—making a quick loop out to the main gate, then turning back to the castle.

"Ship ain't gonna help?" asked one of Castor's men.

"They're dropping help off."

The sound of Vallen Vergun landing on the warehouse roof behind them sounded like a hundred bones being broken simultaneously, then popped back together again a second later.

"Commander," said Castor. "We have a problem."

Vergun scanned the battle below. More acolytes had come charging down one of the avenues and been turned to chowder for their trouble.

"Might be you should go down there?" Castor offered.

Vergun studied the battle a moment longer.

"No."

Castor frowned. "Why not?"

Vergun motioned to the gaping hole in the city wall.

"Because right now the Jaguars still have the ability to retreat."

Vergun produced one of Ward's needles from an inner pocket of his leathers and injected it into his neck. A wave of black scales shuddered across his skin, then disappeared.

"Take that away from them. Then I will kill them all."

91

BRUTUS
The Northern Atlas Coast

After Brutus had been cheated out of a cushier posting by that asshole officer with the tiny teeth, he'd resigned himself to dying in a skyship crash out over the jungle. But it turned out Aeternita's luck was on his side after all.

A week after the swindling, his commanding officer had been snatched off a skyship deck by some horrific yellow dragon covered in poisonous spines. That had been unfortunate for his commander, of course, but since Brutus had seen the incident up close—far closer than he would have preferred—he was tasked with writing and submitting the incident report. When he submitted the report, he also bribed the clerk a hundred silvers to look the other way when he filed a transfer for himself in his commander's name.

With the war on, nobody had noticed the request came from a dead man.

Brutus had spent the last month patrolling the peaceful cities of northern Almira on a coastal cutter, enjoying the summer sun and getting fat off their ample rations. These cities had already endured pacification drops early in the war, so they weren't itching to cause problems. Other than a sudden but temporary failure of their navigation systems a few days back, it had been uneventful in the best possible way.

There were only two substantial drawbacks to the posting. The first was their acolyte, Number 799, who loomed relentlessly on the deck, never speaking and barely moving. Damn thing was the only factor preventing their whole crew from escaping this war entirely.

The second was the terrifying noises that occasionally drifted up from the cargo holds, where they kept three-score of the Madman's feral acolytes, ready to be released onto the coastal cities in the event of a rebellion. Those sounds gave him nightmares.

But Brutus's long string of easy duty ended when an emergency
signal called them back to Floodhaven.

Apparently, the city was under attack.

"What are the idiots thinking?" asked his captain, a man named
Copana. Most captains assigned to soft duty had earned it from successful combat drops, but Copana had earned his posting through
good old-fashioned nepotism. He was son to some famous engineer
on Ward's team. Lucky bastard had never laid eyes on the Dainwood.

"Sorry, sir?" Brutus asked.

"They show nearly impeccable combat discipline for months—
never giving us more than a glimpse at their backsides from the sky—
and then they decide to storm the capital. What did they think was
going to happen?"

"No idea, sir." Brutus scanned the horizons. "I'm just glad there
aren't any dragons to deal with."

"I don't know, it would be exciting to see a few of the really big
ones, at least," said Copana. "All my life, I've heard stories about how
Almira was teeming with the creatures, then I get stuck on the Atlas
Coast, where the Madman's harvesting skyships have already killed
them all. I've been lucky to spot a few of those seafaring breeds from
a great distance."

"Trust me, sir, a great distance away is where you want the great
lizards to be."

"I suppose. Still, I'd have liked to see just one up close. Something
to remember when I retire to Burz-al-dun." He gave a wistful sigh.
"Anyway, set a course for Floodhaven. Full burn. Wouldn't want to
arrive late and miss the massacre."

92

CABBAGE
Gates of Floodhaven

Cabbage had tripped on his way through the breach of Floodhaven's
wall and dropped his sword. Felt like he'd damn near broken his toe,
too, and he'd gotten a face full of dust and debris for good measure.

By the time he'd gotten up, wiped the crap out of his eyes, found
his sword, and gotten his bearings, the Jaguars had taken control
of the area. There were three exploded grayskins that he could see.

The few Wormwrot who were still alive had dropped their weapons and were running away, deeper into the city.

Despite the strong start, nobody was whooping victory cries yet. Willem stalked up and down the line, barking orders to his wardens and moving them into defensive positions around the different streets. Bershad and Simeon were nearby, both already covered in blood.

"Raise your sword if you've still got a bomb!" Willem called.

About half the men raised their blades, Cabbage included. That wasn't bad, but it could have been a lot better, seeing as they'd only made it a hundred strides into the city.

Cabbage reached behind his breastplate and pulled his bomb out, giving the blasting caps a quick once-over to make sure they hadn't been damaged when he tripped. To his relief, everything looked okay.

Cabbage hadn't told Jolan—or anyone else, for that matter—but he'd doubled the reinforcements on his bomb to lower the chances of an accidental trigger, which was quite a bit higher than he or Jolan cared to admit.

After doing that, Cabbage had felt selfish and craven, so he'd gone back and tripled the explosive material, too. Figured that evened things out.

"Why isn't your sword wet, Cabbage?" growled Simeon, coming over.

"I fell down coming through the breach."

"Course you fucking did." He grabbed him by the back of his breastplate. "Stick with me. I'll make sure you get a chance to dampen the thing."

Simeon practically carried him over to Bershad and Willem. "What's next?" he asked, pulling off his helmet with a click and hiss.

"They cleared out in an awful hurry," said Willem. "Might be we were right, they don't have the numbers so they're pulling back." He shrugged. "Might also be a trap."

"Might be both," said Bershad, scanning the rooftops and roadways with suspicion.

"We could scout up ahead," Willem offered. "Get a feel for things."

Bershad shook his head. "The more slow and subtle we are, the harder it'll be for Vera and the others to get into the castle. We need their attention. *All* their attention."

"Guess we're storming forward then?" Willem asked.

"Yeah."

"Excellent," said Simeon, as if he'd just learned a tavern kitchen was serving his favorite meal for dinner. "I'll lead things."

Bershad stopped him with the spear. "Not this time, Simeon."

"Huh?"

"Need you to do something else."

"What else is there?"

"This whole fucking war, you've been bitching that you're always the bait. It's time to switch things up."

"But I—"

Bershad yanked Simeon close, then muttered a few quick words that Cabbage couldn't hear. Whatever he said, it was enough to make Simeon's face go serious. He nodded. Pulled his helmet back on, then trotted down one of the side streets alone.

"The rest of you are on me," said Bershad, heading down the main road.

Cabbage couldn't see the wisdom in separating Simeon from the rest of the army, but he also didn't have a choice but to follow Bershad. So that's what he did.

They moved down the main street with a purpose. Cabbage did his best to check the shadowy nooks and alcoves for hiding enemies, but the city was mostly deserted. The few people that he did see in the windows were clearly civilians, huddled under tables and behind chairs, hiding from the chaos.

Cabbage thought back to his last visit, when the streets had been crowded with soldiers and skyship crewmen and acolytes. Bershad had been right—Osyrus Ward must have emptied the city to make up for the mess Ashlyn made at the Gorgon.

Eventually, they reached a big square, where seven roads intersected. There was no sign of Wormwrot defending the place, so the Jaguars funneled into the square quickly. Cabbage looked around. Remembered the acolyte who had loomed eternal in the center of the square. His stomach churned with panic when he saw a figure standing in the same place.

But this wasn't an acolyte. It was a regular-sized man with long, snow-white hair. He was wearing black leathers and smiling, which didn't make sense to Cabbage seeing as he was facing down an army alone.

Vallen Vergun. Had to be.

"Hello, my muddy-haired friends," he said, scanning their ranks. "I would like a word with Silas—"

Bershad came hurtling out of their line at speed, his spear tucked and shield raised. The sight of the charging dragonslayer seemed to give Vergun an immense amount of pleasure. Probably because while

Bershad was sprinting across the open square, Vergun's right arm was transforming into the familiar and horrible shape of a black dragon claw.

Vergun gave Bershad a lazy backhand with the claw, which caught him on the shield and sent him flying. He sailed over Cabbage's head and landed somewhere behind him with a crunch and clatter.

"Idiot never learns, does he?" Vergun muttered.

"Bolts!" Willem shouted, raising his own crossbow as he gave the order.

Twenty or so bolts slammed into Vergun's leathers. And all twenty of them shattered on impact, as if they were built from glass instead of iron and oak.

Normally, seeing a man survive a volley of bolts would have sent Cabbage fleeing in the opposite direction, but in this moment—with an explosive behind his breastplate—Cabbage managed to dig deep and find a little scrap of courage.

He stepped forward. Pulled his bomb free and wound the timer to five seconds.

"Any man who's still got a bomb needs to throw it!" he shouted, then took a step and heaved.

His bomb clattered to the ground at Vergun's feet. More followed. Vergun didn't move, and he didn't stop smiling. Just stood there amongst a chorus of ticking clocks.

The first detonation set off the rest. Dirt and broken cobblestones blasted into the air in a massive geyser of debris that lingered in the air like fog.

When it settled, Vallen Vergun was still standing in the wreckage of the fountain. His skin had been replaced by black scales that armored his body like dragon's hide. The scales along his ribs and right arm were broken and bleeding, but otherwise the explosives that had turned a city wall to rubble hadn't had much of an impact on him. The scales shifted away from Vergun's face like mud being washed away by a blast of water.

Beneath the scales, Vergun's pale skin was unharmed.

Cabbage decided this was a good time to run away. He turned around, but before he could take his first cowardly step, a group of Wormwrot sprang from hiding places at the edges of the square and locked their bone-white tower shields into a wall that blocked the path of escape.

All around the square, the same thing happened to the other roads leading out of the square.

They were trapped.

"Nowhere to run, little rats!" Vergun called. "Nothing to do but die."

Vergun charged. Blurred past Cabbage with a howl and a thrash that put him on his ass. The warden who'd been standing next to him went down, too. His throat was torn open. Somehow Cabbage had only taken a deep rent across his breastplate. Didn't make sense, seeing as Bershad had gone for a decent flight when he'd been hit. Maybe the bombs had weakened him?

Cabbage didn't know, and he didn't care. He just wanted to run away.

He struggled to his feet just as Vergun made another horrible tear through their ranks, leaving a score of headless men in his wake. Willem was shouting something. The wardens were grouping up, doing their best to form a defense against Vergun's attacks. Dying and dismembered wardens were everywhere.

Vergun charged again, ripping through their meager line and leaving another trail of fallen wardens. He turned back, horrible red eyes searching for a fresh target and landing on Cabbage.

Shit.

Vergun charged. Cabbage closed his eyes. Wondered if it would hurt to have his head cut off.

Instead of finding out, Cabbage heard a bone-crunching thud, followed by a wet shudder.

Cabbage opened his eyes. Bershad had stepped in front of him at the last moment. Vergun's claw was buried in Bershad's shield. And Bershad's spear was rammed through Vergun's chest.

"You and I are gonna finish this," Bershad growled, pulling Vergun closer. "Right. Now."

93

VERA
Castle Malgrave

Concussions sounded off all over the city as Vera, Felgor, and Oromir approached a postern gate of the castle.

"I have a prisoner who needs to be detained in the castle!" Felgor said.

"Prisoner?" the guard asked, looking at Vera. There should have been five soldiers with him, but they'd been peeled off to defend the city. "Are you drunk? We're under attack. Just kill her."

"No, *Private*. I will not just kill her. She's a high-priority asset, suspected of having intelligence on the very attack we now face. Master Ward wants to interview her himself."

The mention of Ward sparked the guard's attention, along with the realization that he was speaking to a high-ranking skyship officer according to the epaulets on Felgor's shoulders.

"Sorry, sir. I didn't realize." He moved aside to give Felgor access to the lock. "Go ahead and use your seal."

"Lost it detaining the widow. Bitches fight like demons, you know?" He motioned to his swollen eye. "Let me use yours. I'll get a replacement after I dump this rabble off in the cells."

The guard clearly didn't like that, but his hesitation was cut short by another huge concussion—far larger and closer than the others.

"Fuck it," he said, digging the seal from his pocket. "I'm going inside, too."

———

"I told you, explosions turn people into morons," Felgor said as they moved up the tower.

"That guard is going to get suspicious eventually," said Vera.

"Anything happening *eventually* doesn't really mean much to us. Now what level are the detention cells on?"

"Thirteen," said Vera. "But Kira won't be there. He keeps her higher up in the castle."

"Jolan might be," said Oromir.

"And Ashlyn," said Felgor. "Trust me, having her on our side will make this whole thing much simpler. She turned a hundred grayskins to tatters on that bridge."

"Fine," said Vera. "Take this hallway to the end."

Felgor continued leading them up the tower. They passed dozens of soldiers and engineers, but all of them were moving through the castle with either a clear purpose or abject panic, and nobody paid them much attention.

When they reached the thirteenth floor, Felgor marched into the detention area.

"Is the queen of Almira in one of these cells?" he asked the lone jailer.

"The queen of Almira?" the jailer repeated.

"Yeah. Dark hair. Blue eyes. Has this metal thing attached to one arm."

The jailer swallowed. "You are not supposed to—"

Oromir drew his sword and stabbed the jailer in the throat. The jailer reeled backward, taking the blade with him. Oromir hopped over the desk and grabbed a ring of seals from the jailer's belt. Moved to the first cell and started trying seals. The first four did nothing, but the fifth opened the door with a clank and a shudder.

"Empty," said Oromir, already moving to the next one.

Felgor wandered around the room. On one side, there was a big crate that he started rooting through, throwing gloves, armor, weapons, and other sundry items on the floor.

"What are you doing, Felgor?"

"This is where they keep prisoners' possessions," he said. "I wanna see if I can find some boots that fit me a little better. These are real tight. Hey, what's this thing? Some kind of whip?"

Oromir froze. He was standing in front of the last cell, the seal to unlock it in his hand. He turned to Felgor.

"Those belong to the prisoners?"

"Yeah, but I have no idea what this thing is."

"I do."

Oromir turned back to the last cell. Started trying seals again. Vera crossed the room just as he got the door open.

Garret was inside. Chained to the far wall.

Oromir's face twisted up with rage. "Gonna kill you."

Oromir rushed into the cell. Started beating Garret to death.

Vera shouted for him to stop. When that did nothing, she came up behind Oromir and put him in a full body lock, then pulled him to the ground. Even then, Oromir kept struggling and shouting.

"He needs to die," Oromir hissed.

Vera tightened her grip. "If you don't calm down, I'll keep squeezing and you'll lose consciousness."

That finally got him to go still. Vera relaxed her grip and let Oromir up, but she stayed between him and Garret. Blood was dripping down the right side of Garret's face from where Oromir had been hitting him.

"How'd you end up in here?" she asked.

"I told Osyrus Ward that I killed you, as promised. Then you showed up and stole Kira."

"Ward didn't appreciate the deception."

"No."

"Well, I did."

Garret shrugged. "So, you came back for your empress again?"

Vera nodded.

Garret turned to Oromir. "And you came to kill me?"

"I came for Jolan. But I'll gladly kill you on the way."

Garret's face was unreadable for a moment. "Do it, if you want. But I'm willing to help you reach Jolan."

"We don't need your help," said Oromir.

The sound of someone inserting a seal into the door rattled behind them. It started to unlock.

"Felgor!" Vera hissed.

"On it," he said, moving to the door and jamming a tool into his side of the lock, which caused a groaning strain of gears. The door opened, but only a hand's width. A man's eyes appeared on the other side, scanning the area.

"It's them! Get this open."

The man's face disappeared, and was replaced by eight gray fingers straining to force the door open.

"You sure you don't need my help?" Garret asked. "Because I'm the only one who can fill that whip with current."

Felgor gave it a test thump against the door. Nothing much happened. "Think he's telling the truth."

Oromir fumed as he looked from the door to Garret and back to the door. He pulled a bomb from behind his breastplate.

Vera stepped closer to him. "You need to save that," she said. "Let Garret help."

The door jerked open another half stride.

Oromir cursed, put the bomb away, then entered the cell and started trying the seals on the machine controlling Garret's irons. "Once Jolan is safe, I *am* going to kill you."

"If you don't move faster, the grayskin's going to kill us all!" Felgor yelled.

The door jerked halfway open. The acolyte shoved through.

Felgor ran away from it, sprinting down the hallway as Oromir finally got the chains open. Garret was out of the cell before they hit the floor. He grabbed the whip from Felgor and slipped his hand into the grip. Squeezed.

A ripple of current shuddered through the whip, bringing it to life.

He snapped it around the neck of the grayskin. There was a blinding light and a hot pop.

When Vera's vision returned, the grayskin's brains were all over the walls.

There were four Wormwrot soldiers behind it. Garret snapped the whip across their faces, killing them in a single sweep.

He turned around to face them. Energy still coursing through the cord. Vera relaxed her muscles. Got ready to dodge an attack, if that's what Garret decided to do.

But Garret cut power to the whip.

"Kira's chamber is the closest," he said. "Follow me."

———————

Garret killed two acolytes and twenty-three Wormwrot on the way to Kira's chamber. Left their steaming corpses littering the hallways and stairwells of Castle Malgrave. But when they reached the level directly beneath Kira's chamber—which was a large, open room occupied by ten Wormwrot and five of Ward's scurrying engineers—Vera stopped him with a hand on his shoulder.

"Leave me one of the engineers."

He nodded. Then went to work.

When it was done, the whole room smelled like burning hair. The engineer Garret had spared was covered in the blood of his comrades and quaking with fear.

Vera approached. Drew her dagger.

"Please don't kill me, I'm just a junior assistant!"

"If you want to live, you need to answer my questions truthfully."

"Anything! I'll tell you anything!"

"How many acolytes are guarding Kira?"

"T-T-Ten."

"He's lying," said Oromir. "Trying to scare us."

"I'm not!" the engineer piped. "After you k-killed the behemoth acolyte, Seven-Zero-Nine, Ward decided a single point of failure wasn't the best strategy, so he stationed ten war acolytes around the room. All angles covered. Always."

Vera turned to Garret. Raised her eyebrow.

"Ten is a problem," he said.

She nodded. Turned back to the engineer. "Is Ashlyn Malgrave in there?"

The engineer shook his head. "Ward keeps her in the upper workshops."

"What about Jolan?" asked Oromir.

"The alchemist boy? He's up there, too. Ward is trying to unlock the system they built, but he's having trouble. A huge amount of re-sources have already been diverted to the upper levels."

Vera tried to think. There was no way for them to get past ten acolytes. Just no way. Their best bet was to draw them out.

She turned back to the engineer.

"Do junior assistants have access to the upper workshops?"

He nodded.

"And do you know a route to the top that has as few acolytes as possible?"

He thought about that. Lip quivering. "Through the amphibian experiments, then up through the tonic refinery. Ward doesn't have enough acolytes left to guard low-priority workshops like that."

"Good." Vera hauled the engineer to his feet and shoved him over to Oromir. "Lead these men up there."

She put a hand on Garret's shoulder.

"I need the acolytes drawn away from Kira."

Garret nodded. "I'll get it done."

94

CABBAGE
Foggy Side Square

Vergun struggled to wrench his claw loose from the dragon-bone shield while Bershad dug and twisted the spear deeper into his chest. While they were locked in that terrible embrace, several wardens tried stabbing and cutting at Vergun with their swords. Their blades bent and broke. Didn't do any damage.

Bershad's spear was the only thing capable of breaking through Vergun's monstrous hide.

Eventually, Vergun managed to pull free from the shield, which sent both men stumbling away from each other in a spray of white bone shards and black scales. There was a big chunk of shield miss-ing, and a massive hole in Vergun's chest that closed in a heartbeat and was replaced by a circle of black scales.

Some brave, stupid warden in an orange mask jumped on Vergun's back, trying to choke him. He got his skull sheared apart for the effort.

That put a stop to the heroics. Instead, the wardens formed a wide ring around Bershad and Vergun.

"I'm glad you survived that little swim down the Gorgon," Vergun said, circling. "After all the times I've tried to kill you, it would have been disappointing for the river to do it for me."

Bershad raised the shield and tucked his spear. "Make your move, asshole."

Vergun dashed forward. Cabbage couldn't follow exactly what happened when they clashed together, but when they separated again, there was another chunk of shield on the ground, Bershad had a hunk of meat missing from his shoulder, and Vergun had a fresh hole in his stomach.

Vergun's wound healed in seconds.

Bershad's just kept bleeding.

"What's the matter, Silas? Running low on that demonic potency?"

Bershad raised his shield again, grunting at the pain it brought.

"Come on. Let's finish this."

They clashed together again and again and again.

Bershad skewered Vergun each time—through the stomach, the chest, even straight through his jaw once. All the injuries healed immediately.

Meanwhile, Bershad's shield got a little smaller each time. Wasn't long before Bershad was holding a broken scrap of bone that wasn't much bigger than a dinner plate. He was bleeding from the arm and thigh and neck. His shoulders sagged. Feet moved clumsy and slow.

Vergun charged again. Pushed the scrap of shield away, then jammed his claw deep into Bershad's belly. He dropped the spear. Vergun squeezed down on his guts, then shoved him backward, leaving a stream of entrails across the square.

A few wardens charged. Got divided by Vergun's claw for their trouble.

Cabbage dropped to his knees. Tears filled his eyes.

Bershad scuttled backward, moving across the square. The ring of wardens parted to let him pass.

Vergun followed him.

"To be honest, I expected more of a challenge," Vergun said. "Some great duel, the two demons of Terra, ripping each other apart while their armies watched!"

Vergun raised his arms, as if basking in the cheers of some unseen crowd.

"It was foolish of you to come for me," he continued, dropping his arms. "You were never going to kill me."

"Wasn't trying to kill you," Bershad groaned. He pointed to the bell tower that overlooked the square. "I was just trying to get you in range of my friend."

Cabbage looked up, saw a flicker of white armor, and smiled.

Simeon jumped off the tower and slammed the entirety of his weight and momentum onto Vergun's shoulders, which dislocated them with a horrific crunch. Then he pulled Vergun into a bear hug and squeezed. Vergun thrashed and struggled against the hold. Simeon's armor strained and wheezed against the pressure—scales and gears popping apart and bouncing along the cobblestones. But Simeon held firm.

That's when Cabbage saw something that shouldn't have been possible.

Silas Bershad stood up again.

He limped toward Vergun, clutching his own guts against the remains of his stomach with one hand. He drew a bone dagger from his belt with the other.

Rammed it through Vergun's throat.

"This is for killing Rowan." Bershad ripped the dagger out of Vergun's throat, slicing the tendons apart. "And for killing my donkey."

He grabbed a fistful of Vergun's hair and yanked.

95

CASTOR
Foggy Side Square

Castor had climbed onto the roof of an abandoned coffeehouse to watch Vergun destroy the Jaguars, so he had a very clear view of the Skojit jumping off the bell tower.

He had an even better view of Silas Bershad tearing Vergun's head off.

The decapitation seemed to sap the last of the dragonslayer's strength. He fell to his knees. Dropped Vergun's head and let go of his own guts.

"Fuck," hissed the man next to Castor. A sergeant named Wren. "Can Vergun heal from that?"

The Skojit answered that question by stalking over to Vergun's head and stomping on it repeatedly, until there was nothing left but a pile of red mush and black scales.

"Not likely," said Castor.

"The fuck do we do now?" asked Wren. "If they all charge the same shield wall, they'll run us down. Only reason they didn't figure that out yet is 'cause Vergun was tearing them apart. Should we fall back?"

"Soon as we break shields, they'll charge," said a private.

"The armada's coming," said Castor. "All we need to do is wait for them."

"If we do that, we're gonna get a bunch of acolytes dropped on us, and they'll kill us same as the Jaguars," said Wren, which was a valid point.

"Pargossian standoff is what we got here," said the private.

"You made that up."

"No I didn't," said Wren. "It's when you got a three-sided standoff."

"We got two sides."

"The skyships are the third side."

"Both of you shut up," said Castor.

Whatever the situation was or wasn't called, it was a bad one. Castor looked at Vergun's corpse, then at the dying Bershad.

He thought of that island off the coast of Dunfar, and the gold he'd amassed through bad deeds with the hopes of buying it. Suddenly, he didn't want the gold anymore. Or the island.

He just wanted to do the right thing, for once in his life.

"Hold positions," Castor ordered. "I'm going down there."

96

BERSHAD
Foggy Side Square

Dawn was breaking over Floodhaven. Skyship engines rumbled in the distance. Bershad was dying.

Goll rushed over with a leather pouch. Pulled out a lump of Gods Moss.

"Ashlyn gave me some for emergencies," he said, pressing it into Bershad's mouth. "Finally, I'll repay the debt that I owe you."

But nothing happened. No warmth. No knitting of his entrails. Nothing.

"What's the problem?" Goll asked, frowning. "Did I do it wrong?"

"No, it's me," Bershad groaned. "Got nothing left."

"Does that mean you're gonna turn into a tree?" Simeon asked.

"I doubt it." He looked at the wardens who'd gathered around, concern and sadness in their eyes. "But you all might want to consider clearing out, just in case."

"What about the plan?" Willem asked.

"If Vera and Felgor haven't gotten into the castle by now, they aren't going to. You did your jobs. No point in getting more of you killed. Rush one of those shield walls. Get out of the city before the skyships arrive."

Willem shook his head. "I'm not leaving you to die alone in this square, Lord Bershad."

"He doesn't have to die at all," came a gruff voice with a Balarian accent.

Men raised swords as they turned around to find an enormous Wormwrot soldier walking across the square. He approached without weapons. Arms outstretched. Bershad recognized him from the battle at the warren, and from Deepdale.

"Who the fuck are you?" Willem asked.

"Castor," he said. Then he looked at Vergun's corpse. "Seeing as he's dead, I'm in charge of Wormwrot now."

"Pretty foolish first move you're making as the commander. You got about five seconds to live."

Castor shrugged. "You lot have a little longer, but not much." He pointed to the horizons, which were now dotted with skyships. "They're gonna fill this city with acolytes when they get here."

"You came all the way down here to give us the news and die with us?"

"No." He pointed at Bershad. "If you let me and my men go without a fight, I'll save his life. Might be he can cut you a path out of this mess."

"Dragonshit," Willem growled.

Castor turned to Bershad. "Back at Deepdale, you gave me the chance to run away for free. I fucked that up. All I'm asking for now is a second chance. And I'm willing to pay for it."

Bershad nodded. "You have it."

Castor knelt by Vergun's corpse and dug a needle out of his pocket. Tossed it to Bershad.

"That was the only thing keeping Vergun from madness. I'm thinking it'll have a different kind of impact on you."

Bershad tried to pick up the needle, but was too weak.

"Got you covered, Flawless," said Goll, grabbing it and injecting the contents into the side of his neck.

The rush of regeneration flooded Bershad's veins. His guts knitted back together in seconds. His muscles filled with the familiar strength of Gods Moss.

"He truly is a demon," muttered one warden.

"I didn't believe it," said another. "Not really."

Castor just stared at him.

Bershad stood up. "Why help me?"

Castor shrugged. "Not like I'm some hero. Just trying to save my own skin. But I figure Terra's better off without Osyrus Ward. And whether you're a man or a demon or something in between, you've got the best odds of killing him."

Bershad motioned to the wall of dragon-bone shields. "Go."

Castor headed back the way that he'd come. The shield wall parted to let him pass. And a moment later, the Wormwrot dropped their shields and retreated down the avenues.

"Any man who wants to follow their lead needs to do it now," Bershad said, motioning to the skyships that were coming from all directions. "Might be you can get clear of this mess."

"Wormwrot might be able to fuck off like cowards," said Willem. "But those skyships'll hunt us all the way back the Dainwood. Personally, I'd rather die making a stand."

The rest of the wardens muttered agreement.

Bershad nodded. Then he took a long, deep breath. If Jolan's tincture had severed his connection to the Nomad, Ward's seemed to be regrowing it. He could feel her again, somewhere to the south. The rush of cool air beneath her wings. The smell of boar blood on her claws.

"I might have a way to even the field a bit," he said, then closed his eyes and reached out to her.

"Um, what's he doing?" a warden asked.

"I think he might be about to turn into a dragon," said another.

"That's not how it works," said Simeon.

Bershad found her. She was two leagues up in the sky, and circling a bend in the Gorgon River that was lousy with turtles and wild boar.

"Hello, old friend," Bershad whispered. "Any chance you're willing to help me out?"

The Nomad stayed in her stubborn circle for a few moments, but eventually veered north, heading for him in a direct line.

Bershad opened his eyes. Skyships were descending upon them from every direction, but the Nomad was flying twice as fast as they were.

"Gather up those shields!" Bershad called to the men.

Everyone rushed across the square to follow his orders. A few minutes later, everyone was back in a line, holding a dragon-bone shield. Willem held his up.

"These are nice and all, but they won't do much good if they bomb us."

"True," Bershad agreed.

The Nomad dropped from the rafters of the sky and slammed down onto the square—tail swishing and eyes focused.

"But she and I are gonna make that difficult to do."

Bershad walked over to the dragon.

"I know that I said I'd never do this to you. You're not a fucking horse. But I promise it'll just be the one time."

The Nomad blinked. Snorted. Then she lowered her head to the ground. He put his hand on the Nomad's neck. The warmth of her gray scales flowed into his bloodstream and bones.

Bershad climbed onto the back of the dragon.

And she took him into the sky.

97

CABBAGE
Foggy Side Square

Everyone took a moment to stare at Bershad and the dragon as they rose into the air.

"Form up in the middle of the square!" Willem shouted, breaking the trance. "I need a circular shield wall and I need it right now!"

Cabbage followed the orders, despite privately wishing that he had dragon he could ride out of this mess. The wardens seemed to click their shields together on instinct, but Cabbage struggled to get his lifted to the proper height.

"This the first time you've made a fucking shield wall?" a warden hissed.

"Yes! I'm a pirate, not a soldier."

He was still struggling when Simeon's white gauntlet grabbed the top of his shield from behind and lifted it into the proper position.

"Don't worry about Cabbage," Simeon growled. "I'll make sure he stays in line."

Above, a skyship was burning directly toward them. When it was about a league away, Bershad and the dragon swooped in and sliced all of the cords around the levitation sack away, causing it to drop like a stone and explode against the rooftops. The second-closest ship saw what happened and veered away.

But before it did, two hulking shapes dropped from the gunwale.

"Were those grayskins?" Cabbage asked.

"Not sure," Simeon muttered.

Ten seconds later, two grayskins careened out of an alley at speed, charging the shield wall.

"Yup, those were grayskins," said Simeon.

"What do we do?" a warden down the line muttered.

"Hold up your fucking shields!" Simeon shouted. "Hold 'em off as long as you can."

When the grayskins were fifty strides from their shield wall, they scattered in opposite directions. One of them hit the shield next to Cabbage with a shuddering impact that nearly tore Cabbage's arm off. The men around him grunted and shouted. The grayskin screamed and clawed at their shields.

Simeon reached over the wall and tore its head off. The grayskin crumpled.

On the far side of their circle, the other grayskin broke through, stomping over two men and raking another man's back apart. Simeon threw the head at the grayskin's legs, dropping it to its knees. Then he charged over, picked up a fallen bone shield, and beat the monster to death with a series of curses and snarls.

"We're so fucked," a warden next to Cabbage muttered.

"No, we're not," Willem said, stepping onto the lip of the fountain. "Close that gap in the shield wall! Stay focused! We can fend them off so long as Bershad prevents them from coming at us in large numbers. Just need to give Simeon enough time to take care of them."

"Works," said Simeon. Cracking his neck and holding the shield like a bludgeon.

98

JOLAN
Castle Malgrave, Level 57

Jolan sat alone in the workshop for a long time, listening to the skyship engines and the screams.

Eventually, an acolyte came for him.

"Follow," it said.

The acolyte took Jolan to a chamber high in the King's Tower. Osyrus Ward was waiting for him in a circular room that was ringed by thick glass instead of walls. There were telescopes set up in various positions around the room.

"Jolan. Welcome to my observatory."

He didn't respond.

"I've brought you here so that we might watch the Jaguar Army's destruction together," he said. "They started off quite well, but I'm afraid the tide of battle has taken a turn. Please, feel free to observe through this telescope."

Jolan approached the telescope and looked down on the battle. His heart sank.

The Jaguar Army had cut a swath of smoke and destruction through the city, but they'd been cornered in a big square, and were desperately trying to hold a shield wall together against the onslaught of the acolytes being dropped by the skyships. There were scores of corpses strewn around the square. Any of them could be Oromir. Any of them could be Willem.

Three acolytes attacked the shield wall. Simeon killed one right away, but the other two ripped five wardens apart before Simeon got to them.

The shield wall got a little smaller as men squeezed closer, filling the gaps left by their fallen comrades.

The Nomad streaked across the sky above, heading directly at a combat ship. The ship turned and released a volley of ballista bolts, forcing the Nomad to duck away. Most of the bolts missed, but one of them tore a line of scales off her back, leaving a bloody ravine from shoulder to tail.

She and Bershad couldn't keep this up forever. And without their protection, the Jaguars would be dead in minutes.

"They have lost," Osyrus said. "But they need not all be killed. Unlock Ashlyn's arm, and I will allow them to leave the city with their lives."

Jolan squeezed his fingernails into his palms, trying to think.

"How do I know you'll keep your word?"

"Because I respect you, Jolan. I respect your intellect, and your accomplishments. I have no desire to kill the warriors in that square, I just want access to Ashlyn's apparatus."

Jolan knew that Osyrus was lying. But he also remembered what he'd said before.

Everyone breaks eventually.

Ashlyn would resist Ward's torture for as long as she could. She might last days, even weeks. But she would break. Ward was simply using the Jaguar's destruction as a chance to expedite access to her power. One way or another, he was going to get what he wanted. The only question was time.

But if Jolan could get into the room where Ashlyn was being held and connect her to the astrolabe, there was a chance she could escape before Osyrus took control of her. A small chance.

"You win," Jolan whispered. "I'll unlock her."

"A wise decision," said Osyrus.

Jolan's mind rushed to come up with a reasonable explanation for what needed to happen next, but he knew he couldn't hesitate. Better to say what he needed and explain it later.

"We had an astrolabe with us on the bridge. I need it back, and I need to see Ashlyn to unlock the bands. We paired the two systems together."

"Impossible. We recovered no such tool."

Jolan knew that Ward was calling his bluff. His only option was to double down.

"You brought me back here on the remote chance I could prove useful, but left our tools on the bridge? We are both extremely intelligent people, Osyrus. Spare me the dragonshit. I can't unlock Ashlyn's arms without that astrolabe."

"That means that should you lose the astrolabe, you would also lose access to her power forever. Why subject yourselves to such a risky requirement?"

"I would have thought that was obvious," Jolan said, stalling for time to come up with a decent explanation.

"It is not obvious to me."

Think. Think. Think.

"We did it to prevent this exact situation from happening," said Jolan. "We knew it was possible for one of us to give up the code, but pairing it with an object makes the system impregnable. It was Ashlyn's idea. I'm the only other person who knows about it. The only person she trusted."

Jolan hung his head in manufactured shame. Osyrus smiled.

"Very well, Jolan. You'll have your precious astrolabe. Follow me."

99

ASHLYN
Castle Malgrave, Level 60

Osyrus had been telling the truth. His spiders were tireless. They'd been shocking her for hours and hours.

Each shock was slightly stronger than the one before it. At first, they made Ashlyn's stomach twist and her teeth grit. Now, they made her bones burn. She was drenched in sweat. Her fingers were shaking.

Ward came and went. He would occasionally remind her the torture would stop as soon as she unlocked her arm, but Ashlyn stayed silent. Eventually, he became impatient and called for one of his lackeys.

"Stay with her, Nebbin," Ward had said. "Let me know when she breaks."

Then he'd stormed off.

That had been hours ago. Nebbin alternated between adjusting different dials and switches on the wall of machinery and watching her with distracted curiosity. The acolyte who still guarded the room stared at her blankly, as her breaths came out ragged and wet.

Ashlyn was trying to decide if it was still worth the effort of trying not to piss herself when Osyrus Ward returned. He'd brought Jolan with him.

"Anything?" Ward asked Nebbin.

He shook his head.

Ward snapped his fingers. The spiders stopped their electrical onslaught.

"Jolan," she said, relief flooding her body, both from the sight of him and the ceasing of the shocks. "Are you hurt?"

"I'm fine." He swallowed. "Ashlyn. The Jaguar Army is being slaughtered in the city. I don't have a choice."

Ashlyn glanced at Osyrus, then back to him.

"No," she whispered. "No, no, no. You can't unlock it."

"They'll die," Jolan pressed.

"If you do this, Osyrus will kill far more people than the ones fighting in Floodhaven. *Please,* Jolan. You have to see the bigger picture."

Jolan's eyes were glassy. He knelt next to her. "You always saw the bigger picture, Ashlyn. And you were always stronger than me. But I can't bear to watch any more of my friends die."

Ashlyn expected him to start turning her bands in the unlocking sequence, but instead, he removed the astrolabe from the pocket of his robes. Set it down next to her.

"I'm going to reverse your kill switch," he said. "I'm sorry, Ashlyn."

She realized what Jolan was doing. And she saw the part that she needed to play.

"You weak fool," she hissed as he wired her to the astrolabe. "You coward!"

Jolan didn't respond. Tears were streaming down his cheeks. She had no idea the boy was such a good actor.

Once the astrolabe was connected, Jolan started turning her bands in the thirty-seven-step reactivation sequence.

Ashlyn used the time to quiet her mind. To focus. She didn't know how much time she would have to find a viable lodestone loop in the room, but she knew it wouldn't be long.

When Jolan reached the final step, he paused. "Please, Ashlyn. Forgive me."

She curled her lip into a snarl. "Never."

Jolan turned the final band. Ashlyn felt her arm awaken.

The astrolabe picked up every lodestone loop in the room. There were thousands of them behind the walls. They ran up and down the castle like blood vessels.

There was nothing to do but pick one at random. She focused on a loop that was emanating from the floor to her left and slipped inside. The braid was long, but it had none of the security measures that protected the acolyte systems.

Ashlyn spun up her bands. She'd have control in ten seconds.

But Osyrus Ward snapped his fingers almost immediately. The spiders released a jolt of current that froze her progress. Then they went to work, weaving through the loops on her bands and taking control of them with a sustained needle of current.

Ashlyn recognized the feeling, because she'd been doing the same thing to Osyrus Ward's systems for months. Now he was doing it to her. And there was nothing she could do to stop him.

A few seconds later, the last of her bands was pulled from her grasp.

"We have her system under control," Nebbin said.

Osyrus crossed the room and yanked the wire out of Ashlyn's arm, cutting her connection to the astrolabe.

Jolan's shoulders slumped. He wasn't crying anymore, but the horror on his face was far more genuine.

"We're ready to begin a purification barrage," said Ward. "Give Kira a full round of steroid injections so she is ready to be harvested. Be sure to amplify her sedatives as well. She will become significantly stronger once the steroid takes effect."

"Acknowledged," said Nebbin, turning a few more dials. He watched them for a moment. "Her levels look good. She's just beneath the threshold of consciousness."

Osyrus placed a hand on Jolan's shoulder.

"You did well. Thank you."

"Call your skyships away from the square," Jolan said, with no hope in his voice.

"Not yet. I need to confirm that Ashlyn is operating at full capacity."

Osyrus adjusted a few of his rings, then snapped out a longer and specific sequence. A series of dragon-bone slats in the ceiling opened, revealing a tunnel that led to the room above. Ward gave another series of snaps, and a glass orb the size of a cookpot descended, suspended by a single metal wire. The top and bottom were both capped by copper, and there were a few dozen lodestones embedded along the glass in an ordered matrix.

The orb landed on an area of the floor with a slight, circular groove. The bottom copper cap slid to the side, connecting the orb to a circular hole that led deeper into the tower. Ward attached a few wires and tubes to the surface, then stepped back.

"What is that?" Ashlyn asked.

"Every loom requires thread," said Osyrus. "It is time for your sister to deliver ours."

He turned to Nebbin.

"Begin."

Nebbin flipped an ivory switch.

The sound of a woman screaming echoed up from the hole in the orb.

A few moments later, the orb began to fill with a thick, milky liquid that Ashlyn had never seen before, but recognized all the same.

Seed fluid. From Kira.

"No," Ashlyn whispered, mind churning with panic and anger.

"Give me a baseline purity reading," Ward ordered. Nebbin pushed a few switches, which caused a small amount of fluid to flow through one of the clear tubes and drain into the big machine on the wall.

"Ninety-four percent," Nebbin said.

"Amazing what such a young, untainted specimen can naturally produce. But, as always, there is room for improvement."

Osyrus snapped.

Ashlyn's bands spun into motion against her will—she might as well have been a puppet. Ward poured her power into the lodestones that were embedded in the orb. She felt their energy swell, then saw miniature flashes of lightning begin to arc between the lodestones, passing through the fluid.

Ward increased the speed of her bands at an exponential rate. The platinum pins that Osyrus had added to her bands allowed him to push her much further than she'd ever gone before. Ashlyn's skin flushed. Her eyes went glassy. The spit in her mouth turned so hot that it burned her gums. The arcs of lightning became a permanent, blurry light, increasing in speed and ferocity with each passing heartbeat.

Ashlyn's hair caught on fire.

Osyrus cursed, then froze her bands. Came over and swatted at her burning hair until the flames were extinguished.

"This is the problem with organic specimens," he muttered, voice filled with irritation. "Nebbin, get another sample while I deal with this."

Nebbin did as he was told.

"Master," he said, voice quivering with excitement. "We're at ninety-nine point seven six percent purity."

That seemed to curb Ward's frustration, but he said nothing.

"We're nearly there," Nebbin added.

"Yes," Ward agreed. "But the final gulch is the most difficult to cross. We'll need to lower her body temperature before resuming. Wouldn't want to break such a productive battery."

Ward grabbed another rubber tube from the wall of machinery, attached a needle, and jammed it into the main vein in Ashlyn's right arm with zero ceremony or gentleness.

"Run the capillary system. Full drip."

Nebbin flipped another switch. The tube filled with a clear liquid that entered her veins. She immediately felt a wave of coolness that started in her arm and radiated throughout her body.

Despite her best efforts, she exhaled with relief. After so many hours of torture, this was exactly what her body was craving.

"Judging from your reaction, I assume that you did not create in intravenous cooling system for yourself?" he asked.

"We used buckets of rainwater."

"Of course you did. Savages."

"You've confirmed that she's fully unlocked," said Jolan, stepping forward. "Call off your skyships."

Osyrus sighed. Then drew a long needle from inside his jacket.

"I am afraid that is not going to happen, Jolan."

Jolan tried to jerk away, but the acolyte stirred from its position near the door and moved behind him. Held him in place with a meaty hand.

"Don't worry, this will be painless," Osyrus said, raising the needle. "I owe you that much, Jolan."

Outside the room, an acolyte barked with alarm. There was an electric sizzle, then a loud pop followed by a violent splash.

The door jerked open.

Garret and Oromir were standing on the far side. There was a dead engineer and a headless acolyte behind them. Garret's whip glowed with current. Oromir's face was painted in Wormwrot red and his sword was covered in blood.

Several things happened in quick succession.

Garret snapped his whip around the acolyte's ankle. Then he sent a surge of current through the whip, which blew the acolyte's legs off and sent the creature to the ground.

With the path cleared, Oromir bolted forward and stabbed Osyrus Ward through the stomach. Ward let out a long, pained gasp. Oromir ripped his blade free and sent Ward stumbling against the far wall of the room.

Nebbin pulled a rectangular controller from inside his jacket, but before he could do anything with it, Garret lashed the whip across his wrist. Nebbin dropped the tool with a scream, then hid underneath his desk.

And Jolan, despite all the confusion, rushed back to Ashlyn and reconnected her to the astrolabe.

Oromir stalked toward Osyrus with the clear intention of cutting his head off, but before he could do that, Ward snapped his fingers and a section of dragon-bone slats peeled down from the ceiling, forming an impenetrable barrier.

"Fuck," Oromir hissed, looking for a way through and not finding one.

"Are there systems in this room that you can breach?" Jolan asked her.

"Hundreds. But the astrolabe is useless if I can't control my bands," Ashlyn said. "The current takes them away from me."

"I know," Jolan said, yanking one of the lead rings Simeon had made for him from his hair. He twisted it around the dragon thread that was attached to one of her forearm bands. "This should block the charge."

"Did you just think of that?"

"I am just thinking of all of this, Ashlyn."

It was a risk, but they had to take it.

"I'll need a second dimension to slip through the loop," Ashlyn whispered. "One of my fingers."

Jolan nodded, already working the second ring out of his hair. He twisted it around the thread controlling the tip of her index finger.

"Is that enough?" he asked.

"We won't know until they turn the purification process on again."

"But that means . . ."

Ashlyn nodded. "You need to leave me here. Otherwise the Jaguars are doomed. We all are."

Jolan swallowed. "You can do it. I know that you can."

Garret stalked over to the acolyte and turned its head to a smoldering ruin with a few quick thumps of his whip. Oromir came over the check the corpse. He and Garret both noticed that Nebbin was crawling toward the wall of machinery with a purpose.

Oromir moved to stop him, but Garret put a hand on his shoulder. "Let it happen. Vera needs that room cleared."

Nebbin reached the console and pressed down nine buttons.

"Hold on, Master Ward!" he called. "I've summoned more acolytes to our position!"

He turned to Oromir and smiled. "You morons are all going to die in the next two minutes."

The raspy grunts of acolytes echoed up from the stairwell, getting closer with each passing heartbeat.

"We need to go," said Garret.

"There's only one way out of this room," Nebbin said, voice full of contempt.

"Not for long," Oromir said.

He pulled a brick-shaped bomb from behind his breastplate and pressed it against the outer wall of the tower. Twisted the timing gear.

Garret took cover behind the acolyte's corpse. Oromir came over to Jolan and wrapped him in a shielding embrace.

There was a flash of light and a blast of hot air, but most of the explosion's force was directed outward. When the smoke cleared, there was a massive hole in the tower.

Garret moved to the hole and looked down. "This will work."

Oromir turned to Ashlyn.

"Vera is going to free your sister." His eyes moved to the threads attached to her arm. "How do we free you?"

"You don't," said Ashlyn. "Just go. The acolytes won't hurt me."

"We need your help."

Jolan put a hand on Oromir's shoulder. "You need to trust her," he said. "Trust me. This is the only way."

The grunts and snarls and footfalls of the acolytes were just below them now.

Oromir glanced at Nebbin, who was cowering in the corner. "Should I kill him?"

"No," said Ashlyn. "Just go. Now."

Garret snapped the tip of his whip against the floor hard enough to embed it in the dragon bone, forming an anchor. "If you two don't get over here, I'm leaving without you."

Oromir's face twitched with stress, but Ashlyn saw the acceptance in his eyes.

"Bershad had a message for you. He said that he wasn't going down the river without you. So you needed to come find him." Oromir put a hand on her shoulder. "I'm hoping you keep that promise, my queen."

Oromir scooped Jolan underneath one arm and ran toward Garret. Grabbed onto his belt.

Garret gave Ashlyn one final look. "Leaving you alive always bothered me," he said. "But not anymore."

Ashlyn had no idea what that meant, but before she could ask, Garret dropped out the hole, taking Jolan and Oromir with him. Ashlyn watched the whip strain against their weight, pendulum inward, then release.

There was no way to know if they survived. She just had to hope.

Nine acolytes swarmed the room a moment later, eyes searching for a threat that was no longer present.

"Status report," Ward groaned from behind the machinery.

"No enemies in sight," one of the acolytes rasped.

Ward snapped his fingers. The protective barrier around him lifted. He was doubled over. Blood was soaked into his beard and smeared all over the floor. Nebbin rushed over and examined him.

"I believe the blade missed your liver and spine, but your stomach is perforated. You need emergency surgery."

"No I don't, you moron." He glared at Ashlyn. "All I need is the loom. Get back to your station. We're nearly there."

When Nebbin was back behind the console, Osyrus snapped his fingers, although he had to try twice before he found the correct sequence to regain control of her arm.

He quickly returned her bands to their previous speed, forcing them to pour their energy into the orb.

All except two of them.

Ashlyn began accessing the lodestone loops in the room at random. With only two bands, she needed to find a simple system, and there was no way to do that other than trial and error. The first three that she tried were too complex to slip through.

"Her charge isn't as powerful as before," Nebbin called over the sound of her roaring bands.

"Fatigue, most likely," said Ward. "I'll move control of her bands to the console."

Ward executed a few snaps. There was a thunk in the ceiling.

"Push her harder," Ward said. "We're almost there."

Nebbin pulled a bunch of levers to their uppermost position. Ashlyn's bands began to move even faster.

With the cooling fluid in her veins and the platinum pins in her bands, Ashlyn's body was able to withstand the added heat and pressure. The lightning arced wild and fast between the lodestones inside the orb. Through blurry vision, Ashlyn watched as the white fluid slowly shifted to a golden color.

"Enough!" Ward shouted.

Nebbin dropped the levers. Her bands froze. Damn.

"Levels," Ward whispered.

Nebbin ran the test again. When he spoke, it was just a whisper.

"One hundred percent. The sample is pure." He looked to Osyrus and grinned. "Truly pure."

"Finally," Ward whispered. "I can begin."

He snapped his fingers. The orb rose back through the hole in the ceiling. The wall closest to him also shifted to form a stairwell that led to the chamber above.

"You are responsible for her now," Ward said to Nebbin. "I will send the orb down to siphon and treat another batch in four minutes. Be ready."

"Yes, Master Ward."

"Five-Oh-Nine, take me up," Ward ordered. "The rest of you, protect this room. Ensure nobody enters, and ensure Ashlyn Malgrave neither causes nor succumbs to harm."

"Acknowledged, Master," they said in unison.

One of the acolytes crossed the room, picked Ward up, and carried him up the stairwell, which retracted behind them. The hole in the ceiling closed. Nebbin returned his focus to the control panel.

"Your friends caused quite the mess," he said, flipping a few switches. "But they've accomplished nothing."

Ashlyn didn't respond, because neither Osyrus nor Nebbin had noticed that she was connected to the astrolabe again, and had two bands under her control.

100

VERA
Castle Malgrave, Level 39

Vera and Felgor waited in the large room beneath Kira's chamber. They used two dead bodies as cover.

An explosion rumbled from the upper levels of the tower. Soon after, nine acolytes came thumping down from Kira's chamber and rushed toward the main stairwell that led higher up the King's Tower.

"They did it," Vera whispered, shoving aside the corpse she'd been hiding under.

"I counted nine grayskins leaving," said Felgor. "Doesn't that mean there's one left?"

"Yes."

"So how are we going to get past it?"

"Just stay behind me," said Vera, already moving toward the staircase.

The acolyte that had stayed behind was a war model with deer antlers. As soon as it saw Vera coming up the steps, it popped a set of claws from its hands.

"Vera the widow," it hissed. "You are not permitted to enter this chamber."

Vera kept walking. She raised the barbs along her right arm like a dog raising her hackles.

The acolyte swiped at her with a claw. She ducked, but raised her arm so that her barbs scraped across the monster's skin. When the acolyte swiped with its other claw, she did it again. Then she skipped backward across the room, putting as much distance between them as possible.

The acolyte howled and charged. But its steps turned awkward and stumbling. It fell face-first into the middle of the room and started twitching. Shaking. It vomited up a puddle of black gore and choked to death on it.

"That was horrific," Felgor said, peering down at the corpse.

Vera pointed at Kira's chamber. "I need that door open."

Felgor trotted over and examined the lock. "How'd you get it open before?"

"With this seal."

Felgor slipped it into the machine. There was a mechanical bark, then it popped back out.

"Code's been changed. But only the last few sequences, sounded like."

Felgor grabbed the seal and gave it a careful once-over.

"Yeah, it's these three imprints," he said, pointing to three holes with visible scuff marks on the edges. "Give me one of your daggers."

Vera handed him *Owaru*. Felgor sat down with the seal in one hand and the dagger in the other. Started carving at one hole with the point.

"Is that going to work?" Vera asked.

"If I can crack a seal with chicken bones, I can definitely carve this one out properly."

"Chicken bones?"

"Not important," he said. "Just give me some time. I'll get this open."

101

JOLAN
Castle Malgrave, Level 55

Jolan had bits of glass stuck into the skin of his neck and cheek. Garret had swung them off the tower and through a workshop window several levels below the top of the tower.

He looked around. Got his bearings.

There were hundreds of miniature humans hanging from the ceiling by hooks. They were each about a stride tall. Their bodies were deformed and twisted, and many of them seemed to have been burned to death by a scrap of dragon thread that was implanted in their arms.

"Gods," Oromir muttered, looking at them. "What is all this?"

"Ward was trying to replicate Ashlyn's dragon thread," said Jolan. "Looks like he failed."

One of the unburnt creatures opened its eyes, which burned with a yellow glow. The creature yanked itself off the hook and thumped to the ground. Released a wild howl.

The rest of them opened their eyes, too.

"Weapons!" Garret hissed, getting to his feet with a wince and a grunt, then activating his whip.

Oromir drew his sword.

Jolan looked around. Found a knife on a workshop table and picked it up.

The creatures swarmed.

102

BRUTUS
Above Floodhaven

Captain Copana was far less confident in the situation when they arrived to find an enormous gray dragon tearing through the skies above Floodhaven, laying waste to any ship that came within drop range of the city.

"That is the biggest fucking dragon I have ever seen," Brutus muttered.

He was tempted to ask Copana if that was a close enough look for
his retirement scrapbook, but decided against it. The man was on
the verge of shitting himself.

"Ballista crews, arm!" Copana shouted. "Arm your fucking crews!"

The men rushed to prepare their weapons, but this was an Atlas
Coast crew. Slow and out of practice and most likely completely in-
capable of pegging a dragon out of the air unless the beast was nice
enough to sidle up along their port side and show its belly, which
didn't seem likely.

Three skyships converged on the city, moving in a tight formation
and launching a volley of bolts. The lizard darted and spun through
the sky with terrifying speed and grace, dodging the majority of the
volley. The few bolts that did connect bounced away in a shower of
gray scales.

"Why isn't it dying? They hit it two or three times!" Copana
shouted to nobody in particular.

"Glance shots," said Brutus. "It'll take a direct hit to bring her
down."

The dragon attacked the three ships that had fired on her. She tore
the stabilizing rudder off one, which sent the ship into a wild spin
that ended in an explosive crash just outside the city. Then the gray
terror swooped along the aft side of another, raking its claws along
the straps that ran between the levitation sack and hull. The skyship
plummeted to the ground like a dropped stone.

"I've never seen one attack with that kind of precision before,"
said Brutus. "Dragons don't do that. They treat the ships like prey."

Brutus raised his lens to get a better look. Didn't believe what he
was seeing.

"There's a man riding it."

"What?" Copana raised his own lens. Paused to train it on the
same spot Brutus was looking, where a small figure was crouched on
the back of the dragon's neck, positioned like a man riding a horse
at a hard gallop.

"That's impossible," Copana muttered.

Brutus didn't say anything, but it was clearly possible, seeing as
they were both watching some crazy bastard do it.

The dragon swooped toward the next skyship, which was a heavily armored combat dropship. Those were designed to take abuse
from three or four dragons at a time. No way could a single lizard
take her down before they got off a clean shot.

This was it. Had to be.

But instead of attacking, the dragon winged past at an angle so the man riding it could jump onto the skyship, then it rolled away, dodging the volley of bolts.

The man stalked toward the foredeck with a purpose.

"He's going for the pilots?" Copana asked.

"I guess. But he's gonna be disappointed. Their cabin is protected by a stride of dragon bone."

The man stopped when he was directly above the cockpit, planted his feet, raised a spear over his head with both hands, then rammed it down on what seemed like a very specific location. He yanked the spear free, moved to his left a little, then did it again.

The ship lilted hard to the south, tugging away from the battle-field like a fish caught on a line. As it careened toward the ground, the man leapt off the side of the ship.

The dragon swooped beneath him, catching him a heartbeat before he slammed into the ground.

The dragon rose in a straight line, which gave Brutus the chance to keep his lens on the rider just long enough to mark the massive line of tattoos running up his right shoulder.

Brutus lowered his lens. "That's the Flawless Bershad," he whispered.

"What do we do?" asked Copana, who seemed to have forgotten that he was the captain of the ship, and deciding what to do next was, traditionally, up to him.

But Copana's uncertainty gave Brutus an idea.

"Sir, if I may make a suggestion?" he said, lowering his voice.

"Please, Corporal," Copana said with an eagerness that was almost sad.

"Osyrus called back the *entire* armada. This whole situation is pure chaos."

"What's your point?"

"We don't need to engage directly. We just need to *appear* to be engaging directly. Let's just hang back on the outskirts and wait for a different skyship to—"

"Corporal Brutus," rasped Acolyte 799, putting a meaty hand on his shoulder. "You will cease to spout treason from your mouth, or I will tear off your jaw."

Brutus swallowed. "Uh, I was merely—"

"Master Ward ordered this ship to drop its cargo in the center of the city," Acolyte 799 continued, turning to Copana. "You will follow that order, Captain. Right. Now."

"M-M-Make a heading," the captain said to the pilot, voice hushed. "Full burn, straight into the city."

The skyship kicked forward. Brutus felt a sudden and urgent need to shit.

On their starboard side, a skyship with its entire levitation sack in flames careened into the ground. To port, another simply exploded, raining hot shrapnel and ignited men onto the city below.

The dragon seemed to be everywhere—screaming up and down and across the sky. Somehow, their ship remained unscathed. The square came into view.

The Jaguar Army had been pressed into the middle of the square so tightly that half of them had boots in the fountain. They'd formed a tight shield wall. There were at least a score of headless acolytes scattered around the perimeter.

"How did they kill so many of them?" Brutus muttered.

The answer to his question came a moment later when a grayskin stormed out of an alley and slammed into the shield wall. Before he could press through, a man in bone-white armor reached over and tore his head off.

"What the fuck is that?" Copana asked.

Acolyte 799 moved to the gunwale, shoving a crewman aside. He looked down at the man, eyes bulging with sudden lucidness and rage. Then he rattled off a series of words that made no sense.

103

ACOLYTE 799
Above Floodhaven

"Skojit. Skojit. Skojit. Simeon. Simeon the Skojit. Ghalamarian blood. Pus. Heads. Sergeant Droll. Shoes. Shoes. Shoes."

What is your name?

"False."

What is your name?

"False."

What is your name?

A shock of clarity flooded his thoughts.

"My name is Rigar. And I am going to kill that fucking Skojit."

104

BRUTUS
Skyship

After roaring that stream of incomprehensible jargon, Acolyte 799 jumped off the side of their skyship with a howl. It dropped straight through the roof that it landed on. There was too much smoke and debris to tell if it survived.

"What was that all about?" Copana asked.

"No clue, sir," said Brutus. "But I say we drop our ferals right now, then get the fuck out of here. Without that acolyte on board, there's nothing to stop us from a hard burn across the Soul Sea and putting this mess behind a horizon or two."

Captain Copana swallowed. "I agree."

105

CABBAGE
Foggy Side Square

After Simeon tore the twenty-ninth grayskin's head off, Cabbage started to hope. Hope that they could keep going like this long enough for Bershad or Ashlyn to save them. Hope he might somehow live through this mess. Hope that he might see Jovita again.

But when a skyship broke through Bershad's line of destruction and dumped scores of deformed creatures onto the rooftops around the square, that hope died.

The monsters that scuttled off the rooftops and into the square weren't as large as the normal grayskins, but they were horrific and wild—all tumorous flesh and jagged spikes. Mouths and eyes in all the wrong places.

They were the stuff of nightmares. And there were so many of them.

The Nomad made a pass across the rooftops, dragging her tail behind her and smashing a score or two to bloody pulp. But a volley of ballista bolts forced her to duck away before making another pass.

A group of about thirty monsters poured into the square. Cabbage tightened his grip on the shield. Braced for impact.

He bit his tongue when the first creature crashed into his shield. Felt his mouth fill with blood. The creature kept bashing at his shield. Over and over. His shoulder burned. His fingers were numb from holding the shield so tight.

Cabbage screamed. Grunted. Stabbed at the creatures as best he could, ramming his sword between the little gaps in the shields. A monster snuck its claw beneath Cabbage's shield and hooked him in the foot. Cabbage cursed. Sliced the claw off with a swipe of his sword. Nearly fell over from the effort.

More screaming and grunting and stabbing. Cabbage managed to create a little pile of corpses in front of him, which was fantastic until a monster used those corpses to climb up the shield of the warden next to Cabbage, grab his mask, and ram a jagged thumb through his eye.

The man howled in pain. Cabbage hacked at the monster's arm, severing it at the elbow. Problem was, that sent the warden falling backward, taking his shield with him. The gap in the shield wall was quickly filled with a surge of deformed limbs and screaming faces. Cabbage tried to hack at them, but his foot slipped against the bloody cobblestones. He landed hard on his ass. Dropped his sword.

He tried to get up, but the monsters charged over him, pressing the shield into his face. He tried to shove it off. Failed. The shield pressed down harder. So hard he couldn't move. Couldn't breathe. Couldn't do anything besides register the strangely clear thought that this was how he was going to die—trampled to death by a bunch of monsters.

His lungs burned. His nose hurt. Cabbage was about to black out.

Then there was a guttural howl and the wet pop of limbs being torn from their sockets. The pressure let up.

Cabbage pushed the shield away. Took a deep gasp of air. Then another.

The shield wall was broken. It was chaos. Wardens were snarling and stabbing and dying all around him. Something grabbed him by the back of his breastplate and hauled him to his feet.

Simeon.

He punched and kicked his way through a horde of monsters, then sprinted toward the buildings that ringed the square, carrying Cabbage with him.

"What are you doing?" Cabbage shouted.

"Saving your fucking life, you idiot."

Simeon dropped a shoulder and careened through the door of a coffee shop. Threw Cabbage over the counter.

"Stay there till it's over," he said.

"I can fight. I want to—"

"Simeon!" boomed a voice.

They both turned. There was a massive grayskin filling the doorway.

"How'd you know my name, asshole?"

"Fallon's Roost," the acolyte rasped. "Survived."

Simeon laughed. "Rigar. You Ghalamarian bastard."

The grayskin's claws extended from between his hands. "Should have . . . killed . . . me."

"Yeah, but that's an easy mistake to correct."

Simeon crossed the room with a roar. Rigar raked his claws across his chest, sending dragon scales spraying everywhere. Simeon grabbed Rigar's shoulders and head-butted him. Once. Twice. But before he landed a third, Rigar rammed his claws into Simeon's stomach and twisted.

Blood splattered all over the shop floor. Simeon howled.

They went down together. Simeon gurgled. Cursed. Grabbed a broken chair leg and shoved it through the acolyte's neck, which did nothing to stop Rigar from pinning him down with one claw, and tearing him apart with the other.

Cabbage didn't think. He just hopped over the counter. Dodged one of Rigar's backswings, then ripped the chair leg out of his neck and rammed it through his eye. He punched the end of the stick as hard as he could, burying it in Rigar's skull.

The acolyte wavered. Twitched. Then fell back dead.

Cabbage turned to Simeon. His whole chest had been torn open. He was bleeding all over the floor and struggling with the clasp of his helmet.

"Help me get this off," Simeon muttered.

Cabbage did as he was told. Then he sat down. It made his heart hurt to see the wreckage of Simeon's guts.

"Don't look so morose," Simeon said. There was blood all over his lips. "I didn't deserve to survive this deal." He looked at him. "But you *do,* Cabbage."

Cabbage tried to speak, but couldn't form any words.

Simeon shifted with a groan. "Do me a favor. You get out of this mess, you take that trip to the Razorbacks. To the highlands, where you can see all the way to Pargos. It's . . . really something."

Cabbage swallowed. "I will."

106

VERA
Castle Malgrave, Level 39

Vera couldn't see Kira, but she could hear what was happening in the dome. Listening to Kira scream while Vera stood helpless outside made her want to cut her own fingers off.

After the third round of torture, Felgor was still carving out pieces of the seal, trying it in the machine, then carving some more when it was rejected.

"Felgor, if you can't get this thing open, you need to tell me."

"I can do it," Felgor said, face grim and covered in sweat. "I promise."

Vera gave him another minute to carve and whittle in silence—keeping her eyes fixed on the stairwell behind them, praying that the other acolytes didn't return.

"Okay, this is definitely the one," Felgor said, blowing some dust away from the seal, then muttered what sounded very much like an honest prayer to Aeternita. He straightened up and inserted the disc.

Click. Click. Pop. The door opened.

Felgor slumped back on his heels with a sigh of relief. "Thank fucking Aeternita. I had no idea whether that was going to work or not."

Vera rushed inside. The chamber was humid and hot and smelled of salt and harsh chemicals. Kira was on the table in the middle of the room, stripped back down to wearing only the bandages. There were scores of rubber tubes running in and out of her body.

Vera sliced the tubes apart with quick jerks of her dagger, then pulled them from her skin. She watched as the wounds where the tubes had been inserted knitted together and disappeared. Not even a scar remained.

Kira's eyes opened.

"Ki, it's me. It's Vera."

Vera moved to help Kira, assuming she'd be weak like last time. But Kira bolted upright and looked around the room with sharp eyes.

"I am going to kill Osyrus Ward."

Vera was so stunned by Kira's strength and alacrity that she didn't react as Kira hopped off the table and stalked toward the exit, walking over the dead acolyte as if it was a carpet.

Felgor's jaw dropped when he saw the nearly naked empress walk past him.

"Kira, wait!" Vera said, finally conquering her surprise and following her down the steps, back to the big chamber where she'd waited with Felgor. "We need to get out of this tower."

"I'm not going anywhere until that greasy-haired motherfucker is dead."

"You're in no condition to fight."

Kira ignored her, but a series of howls and screams echoed down the stairwell she was walking toward.

"By Aeternita," said Felgor. "What now?"

Jolan came sprinting down the stairwell with some kind of creature on his back. It was about the size of a monkey, but shaped like a deformed human. Jolan was screaming and stabbing at its legs with a dull knife.

Kira grabbed the creature by one leg as he ran past her and threw it against the wall so hard that it exploded. She turned back to Vera.

"You were saying?"

Vera just shook her head.

Garret and Oromir came down the stairs a moment later. They were both panting. Both covered in blood.

"More coming!" Garret shouted, turning around and charging the whip. "A lot more."

Vera raised her barbs. Felgor and Jolan took cover beneath a broken table.

The creatures descended from the stairs in a tide of snapping jaws and razor-sharp claws. Garret slung his whip across the stairwell, toasting a good chunk of them in a single swing. But he was pulled to the ground by three of the creatures before he could tear through them again on a backswing. More piled on after that.

Oromir started hacking at the creatures with his sword. Kira tore them apart with her bare hands. But they were both too far away to help Garret.

Vera rushed over to him—kicked one creature away from his face. Another from his stomach. Then she draped herself over him and flexed her muscles so that only the barbs along her back spiked outward. The creatures continued to attack, but impaled themselves on the poison barbs, recoiling and gagging and dying all around them.

Eventually, the creatures stopped coming down the stairs. Oromir moved around the room, stabbing any survivors. Kira helped Felgor and Jolan out of their hiding place.

Vera looked at Garret. "Does this make us even, or do you owe me again?" she asked.

"Not sure."

Vera retracted her barbs and got up. For a moment, the five of them just looked at each other.

"Where's Ashlyn?" Felgor asked.

"Still at the top of the tower," said Jolan. "But she isn't going to stay there much longer."

107

ASHLYN
Castle Malgrave, Level 60

While the battle raged in the sky above and the city below, Osyrus had sent the orb down to be refilled and purified three times. Ashlyn had been desperately searching for a lodestone loop that was simple enough for her to slip through with only two bands, but hadn't found one.

She was starting to lose hope. But as Nebbin filled her bands with power and began another purification round, Ashlyn forced herself to calm down and focus. She just needed one. A single foothold. That was all.

The first five loops were, once again, too complex. But the sixth was just a two-pronged orientation.

Finally. This was her way in.

Ashlyn wrapped one of her bands between each prong, then slipped the second through it in the opposite direction and pulled.

The first lodestone was hers.

Behind it, there was another one. Ashlyn slipped through the same way.

Another behind that one. And another.

She followed the trail of lodestones, which led straight down. She must be connected to some kind of pipe. The lodestones felt like they were used to control the direction of flow. That's why they were so simple, they only moved in one of two directions.

To take over the entire lodestone loop, all she needed to do was reach the bottom.

Ashlyn worked as fast as she could. She'd made it through

thirty-four lodestones when Nebbin throttled everything down, halting her progress.

Shit.

The orb rose into the ceiling again. She could hear Osyrus's loom working overhead. The sounds were like nothing she'd ever heard before—a kind of wet stitching and bone-crunching hum that made her skin crawl.

Ashlyn caught glimpses of the Nomad ripping skyships apart through the hole Oromir had made in the wall. She heard the screams of the wardens as they were torn apart by the ferals.

She was running out of time. When the orb came down again, she needed to make it all the way through the loop, no matter what.

"Engineer Nebbin?" she said, lips and mouth dry. "Could I trouble you for another round of that fluid? I feel as if I'm about to catch on fire again."

Nebbin glanced up at her. Then squinted at a few different dials.

"Your temperature *is* high," he said, then flipped a switch. The tube in her arm filled with the cool water. Relief flooded into her body.

"Thank you."

Nebbin ignored her.

The orb came back down a few minutes later. The copper cap shifted away, ready to be filled by Kira.

Nebbin flipped the switch that would harvest Kira, then ramped Ashlyn's bands up to a low hum in anticipation of the fluid arriving. Ashlyn immediately started working her way back down the pipe—moving as fast as she could without risking a mistake.

But this time, the orb didn't fill. There were no screams, either.

"What the hell?" he muttered to himself, flipping the switch again.

Still nothing.

Nebbin snapped his fingers at two of the acolytes. "There is a problem with the Seed's fluid production," he said. "Go down to her chamber and confirm the specimen is properly situated in the dome."

"Acknowledged," they said in unison. Then departed.

Ashlyn continued moving down the pipe—past the forty-seventh and forty-eighth lodestone.

Nebbin seemed lost in thought for a moment, but his focus returned when he realized that Ashlyn's bands were still powered.

"Might as well conserve your energy until the issue is corrected," he said, moving to the levers that controlled her bands.

"Engineer Nebbin, I would like to make you an offer," she said quickly. "If you were to release me from confinement, I would be willing to give you an extremely valuable reward."

He stopped. Turned to her with an amused look on his face. "If you're referring to a sexual exchange, you're wasting your time."

She unlocked the forty-ninth stone. Moved to the fiftieth.

"No. I'll tell you the one thing that Osyrus couldn't figure out."

"Which is?"

"The method I used to attach this dragon thread to my body."

Nebbin laughed. "You don't understand what we're doing here, do you? Your arm will soon become a relic of the past. A rusted, useless tool. Master Ward will restitch the very fabric of this world. There is nothing of value you can offer besides the power in your arm, which you are already doing."

Ashlyn unlocked the fiftieth lodestone. Instead of granting her a path to a fifty-first, the entire system shifted like the tumblers on a lock. She ripped her strand out with a hard tug, taking control of the entire loop.

"Too bad," Ashlyn said. "Now I'm going to have to kill you."

"Oh?" Nebbin smiled. "And how do you plan to do that?"

She used the two bands in her control to rip the top lodestone out of the floor, where it hung in the air at head level.

"With this."

She didn't have much control over the lodestone with only two bands, but she had enough to push it straight through Nebbin's forehead.

His brain matter sprayed across the wall behind him. His body crumpled to the floor.

The acolytes stirred at the engineer's sudden demise. They looked between Ashlyn, Nebbin's corpse, and the bloody lodestone hovering in the air. None of them seemed to understand what had happened, but they knew Ashlyn had done it.

"Stop," they rasped in unison. "Cause no harm."

Ashlyn nudged the lodestone to the left, then reversed her polarities, yanking the lodestone backward, severing one of the dragon threads attached to her arm and giving her access to another finger band.

With three bands, she had three dimensions of control.

And that made all the difference.

She zipped the lodestone back and forth, severing the remaining threads in seconds.

Her arm thumped against her hip.

Finally, she was free.

The manacles around her ankles were made of iron, so Ashlyn tore them apart like paper. She stood up, wincing at the pain of blood rushing through her legs again.

"Directive required," the acolytes rasped, staring at her.

"Your master is occupied," Ashlyn said. "You'll need to decide my fate for yourselves."

They blinked in unison. Then their claws extended from their fists.

Ashlyn smiled. "That's what I thought."

She roared her bands to life. Poured their power down the length of the pipe, activating the other forty-nine lodestones in the loop. With the platinum pins Osyrus had given her, manipulating them was as easy as juggling a pair of apples.

The lodestones swarmed out of the floor like locusts. Ashlyn set them on the acolytes, reducing them to ruined skeletons in seconds.

When that was done, she turned the lodestones toward the ceiling, trying to break through and kill Osyrus. But there was some kind of repulsion on the ceiling that sent them skimming away, smashing against the walls and floor instead.

Ashlyn halted the onslaught. That wasn't going to work, so she shifted her attention back to the astrolabe and used it to access the other lodestone loops in the room. Now that she had control of all her bands, none of the loops were too complex for her to slip into.

First, she tried to find a loop that led into the top of the tower, thinking she could crush Osyrus Ward and his loom with the dragon-bone walls. But everything that led into the ceiling had been severed. Whatever Ward was doing up there, it was now a completely independent system, one that didn't rely on lodestones at all.

She didn't know what that meant, she just knew she needed to destroy it.

Ashlyn shifted her attention back to the room she was in, where there were still scores of lodestone loops running down the tower. She picked one at random and slipped inside. It only took her ten seconds to take control of the loop. She moved to another.

And another.

And another.

Within a few minutes, she'd taken control of half the systems behind the tower walls. Thousands of lodestones were under her command.

If she couldn't crush the upper chamber, she would pull the whole castle down, instead.

But before she could begin the destruction, she heard the Nomad howl in pain.

Ashlyn ran toward the hole in the wall just in time to see the Nomad tumble to the ground with a ballista bolt through one wing. She landed in the middle of the square with a crunch. Tried to get up, but failed. The bolt was lodged in her wing, hampering her movement.

Ten skyships were closing in on the square. Feral acolytes were everywhere. Ashlyn couldn't see Silas, but she knew he was down there with the dragon and the Jaguar Army. Unless she helped them, they would all be dead in seconds.

Osyrus would have to wait.

Ashlyn jumped out of the tower.

108

CABBAGE
Foggy Side Square, Coffee Shop

Cabbage couldn't bring himself to look at Simeon after he died. And he couldn't stay in that coffee shop with his corpse. He didn't care what he'd promised Simeon about surviving. He'd been a coward his whole life. All he wanted to do now was die fighting alongside the only friends he had left.

So he limped back outside.

The fight was still raging. The monsters were winning. Smokey had finally take a ballista bolt and crashed into the square. She was trying and failing to get up. Bershad was nowhere in sight.

Cabbage only made it a few dozen strides before something jumped onto his back. Bit into the meat of his shoulder.

He fell over. Bashed the creature in the face with Simeon's helmet, which he hadn't even realized he was still holding. The helmet broke three of the creature's teeth. He hit it again. Broke its jaw, which sent it hopping backward with a snarl. Black goo dripped down its mouth.

The creature crouched. Got ready to pounce.

Cabbage got ready to die.

There was a sharp crack from the big castle tower, loud enough to snatch everyone's attention, even the monster's. Cabbage squinted at the castle and saw something that didn't make sense.

A long seam of broken pipes and hissing steam was cutting down the side of the tower and leaving a streak of ruination in its wake.

The surge of shrapnel neared the ground, but didn't hit it. Instead, everything gathered in a cloud at the base of the castle. There was a strange moment of confused peace, where all the wardens and monsters were equally transfixed at the sight.

Then the cloud rushed toward them, skimming across the rooftops of Floodhaven. As it got closer, Cabbage saw that there was a person in the middle of it.

Ashlyn Malgrave.

The skyships had tightened their perimeter around the city. Ashlyn rose to their level and flew a tight loop around them. The shrapnel in her wake shredded their levitation sacks in a series of gaseous pops. Cabbage could smell the chemicals and he could see the ships falling to the ground. All of them.

After the armada was destroyed, Ashlyn flew to the square. Hovered in the air above, her bands spinning.

Every acolyte in the square went rigid, backs arched and limbs frozen in twisted postures of pain.

"Awaiting command," the ferals said in unison.

Her bands spun faster, turning into a wild, roaring blur. The windows of the shops ringing the square shattered. Cabbage pressed his hands against the sides of his head, glad for once that he didn't have ears.

Ashlyn's bands stopped. The square went quiet. When Ashlyn spoke, it sounded like a whisper.

"Execute annihilation protocol."

"Confirmed," said the chorus of monsters.

A moment later, their heads collapsed into themselves—skin and bone and eyes pressed into a red ball the size of an apple. Their bodies twitched, then slumped over. Dead.

Cabbage couldn't believe it. She'd killed them all.

Ashlyn dropped to the ground. The lodestones around her hovered for a moment above her, then fell around her like hailstones.

She ran toward the fallen dragon. Cabbage followed her.

Silas was already crawling out from beneath her damaged wing when he got there. He was covered in his own blood, but whatever wounds had caused the injuries were already gone.

"Hey, Ashe," he said, standing up and cracking his neck. "We came to rescue you."

Ashlyn gave him a look. Smiled.

"I thought you said you'd never ride her."

"Yeah, well. Alternative options weren't exactly jumping up and down, waiting to be chosen." He turned his attention to the dragon's wing. "Think you can help her out?" he asked Ashlyn.

"If she'll let me."

The dragon begrudgingly extended her wing.

Ashlyn's bands whirred. She guided one cluster of lodestones near the ballista tip, and another to the metal nock. Her bands increased speed with a high-pitched whine, and then the bolt was ripped in half and pulled free from the wing without causing further damage.

The dragon stretched her wing experimentally, seemed satisfied, then started licking her wound.

To the east, the sound of a skyship's engines boomed.

They all turned to see the final skyship in the armada burning hard to the east.

"Looks like you missed one," Bershad said.

"Forget the skyship," Ashlyn said, turning back to the tower. "Osyrus Ward is still alive, and he's doing something very problematic. I can destroy the tower, but Kira and the others are still in there."

"So what do we do?" Silas asked.

Ashlyn looked to the tower.

"I'm not sure."

109

GARRET
Castle Malgrave, Level 39

Ashlyn Malgrave tore a section of wall off the side of the castle when she came down, giving them a clear view of the ruination she then brought upon the armada.

"I knew she could do it," Jolan whispered.

There were hundreds of broken pipes pouring different kinds of liquid all over the floor. Garret's nostrils filled with harsh chemicals and acrid smoke. His eyes blurred. Everyone started coughing and choking.

"Can't stay here," Garret rasped.

"I'm not leaving until Osyrus Ward is dead," the empress said.

Vera grabbed her. "All of us will die if we stay here, Ki."

The empress continued to seethe. She alone seemed unharmed by the chemicals in the air.

From above and below, the grunts and howls of more acolytes surged through the tower. Oromir moved to the massive spiral staircase and looked down it. There were scores of acolytes moving upward, trying to reach their master.

"Not getting out that way," said Oromir.

"The *Blue Sparrow* is still docked on the far side of the Queen's Tower," said Garret.

"Can anyone fly it?" Jolan asked.

Vera looked at Kira, who took a large breath in and out, quieting her rage.

"I can."

———

One of those miniature monsters had chewed through Garret's left boot and made a mess of his toes. Each sprinting step that he took across the massive skyship platform sent shocks of pain through his foot and up his leg. Halfway across the platform, Jolan fell down. He was winded and exhausted. Oromir and Garret hauled him back to his feet. By the time they reached the *Blue Sparrow,* they were essentially carrying him.

As soon as they were on deck, Kira hopped into the pilot's cockpit and started flipping switches and cranks.

"Drop the aft and port levitation lines!" she shouted at Felgor.

"The what?"

"Cut those fucking ropes there, there, and there!"

Felgor rushed to follow the orders. Above them, the levitation sack began to inflate.

"As soon as the sack is filled, I can get us out of here," Kira said.

Everyone relaxed for a moment. Jolan and Oromir embraced each other. Felgor threw up over the side of the ship. Garret pulled his boot off and looked at the ruination of his foot. Tied his sock around the worst cut and pulled the boot back on.

When that was done, he saw that Oromir was staring at him. Hand wrapped tight around the grip of his sword.

"Guess we got that done," Oromir said.

"We did," Garret agreed.

"Means you and I have unfinished business to clear up."

"Yes."

"Wait," Vera said. "You can't still . . . after everything he's done for us?"

"Doing something good in the present doesn't change the past, does it, *Garret*?"

"No. It doesn't."

For the longest time, Garret had believed that nothing anyone ever did mattered. Not when you looked at the big picture. The greater motions. But there on that skyship deck, with the skies full of chaos and the few people in this world he cared for all huddled together, wounded and bleeding and desperate, he realized that he'd been wrong. All this time, he'd been wrong.

"The man that I killed. What was his name?"

"Jon Cumberland."

Garret nodded. He dropped the whip on the deck.

"If you want your revenge, take it. I won't stop you."

Oromir drew his sword halfway from its sheath. Squeezed the grip even tighter. Then he shoved it home with a growl and a curse. "Keep your life, asshole. I don't want it."

Garret turned to Jolan. "What about you, kid?"

Jolan's jaw tensed. Garret could see the roil of emotions and conflict behind his eyes.

Before he could answer, there was a wave of wild howls from the castle. Everyone looked back across the platform.

A pair of glowing eyes appeared in the darkness. Then another. And another. And another.

Acolytes. Five. Ten. Then too many to count.

"How much longer until we can get out of here?" Vera asked.

Kira looked at her dials. "Seventy-seven seconds. If we lift off before that, we'll drop out of the sky like a rock."

The acolytes charged. Crossed half the platform in ten seconds.

"We're not going to make it," Vera said.

Garret picked up the whip. "Yes, you are."

He hopped onto the gunwale. Turned to Jolan.

"It's better you didn't answer, kid. And it might be that looking back, you'll figure that meeting me in the woods that day and saving my life was the worst thing you ever did. Might be that's true. But I'm glad to have known you, Jolan. I'm glad you'll outlive a wretched thing like me."

110

JOLAN
Aboard the Blue Sparrow

Garret jumped off the ship. He uncoiled the whip as he moved to meet the acolytes and filled it with current.

Jolan dug his hands into the gunwale so deep, his fingernails threatened to snap off.

When the first acolyte swiped at Garret, he lashed his whip around its wrist and used the momentum to swing into the air before blasting the acolyte's arm apart in a spray of gore. He landed on another one's back, strung the whip across his throat, and yanked the creature to the ground.

"Twenty more seconds!" Kira called.

One of the acolytes rushed past Garret, focused on the skyship. His whip lashed out. Blew the creature's knee apart and sent it sprawling. Realizing they couldn't reach the ship without getting past Garret, the others descended upon him in a horde. Garret whirled around in a swirl of current, somehow keeping the creatures at bay.

"Five seconds!"

Jolan couldn't watch the rest. He collapsed to the deck. The sizzle of Garret's whip stopped. Got replaced by the sound of tearing meat, followed by the thump of acolyte feet thundering toward them again.

And then the roar of the skyship engines drowned out everything else.

The ship jolted into the sky.

111

BERSHAD
Foggy Side Square

Everyone was still arguing over what to do when a blue skyship fired its engines and pulled away from the castle.

"Is that them?" Ashlyn asked.

"Not . . . entirely . . . sure," said Cabbage, lens focused on the skyship. "My eyes aren't so good. Everything's blurry."

"Give me that," Bershad snapped, snatching the lens and glassing the ship. He could see people moving on the deck. Couldn't make any of them out except for one.

Felgor. Grinning like an idiot and waving at him.

"That's them," Bershad said.

Ashlyn's bands whirred to life. The lodestones rose in the air around her, and she rose with them.

"What are you going to do, exactly?" Willem asked.

"Silas always said I'm no good for castles."

Ashlyn tore across the city. When she reached the castle, she wrapped around it in a blur of destruction, ripping the walls and structural beams apart as she spiraled her way to the top of the King's Tower, leaving nothing but a skeleton of bent support beams in her wake.

When she was done, she flew back to the square and landed next to Bershad.

Everyone watched the broken tower as it teetered in the wind.

Bershad cleared his throat. "Think you might have needed a few more passes."

The tower snapped in half at the middle, sending up a massive cloud of dirt and smoke that washed over the city. Bershad shielded his face against the grains of dust that came sweeping through the square.

"You were saying?" Ashlyn asked, doing the same.

"Nothing."

Bershad smiled at her, but his happiness disappeared as the dust settled.

The tower was gone. But a strange, golden orb the size of a castle room remained. It was floating in the sky, unharmed and unaffected by the removal of the tower around it.

"What is that?" Bershad asked.

Ashlyn swallowed. "Osyrus Ward's loom."

"Loom? The fuck is he sewing?"

"Anything that he wants."

"That's not good."

The orb released a low hum, like a whale's song in the deep of the ocean, then tore through the sky—heading east.

"What now?" Bershad asked.

Ashlyn's bands started churning again. "We go after him."

112

JOLAN
Above Floodhaven

Jolan felt like he was going to puke. His head was awash with the horror of Garret's death, the chaos of the castle's destruction, and the cold realization that Osyrus Ward was still alive.

"Should I land?" Kira asked.

"Don't think that's necessary," Felgor said, pointing down in the city. "They appear to be coming to us."

Bershad and the dragon took to the sky. Started circling the skyship.

Ashlyn flew up to the *Blue Sparrow* amidst a cloud of lodestones. Landed on the deck with a clatter.

"Jolan," she said, coming over and pulling him into an embrace. "You saved my life."

"You saved us all," Jolan replied. "But we're not done yet."

"No," Ashlyn said. "We're not."

"I think that Osyrus tethered the orb to that skyship that burned eastward. Once he reaches it, he'll only be able to go as fast as the ship."

"I think you're right," said Ashlyn.

"The *Sparrow* can fly twice as fast as that cutter," Kira said from the pilot's seat.

"Kira. When did you learn how to fly a skyship?" Ashlyn asked her sister.

"Ashe, it's been a long time and it's good to see you, but if we start asking each other shit like that, we're gonna be here all day and Osyrus Ward is going to escape."

"Fair point."

Ashlyn turned to Felgor. "Sorry about this, Felgor. But I promised Silas."

"Promised what?"

Ashlyn zipped a lodestone beneath each of his armpits, then hauled him into the air and down to the city below. He was screaming the entire time.

When that was done, she looked back at everyone else.

"Anyone who stays is unlikely to survive. This is your last chance to leave."

Nobody said anything.

Jolan turned to Oromir. "I've made a lot of mistakes in my life, Oro. I've gotten people killed. I've killed people myself. But this is one thing that I can do right." He turned to Ashlyn. "Take him."

Oromir's eyes widened with realization. But before he could say anything, Ashlyn slipped five lodestones beneath his armor and carried him down to the city. His was less of a scream and more of an angry growl.

Jolan didn't care if Oromir hated him forever. He just wanted him safe.

"You're sure you don't want to go with him?" Ashlyn asked him.

Jolan nodded. "I'll see this through to the end. I have to."

She turned to Vera. "And you?"

"I promised someone that I would kill Osyrus Ward. That's what I plan to do."

Ashlyn nodded. Motioned to Bershad, who guided the Nomad east, over the Soul Sea.

They followed.

113

BRUTUS
Above the Soul Sea

Brutus didn't see where the orange orb had come from, exactly. He'd been too busy celebrating their narrow escape from Floodhaven with the crew—slapping backs and bumping bracers. Dumb shit like that. Captain Copana was the one who sighted the thing, which hung on their tail as if tied there by an invisible string.

"What the fuck is that?" Captain Copana asked, pointing.

"No idea," Brutus admitted. "But I think we should try to out-run it."

"I'm already at full throttle," said their pilot. "And before you ask, no, there isn't a way to speed up beyond full throttle."

The ship lurched and shuddered as their speed decreased with a level of violence that couldn't possibly be good. They also began to change course, lilting to the north.

"Well, you can certainly speed up now!" Copana yelled. "And why are you changing course? That will just—"

"I haven't done a fucking thing, Captain," said the pilot, who appeared to be the only man capable of remaining calm in the face of this terrible situation. "I'm not in control of this skyship anymore."

"How is that possible?"

"Dunno. But I'd venture to guess that giant golden orb is a factor."

"Where is it taking us?"

The pilot consulted his instruments. "Shit."

There was nothing to be done while the golden orb directed them toward the Heart of the Soul Sea.

Well, there was nothing useful to be done. The men alternated between futzing with the controls—which were completely locked—screaming at each other, hitting each other, crying, shooting arrows at the orb, and crying some more. Going to the Heart of the Soul Sea was a death sentence.

For Brutus's part, he just kept an eye on their heading and waited for the source of his demise to appear, which took about thirty minutes.

He'd skirted the dragon-infested islands that made up the Heart of the Sea dozens of times during the war, and always thought of them as looking surprisingly small, given their dismal reputation for dealing out death and destruction. He soon realized that was just a trick of perception.

The general orders were to avoid coming within five leagues of the Heart. But the orb sent them careening inside the five-league threshold with a purpose, and Brutus saw that the islands were actually enormous and varied in their landscape. Some were covered by rocky ridges that were all cut up with raging rivers that poured into the ocean. Others were all heavy forest with deep valleys covered in thick canopy. Others still were dominated by flat meadows filled with tall, wild flowers.

And all of them had hundreds of dragons swarming above.

When they were about a league away from the nearest island, the skyship lurched upward at a threatening angle, which sent the crew grasping for handholds. A few men were a little slow, and went tumbling off the back of the skyship and into the sea. Brutus wasn't sure whether that was a better or worse way to die than being eaten by a dragon. He debated letting go of the rail, but some idiot aspect of his brain insisted on stubborn survival.

They climbed for a full minute before leveling off. The orb shifted around to the bow of the ship so that Brutus had a close-up view of the thing. He squinted at the golden surface, which was just translucent enough for Brutus to see that there was a man in the middle of it. He had a bundle of golden appendages pouring from a gash in his stomach. They snapped and writhed like the tentacles of an octopus, attaching to different places on the orb, making what seemed like instrument adjustments, although there were no controls or dials, just fleshy pockets of liquid that shifted in an oddly systematic pattern.

"I think that's Osyrus Ward," Brutus said, squinting at the man.

"Well, if anyone was going to drag us across Terra while riding inside a massive bubble, it'd be the Madman."

Osyrus made a few more adjustments, and then all the tentacles pouring from his body were sucked back into his stomach. They formed a golden splotch against his skin that rippled like a pool of water. He turned around and scanned the skyship, eyes searching. By that time, most of the crew had joined Brutus at the bow.

Ten of the golden tentacles snapped out of Ward's stomach and grabbed ten men by their faces—one of whom was Captain Copana—and sucked them into the orb.

Their bodies weren't exactly torn apart as they moved through the orb's film. It was more like being shucked. Their armor was peeled away into long strips of metal and leather that gathered in pools at the base of the orb. Men's skin separated from muscle, muscle separated from bone. All the errant parts were siphoned into a hole in the middle of the orb that looked disturbingly similar to an asshole.

The entire orb swelled a little in size. A mixture of steel and bone formed on the bottom. It looked a bit like an upside-down acorn.

Ward pointed a bony finger toward the ground.

The orb plummeted from the sky.

Brutus leaned over the gunwale to get a look. The orb landed on a forested island. Trees in a two-hundred-stride radius were snapped at the base of their trunks, creating a big clearing and sending scores of dragons into the air. They darted away at first, but they quickly started to swarm around the orb. Tails flicking and teeth gnashing.

"Maybe the dragons will destroy it?" Brutus muttered to nobody in particular.

His optimistic idea was quickly put to rest when more of those golden tentacles lashed out and sucked the dragons into the orb. They were torn apart, just like the men. Again, the orb swelled in size, threatening to burst this time from all the extra material. Then the membrane of the orb broke like the yolk of an egg, and an array of strange machinery made from organic material spread across the forest clearing. Each of the bulging compartments was connected by a narrow tube, like the way wasps are held together.

"I have control again!" the pilot shouted. "Engines, instruments, and levitation mixtures."

"Then by fucking Aeternita, get us out of here!" Brutus shouted.

The pilot fired the engines and throttled up. But just as they were beginning to move away from the horrifying scene below, one of the larger sections of the machine started to expand toward the sky. It looked like the cone of a conch shell, and within a few seconds it stretched halfway between the ground and the skyship. The tip opened to reveal another one of those asshole-looking siphons that had eaten both dragons and men.

Brutus cursed. Dug his seashell out of a pocket. Said a prayer to Aeternita.

With trembling fingers, he placed the seashell in his mouth and closed his eyes.

114

ASHLYN
Above the Soul Sea

As the skyship they'd been chasing was pulled toward the funnel of Osyrus Ward's loom, it began to break apart.

At first, it was just small fragments pulled from the rigging and the hull. Then great chunks of machinery were sucked from the guts of the ship. Men started jumping overboard and plummeting toward the ground. They splashed into the water or slammed into the forest below.

Hundreds of dragons rose from the nearby islands, swarming the sky and moving to attack.

They were pulled into the siphon, too. Every last one of them.

When it was done, and the sky was clear, Ashlyn could see Ward's machine swelling across the island. The structure was a hideous amalgamation of tissue, dragon bone, and skyship steel that rippled and shuddered like a living creature.

Bershad and the Nomad came up to the port side of the ship. Glided alongside them.

"What's the plan here?" Silas called.

"Destroy the machine," Ashlyn said. "Kill Osyrus Ward."

"He just turned a hundred dragons and a skyship into chowder," Silas said. "Don't think he'll have much trouble doing the same thing to us if we get much closer."

"The siphon didn't capture the men who jumped from the ship. The key is to approach at speed. I can get down there first, but I can't kill him alone."

"I'll go," said Kira, already working her way out of the pilot's seat.

"No, you need to fly the ship. You're the only one who can do that."

Kira's lips tightened. But eventually she nodded.

"Good. Bring us higher, but don't get any closer."

Ashlyn tried to think. She judged the angle between them and the ground. Then she looked from Silas to Vera.

"We'll only have one chance at this," she said. "And everything needs to go perfectly."

115

OSYRUS WARD
The Heart of the Soul Sea

Osyrus Ward picked up an errant human leg and tossed it into one of the loom's fuel cavities. The crunching whir of mulched bone and sinew gave him an immense amount of comfort. Like the first sip of a warm drink on a cold, rainy day.

Ashlyn Malgrave had caused quite the commotion at Floodhaven, but she was too late to cause any real harm. The loom was now fully functional, producing its own synthetic Seed fluid on an infinite loop. All it needed was more organic material, and these islands provided a surplus.

The loom worked the materials apart, dividing everything into their most basic elements, and then braiding them together according to the designs that lived within his mind. Ward dabbed a finger in the loom fibers that were adhered to his stomach and spine, running along his entire nervous system. The loom was a part of him now, and he was a part of the loom. No need to fuss with spiders and snapped fingers anymore. His thoughts were enough. There would be no more slow, iterative improvements, earned through years of toil and failure and setbacks.

Finally, at long last, the perfect engine of creation rested fully within his grasp.

His mind wandered over the possibilities before him. First, he would produce several updated acolyte models. A few mobile minions to gather materials from the different islands while he gave the loom further instructions. After that, there was a truly endless array of applications. Ward envisioned a floating city strung beneath an artificial cloud on impossibly fine thread. Another city could go deep beneath the sea, where a bubble of atmosphere was fortified by a set of heaving lungs the size of a castle.

Neither were impossible anymore. Neither out of reach.

He would need to design a new type of person who could live in such climates, of course, but that was not an issue. The cities of Terra had plenty of organic material with which he could mold his vision.

The loom gurgled and retched. The emissions gasket dilated. And the first of his new acolytes emerged, exactly to specification.

The creature was no longer bound to the rules of corporeal form. Its torso was a harvesting pouch the size of a warhorse's chest. It had four malleable limbs, but no eyes or ears or nose. The loom had imprinted a skin of input sensitivity that was far superior to any sensory organ built by thousands of years of trial-and-error evolution.

"Omega One," said Ward. "Welcome to existence."

A Yellow-Spined Greezel the size of a Ghalamarian bull emerged from the underbrush at the fringes of his workspace. Its predator eyes focused on him.

"Ah. Our first field test."

The lizard charged.

When the Greezel was twenty strides away, Omega One's enormous maw spread wide and sucked the entire dragon into its harvesting pouch like a frog snatching a lake fly. The acolyte's sides swelled to adjust to the specimen's size, then compressed. It coughed up a ball of concentrated organic material the size of a cantaloupe, which Osyrus tossed into the loom.

"Excellent. I'll have another one just like you, I think."

Ward gave the production orders, and his mind wandered again while the loom did its work.

Beyond placing cities in the deep of the ocean and the heights of the sky, he dreamed of piercing the aether film that imprisoned them upon this hunk of rock. He would leave this planet and travel across the vastness beyond, where thousands upon thousands of other worlds waited for him. He would visit them all, and give creation to each of them. Write a destiny and future upon the multitudes of lifeless minerals.

The loom had just finished printing Omega Two when Osyrus felt the familiar magnetic hum of Ashlyn Malgrave's approach. She was moving too fast for the loom's siphon to catch her, but that was not a real concern.

She crunched to the ground behind him, surrounded by her archaic shroud of lodestones.

"What do you want?" he asked over his shoulder. "I'm very busy."

"I won't let you do this."

"This little game of ours is no longer particularly interesting to me. Leave me to my work, or be re-formed by the loom."

Ashlyn's bands churned into motion. The lodestones orbiting her body blurred with speed.

Osyrus shrugged. "Very well. Another redundant test, then."

He ordered Omega Two forward alone, figuring that he could at least confirm its configuration and reactions were up to specification so this interaction wasn't a complete waste of time.

Omega Two charged, its maw opening and preparing for suction. However, Ashlyn released three lodestones from her system at a surprisingly high velocity. One careened into each of the Omega's mouths, and one careened into Ward's stomach.

"Hm."

Ward focused on the foreign object in his belly. Wrapped it in fiber from the loom. That was good, because Ashlyn overloaded the lodestones a moment later, causing a relatively powerful reaction. Ward was blown in half, but the loom's fiber prevented any damage to his vital organs. The Omegas were not as quick to protect themselves from the foreign object—a minor design flaw he would rectify once Ashlyn was dead—and were each reduced to shreds of loom fiber that scattered across the broken tree stumps lining the area.

"Does your test still feel redundant?" Ashlyn asked, moving toward him.

Osyrus turned off the loom's siphon to conserve energy, then issued a new set of production orders. "Yes, Ashlyn. I would still characterize that display as a waste of my time. But not a complete loss. The platinum that I drilled into your arm is quite rare. I will put it to good use."

The loom sprayed a swarm of mosquitos into the air around Ashlyn. The insects latched onto her lodestones and exploded, expelling a mucus that reprinted her lodestones with a corrupted orientation system on contact. The stones fell to earth with a series of thuds.

Ward then ordered the loom fibers on each half of his body to tug back together. His legs fused to his spine with a satisfying pop, similar to cracking one's knuckles. His nervous system self-healed, and he stood up. He ordered the Omegas to pull themselves together, too, but given their fragmented condition, that would take several minutes.

Ward ordered the loom material in his stomach to form into four tentacles and latch onto Ashlyn's wrists and ankles, which they did with perfect accuracy.

"Good-bye, Ashlyn Malgrave. I promise to turn you into something more useful."

Before he could reel her in to the machine and out of existence, that irritating Gray-Winged Nomad swooped through the clearing and severed the tentacles with her tail. The lizard departed again before he could order the loom to mulch her, but Silas Bershad leapt from her back in a rather improbable feat of athleticism and attacked him with a spear that Ward was pretty sure he had designed on Ghost Moth Island.

Ashlyn Malgrave had been powerful enough to cause a mild inconvenience, but Bershad's attacks were simply useless. Ward's loom-skin shifted across his body in automatic waves, nullifying each prick from his spear regardless of how rapidly they might have been arriving. Bershad growled and yelled and grunted, but it made no difference.

Seeds. Such wild creatures.

Ward allowed the attacks to carry on for five seconds while he moved a wire of loom fiber to the tip of his right index finger. He pointed the finger and stabbed Bershad through the heart, which paused his futile onslaught. Ward then twisted his finger in a tiny arc and sliced off both his legs.

They began to regrow immediately, of course. Ward slipped a tendril of loom fiber into Bershad's body, immediately recognizing the steroid of his own design flowing through his bloodstream.

"I see that you have commandeered Commander Vergun's tonic. While its impact on your body is certainly noteworthy, the time for my experimentation with Seeds has come to end. For once, I think it best I revert you back to your natural state."

Ward siphoned the steroid out of Bershad's bloodstream. His lost limbs stopped regrowing. Instead, bundles of roots began to spread from his leg stumps. The transformation was upon him.

"Normally, I would allow you to complete your cycle, but I am using this area for my own purposes, so I'm afraid you'll need to be mulched. Apologies, Lord Bershad. You were a very amusing and interesting specimen, but all things must come to an end."

Ward attached his tentacles to Ashlyn's and Bershad's ankles. Pulled them closer together.

Ashlyn's bands whirred to life. She reached out to Bershad. Osyrus wasn't sure what she was planning to do, given there were no more lodestones for her to play with. Then, two hunks of metal that appeared to be crossbow bolts were pulled from Silas Bershad's back. Ward dropped the fibers and prepared countermeasures, but Ashlyn zipped the metal chunks through Ward's chest before he could properly defend himself.

The damage to his heart was swift and catastrophic, but also repairable.

Ward sent half of his loom's skin inward to repair the mortal wound and redirected the rest into a coil that would kill Ashlyn Malgrave.

That left him unprotected when something landed on his back and injected a score of copper barbs into his skin.

"Caellan sends her regards," whispered Vera.

Poison flooded his veins.

Ward spun the fibers into more countermeasures—ordering them to identify the substance and process an antidote. But the system balked and choked. The loom returned a salvo of errors in the identification stages, then turned against his flesh and organs.

His half-repaired heart sagged apart. The toxin roared through his neural pathways, toward his brain.

In his final moments, Osyrus Ward thought once more of the cities he could have built. Buried in the ocean deep. Hung beneath the glistening clouds. And nestled among distant stars.

116

BERSHAD
The Heart of the Soul Sea

Vera shoved Osyrus Ward to his knees. Retracted the copper barbs of her cloak. Osyrus vomited an astounding amount of black liquid onto the ground in front of him. Blisters rose on his neck and arms and cheeks. The golden patches of his skin turned black, then a cold gray—the color of dead bamboo.

Osyrus released a guttural, pained moan. Tried to mumble something around blackened teeth, but they fell out of his rotting gums as he spoke, muffling whatever his final words would have been.

His head slapped into the puddle of his own vomit, and that was where Osyrus Ward died.

Bershad looked at himself. There were vines and roots radiating out of his leg stumps and stretching into the ground.

"Well, that's not good."

Sensation exploded from the places where the roots worked into the ground. He could feel the soil like it was his own body, filled with worms and burrowing animals. The Nomad slammed back down into the earth and released a bone-rattling howl. He felt her pulse shift to match his own. Felt the change finally coming.

And then he felt Ashlyn's familiar hand on his cheek and neck.

"You have to hold on, Silas. Hold on for me."

"Think we're past that point, Ashe." He winced at the feeling of his roots spreading deeper into the unfamiliar ground. "Just wish it wasn't happening here. I wanted to die in Deepdale."

Tears were streaming down Ashlyn's face. She looked up at the sky, where the last skyship in Terra hovered. Then she looked at the Nomad.

"We can make that happen, Silas. But you need to *hold on.* Can you do that?"

He nodded, but he didn't think he could. Not really. He was so fucking tired.

"I love you, Ashe," he muttered.

117

ASHLYN
The Heart of the Soul Sea

"Always have," Silas finished, then lost consciousness in her arms.

"Jolan!" Ashlyn called to the skyship, which Kira was guiding to the ground in fits and starts. "Jolan, I need you down here now!"

Once the skyship was a hundred strides off the ground, a rope dropped. Jolan skimmed down it and ran over. Vera paced around aimlessly, face pale and eyes glassy. When Jolan reached them, he stopped. Stared.

"Do something!" Ashlyn screamed, chest brimming with panic.

Jolan's eyes filled with tears. "There's nothing we can do, Ashlyn."

Ashlyn shook her head. "No. No, I won't accept that."

She looked between Silas and the skyship, then to the loom that Osyrus had created. There was a small shred of golden fabric on the ground near her foot. A remnant that had come off Osyrus Ward before he'd died.

Without thinking, Ashlyn pushed it between the seam of two bands. Let it sink into her.

She could feel a connection between the scrap and the loom, and inside the loom she felt a power that existed beyond lodestone loops or dragon threads. A churning of possibilities that seemed both fundamental and endless. It scared Ashlyn to her core, but it also let her see the parts of Silas's flesh and blood and bone that were transforming. It showed her how to stop it.

All she needed to do was make the smallest of changes.

One change.

Nothing more.

ONE MONTH LATER

118

JOLAN
The Heart of the Sea

Jolan stood with Ashlyn on the deck of the *Blue Sparrow*. The bands on her arm rotated and whirred as she moved the final piece of the sarcophagus into place, sealing Osyrus Ward's loom under seven layers of steel and bone and concrete.

They'd tried to destroy it, first. But whether they used Jolan's explosives or more lodestones from Ashlyn, the loom only grew larger. More powerful.

So, they decided to cover it up. Hide it from the world.

Jolan and Ashlyn had designed the structure together. Mapped out the places they would need to source the materials. And then, over the last month, Jolan had stayed with Ashlyn in the Heart of the Sea while she built it.

When the final cap of the dome was in place, Ashlyn's bands went still. They both gazed out at the massive structure for a while.

Eventually, Ashlyn looked down at her arm. Touched a few of the bands with her good hand.

"It's time," she said.

A week ago, Ashlyn had told him what she planned to do when the dome was complete, and he'd been dreading it ever since. "You told me once that a day would come when we could use your arm for something good. Do you remember that?"

"I do. But I was wrong. This is too much power for any one person to wield."

"Are you sure that you don't want to wait a little longer?" Jolan asked. "There might be an issue with the foundation as it settles. Or support struts that require a patch."

"The foundation is strong, Jolan. The support struts are perfect.

There is just one last thing required to clean up this mess. Then it's done."

Ashlyn had used her arm to move the massive slabs of steel and iron into place with lodestone anchors. But Jolan also knew that Ashlyn was using something else. A part of the loom itself that allowed her to morph and change the raw materials they brought by skyship. It was the same power that Osyrus had held before they killed him.

That was why she wanted to get rid of it.

"I have everything ready in the cabin," Jolan said.

Jolan used a circular saw that was powered by dragon oil to cut off Ashlyn's bands. He stacked them in a pile, and stopped after each segment to apply a moss poultice to the flesh beneath, which barely looked like it belonged to a human. Her muscle and bone were twisted together with the dragon thread in a tight braid.

When all her bands were removed, Jolan put them into a steel locker. He moved to disassemble the circular saw.

"You're not finished with that yet."

"What do you mean?"

She held up her arm. "This isn't a difficult choice. The loom wasn't just in that machine we covered up, or the bands you just removed. It's in me. And it will never stop spreading through my body if we don't do this." She gave him a gentle smile. "There is also no way that I'm going to let Cormo amputate my arm. He'd probably saw off the wrong one."

Jolan knew she was trying to cheer him up. It didn't work.

"There has to be another way."

She paused. "I've put an unfair burden on you, Jolan. You, more than anyone else. But I need you to help me with this. Please."

Jolan gave her a long look. Then he moved to his bag. "I'll prepare the numbing tonic."

When it was done, Ashlyn put her own severed arm into the same locker as the bands and secured it with a Balarian seal. Then she walked to the stern of the ship and threw it into the sea.

She waited another full minute before throwing the seal to the lock into the ocean.

"What will you do now?" Jolan asked her.

"The loom and my arm needed to be destroyed, but there are a thousand applications for the lodestone systems that will improve the world. Windmills. Plumbing. Skyships that are built for travel and trade, instead of war."

"Sounds like the job of a royal engineer."

"Empress Kira needs one."

Jolan nodded. But he couldn't help thinking about how easily he had retrofitted the lodestone technology into bombs. As long as the technology existed, there would be people who would use it for violence and destruction.

Floodhaven came into view ahead of them.

"There's a place for you in the court," Ashlyn said. "At this point, I can't imagine working without you."

"I want to, Ashe. More than anything. But I left something undone a long time ago. Before I move forward, I need to go back and finish it."

"I understand." Ashlyn put her remaining arm on his shoulder. "You have a brilliant mind, Jolan. And a good heart. That's a rare combination. Whatever you do with the rest of your life, I know in my bones that it will make the realm of Terra a better place."

He nodded.

And in that moment, he believed her.

119

VERA
Floodhaven

On the day that Ashlyn and Jolan returned from the Heart of the Soul Sea, Vera burned her widow's armor in the rubble of Castle Malgrave. Kira helped her make the fire.

As the armor that Vera had spent most of her adult life wearing turned to ash, Kira took Vera's hand and squeezed it.

"How do you feel?" she asked.

Vera thought about that. There were so many things that she had done in that armor that she wasn't proud of. Wretched things that she could never take back.

"I once told someone that you can have black deeds in your past, and keep moving forward. It's time for me to move forward. With you, Ki."

Vera kissed her. Got lost for a moment in the softness of her lips.

They broke apart as the *Blue Sparrow* began its landing sequence.

Now that the skyship was back, it was time for Kira to start rebuilding the ruined relationships with the different countries of

Terra. They were planning to leave first thing tomorrow, once the *Sparrow* was resupplied. First to Pargos. Then Dunfar, Ghalamar, Balaria, and Lysteria. All of the countries that Osyrus Ward had conquered.

"Ashlyn will need me for a while," said Kira. "She won't admit it, but she will."

Vera nodded. "I need to track down the others, anyway. Make sure that Felgor hasn't stolen anything too valuable."

"I'll see you tonight, then." Kira kissed her again, longer this time, then whispered in her ear. "I want one more night to ourselves in a proper bed."

Vera walked through the ruins of Floodhaven. All around her, people were still rebuilding and repairing the destruction that had been caused during the final battle for the city. Some people had refused to use any of Ward's materials to repair their homes and shops, others had embraced it. The result was an amalgamation of rock, slate, metal, and dragon bone.

She made her way to a large coffeehouse on Foggy Side. The roof had been torn off in the battle, but repaired with slats of cut dragon bone. There was a freshly painted sign over the door.

The Cat's Eye II

Inside, Felgor and Goll were at the bar. There was a jug of rum between them, and a young girl behind the bar polishing a glass and listening to them with wide eyes.

Goll burped. Slammed down an empty cup. "So anyway. The mushroom demon sends Flawless flying through the garden like a pebble skimmed across a lake. He leaves a huge rut in the ground. Course that doesn't really deter Flawless much. He stands up and he says—this is a direct quote, mind you—he says 'Hey asshole. Gonna take more than a tap to kill me.'"

"No!" the girl said, smiling. "He really said that?"

"He did. Course in that particular situation the heroic deeds were split pretty even across all parties. Right, Felgor?"

"Incorrect. I pretty much always hold a lion's share of the heroics," said Felgor. "And I very rarely receive acknowledgment or compensation for them. Ashlyn Malgrave personally owes me five hundred and seventeen thousand gold pieces."

"Don't listen to these two liars, Grittle," said an older girl, coming up from the storeroom with a basket of apples. She had a pink scar along one cheek.

"We're not lying, Nola!" Felgor said.

"You're telling her stories about mushroom demons."

"Yes. They were created by an insane alchemist who discovered immortality from these rare mushroom spores that only grow on a distant island in the—"

"Enough. You'll give my sister nightmares."

"You two causing trouble again?" Vera asked.

"Oh, hey, Vera. No, we're just telling stories about Silas. Come have a drink with us."

"We have food, too!" said Grittle. "Vegetable pie. Black bread. And all kinds of jams."

"Vegetable this. Bread that. What kind of tavern doesn't serve meat?" Goll asked.

"This kind," said Nola.

"Why is that?"

The older girl's face changed. "We just don't."

Goll seemed to recognize the shift in her tone. "Sorry. The jam *is* delicious."

Vera took a seat at the bar. Motioned to Grittle for a glass.

"The two of you make for a sorry pair of diplomatic envoys," she said.

"You don't know the half of it," said Kerrigan, who was sitting at a table near the window, poring over a ledger. "That is their third jug of rum today."

"Lysterians have very high tolerances," said Goll.

"And Balarians?"

"We just like to have a good time," said Felgor.

Vera took a sip of the rum, which was full of spices. "Well, whatever the case, this is the last drink. I don't want you idiots to be hungover when we leave tomorrow."

"What's our first destination?" Goll asked.

"Pargos," said Kerrigan from the corner. "Then Dunfar, Ghalamar, Balaria, and Lysteria."

"Kira wants to add one more, actually."

"Where?"

"Juno."

"The lands beyond Taggarstan?" Goll asked, scratching his head. "I've never been fully convinced they exist."

He took a big gulp of rum.

"You just drank a bunch of spices that came from Juno," said Felgor. "If the spices are real, it stands to reason that the city is, too."

Goll studied his jug. "Another one of your proxy laws, is it?"

"I'm nothing if not consistent," Felgor said.

"I'll add Juno to the list," said Kerrigan.

Felgor leaned over the bar, motioning for Grittle to come closer. Then he whispered to her. "See those feathers on Vera's cloak? She can use those to fly."

"Really?"

"I told you to stop filling my sister's head with lies," Nola warned. "Next thing you know she's going to tar herself with pigeon feathers and jump off my new roof."

"It's true!"

Nola and Grittle both looked to Vera. "Well, it's more gliding than flying."

"See!"

"But you need special feathers for it," Vera continued, looking at Nola. "So don't get any ideas related to pigeon feathers or rooftops."

Grittle nodded solemnly.

Vera emptied her glass and pushed it across the bar. Stood up. "All right, both of you stop drinking, and be ready to leave tomorrow. Got it?"

"Aw, come on, Vera, drink with us for a while," said Felgor. "We're telling stories about Silas and you've got a bunch of good ones."

"You do?" Grittle asked, eyes widening with excitement. "Will you tell me one? A *true* one."

Vera hesitated. Felgor refilled her cup and pushed it toward her. Raised his eyebrows.

Vera sighed. Took the glass. "Fine. But just *one*."

120

CABBAGE
Razorback Mountains, Skojit Territory

After the war, Willem had offered Cabbage a warden's position in the Dainwood Army. It was some great honor, apparently, since the Jaguars had never allowed a foreigner into their official ranks before. They even introduced him to the carpenter who would carve his mask.

Cabbage turned it down. He'd made a promise to Simeon that he meant to keep.

But a month after leaving Almira, huffing his way up yet another windblown peak in the Razorback Mountains, Cabbage was starting to regret his decision.

"C'mon, Cabbage!" Jovita called from the shelf above. "Thought you were supposed to be some legendary warrior."

"Wasn't this much climbing involved in the war," he gasped.

"Well, climbing's all that's involved now. Keep up!"

She disappeared around a ledge.

They kept on, heading deep into the hinterlands. They'd been stopped by four different Skojit tribes on their way through the mountains. Each time, it had only taken one look at their cargo before they were granted safe passage. One tribe even offered them a shank of goat and directions to good water.

Simeon had been gone from the Razorbacks for years, but he was still remembered.

By the time Cabbage caught up with Jovita, she'd laid out a blanket and prepared slices of bread, goat meat, and cheese for dinner. She waved a jug of wine at him as he approached.

"Thirsty?"

"Too tired to be thirsty," he huffed, pulling the sack off his shoulder with a wince and setting it down.

"I can carry it for a while tomorrow, if you want."

"That's okay."

"I ain't squeamish about hauling a head around, if that's what you're worried about."

"It's not that," said Cabbage.

Jolan had filled it full of chemicals to prevent a smell, which Simeon would have probably taken offense to, but there was no way he was carrying a rotting head up the mountain.

"What then?"

Cabbage stalled for time by jamming a piece of bread into his mouth.

"It's my burden to carry, I guess. I'm just thankful you agreed to come along."

Jovita shrugged. "I always wanted to travel." She took in a big breath of air. "The air's so clear here. So thin. Nothing like the soup of the Dainwood. I love it."

"You Almirans are all insane, you know that?"

"Yeah," she said pleasantly. "We know."

They ate for a while. Cabbage got a fire going. Jovita snuggled into her blanket.

"You have a spot in particular you need to reach?" she asked. "Not trying to cut things short. I like the mountains. Just curious how much longer I'm gonna have to listen to you huffing and puffing on my backside."

"We're getting close, I think. But I won't know for sure until we get there."

Jovita yawned. "Sounds like some kind of pirate riddle related to buried treasure."

"We never buried treasure," said Cabbage. "Ground was too cold for it at Ghost Moth."

"Ah, well. The ground's awfully cold here, too." She lifted her blanket. "I could use some help staying warm."

Three days later, they passed the tree line. From there, Cabbage guided them south along the bald ridges, figuring that was his best chance at finding the perfect spot.

There wasn't a cloud in the sky. A few Red Skulls were circling, but they were far off. Cabbage wasn't worried.

Near midday, they cleared a pass, and the flatlands of Ghalamar opened up below them, stretching out for leagues and leagues and leagues. Cabbage thought of all the crimes he and Simeon had comitted in their lives. He still wasn't sure that he'd deserved to survive. But seeing as he had, he was going to try his hardest to do something good with whatever time he had left.

"This is it," he said.

"You're sure?"

"Definitely."

Simeon had been right. He could see all the way to Pargos.

121

JOLAN
Otter Rock Village

On the morning that Jolan returned to the apothecary at Otter Rock, he woke up an hour before dawn to make the coffee.

He'd arrived after dark the day before, and slept in the back of the supply cart Ashlyn had given him when he left Floodhaven. His donkey was already grazing around the field, straining against his hobble.

Jolan got a fire going and put a pot of water over it. The nights were turning colder with each day, and Jolan huddled underneath his blanket, shivering while he waited for the water to heat up. Once it was boiling, he added the coffee grounds. Jolan blew on his hands while it steeped. Added another log to the fire. Listened to his donkey chewing.

He sipped the coffee while the sun rose over his old home.

The charred skeleton of the apothecary was still standing. Weeds grew chin high in the main living area. The cast-iron stove and oven was still there, too. He walked around the burned-out building. The donkey followed him.

Out back, the glass panes of the greenhouse had all been stolen. He'd need to travel to Valmont to purchase replacements.

Jolan spent the morning clearing the weeds out of the apothecary. He stacked them in little bundles that the donkey happily ate.

When that was done, he returned to his cart and started unpacking supplies.

Ten glass vivariums. Five distillation vats. Seventeen beakers of various volumes. Enough rubber hose to wrap around the apothecary a dozen times. And fifty jars of various alchemy ingredients, which he stacked inside the oven for now. He'd build a proper shelf for them later.

Then he went down to the river and gathered a score of red-shelled snails. Brought them back. Placed each of them in a vivarium.

Jolan knew that he might have been able to sift through the rubble of Castle Malgrave and recover Osyrus Ward's antivenom. He didn't care. He wanted to solve the problem himself. With his own mind. And his own resources. He wanted to finish what he and Morgan Mollevan had started so many years ago. He needed to finish it.

An hour later, Jolan was squatting in the middle of the apothecary, struggling to get one of the distillation vats adjusted, when a shadow fell.

He looked up through the rafters. Squinted at a circling dragon.

"Needle-Throated Verdun," he muttered. About the same size as the one Silas Bershad had killed on the day they'd first met. Maybe a little bigger.

Jolan went back to work.

A few minutes after that, Jolan heard the whicker of an approaching horse. He stopped weeding. Stood. Turned around. His pulse went wild.

Oromir wasn't wearing armor. No mask. No sword. Just a pair of simple linens and good traveling boots. He dismounted his horse and crossed the field. Stopped outside the burned-out door frame.

"I looked for you in Floodhaven. They said you'd gone north."

Jolan nodded.

Oromir put a hand on the door frame. "That was some shit you pulled on the skyship."

"I didn't want you to die."

The donkey came up to Oromir. Sniffed his boots. Oromir put a hand on his snout.

"Did you give this one a name?"

Jolan swallowed. "Cumberland."

Oromir took a breath. Spoke his next words very softly.

"After he died, I was so angry. At Garret. At Wormwrot. At everything. And I needed a place to put it, so I put it on you. I said such terrible things to you. I'm sorry for them. I'll *always* be sorry for them."

A tear streamed down Oromir's cheek.

"I still remember what it felt like before," he continued. "And I want to get back to it so badly. It's all that I want, but I can't find the path. I'm not sure there is a path left for me."

Oromir broke down crying. Wiped the tears from his eyes, but more came pouring down.

Jolan crossed the room. Put both hands on his shoulders.

"I'm not sure, either. But we can look for it together."

Jolan kissed him. Again and again. Kissed the tears from his cheeks and lips and eyes until his whole mouth was salt.

"Where do we start?" Oromir whispered.

"With something easy," Jolan said. "Your horse needs a name."

122

ASHLYN
Ruins of Deepdale

Ashlyn walked to Deepdale alone.

Kira had been aflutter with worry, trying to force an entourage of wardens to go with her for protection.

"You just had your arm cut off," her sister had said. "How will you even feed yourself?"

Ashlyn had laughed it off and refused any company. The truth was, her left arm hadn't been very useful for anything besides widespread acts of destruction for a long time now. She was glad to be rid of it.

And she enjoyed traveling alone. For almost her entire life, she'd been surrounded by other people. Courtesans. Servants. Bodyguards. Solitude had always been a precious and rare commodity. She savored the days of quiet, knowing that when she returned to Floodhaven there would be a lifetime of public projects and bureaucratic meetings waiting for her.

Ashlyn reached the ruins of Deepdale near sunset.

Even though the city had only been abandoned for a few months, the jungle had swallowed most of the structures.

Heavy vines and thick ferns covered the walls—orange and blue and yellow flowers sprouted from the fecund morass, attracting bees and butterflies and zipping hummingbirds with iridescent, green wings. Ashlyn could see the feline shape of a few old jaguar statues along the overgrown walls. She could also see the glowing yellow eyes of living ones, lounging alongside their stone counterparts.

Ashlyn scanned the sky, where three Nomads were turning slow gyres above the clouds.

She entered the city through the remnants of the eastern gate, which had been reduced to a bed of soft, rotting wood covered in moss. Headed toward the lake in the middle of the city.

She passed the skeletons of animals the Nomads had eaten. Deer, tapirs, and okapis. There were also plenty of living animals that were too small to warrant the large dragons' attention, and they thrived in the city that was devoid of men. Red and blue frogs the size of apples. Clever white-tailed coatis. Half a hundred different species of birds nesting in the collapsed roofs.

The lake's water was crystal clear and filled with hundreds of brightly colored fish that swam between the lilies and reeds. Their mouths popped out of the water to snatch at mosquitoes and flies, then disappeared back into the depths. Painted turtles sunned themselves on smooth rocks. Chameleons stood on their shells, hunting butterflies.

In the middle of the lake, there was an island dominated by willows—their weeping leaves dangling in the current so they swished and shuddered like dancers moving to music.

Ashlyn raised a hand to her eyes, shielding them from the setting sun.

She could see the familiar, gray outline of the Nomad. She was napping in the wet mud. Her chest rose and fell in a steady rhythm.

Ashlyn pulled off her boots and clothes, then waded into the lake up to her ankles. The fish darted away from her, and the disturbance was enough to wake the sleeping dragon, who rolled farther onto her back and considered Ashlyn from an upside-down, lazy posture.

"I see you're still quite the terror," Ashlyn called.

The dragon licked her lips. Snorted. Closed her eyes again.

There was another flicker of movement in the trees. A familiar silhouette.

Silas Bershad walked out of the shadows and smiled at her.

Ashlyn didn't regret the changes she'd made to him in the Heart of the Soul Sea. In that moment, she would have done anything to save him. To let him finish his life in the quiet and peace that he'd been denied for so many years. To let him be surrounded by the animals that he loved, and hidden away from the people he disdained.

Hidden away from everyone except for her.

Ashlyn dove into the clear water and swam toward the island.

THE ANIMALS
OF DEEPDALE

(Orally recited by Silas Bershad, Recorded by Ashlyn Malgrave)

The Chickens

Those terrorists live in the ruins of Nola's old tavern. Little squawkers turned the whole attic into their private coop.

There are five of 'em. The two white ones are Sun and Snow. They're sweet. The brown one is Cranberry, because she'll throw a huge fuss if you don't bring her some berries at least once a week. The yellow one's Dimwit, on account of her getting trapped underneath the stairs on a regular basis.

And then there's Witch Queen. She's the black one who runs the whole show.

Ashlyn's Note: I do not love the fact that—of all the animals who have moved into the ruins—Silas decided to name a chicken after me.

The Rooster

Not even gonna give that asshole a name yet, because he throws himself into a murderous rage every time I come up there for my morning eggs. I understand he's gotta protect them, but if I can convince a dragon that I'm not the enemy, one stubborn rooster should get the picture, too.

If his attitude doesn't improve by the next full moon, I'm gonna eat him for breakfast. The chickens will be fine without him. They can run their situation like Papyrians.

The Jaguars

There are two of 'em in the city. Brothers, I think. They sleep in the castle during the day and prowl the wilds beyond the city at night. I named the bigger one Leon, after my father. The smaller is Gregor, after my uncle.

I'm glad to have them looking after the castle for me. I don't go up there much.

Ashlyn's Note: Jaguars are normally solitary creatures. It's unclear why these two have formed so close a bond, but I must assume Silas's presence is a factor.

The Paku

I didn't name her, because paku are delicious and I was planning to catch her for dinner on a special occasion, but a certain someone spotted her during their morning swim and named her Gertrude and now I can't stomach the idea of eating her. Poor fish. Only thing uglier than her face is the name you gave her.

Ashlyn's Note: I regret nothing.

The Wild Dogs

They took over the livestock pens. They like to gnaw on the pig bones that're still lying around.

You want me to list all their names? It's twenty dogs, that'll take forever. My favorite is Lola—she's the big black one with tall ears. All the other dogs are terrified of the dragon, but not her. She comes up every few days to swim in the lake. I throw sticks for her to chase down, which she never gets tired of. Yesterday, I had to swim out and haul her to shore because she ran out of energy in the middle of the damn lake.

She'd make a good war hound. But I'm glad she doesn't have to be one.

The Howler Monkeys

That whole crew's real ambitious. They came down from the eastern hills last month and took over the whole rampart area from the spider monkeys who'd claimed that spot originally. Their leader is the big one with the white shock of fur on his head. I call him Simeon. Yeah, yeah, save it. I'm a sentimental bastard and always have been.

Simeon and his crew better watch out, though. I can still smell the spider monkeys out west. They're planning their revenge.

Ashlyn's Note: I can't tell if he's making this up or not.

The Sloth

He lives in the big Dainwood that fell over and caved in the southern wall of the city. His heartbeat might as well be made of molasses, and he only shits once a month, on the full moon. I suspect he's working on some kind of fecal sorcery, so I named him Kasamir.

I don't know what he's hoping to accomplish, Ashe. I just know he's up to something.

Ashlyn's Note: I keep on telling Silas that sloths typically have one bowel movement per week and the moon's cycle has nothing to do with it, but he refuses to see reason.

He might be messing with me, or it's possible that Silas has a few mushrooms growing in his brain from that business on Ghost Moth Island.

The Coatis

They're a bunch of outlaws. They steal my private stash of nuts and berries constantly, and they're always snatching turtle eggs from around the lake, which vexes me seeing as the turtle pulses help me sleep at night. I've asked the Nomad to murder them on several occasions, but she says they're too small to bother with. I'd do it myself, but their meat's stringy and gross, and I don't kill animals that I'm not going to eat.

That makes me think, though. The only thing preventing the coatis from getting at the chickens is probably that vicious rooster. Maybe I won't eat the crotchety bastard after all . . .

The Lightning Bugs

Can't really name a bunch of insects individually, but they gather over by the castle wall, where I got shot by that ballista bolt. Whole big swarms of them, most nights. I like watching them. There's a peace to it, watching those lights pulse, steady and slow. Kind of like the earth's heartbeat, spread out across a bunch of tiny bugs.

Why was that a weird thing for me to have said?

Ashlyn's Note: Again, I think I need to check Silas for mushroom growth in his brain.

The Eyelash Viper

That yellow demon lives in Cuspar's old manse. He bit me in the throat the first time I came through there. I blacked out. Woke up outside a few hours later. Must have got dragged to safety by one of the friendlier animals. Lola, or maybe Leon. Anyway, I couldn't eat anything without vomiting for a week.

You're damn right I named him Vergun. I don't care if it's unoriginal. I also plan on tearing his head off in the near future and eating him. How's that for unoriginal?

The Ocelot

He's a sneaky bastard, but I respect him. He lives in one of the old dragon watchtowers, but doesn't even bother hunting. He just creeps into the castle at night and steals leftover scraps from Leon and Gregor. Might get himself killed for that one day, but for the time being, he eats like a king and spends all day napping in his tower.

Yeah. That's Felgor.

The Gray-Winged Nomads

Speaking of Felgor, don't tell him that I finally bought into his nickname for the Nomad. Of course she still hates it, but if we're doing this whole record, there's no sense in coming up with a new name for her. You want me to say it out loud? Fine. Smokey. I call her Smokey.

The Dainwood is her main territory, but she's been ranging further west recently, out over the Big Empty. She likes the smell of the salt, and the cool of the breeze. I do, too. After you return to Floodhaven, we're thinking about making a trip across the Big Empty together, just to see if there really are fire-breathing dragons on the other side. We're both skeptical.

Don't worry, we'll be back before your next visit. I promise.

Her sons? I named them Rowan and Alfonso.

Unlike her own name, she likes those quite a bit.

ACKNOWLEDGMENTS

I must first thank my agent, Caitlin Blasdell, and my editor, Christopher Morgan, for their wisdom and guidance every step of the way.

I would also like to thank Matt Rusin, Desirae Friesen, Laura Etzkorn, Molly Majumder, and the talented team at Tor, as well as Bella Pagan, Georgia Summers, Jamie-Lee Nardone, Rebecca Needes, and everyone at Tor UK.

Steven Brand deserves a massive shout-out for giving the Dragons of Terra series a wonderful voice.

A big thanks to the crew of Old Chicago, for providing liquid inspiration on many an afternoon.

I would like to acknowledge the authors, book reviewers, and digital friends who have supported me along the way. Your enthusiasm and support have meant the world to me. Specifically, I would like to thank Nils Shukla, Mike Shackle, Angus Watson, Sebastien de Castell, John Gwynne, Peter McLean, Django Wexler, David Walters, Jenn and Mike Lyons, Petrik Leo, Andrew and the Quill to Live Team, and Alex at Spells and Spaceships.

Lola—my brave and stalwart German shepherd—once again came up with most of the good ideas in this book, while also defending the household from squirrels 24/7. Quite the feat.

Lastly, I owe an enormous debt to Jess Townsend. Not only did she tolerate and support me while I worked on this book, but she did it during a time in our lives when we were essentially trapped in a house together due to a global pandemic. Without you, none of this would mean anything.

ABOUT THE AUTHOR

BRIAN NASLUND is an American fantasy author based in Boulder, Colorado. *Blood of an Exile* was his debut novel, and the first in the Dragons of Terra series. He grew up in Maryland and studied English at Skidmore College in New York. Naslund is now a product director for a tech company, and first started writing about dragons to escape the crushing boredom of his incredibly long bus commute. When he's not writing, he's usually griping about video games on Twitter, hiking with his dog, Lola, or whitewater kayaking in the mountains. The last activity makes his mother very nervous. You can connect with him at briannaslund.com.